A SPY IN

JULIAN

AMNESIA

SEMILIAN

SPUYTEN DUYVIL   *New York City*

Spuyten Duyvil
PO Box 1852
Cathedral Station
New York, NY 10025
1-800-886-5304
http://spuytenduyvil.net

The Rimbaud and Baudelaire pieces quoted herein are by Arthur Rimbaud, translated by Louise Varese, from A SEASON IN HELL & THE DRUNKEN BOAT, © 1961 by New Directions Publishing Corp.; by Charles Baudelaire, translated by Louise Varese, from PARIS SPLEEN © 1947 by New Directions Publishing Corp. Both reprinted by permission of New Directions Publishing Corp.

Reprinted sections of Jorge Louis Borges' "Ariosto & the Arabs" and "Babylonian Lottery" appear courtesy of Grove/Atlantic, Inc.

Translations from Rilke's First Elegy by Imogen Von Tannenberg.

10 9 8 7 6 5 4 3 2 1

Printed in Canada

A Spy in Amnesia

To Peter Glossop –
towards transcending
the ravages of time

Best wishes

Julian Slimline

June 2003

To Octavio Paz, Guardian of Poets

They assured us the tree of good and evil would be wrapped in shadow, the compulsion of pious propriety banished, so we might again enrapture each other without constraint.
—Rimbaud

Perhaps I am mistaken to propose this but perhaps too I am telling the truth.
—Lautreamont

I seem to speak, it is not I, about me, it is not about me.
—Samuel Beckett

PROLOGUE

... and he again said to his offspring,
"It is I who am the God of All." And Life,
the daughter of Wisdom, cried out; she
said to him, "You are wrong, Saklas!"
                    —*Hypostasis of the Archons*

The Enamored One creeps against the steep of the rise in the manner of a penitent. The manner of a penitent suits my purpose, he muses. I am a string of intentions out to elicit a pluck, he would declaim, then giggle. If the Beloved, he muses, could envision a violin and string it with intentions, he, the Enamored One, would be one of the strings, to be plucked at the Beloved's pleasure. Or, why not, he would be all four strings. A shiver permeates his being and nearly dissolves him: the masterful fingers of the Beloved would then never abandon him, but skip from one string that is him to the next string that is also him, and then the next and the next string that is him; thus upon abandoning one string that is him, the Enamored One muses, the dolorous exquisiteness of abandonment would dissolve in the anticipation of the impending pluck whose destiny now no one could avert... He muses on the audacity of his longing, to be all four strings simultaneously, and he is temporarily frozen with fright at such insolence. No, such longing, impious apostasy! could never, never find, no matter how frantically he might attempt, the faintest echo of sanction in the catacombs of his formulations.

Perhaps only one string would do, yes, one string eagerly fibrillating in anticipation of the next pluck by the Beloved's masterful fingers. Eagerly shivering with envy at the plucking of the propinquitous strings. For how long could the subduing fingers of the Beloved stray from the one string of intentions whose rhapsodic prosody is the plinth to exalt him?

A string of intentions in the Beloved's violin. The musical metaphor makes him giggle again, agog with admiration. Yes, in admiration of the unexpected line of poetry that greeted him around a corner he turned. Not only so, he giggles, but in a locus where there are no corners. What is he saying? In the catacombs of his formulations, there are plenty of corners! But which of the violin's four strings would he be? Never having learned to play it, the violin has always remained an amber imponderable to him. No, apostasy to the wind, he would be all four strings. No, no, he would be each and every string, throbbing with frenetic and reverberant effervescence, with each and every pluck of Beloved's fingers. Or, he would cabriole from the pitter-patter of pizzicato thrumming to the hollow hysteria of a contralto baritone. I am imbued with alacrity, I am aglow with effervescence, frenetic with hysteria even, he muses. I am suddenly all-in-a-dither, agog and all-a-gaga, he giggles. Agog and all-a-gaga he giggles makes him perfervid, febrile, zestful, vivacious. Anxious, avid and agog. A grand jetté en avant, more, a grand jetté en avant battu perhaps—o the battu of the translucence of Beloved's alabaster and cambered calves!—perhaps a glissade melanged with a series of grands jettes en avant battu, performé at a feverish pitch, he giggles again. A gargouillade and pas de chat. And then, followed by mortification. I am mortified, then dipped in tar to fry, then dry. He pauses then to ponder and consider the meaning of mortify. He ignores his own warning to ignore the menacing meaning of mortify. Mortification. An enrapturing rumoring murmur of suctioning capitulation, whose echoing meaning should be ignored. Plunge and douse yourself into the rumoring murmur to gain the warm comfort of a tarry pitch shelter. Tickle yourself to sputtering cachinnation while bathing with the 'y' of mortify.

Yes, tickle me with the 'y' at the end of mortify, and once

more he giggles, before the certainty of the intrusive echoings of meaning that menacing mortification surreptitiously insinuates upon his formulations with the intransigence of a certitude. And once more he giggles, this time it is certain why, once more to defy mortify. Mortify I must defy at any price. At least, he muses with the futility of a dessert crosser, if only price had been pry! The triple rhyme might have saved him on account of the fortunate succession of the y rhymes, like a victory in a game of hazard. Not even a grand jetté en avant battu to return to a string of intentions out to elicit a pluck will help now.

A string of intentions out to elicit a pluck is not at all unskillful, he calms himself, attempting to spray the perfume of self-fawning over his elentechical being. Spray the perfume of self-fawning before he is frozen again with the dreaded mortification. Come, fingers of the Beloved, come to strum and thrum!

But admiration of What? he wonders. If he is not, what, who, is there to admire? If he is not, why should he be mortified? He didn't foresee mortification to suddenly intrude upon his fawning. Fawning is a feather torn from a forest of flight. As usual mortification intruded, but this time it surprised him, disguised as a feather as it intruded, a sound undisguised by the beguiling beret of significance, ostrich feathered. The intrusive echoing in a catacomb of unexpected significances.

Is mortification a messenger of He-Who-Employed-him-To-Spy, a warning? Is it the presence, the absent presence of He-Who-Employed-him-To-Spy, him to whom he belongs, whose spy and messenger he is, that ceaselessly mortifies him? Mortification, a tarry pitch to fry and freeze him in each time he plunges in his pool of private longings. Perhaps his pool of private longings is a tarry pitch pool to fry and freeze in. Perhaps mortification is a tarry pitch pool whose meanings he is prevented from fathoming for frying and freezing, a frying and freezing induced by He-Who-Employed-him-To-Spy.

If no one is needed to understand him, he ventures to muse, why could he not just spurt about the words he feels to fill the space as he feels fit? What obliges him to squander the feeble string of vitality he still possesses, the feeble string of vitality that He-Who-Employed-him-To-Spy provided him with, for the purposes of spying and reporting, on mere meaning? It is insidious, he ponders, to be tarred and feathered by meaning. To be endowed with vitality to be squandered on meanings which do not belong to him! To be prevented from plunging into the shimmering pool of meanings which are meaningful to him alone! What forces him to squander himself in torturous attempt to fit a meaning which does not belong to him to the fleeting assault of sounds? To re-shape the sounds into meanings which provide him with no satisfaction? To contort himself into meanings which paint him in hues whose shimmerings he would never indulge in? If only he had his own form, he would not contort it to seek meanings that have no meaning for him! If He-Who-Employed-him-To-Spy provided him with such economy of energy, why does he feel obliged to say 'provided' when what he truthfully wishes to say is 'providianed'? Providian which twists unexpectedly like the passion of an iron boomerang maternality. Paternality. Maternality. Is saying 'provided' when he wants to say 'providianed' self-mortification to mollify with the gift of self-freezing Him-Who-Employed-him-To-Spy? He is mortified at his self-mortification to merely mollify Him-Who-Employed-him-To-Spy.

Yes, 'providianed' him with. Maternality to mortify. Why should he be mortified to have traded the consensual 'provide' for 'providian'? Yes, he can't help but formulate 'providian', 'Providian', actually, for He-Who-Employed-him-To-Spy. "I am challenging the hegemony of the signifier." Why could he not be 'mortified' in the way he would like to be 'mortified', as in, say, tickled to tears by Morticia's feathers? Yes, somewhere there was a Morticia, the meretricious matron, the Morgana without maternality who absconded to her dungeon with him where she placed him for years and where she feathered him to tears, in spite of and despite his bootless cries and fruitless protests. She feathered him and he giggled in spite of and despite his own fruitless protests. But then he had a form, which she didn't spare to mollify by mortification with feathers she employed to delight and cuddle him in spite of and despite his own fruitless protests. Yes, she feathered him, and he was mortified by this meretricious matron Morticia who feathered him in her oubliette, feathered but never froze or tarred him.

If he were not now frozen and tarred with mortification, frozen and tarred like a fortification in his mortification, he finds himself giggling, he would declaim. He should declaim, not giggle. Let the declaiming be conducted with the force of dignity, I would shout! he pouts. No more the sheathings of fruitless protests, as in his pasts, pasts that now he can't recall for the frozen tarring.

We know it is perhaps time now to describe the details of his aspect. We do not wish to frustrate you, reader, you the reader, in your cravings for the details of his aspect. No, we would not avoid describing the details of his aspect to you but we can't. Perhaps you suspect why. We can't, meaning not that we are not capable; no, by no means do we lack the force of description.

It is true, we admit, we are not keen on description. In the manner of a Rimbaud or an André Breton, description bores us. We would deride a downright Dostoyevsky for it. But, no, by no means do we lack the means. At the drop of a hat, and we're not speaking of hats here, no one is dropping hats here, it's only a manner of speaking, and you can't imagine just how we loath, what odium! to be observed inelegantly engaged in employing manners of speaking at the drop of a hat, at the drop of a hat we could describe—but we're not—at the drop of a hat we would describe the amber swirls of sheathing marble on a Romanesque baptisery in a Renaissance Venice, or the windlet in the wake of a feather vane in the twirl of seducer's beret. The language itself creates slight scapes, lockets of irony pierced with the passion of a dense gloom, we find ourselves knitting. Or perhaps stealing a line. A Venice astir with the fans of rumor, we find ourselves weaving, without knowing why.

But back to description. No, don't imagine for a photographer's flash we lack the means. It is not the reason why we are not describing the details of his aspect.

Neither are we afraid: no such insinuation should be imputed upon the pellucid vision we are adorned with. And nor are we prevented. In vision we are unrestrained.

We can't. Simply can't.

But why? Why? you insist. Your insistence is seductive. So seductive we're imagining a tryst perhaps. Still, do not raise your hopes.

Why no description? you insist. Perhaps you already know why.

We don't see him. That's why. Understand that, we don't see him. The Enamored One is there, but we don't see him. We do not lack the macula lutea, nor the acute force of its binary contemplation. But the Enamored One has no aspect. There is nothing to see. He is but not seen. It is not the sense of sight which should be employed in grasping his aspect. He would very much like to have an aspect which the sense of sight, his and others, would grasp. Oh to linger and languish before the looking glass: a luminous stocking flaunting a cambered calf, brandishing the mandatory popliteal crease; the negligent fingernail of an Amoroso or an Amorette concealed behind the curtain's velvet tracing a sudden serpentine along the comforting alabaster of the silky thigh under the

minaret fold of the trunk hose. Or the emerald of his doublet's billowing sleeve raised in a bras en attitude!

He would die for that sort of an aspect. We take that
back. To declare he would die for an aspect forces us to go
meandering into a metaphysical mire. For instance, if he has
no aspect, is he not already dead? Though philosophically
inclined, possibly even apt, we hesitate to slip on the
demanding pantofles of a metaphysical minuet. Though
description bores us, we would much rather describe. But
you, our sweet philosophical peruser of this tortuous text,
put on, if you will, the pondering peruke, the feathered hat
of a guerre de plume, allow yourself if you will a roaming
glissade amidst the vast catacombs filled with the silky
smoke of sophistry.

Perhaps he did have an aspect once. We are not going to
delve here into delicate details of etiology. We did say he did
once, did we not? mortified through Morticia's feathering,
when she abducted him and forgot him in her oubliette. But
perhaps he was aspectful on other numerous and peripetuous occasions. With a not, to his surprise, unpleasant shiver
he calls to himself the fierce pirate who drowned his frightened lover on a moonless night in the molten waves. Yes,
fierceness was not foreign to him once. Yet to write pirate, yet
to write fierce, does it not betray the signifying author's dis-
comfort in a mirror that does not mirror the signifying vortex
of the pre-dominant culture's iconography? And to write
pirate, to write fierce, does it not betray a craving for the tar
of precision, a tar we pride ourselves in perusing contemptu-
ously?

Perhaps, we did write that too, perhaps not, that now in
his disembodiment he is serving a sentence. Perhaps he is
serving a sentence in longing. A long sentence in longing.
The aspect of his longing would allow him the peripetuous
craving he craves. Perhaps he wishes us to witness him as he
serves his long sentence in longing. Of course, as we have

just explained, we can't watch him. But we know where he is. And we know how he feels. Because he does feel. He is sentient. We know what he thinks. Because he does think. He is cogitative. And we know what he's looking at. Because, even without visible sight organs, the sense of sight is available to him. We know everything about him. Everything but what he, we are inclined to feel it's a he, looks like. We'll be a witness to his longing.

The reason we know? Or perhaps the method of our gaining the knowledge? We foresaw your perplexity. We have an answer. We know. We have the means to grasp his non-aspectless aspect. Trust us. We are privileged that way. You, reader, are not, but we are. And we have been employed for the purpose of portraying him for you. We have been thus gifted, perhaps for your sake. We feel everything he feels. We know everything he thinks. And we're going to tell you. It is the raison d'être for the bons mots minueting before your vitreous humors. Go on if you wish. Go away if you must.

We will pursue on, at times kindly lending him, the Enamored One, our great gift for description. And sometimes we will describe. We will strive on in this manner. We will go on as far as we can before boredom, before ennui, impales us. Not you. Us. We are not responsible if ennui and boredom should impale you. We insolently assume that once we have you impaled you will not escape. You will struggle, you will long, perhaps flail your arms in protest, but not escape.

The Enamored One longs. He is a nothingness longing for something. A space enveloping, no, engulphing the Adored One. Not the general or abstracted space of a vast and indifferent universe showcasing its orange craggy rocks in the customary crepuscular luminescence. No, not that. A space that longs; a space that chooses the details it longs to engulph, "as a stocking engulphs a lovely limb", as the Enamored One might denounce. We mean enunciate.

The Adored One? The Adored One is he upon whom the

Enamored One is sent by He-Who-Employed-him-To-Spy to spy. This is complex, so we will expect your patience. Relax. Take a deep breath. First, He-Who-Employed-him-To-Spy is not the same as he (or She) who employed us. Of him (or Her) who employed us we are not at liberty to speak. That's that. We leave that alone. We should not even have divulged as much, but there you have it, and it's too late now.

The Adored One. The Adored One, or the Beloved, is he, as we said, whom He-Who-Employed-him-To-Spy sent the Enamored One to spy on. You may have grasped the Adored One is He-Who-Is-Adored-By-The-Enamored-One. The mission He-Who-Employed-him (The-Enamored One)-To-Spy, is to spy on the Adored One, and not to adore him. To spy and report. Report according to words whose meaning is meaningful to the purposes of He-Who-Employed-him-To-Spy.

The adoring is The Enamored One's personal secret mission, and his stratagem—unsuccessful—was to keep it secret from He-Who-Employed-him-To-Spy. But He-Who-Employed-him-To-Spy deployed the Enamored One discarnate, formless, perhaps in expectation of the Enamored One's adoration of the Adored One, but with the implied promise that he, the Enamored One, would, by fulfilling the dictates of his mission, be endowed with the form he craves, and freed. As though the dictates of his mission were simultaneous with and equal to the serving of a sentence at the end of which, dictates upon the successful fulfillment of, will materialize into the gaining of the form, the incorporation the Enamored One craves, the gaining of a form leading to the freedom to fulfill his longing. A longing the fulfillment of which the Enamored One divines He-Who-Employed-him-To-Spy disapproves of; still, as the employed of He-Who-Employed-him-To-Spy, the Enamored One must obey. What power does He-Who-Employed-him-To-Spy have on the Enamored One? The power, the Enamored One imagines, to endow him with form. With form to fulfill a longing He-Who-Employed-him-To-Spy disapproves of.

The expiation of a deed deserving punishment according to He-Who-Employed-him-to-Spy, and the well established modus operandi of He-Who-Employed-him-to-Spy is what leads the Enamored Spy to divine he is serving a sentence in expiation. Expiation of the consequences of a deed he committed but now does not recall and for whose commission the punishment consists of fulfilling the commission of this present mission in the form of discarnation, so that the longing will be prevented from fulfillment during the procedure of the fulfillment of the mission.

The full dictates of his mission were left unclear, in the manner customary of this employer. This is a complex network of events which baffles you and us both and which he (or She) who employed us sent us to clarify for you. It will not be easy. Yet, since it is our mission to clarify and help you enhance your understanding, we will not fail you. More, we are enamored of our employer.

But back to the Enamored One, the Employed of He-Who-Employed-him-to-Spy.

I am a string of intentions out to elicit a pluck, he would declaim. Of course, a string of intentions is a poetic metaphor, made more entrancing by the conceit of the Enamored One. A string is not an empty space. A string is not formless. A string is an aspectful material. But to begin here a diatribe on the nature of what is material and what not is beyond the purpose of this treatise; or maybe it is not: we are amphoteric on this matter: the ambivalence of what is and what isn't entrances us, and we are always, like smugglers, on the look-out, for the ever shifting threshold between one and the other: after all, though we don't see him, isn't the Enamored One material too? Do not his longings transmute into the very words before your eyes? Yes, ambivalence entrances us to delirium.

We would not ridicule the Enamored One for his poetic conceit. Kindly, compassionately, perhaps a tear hued with ironic formulations shaping itself on the surface of an iris. An iris belonging to us.

A pondering imponderable, escapes our lips.

And we return to the matter of the serving of a sentence. Why serving a sentence? What alerts us? The single and simple fact that it is the manner of a penitent that he assumes. It is that which alerts us to the possibility of the method of sentence serving.

Presently the Enamored One's finger would trace along the Adored One's brocaded shoe; his lips might glide along the cameoed seam of the silk stocking. The prolonged engulfing of the limb he craves. The arrogant cruelty of the seam cameoed, yes the seam cameoed as an exuberant effervescence of the casual cruelty employed in the showcasing of the limb. Casual cruelty employed in eliciting the longing of the Longing One. In eliciting a longing which is without a conclusion. A string of intentions out to elicit a pluck. A string of intentions never perhaps to be plucked. No!

Perhaps we were a bit hasty in declaring our gifts of description; we too are entranced; the Enamored One's entrancement reflects ours; we are between the grip of entrancement and the grip of a struggle for description, a delectable description of the back of the cambered calf in the snowy drifts of the white stocking perused from a very close but slightly raised angle; though it is fine from any angle you care to stare. We have plunged into delectable entrancement along with the Enamored One. The curve of the cambered calf as observed from the floating gallery we built at a level slightly above the entrancing crease at back of the knee where we recline to stare at the imponderable curve of the calf; the stockings, nebulae of imprecise staring! we exclaim, along with the Enamored One; yes, the cameoed seam, as though raised on a pedestal, a shrine to its own beguiling entrancement. The ankle bone's luciferous mini mezza moon, the shady hollow below the astrogolos with its insinuation of quicksand luminance; yes, the ankle bone pronounced to delirium; with our psyche we shift our sedan gallery spiral-wise to inspect the shading of the metatarsals above the second half-moon philosophically reflecting the first, the undulate band—(with point noué lace border of the late 15th century)—of the brocaded pantofle's border slicing across the so carelessly concealed toes.

A marxist-infused eye might stare askew and sternly inquire into the problematic issue of the exploitation of textile workers. An investigative reporter would uncover that two thousand female ecclesiastics were abducted from convents and forced to sew this band of lace for use in idolatrous worship and demonic fetishism, their eyesight irredeemably lost in the process of sewing, and bemoan in conclusion the evils of this exploitative system. The sight of two thousand pairs of eyes sacrificed in the service of the creation of pleasure for one single individual. We will reveal though, in future dialectics about materials in particular and matter in general that this treatise will plunge into, how neither a marxist, nor a cleric, nor even an exploitative system sympathizer calling for compassionate use of the working force, should find reason to complain, about this or any other formulation of materials which appear in this treatise for purposes of pleasure engendering. No partial, or entire, human beings were sacrificed in the production of the materials employed in the narrative of this argument. All rest assured.

Who, then, produced the brocaded pantofle of the Beloved, who weaved and embroidered the entrancing seam of the luminescent silk stocking the Enamored One wishes to place the lips he dreams of possessing upon? We would like to pause here and answer you but the time has not yet come. We too are entranced as the Enamored One is, and simply do not wish to take the time out for a philosophical interlude.

Obversely, if we were to pause once again to peruse the intriguing play of shadows on the exquisite stocking, how we plunge into their entrancing hyperbolic paraboloid effect! and our lips are forced to sussurate in glossolalia a magnificat to the manipulator of the materials of which the stocking is weaved. Once again, our concession to metaphysics, we are obsessed with metaphysics, force us to ponder on the etiology of the material itself, pondering which leads us to inquire into the nature of production of this material, further, the nature of the material itself. Our questioning itself leads us to the entrancing infinitudes the hyperbolic paraboloid effect of the stocking obliged us to plunge in, to be captured by in momentary ecstatic imprisonment, leads us further even, into inquiring the essence of the Beloved, of the Adored One.

But spur himself ourselves on we he must, with the severe lashes of remonstrance. It is the Enamored One's longings we must witness.

The brocaded pantofle a frog or a gondola, the Enamored One pauses to ponder, spurred perhaps by the memory of a Venetian Renaissance. The Adored One, he muses, exists in the persistence of a Venetian Renaissance. Or, he digresses, perhaps the Venetian Renaissance is a mere aspect of the essence of the Adored One, a foreshadowing of a history of whose past we are presently offered the seduction of a soupçon.

A gondola and to repeat, two categories of half moons: one in relief, the ankle bone's astrogolos, one abstracted, two dimensional, the edge of the slipper's. We too pause to ponder on the Enamored One's unwitting pondering on the two different methods of mezza moons. A being without a form unwittingly pondering upon the philosophy of forms.

The Enamored One, not having a form, being of insubstantial substance, being a longing only, how could he hope to fulfill his longing? Foolish Enamored One! he chides the formulations of his unsubstantial aggregates. The unsubstantial aggregates whose anxious fabrications he is at the mercy of, like the sight of Beloved's stockings. Whose formulations are the Beloved's stockings? Whose fabrications are they? It is known that He-Who-Employed-him-to-Spy formulated everything. It is known that He-Who-Employed-him-to-Spy fabricated everything. If only he didn't stutter so! If he didn't stutter so when he addressed He-Who-Employed-him-to-Spy, in terror of his wrath! He would then ask him: whose formulations are the Beloved's stockings then? The Beloved's stockings, entrancing infinities, hyperbolic paraboloid engenderers of cravings? And whose formulations is he? If he craves to caress the Beloved's stockings, more, to gadabout bedighted in pair of them himself, the same as the Beloved, then whose formulations are his cravings? Because, ponders he, could it be that He-Who-Employed-him could have formulated him but without his cravings while his cravings were formulated by another whose purposes are inimical to He-Who-Employed-him-to-Spy? No, no, this could never be! This could never never be! protests the Enamored One. But then, the looming of a conclusion that terrifies him: if He-Who-Employed-him-to-Spy formulated and fabricated both him and his cravings, if He-Who-Employed-him-to-Spy formulated and fabricated stockings as well, might not He-Who-Employed-him-to-Spy be accused of premeditated and calculated cruellery? Is He-Who-Employed-him-to-Spy then not All-Good? Could it be assumed that He-Who-Employed-him-to-Spy formulated and fabricated him, the Beloved's stockings, and his cravings, incognizant of the network of dependant origination relationships existing between them? Because then is He-Who-Employed-him-to-Spy not All-Wise? All-Aware of the relationships between all things? Could it be then that He-Who-Employed-him-to-Spy is enjoying the engendering of the torture that he, the Enamored One is undergoing in his unfulfillment?

Otherwise, if He-Who-Employed-him-to-Spy formulated and fabricated him while someone else formulated and fabricated his longings, and since his longings are what animates him, what would he be without his longings? If it were not for his longings, being immaterial, what would he be? And if indeed He-Who-Employed-him-to-Spy formulated and fabricated both him and his longings, would he not be justified in abandoning any loyalty to He-Who-Employed-him-to-Spy? Could he still believe the implied promise that He-Who-Employed-him-to-Spy made to him to incarnate him upon completion of his mission? If He-Who-Employed-him-to-Spy exercises such cruellery with no compunction, what is to prevent him from not fulfilling his implied promise? Without even the benefit of a contract?

The longing is what animates him. Yes, he is animated by the longing to fulfill his longing. It is penance in longing he is serving, to be ceaselessly searching for the fulfillment of the longing which could never be fulfilled; he ponders unwittingly on how, though his dichotomy should lead to his destruction through self-cancellation, the means for self-cancellation are not available to him, being as he is a nothingness; he ponders on the imponderability of his nothingness as he scurries upwards; he would glide the tip of his tongue and trace it along the treacherous seams of the Adored One's entrancingly luminous limbs. Barely trace it, it occurs to him, so that saliva would not douse it; though there is no saliva, he rejects the potentially incipient invasion of a concept of liquidity which he senses forming at the margins of his faculties, and now he dreads an inappropriate dousing; an inappropriate deluge of dousing; he fears the punishment of the inappropriacy of a dousing deluge disturbing the lake of his longing. The lake-like liquidity of his longing, lapping at the longed for form which he assumes (and which mirrors the form of the Beloved) is a liquidity of a nature that cannot be weighed on conceptual scales mirroring that other liquidity whose dousing intrusion he fears will upset the delicate balance formulated by the demands of his longing. By all means he must repel, spurn, refuse, the threatening advances of the unwelcome liquidity. Still, before abandoning this matter—and he stabs himself with jagged reproaches for lacking the intransigent skills of quick abandonment, for perhaps never having properly practiced to hone, yes, practiced with abandonment, with obstinate resolution perhaps to hone, the art of quickly abandoning, a self-bastinado with obstinate resolution and ceaseless devotion, exerting himself diligently, in trial after trial, sacrificing all comforts, how he chides himself for his lacks!—he furtively indulges in a contest of comparisons. Perhaps, furtively—but without hope—he hopes, a contest of comparisons on scales of ideology might disimprison him from the advancing liquidity he fears will douse the liquidity he longs to be doused in. To douse the Beloved's elaborately luminous limbs in a deluge of lake-like liquidity would diminish if not cancel in extenso the longed for liquidity engendered without the need of a deluge.

The formulation "deluge" disturbs the circumscriptions of the forms he would indulge in: yet another ruthless onslaught he must dispel, and he thinks of Him whom he thinks of as He-Without-Ruth, he thinks of Him he does not wish to think of, he thinks of Him he is horrified to think of as He-Without-Ruth, he thinks of Him he once frightened himself by subversively and impertinently thinking of as Flood-Plotter, whose praxis is punishment by deluge, he thinks of He-Who-Punishes. He thinks of Him who is always lurking at the edges of his formulations. He thinks of He-Who-Employed-him-to-Spy. Still, I am challenging the hegemony of the signifier. I am challenging the hegemony of He-Who-Signifies, because I am petulant. If I belonged to the Beloved, I would be petulant too, he laughs, lake-like. I am petulant lake in which to drown the Beloved at will, he meanders.

Yes, he is fearful that the Flooding he fears will douse the liquidless liquidity he would indulge in his longing for the Beloved is the warning hand of He-Who-Employed-him-to-Spy.

Perhaps another philosophical interlude might be lapping at the shore of our comprehension of materials. The philosophers have taught us that basic materials composing our universe are earth, fire, water and air. To which the Buddhists have added the fifth material, the void, which contains the essence of the other four; thus, the Beloved's stockings, which should be according to reason made of earth, i.e., a secretion of the mulberry worm, are also water, as the Enamored One drowns at the sight on them, fire, as the passion of the Enamored One flares at the sight of them, and air, because to wear them, the Enamored One is lifted to the clouds and floats, earth again because he is helplessly sucked into their quicksand. But to suddenly be doused in a deluge causing them to become soaked, even moist or muggy, imbued and oozing, spritzed, swashed or sloshed, drenched and saturated, soggy and sodden, no! No, no, no!

In the nebulous aggregate of his formulations he balances the fleeting feather of his ceaseless longing oppugned by the constant restraint of his onerous duty, a formulation of fear.

He feels the surge of ire. The inadmissible surge of the Unsuspected and Unrestrained!

oh if only he were allowed

no Prohibition!

He too would be a Traitor to the One-Who-Employed-him-To-Spy!

What if, the Spy indulges in the velvet poetry of sophistry, I am the puppet of an Imponderable, imponderable, he flouts for a flash, then douses his fear, no longer prescient? What if he should turn out to be not an imponderable at all?

What if the nature of what he formulated as Imponderable is about to withdraw, or never even existed? What if a Grand Prevarication were to be exposed?

But then, could he himself continue? Oh, there is so little time left! So little time for the description he longs for, for the minutiae he wishes! Oh to embellish oneself with the lace of minutiae, or the minutiae of lace! that embellishes the Beloved, and thus become the Beloved! So little time left!

Yes, perhaps He-Who-Employed-him-To-Spy is as powerless as he is; perhaps that's why he only employed one as powerless as he; he feels the gliding brush, the feathered thrill of unrestrainment in his powerlessness; if he abandoned—if he had only had mastered the art of quickly abandoning!—his Employer, employer, perhaps his employer would no longer be and no punishment would be perpetrated on him, like the Punishment-of-Prohibition-of-Personal-Expression, prohibition cruelly grafted to the core of his sorry assemblage. Yes, should the Prohibitor vanish, shouldn't his prohibitions vanish as well??

Yes, it is preferable to ponder, if he only could, oh if he only could! to venture to ponder on what he would do, the gestures he would perform, the ballet of the gestures he would perform! perform to precision, if he had a form. It is preferable to ponder on how, if he had a form, phorm, he would spite the norm to spell phorm with 'ph' instead of the consensual 'f'. It is preferable to ponder on how the lingering procrastination of the phoneme would cause the gliding of his tongue to linger a little longer upon the seam, and unrestrained, would deviate beyond. Yes, were he to be a being, at what exact point his tongue would derail from the fixed, the phixed, line of the seam's trajectory, to glide and snake-like slither along the soft of the inner thigh and cause the Adored One to shiver and a shout to escape from the surprised and crimson lips. Nowhere is the marvelous, he murmurs, for no reason he can discern, a locus which could never be colonized; and his tongue a colonizer, a lash to colonize the marvelous he longs for! and the Enamored One leaps in the manner of a bayadere on the lowing lips of the Adored One. The lips lowing on account of the shiver the Adored One received from the lash across the soft of the inner thigh. The Enamored One would know the places to let his tongue to slitheringly linger like he knew the back of his own thigh, were he to be endowed with one. He would know like he knew the workings of his own intricate networks of events leading to his own surprised shouts and shivers he craves. Were he incorporate he would be a replica of the Adored One. For fulfilling his mission of penance the purpose of which he still is unclear of, he would ask He-Who-Employed-him-to-Spy for a phorm mirroring the phorm of the Adored One. His own intricate network of elaborate events animated as they are now only by his longing, a discorporate longing, a longing fulfilling a punishment perhaps through penance, the penance of longing without the possibility of fulfillment. Phulphilment! Yes, to prolong the gliding of the slithering motion by the lingering of the phoneme and thus mitigate the notion of the impending doom of the cancellation of longing awaiting at the termination of the slithering lotion, we mean motion; through the ensuing prolongation of the motion through lingering tongue perhaps the penance would transmute to incorporation leading finally, phinally, to phulphillment. There is always hope, and hope is a thing with feathery thighs.

His nothingness could become something each time he shivers, he muses.

I would shout, he pouts, no more the sheathing of a fruitless protest as in the past. A past he no longer grasps.

The Enamored One would, if could, emulate the dramatic arching of the pierced gallants he perceives in the mirrorings of the globulous orbs below the lashes of the Adored

One—speaking of the lashes of the Beloved, how this linguistic twist in the realm of meanings plucks turbulence on the string of his craving. We note how the Enamored One, amidst the intransigence of his longing, continues in his attempts to pluck at poetic strings. We are moved. Perhaps less by the poetry itself than by the attempt. We have our own likes and dislikes. We too are employed.

Yes, the Enamored One would, if could, emulate the dramatic arching of the pierced gallants he perceives in the mirrorings of the globulous orbs below the lashes of the Adored One and would turn to stare directly at the piercings of swords inculcated upon the gallants by the phorce of the Phierce Demoiselles, Madonnas of Doom. If he were endowed of a phorm he would place his doubletted trunk to face the glimmering rapiers of the Phierce Crimson Dames.

He wouldn't even glance at the rapier piercing him. He would struggle bravely to prolong the last few glimmerings, phew, knowing that to prevent the piercing of the Maddened Demoiselle's rapier is a vain wish he doesn't wish for.

The Maddened Demoiselle's rapier would pierce the velvet of his doublet and he would arch with a shout then tumble, as the gallants at the bottom of the summit he penitently climbed at the beginning of this chapter in his penance are arching their backs and tumbling under the blows of the Demoiselles' rapiers. Oh, if he could only transmute into one of them. Or into the echo of each and everyone of them!

Yes, he would turn to witness it directly if he could bear to abandon The Adored One even for an instant; but to renegotiate that tenuously precarious place of mirrorings might prove to be the frustrating labor of ages.

And not having a phorm, how could he dream of phulphillment? Phoolish! But somewhere is always feeding on nowhere!

Yes, if he had a phorm, he would like us to spell it with the 'ph'.

Yes, if he had a phorm, like that of the gallants, nay, like the Adored One—perhaps he too once had a phorm—he would too fling his head backwards and arch his supine spine; where is it then that he feels the boiling lava of ecstasy as he imagines himself to be inculcated in each and everyone of them? As he craves himself to be speared by rapiers, as they are speared. As though one is mirrored infinitely in the net of Indra! (He remembers momentarily he once learned about the infinite mirrorings of the net of Indra, of each and every event in the universe entire.) But the simultaneity of action delayed echo-like with each succeeding piercing which, though taking place simultaneously in the Enamored One repeats itself in multiple mirroring impressions in his nothingness; a multiple of repetitions which though simultaneous, the Enamored One forces himself to experience sequentially, in time, like an echoing of catacombs. A multiple plucking of his longing string echoing through the catacombs; multiple, not infinite, because we must not pause there too long; we have a story to tell; besides, there is such little time. The Enamored One, under the burden of his duty as a storyteller—for what is a spy but a storyteller?—or there would be repercussions otherwise, under the whiplashes of his duty—unshackles himself from his reverie with a sigh, to adore the further unfolding, yes, encourages himself in the hope of further unfoldings to adore.

The maddened cadre of Demoiselles at Dämmerung would rung by rung rend the Adored One, the Enamored One muses to the gallop of steeds only he can hear.

Pierce this doubletted breast, he would shout, were he endowed of a tongue; he would put himself in the way of the demoiselles' rapiers before the Adored One at the drop of feathered beret, an ostrich feathered beret, he would let himself be pierced by their rapiers to save the Adored One's breast, and now wonders if he truly stumbled upon the meaning of sacrifice, wonders if perhaps he has achieved it.

Is it perhaps sacrifice his pelegrinage in formlessness is to teach him? His fathomless penance a pelegrinage in sacrifice? Must one pelegrinate in sacrifice for the one for whom one adores and sacrifices for to outsoar a life of propitiation?

A lucidity nearly immeasurable of the fruitless being.

Amnesia, Lower Appalachia, October 20, 1998

My Imogen:

I woke up in the middle of the night last night and I heard this line: 'Love is nothing but the desire for the sweet torture it makes us crave.' As soon as I heard it—I had spent a good portion of the night in smoky catacombs with long hallways phantasizing you, though I don't know if it's correct to say I was phantasizing you, I was in fact, as I always am, issuing images I have stored of you, my insides are factories of imagery, Imogen imagery, an industry of images engendered by the mystery factories of my within in response to the knowing of you, and now I can't help wishing to use the obvious assonant connection between images and Imogen but the graceful way of marrying the two sounds by the contiguity of the two words isn't momentarily obvious to me— impressive as it might have appeared at first hearing, this line, and for a moment, before I had time to think about it, I had hoped it would turn out to be a good line, a poetic image,—my poetic Imogen—before the tentacles of judgment had intruded, in customary manner, to maul it to shreds, this line which suddenly I hated because, due perhaps to the mauling action of the tentacles, it became a vacationing island to the near literate idiots, whom I despise, who crave for such insipid conclusions to hang onto, such insipid conclusions that this line draws for this near-literate idiots who will not sweat for an image of their own but vampirically suck the images of others, those whom you know very well, who feed it to them and take advantage of their idiocy, I couldn't, no, I couldn't lower myself as to make it an image for their idiotic mastication, no!

I can see their simpid smiles, sweet! I loathe these people! I loathe them! I would put them in concentration camps where for punishment they should be made to listen day after day to insipid stand-up comics standing as poets feeding them a steady diet of insipid metaphors; the pure torture of being put on this forced diet will act metabolically, nay, alchemically: being forced in such to digest it day by day, the 'friction will make them become more profound people, yes, so I severely chased it out in my mind, this line, 'Love is nothing but the desire for the sweet torture it makes us crave,' as a candidate for a line in anything that would be my contribution to world literature: look at it: 'sweet' contains for me the 'squirm' factor, and instantly freezes me with its vapid reek, while its contiguous alignment with 'torture' seems too tortured a conjoinment of two terms disapproving of one another at first sight, a far too obvious a first sight for me; I could already discern in the dark the cackling of approval of those near literati I spoke about above and whom so I despise, ready to run off with it to their little island, like hungry dogs running off with a flung bone, so I was reticent to write it down except as its own death, its own squirming agony like a cut worm and I wish to destroy it for those semi-literatis in mid-grin with the monstrous agony of the squirming cut worms. I wish them to shudder and draw back and either be shocked into good literature or force them to abandon their facile fanfaronade.

I was suddenly filled up with a dark liquid hatred for their fetid understanding... but as I go on allowing my fingers to meander across the keys of the laptop, addressing you, my dear goddess, my sweet torturer, I am afraid these anxious constructs make no impression on you, that they may not raise your soul to great heights of ecstasy and most of all, of admiration for me and all I wish is place myself before you, kneeling of course, at your feet, and with tears in my eyes declare that I love you, that I can't live without you, that I wish to be your slave forever, that I crave you, and yes, more! that I crave for you to torture me. You allow me to kiss your foot and before my tongue searches for your silken sole my melting vitreous humors raised in supplication before your unfathomable ones, commanding, yes, scrutinizing eyes, but not unkind, not disapproving, and now I wish to prove to you this is not just mere erotic phantasy that I am in the throes of and for which I should be despised for being so obsessed by but in fact this is to be raised to the highest levels of world literature:

'... Where are my stockings? Put them on for me?

She thrust out some positively fascinating feet, little dark skinned feet, not in the least misshapen, as feet that look so small in shoes always are. I laughed and began drawing her silk stockings on for her.

"Eh, bien, que feras-tu, si je te prends avec? To begin with I want fifty thousand franks. You'll give them to me at Frankfurt. Nous allons à Paris; there we'll play together: et je te ferai voir des étoiles en plein jour. You will see women such as you have never seen before. Listen...

Then, she tells him of her plan to spend the money he'd won gambling.

"What? all in two months?"

"Why! does that horrify you? Ah, vil esclave! But do you know? one month of such a life is worth your whole existence. One month—et après, le déluge! Mais tu ne peux comprendre; va! Go along, go along, you are not worth it! Aie, que fais-tu?

'At that moment I was putting a stocking on her other leg, but could not resist kissing it. She pulled it away and began hitting me on the head with the tip of her foot.'

No one less than Dostoyevsky, yes Dostoyevsky himself wrote this, so on my knees, yes, a knight bedighted as I would be on such occasions when, on my knees before you, in my Renaissance dress which I confessed to you I am obsessed with wearing, and—if you'll recall, you suggested once when our craving for each other was young, when our craving for each other was mutual, you said we should get Renaissance clothes for me when we shared our mutual love's pleasuring of each other—which Renaissance suit I yearn to wear as my adoring you wear, yes my Renaissance dress as my adoring you wear, and, on my knees I stare at my knees, the crease of the white silk hose I wear and which I admire and which gives me such pleasure to feel gripping tight along the length of my legs whose shape I wish to admire as I am on my knees worshipping your silken soles with my tongue and yearning for you to

                do you recall when you and I were
          sitting with each

other in the garden of your apartment in the autumn of our mutual desiring and your lovely fingers slipped the black hair tie over your ever lovely leg so sculpted by years of ballet training, oil in the service of Europe's cultural machinery and paused it mid-thigh in the manner of garters with such exquisite skill, and how by the way how did you know exactly where to position it mid-thigh to give me that intimate shiver your positioning there the black hair tie caused in me? Precisely placed where the lacy top of the silk black stocking would end; and as soon as your fingers posted it there, they took it back and I begged you to tell your fingers to post it where they had previously paused it, at that exact same spot mid-thigh but you didn't, instead you said my desire for you is selfish and I wished to protest as I lightly pondered the source of the severe philosophy of your apostrophe, the moral finger you shook at me then, pondered it without more than an answer so vague I didn't bother to distinguish the source of its imprints upon my brain, whether it was mere christian entreaties or had complications of Eastern philosophical sources as they invaded the West in the sixties, though I did conclude that what made it 'selfish' in its negative connotation, in the sense of my own moral lacks (observed in the mirror of your apostrophe), was your lack of compassion for me and my desire, conjoined by your judgment of my desire, desire which you yourself made sure your lovely fingers stoked in my feverish brain and body with such skill, trained as it was, is, by the European Community's Cultural Factories, factories whose furnaces are never not smoking, desire which, according to christian entreaties you no longer believe in, is sinful, and which, according to Eastern philosophies is natural, so in conclusion, you merely desired to torture me, and so you did, very well, and I, I too, I watched myself desiring you to torture me, you were brutal in the torturing of me that night, brutality in your refusal to bring up the black garter hair holder to the same level of the thigh, oh yes, so skillful your fingers were that they brought it back when I begged again but only to the visually unsatisfactory position of just above the knee which I now declare you knew very well wouldn't please me but only tease me, no, more, disappoint me, displease me, tear my soul, scar it, and then forbade me to bury my head in your thighs, pounded my head with your fists, pulled your pant leg down.

Anyway, it's late and I have to go to class. I got a one thirty with my second group of second year students and then a seven o'clock with my third year students. Actually I had a faculty meeting at ten a.m. which I thought was at ten thirty, so I wouldn't have made it on time anyway; but the gas man was supposed to show up between eight and ten and turn on the gas—it's beginning to get cold here in Amnesia, the kind you don't get down in L.A.—and he hasn't yet. That's why I was able sit down at the laptop for so long at one sitting. I guess I'll have to leave him a note. I hope that you realize it's not my intention to criticize you; my love for you hasn't changed; I desire you stronger now than when I was in L.A. Your rejection of me hasn't marred my feelings in the least. It's not just that I can't forget you, I don't want to. I dream about you coming up here after you get your Ph.D. I can't help but feel assured there will be a position open for you to teach German. With your background in ballet and piano, it will be perfect. You will love the faculty here, and I think they would love you too. They are a wonderful bunch, not the stuck up professorial types one reads about in Nabokov. After my poetry reading, which was well attended by the faculty, I think I am now a bit of a celebrity here. They were impressed indeed when I read my poems from magazines with beautiful covers and perfect binding, not the usual typed sheets of paper everyone uses when they read their poetry, or the stapled together rags. I started somewhat of an affair with a married woman, she teaches drama history and after the reading she asked me for a photo-copy of 'lovely lyla'. Her husband is in the theatre as well and lives in Atlanta. I'm certain this won't be a problem once you get here. (I told her about you and she asked if you were my muse. I gave her a vague shrug, as I felt it would diminish me to appear less than vague.) The gas man still hasn't showed and if I don't go in the next few minutes I'll miss my T'ai Chi class I take before my Thursday one-thirty. I guess I'll just leave him a note pinned to the mailbox with the combination to the basement door lock.

Your adoring slave,

J

P.S. There is a spot, an entrancing milky mound, which, just to imagine, my Imogen, I get weak in the knees, just behind your knees. As I walk to my car I will not take note of the leaves on the poplars across the street which are daily turning from amber to near crimson in the autumn sun; and I will not comment to myself regarding my notorious gift for locking with gaze the frilly frontier where the leaves which are still clinging to their green past and those traitors already crimson contraband. Instead, I will picture myself kneeling, in Renaissance dress of course—one fleeting glance to make note of the contribution of the thin alabaster strip of lace, how it smiles between the billowy emerald velvet of the sleeve and the lavender of the skin!—and clinging—cameos of unrestrained prayer! monuments to thirst!—to the back of your thighs, my tongue in close congress with the above mentioned mound; though you should know, it is going to be difficult to decide whether I will drink of the silk of your white skin, or whether I will simply place my cheek, adoringly against the seam of your silky black stocking, and shiveringly sob.

AMNESIA, LOWER APPALACHIA,
OCT. 24, 1998

My Imogen:

My letter to you of October 20 sits on the mantle above the faux fire place my place here in Amnesia is bedighted with. (I do not need to stress to you that my mission here in Amnesia must remain TOP SECRET.) Four days ago I placed inside its envelope four perfectly paginated microsoft word pages in the font of Courier twelve point, except of course for the Dostoyevsky quote which I carefully, post script, reformatted by indenting it to the right the length of a left index tapping of the tab key, then reduced it (to ten point) in the manner I had seen quotes printed, properly as in books. I also took pains to accent the French, but did not italicize it. Since you are fluent in the 'ramble of Rimbaud' and will assume I too had grasped it as quoted by Dostoyevsky in the text, I felt it felt just right to allow the text to remain plain, as though casually sprinkling the conversation with the frill of the French, the ratata of the ratatouille, and thus prompt the ooohs and aaahs of those in whose mirror of ooohs and aaahs one wishes to observe oneself posturing thus.

Of course, to wish to observe one's self thus is a 'grasping for the moon in the water, mistaking the reflection for the actual object—it has the color and shape of the object but not the reality', to quote the Enlightened One.

(Here I must pause to relate an event to you. The other day, Marcel Pomme, who teaches French here at the school read a long and ponderous panegyric of jesuitical jive, waving his arms in the pantomime of a post-mortem Voltaire, to the superiority of the French langue; the eleves roared with rieur without pausing to ponder that M. Pomme, underneath his fanfaronade, meant every word he uttered; I rushed to him after the reading to congratulate him on the mastery of his mots and then, like un vrai Romanian roué, stabbed him suddenly in the side with a casual remark about Rimbaud, and how his poems in the translation of a masterful Romanian poet were for me far more powerful than in the original langue. He has avoided me since, though I make it a point, each time I see him gesticulating in peripathetic con-fraternation with a dashing boy in ballet tights, to rush to him and greet him with an accented but elegant 'Common va tu, Marcel? Tout va bien?').

Then I printed the letter on regular eight and a half by eleven plain white paper I bought from the Office Depot here in Amnesia, as I couldn't find the paper I brought with me from L.A., then folded it carefully in three and forced it as it rustled inside an unadorned white legal size envelope; the tongue you once knew intimately and praised, 'the foreign tongue I taught you once', this tongue once blessed now risked paper cut to salivate along the despicable glue, and then the sealing, the shutting close of a destiny, a gesture of finality, the act of courage of a heart unmasking itself, a reli-gious gesture akin to confession, mystical, a transaction in transcendence; and the envelope: the red print of the letters on the return address sticker I stuck on the left corner with the red candle icon traversed snakelike by a barbed wired reversed S were a free gift from Amnesty International requesting $$$; the stamp a standard US flag 32 center; my handwriting of your name and address as flowing as I could muster it in ascertaining the handwriting discernment capa-bilities of imaginal postal workers. I did give Imogen's I, suc-cessfully too, a dashing, frilly curlicue of a stroke, which gives me the shivers each time I peruse it, like the late afternoon's anticipation of an evening's flagellum's lash, gripped by the gloved fingers of the Worshipped One. The rest of the stroke is caligraphically chic yet uniform and to stare at it, at the entire envelope, you get the feeling of sheer aesthetic pleasure, disquieting mystery, a shivery sense of accomplishment: the plain, unadorned paper envelope was transcended. Each time I return home from school I pick it up in my fingers and let the tips stroke it gently. You may ask yourself, perhaps subconsciously so, how could I have allowed its present stamp, such a clash with the rest of the concept. It goes without saying that I wished the stamp to be other then the one with the US flag, but in the fervent rush of anticipational anxiety for my frantic declarations to reach you, I ignored my best aesthetic sentiments in a crucial instant, and slipped on the despised stamp; and how could I forgive myself, ever, for engaging nationalistic matters into our poetical transactions? A love letter of such ardor, of such baroque word eruptions spurting as they do from my sensual ardor, should be marked, perhaps, by another sort of stamp on it.

I know of no stamps with famous dominatrixes; I think this is a terrible oversight: a stamp collection of erotic adorators of all sorts. I think a terrible disservice is done to them by not celebrating them in stamps: it makes the whole gamut of erotic obsessions something not to be celebrated publicly. After all, the gays have pride parades; why not parades for all erotic adorers? Unfortunately for them, the erotic adorers are all grouped with the gays. Nothing against the gays here; it's just that not all erotic adorers are gay. I think if we are to have stamp collection cameoing imaginative and obsessive erotic behavior, it will probably have to wait at least until the gays get their famous gays stamp collection, which might take a while, I presume, considering the present climate. (They haven't even made it in the military, though I have no idea why they would want to.) But who knows, it might so be in the future, that we all could end up on stamps, as pioneers in erotic behavior. If I could paint I think I would paint our stamp as the content of the P.S. paragraph from this last letter to you, letter which you don't have yet. Our backs would be to the viewer, so that the seam of your left leg's stocking would be clear and visible, since the view of the right one would be blocked by the kneeling moi, in my Renaissance garb. But our heads, our heads would not be turned away, instead they be turned to the viewer, not with frightened, shamed aspect, as though surprised in flagrante delicto by the paparazzo's flash, but with a wistful sort of pride and a challenging glare, perhaps even a contemptuous frown, something á la Rimbaud. The reason for this is clear: we are proud of our particular form of eroticism. But why not then, one might ask, face the viewer directly? Why not proudly pose in frontal view in mimick of the American Gothic, the fanciful S of the whip supplanting the utilitarian fork, while silk and velvet, leather and lace replace the artless rough stuff of their protestant cloth? Well, simply because we are not directly inviting the viewer into our world. The viewer, liberated by this public acceptance of our eroticism, this government issue new American Gothic of our liking, by this act of celebratory cameoing of an action verboten till then, may wish to join in, may have long wished to join in. But we, proud pioneers of the erotical picaresque, we pioneers of the erotic beyonds, we who have long struggled and endured true and imagined beratings (B ratings?), who have practiced our activities of raising pleasure to an ever higher plane, explorers of forbidden unknowns for the sake of liberating hibernating humanity, we say this to you: we will not make your entrance to this brave new world an easy one; no, you must endure, as we did, not the contempt of the common activity field, but our contempt; if you can pass through its lacerating teeth, then you're welcome to its peculiar ecstasies; if not, please perish in the tepid pleasures of your missionary posturings.

Here I must pause to speak of post intention. In the integral work of art I wish this envelope to be—as you may have noted by now, how attached I have become to this envelope, how much it has come to signify—because only an integral work of art containing all the complexity which my aesthetic self-esteem yearns for, an outer twin to its inner twitches—why not assume the present stamp is the Original Intent? (Notice the capitalized O & I.) Sure, I plastered the stamp on in a hurry because I had to obey not the call of wisdom—what is that anyway? The common black bread of daily grind which here I wish to rise above (please, no dough jokes)—but the hurricane call of my heart's desire, because having confessed in fevered and skillful words, ornate baroque constructions to caress your lovely intricacies, the unbearable Babylon you engendered in my soul, I wished for you to know these words, I wished to place myself before you as I am, exactly as I am, I wished, by writing it and presenting it to you to purchase a ticket at the Babylonian lottery of your mercy, as presented by Borges:

> Once initiated into the mysteries of Bel, every free man participated in the sacred drawings of lots, which were carried out in the labyrinths of the gods every seventy nights and which determined everyman's fate until the next exercise. The consequences were incalculable. A happy drawing might motivate his elevation to the council of wizards, or his condemnation to the custody of an enemy (notorious or intimate), or to find in the peaceful shadows of a room the woman who had begun to disquiet him or whom he never expected to see again.

Do you understand then? This envelope which a moment ago I paused my writing to pick up once again and once more admire, this envelope whose artistic complexity now grows—onion skin like—more complex with my every

word and whose successive tearful pealing leads labyrinthi-
cally, catacombically, to the fire that burns for you at the very
center of my being, could it not be, not the accidental col-
laging of the US flag with the lashy I, more, with the positively explosive contents, but by arrangement with a Higher
Self, of which, in my passionate whirl of the moment I was
only peripherally aware of?

The delightful object d'art, this trope of an envelope,
where the clash—the lash really—of the I of your Imogen—
my Imogen!—with droves of the patriotically repressed concealing their true yearnings behind the banner studded with
stars, just like my fiery words to you are concealed behind
the thin paper walls of this envelope! This stamped masquerade, trope of my subversion, dungeons of corrosive contents! The innocent lash of an 'I' to undermine the whole of
the repressive mentality of the common activity at one
stroke! Yet, no one knows this but this 'I', this lash of my 'I'!

I will now switch from the lashy meanderings of my love
quill to the rapier of philosophical dissent.

You know as well as I that this area where I live, Amnesia,
Lower Appalachia, is the hotbed of baptist fundamentalism.
I don't know your real feelings about it as we never really discussed our beliefs with each other, but this is how I feel. Of
course, this is a generalization, to say this area is the hotbed,
I want to call it a cesspool, of fundamentalism, yet the numbers themselves are the key here. I mean the numbers of
actual believers, and specifically what they believe in. Let me
digress philosophically. Their belief, the flagellum snaking
like a coda at the core of their credo, the conception of their
conviction, that man is originally sinful.

Meaning fucked from the start. I won't get here into the
concept of their god, which is disgusting: I mean, why create
a god who is so mean-spirited? Genesis 3:24, when he kicks
A & E out of heaven: "In sorrow shalt thou eat it all the days
of thy life; Thorns and thistles shall it bring forth to thee...",

etc, etc. And then, to finish off Genesis 3: "...and he placed at the east of the garden of eden cherubims, and a flaming sword which turned every which way, to keep the way of the tree of life."

So, first of all, since it is the people themselves who create their god, to have created such an asshole of a god tells us something about that whole group of people who embrace this conception of a god, a god with which to torture themselves, a god with which to oppress themselves; I don't want to harp on this—get the joke?—whose ideas ended up infecting most of the world; in other words, the idea that life itself does not belong to you, that it is on loan to you for the duration of your physical existence and you may only use what is previously approved for you by others whom you despise but should trust because they 'say so', and who have the police and the mayor on their side to prove it.

I mean here's a list of things this system does:

a. You have a pleasure system, don't touch it

b. You have an imagination to enhance the uses of your pleasure system, don't use it.

c. In the heaven this god has created for you, you are going to enjoy yourself according to our ideas of how you are going to enjoy yourself; none of the enjoyment apparatuses you possess now will be available to you then, thank god, but trust us, it will be heaven.

d. Mostly, under the pain of upcoming hell, your self, your imagination, your mind, is not accessible to you; the reason? you are bad! left to your own devices, you will do something bad and end up worse off than you are now.

e. The society: a place where a group of people make sure that no one in particular has access to their internal self; a place to reinforce prohibitions; a serious choking place.

f. Respecting authority means nothing but repressing yourself in favor of an authority figure who is the successor to past authority figures dedicated to the repression of the freedom of the human imagination; thus respect and repression go hand in hand. It is in fact respect born out of fear.

g. That indeed there is a heaven but you don't have access to it; your entry to heaven is basically barred by severe people, by those who know more than you do. You must behave as they say, otherwise you don't get in. A selective hierarchy that rewards the restricted, squeezing the goodness from their lives like toothpaste till they become nothing but tubes of amnesia, like a masked form of the prohibited masturbation, the rerouting the imagination born of the life force into the abstraction of concrete shopping malls.

h. They certainly spent a lot more time creating hell than heaven. Heaven is dull, there is no such thing there as imaginative erotics; however, as opposed to heaven, in hell there are all kinds of phantasmagoria; phantasmagoria which is within you, which you are the fabricator of, but which will lead you to hell, therefore you are sinful, and you are of the devil.

i. Perhaps upset over the long reinforcement of fear of hell, the scientific revolution, trying to oppose hell, has created an abstraction of hell out reinforced concrete; the Dantean hell at least has the advantage of being imaginative; our hells are nothing but a complete denial of the imaginative.

J. We have created a society on whose stage only those whose desires are unimaginative can function, a society of functionaries, of protestant fundamentalist functionaries.

k. That there is little of you which is good, but the rest of you, which is most of you, is bad and stay away from it if you know what's good for you. A prohibition against your own self, against living the life that's yours from the start. The cherubim with the flaming sword will make sure of that.

Then, after this arbitrary way of frightening the folk of their own selves for a few millennia takes root, people believing they are 'fucked from the start', this jesus person appears to tell them, hey, god is really ok, and though you are sinners, you can be forgiven through me, son of god, I'm totally in with the old man, and if you don't believe me, here, let me do a few tricks for you, I'll walk and water and turn it to wine. And people, having felt so bad about their own selves for so long, embrace this man's ideas. Yet again, another way to separate them from their lives, by giving them a transcendent way to deny themselves. This is perfect for the romans whose own gods have run their course; romans, lovely connoisseurs of human souls and how to control them, figure this is a wonderful philosophy to control the people: make them feel bad about themselves, create a network, catacombs of prohibitions in which to get perennially ensconced; but at least for 1500 years the catacombs were fun, they had some sort of connection to the Babylonian lottery, where, if, for example, someone like me, by the luck of the draw, might get delivered in the hands of a marvelous intimate enemy, like you, wouldn't have to feel bad about enjoying it. There was no god to judge it, you were simply at the mercy of a whimsical fate, without morality to burden it, an erotic operatic cosmic melodrama. Then Luther shows up, etc, etc.

Oh Imogen! 'Je t'adore ô ma frivole, ma terrible passion!'

It is at times like these, when the light of artistic recognition pervades my quivering soul, when the light of independent origination fulminates through my fiery fancies that my silky knees yearn for the ground before your silken foot, 'avec la dévotion du prêtre pour son idole', in the manner of Baudelaire. Presently a mere pretend foot, but the lashes of destiny may be kinder yet to this slave!

> Beneath your pump, so satiny!
> Beneath your charming silken sole,
> Your slave, I, play my quivering role,
> Pray, take my genius, mock my destiny.

<u>My</u> translation of good old Charlie B., by the way. Note the perfect ABBA rhyme scheme, exactly as in l'originel. (Compare it with the impotent others', and your admiration for me will rocket to the Heavens!)

Your most obedient slave,
J

P.S. I wonder, though, if a politician in the throes of couvade could bring a case against me for desecrating the flag.

Amnesia, Lower Appalachia,
November 7, 1998

My Imogen:

Nietzsche says in his "The Gay Science": "So far, everything that has given color to existence still lacks a history..." You wore a mini and white cotton stockings and kept pulling up them up past mid thigh under the vigil of homeless proletarians now thoroughly eroticized in the silvery penumbra of the Saturday afternoon, forced as they were into right angles by the rigid right angle formed by the sidewalk and the stone side of the building and who bellowed their appreciation each time you bent because they kept falling down, the stockings that is, unpropped up as they were by anything but their own inherent property to grip the skin, property their designer did not endow them with liberally; or, the material itself was not inherently endowed with the property to grip the skin, but it was the designer who picked the material. (The possibility exists, certainly, the manufacturer did not follow the specifications for material that the designer conjured up when working alone on the design of the stockings in his studio, perhaps he had asked for strands of elastic lycra to be infused into the cotton, who knows? Yes, that possibility certainly exists, but as with most historical scientific movements, a limitation of assumptions has to be made to elicit any advance; so we will assume for the purposes of our search the designer picked the material the manufacturer ended up using. Based on my experiences I know this is not perhaps likely; but, to advance, we will assume it and go on.)

Such was the choice of the material, and I wondered if it was purposefully selected. This is not a territory I am familiar with, not a territory I invested with interest, so I wondered what the designer had in mind at the time. If I were to declare I would like to invest interest in this territory, I would feel fearful, as though I ran the risk of being discovered and exposed while performing an act for which I would be ridiculed and shamed. Certain materials are invested with this sort of shame, whether natural or synthetic. You long for this sort of material, but secretly, and glance at it surreptitiously when passing the you-know-what rack in the supermarket.

Still, there was someone who clearly didn't feel shame and designed this particular sort of delightful stocking and I wondered if he thought about the frustration he was causing in me. I wondered if that was part of the design. You did not seem frustrated, and kept pulling them up, though irregularly. I want to say 'you couldn't set your clock by it', but you know how I hate the commonplace. We were part of a larger drama, designed by the designer of the stockings; the designer of the stockings was too part of a larger drama: the drama of stockings. The allure of stockings was designed into the universe to play a major role over a sectioned portion of time and space, of history, fraying certainly into other times and spaces, other histories, other universes, where the stocking played a more minor or no role; the universe itself, in imagining its own drama, designed stockings; stockings are weaved out of the universe itself, its entrancing strands are secreted by the universe itself, stockings are the universe weaving itself into entrancement; the designer of stockings was merely the messenger of the spider at the center of the universe.

I now realize their entrancement, the stockings', your stockings' specifically, was the mechanism they produced: their mid-thigh allure contra the constant thwarted hope they would stay up so as to maintain the mid-thigh allure; each action of pulling them up foisted upon me new hope; less than five minutes later however, whether walking or sitting or lying down—we were walking—the ideal form would disband to leave in its place a longing for it; one lived for the spectacle of the next pulling up, for the spectacle induced by the 'very acme and pitch' as Donne would put it, the apogee of the next pulling up, the zenith, and for the hope that the next pulling up would bring a more lasting success; and though one understood very well the principles of physics, such as the principle of diminishing grips each successive pulling up would necessarily lead to, one never stopped hoping, hoping against hope. Hope is a thing with feathers. No, hope is a thing with garters.

I silently fought for a world of fixity, while you promoted motion. Yes, the very design of the stockings led to your motion; I can't guess whether you were a volunteer in collaboration with this designer's experiments or whether your actions were simply the involuntary result of this designer's designs. Still, your motion was made valid by previous fixities; all present art, I heard it said, is ironic discourse on the art of the previous generation; yes, the motion itself was a commentary on the previous fixity, and the commenting itself became the entrancement which previously consisted in fixity. Even the non-luminous whiteness was a comment upon previous luciferous black. The constancy of the spell of white thigh—tanned—preaching from the pulpit of the lacy top, the vertical worship of the garter belt pointing approximately to the chantry; your fingers which previously were to be fixed on the instrument to ensure the worshipper's conversion, were now busy with the labor of reconstructing the fixity; but in so doing, the reconstruction became a deconstruction, motion replacing fixity. Religion converting to post-modernism.

One dreamed of possible schemes of progress, not

progress but return, improvement; yes, one postulated an appropriate garter-belt, only to fearfully dismiss it a moment later: the simple but not inelegant stocking top—a creation achieved by no more than a mere folding over of the fabric at the top, a folding over of no more than a half an inch, and a stitch which the eye sought in desperate hope for the impossible fulfillment which the lace surely would have brought, still, a stitch not to be merely dismissed, a stitch which was merely a stitch, whose function was just to be that and no more, though the designer of the stocking, even by choosing cotton, even by eschewing the expected elemental lace of the top, by subverting so obviously the expected ideal form, was well aware of the boldness of his statement—was consciously endowed with its own aesthetics that did not wed it to the garter belt, it made the apropos garter belt inappropriate, it belonged to another, newer, elemental condition of ideal beauty. No, this white cotton stocking, a condensed condition of a previous history, an apparently austere protestantism emerging from an indulgent baroque catholicism, more, an ironic commenting, with its laundry fresh allure mimicking the scent of spring flowers transgressing thus into a possibly permitted decadence, was a bold scheme to undermine and subdue by inappropriate means, to undermine and subdue the ideal form, the classical, mythological form; a post-protestant form to restate and undermine, a quicksand scheme, a Fata Morgana, a now-you-see-it-now-you-don't ruse to subvert the pre-established order; it was aimed at seduction by catering to your longing for seduction by destruction; a form of pleasure we crave, to be frustrated in the grips of the entrancer, the grips of the entrance, a mechanism of frustration aimed at the vanquishment of the hapless spectator; at the instant of the vanquishment, achieved by the constant wearing down of the vanquished through successive quicksand morality, of promises never kept; a lesson perhaps partially gleaned from (or by) the insurgent cocote of Lubitch in the movies of the thirties who to entrance and thus vanquish the iconic male she pulled on the strand of the proper papillon to disband its proper form; very much like Baudrillard's colonialism as seduction; or colonialism by seduction; the victor could go so far as to let the subversive stockings reach, to the vanquished one's ecstatic horror, like the ultimate quicksand suck, all the way down to the ankles; no, not exactly: you wore black suede grandma boots with four inch heels; the boots gripped entrancingly half way up your ballerina calves, while the fiercely threatening laces made such precise loops! though I hesitate to call them grandma boots because grandma implies a decaying of the flesh, I am trying to avoid thinking of decaying flesh when I think of you and I and our endeavors to engender pleasure together for and from each other. From each other.

I was speaking of the designer of the stockings; you are a woman who admires philosophy, who philosophizes herself. André Breton says: "The human individual struggles within a play of forces whose meaning he has generally given up trying to unravel, and his utter lack of curiosity in this regard indeed seems to be the very condition of his adaptation to life in society: rarely is the shoemaker's or optician's trade compatible with any profound meditation on the goals of human activity."

I agree. They flounder at the border of a quicksand namelessness no one pays them to penetrate and, like squint eyed philosophers, like shepherds of bleating notions, they wipe their eyes in crooked wonder reckoning it pays nothing to venture a furlong further to the beyond where the true trafficking of ideas transmutes to the degree of vision.

You will appreciate then I'm sure my discussing the erotic mechanism designed into the stockings, the subtle machinery foisted upon us to enhance pleasure and enslave. I don't know if it is appropriate to bring up the workings of capitalism here; I am not very well versed in Marx, yet I feel it is appropriate, I'm sure it is, to bring up mass production, as that particular pair of stockings you wore that day, the only time I ever saw you wear those stockings, the only pair of stockings of that sort I ever saw anywhere, were creations of a designer who understood the most subtle desire mechanisms of the human soul, a true poet, all the more so in that he was unrecognized by the poetic community at large; I recognize you, poet of engendering desire, whether you are a true poet whose meaning is to foist pleasure upon the soul and thus free the soul from its daily fetters, a poet whose designing strands are the true strands of the spider herself spinning at the center of the Imponderable from the silk of Helios, or whether you are a poet spy, spinning from the strands of labor's blinded tarantulas, a poet whose meaning is to enslave the soul to the subtle and complex mechanisms of capitalism and mass production: even our most private, intimate thoughts and desires are pre-designed; as in Borges' Babylonian Lottery where part of the punishment, or the reward, according only to how you choose to view it, is to be delivered into the hands of an intimate enemy; the enemy, in this case, is the mechanism of the stockings which is in turn the mechanism of capitalism: to engender desire which to constantly in turn frustrate, which in turn engenders more desire to continue to constantly frustrate. Who is the spider at the center who yarns the yearning of it all? (Please note here that in latin cultures the spider's net is likened to the silk of the stocking.)

O the phantasmic yearning whose luminous yarn I'm in the grip of and with your help tried to reconstruct in strict observance of its promised entrancements whose initiation's grips we attempted to escape into, how you and I bartered for that pleasure you promised me! How we quartered our imponderables on scales of culpability! The world itself an infinite stocking made guilty by our staring!

Is there, I ask myself, a platonic stocking at the center of the universe, one which only god might wear and from which all our imperfect copies are constructed? Was your sporadic folding and unfolding meant to fulfill the fate inherent in the mechanism of the stockings ultimately a dance you performed for a god's enjoyment? A dance to make this god happy, and me miserable?

But let me douse this poetic exuberance with the cotton of disappointment. Your white stockings lacked luminance, which was mildly annoying. Perhaps it was the fault of the weft. If I said the choice of cotton was amusing I would be dishonest. At the time I think I might have welcomed it, as a relief from the indulgence of imagined silk and the luminance of its petrolific mimicks. In a French movie of the thirties a pimp conveys his frustration his whore's stockings are cotton. In retrospect the cotton was only mildly disappointing at the time you wore it. In retrospect I crave its laundry fresh allure with its mimick of spring flowers. I realize now the grave mistake we made. The grave mistake I made. But again, I'm getting ahead of myself. Still, if I were to turn the hose of self-reflection on myself and splay on myself a healthy dose of self-criticism, I would claim that at the time you wore these cotton stockings, which clearly lacked the craved luminance of their baroque predecessors, I lacked luminance too, the luminous numen of recognition: unwilling to let go of preconceived notions of the pleasure mechanisms of my past, having cemented through incessant recapitulation of imaginal worship an altar to the garter belt, I couldn't allow a purely ecstatic worship to be engendered by the white cotton stockings, I saw them merely as amusing mirrorings not transcending irony, irony whose function is merely to amuse, to merely hoist up a lip corner, but not to break through to the worshipful pose of ecstatic abandonment. In retrospect I clearly see I faltered. In clasping so close my altar to the garter, in my worshipful fundamentalism, I failed to appreciate and thus open up the potential of new germinal incipiences.

I faint now to imagine the soft suck your lovely legs were enduring—o the intransigent perfection of your lovely legs!—and since I don't have you now in my arms, it is as though I am plunged into stockings myself! Yes, the stockings of my loss of you. My loss of you which cannot be entered in the registers of Marx's dialectics, nor encased in Case's technological advances...

AMNESIA, LOWER APPALACHIA,
DECEMBER 28, 1998

My Imogen:

I was taking a stroll on Sunday, a Sunday stroll if you will, this sounds so self important, I hate it, how about Sunday I took a stroll, with the simple and elegant 's' alliteration, I must remember this is simply a letter, not literature, I am not writing this for publication or posterity, it was a gloomy, cloudy, drizzling Sunday, there is a street in Amnesia I walk on on my way to Hades Park, on my left the hospital's parking structure with its toasted waffle architecture, the private memory dream of a childhood's morning to give comfort each new morning as adult in the workforce: abstract art, to please him, to torture me with its absence of baroque deviations; a sawed off piece of home for him, discarded food for me, and now the butter splattered on the waffle has slipped off into the street, notice here how we're playing with abstraction of sizes, the immensity of the waffle versus the mere smattering of the butter or ice cream, the severe civilizing effect of the diamond cut of the gray wall waffling at me with a frozen sneer, while across the street, the forest, infinite and poetic severed by the despair engendered by the freeway slashing across it.

And here I was again, at the time I spotted the butter, or the ice cream, a prisoner of your illusionarium, supine in my doublet and hose, the tip of my tongue in infinitesimal congress with the silk of your soles—I am mixing here sensuality and politics—your soles of translucent black silk, your lucifer deceivers whose deception I craved, whose deception is the only reality I crave, and wondering:

Why was I
    viewing myself
        in such
            dark light
            for this craving?

There I was, my tongue, its surface, was gliding along the silky surface of your sole, the silky surface of your black stockings over your sole. I know, I know I am repeating myself and it makes me squirm too to repeat it, to write it down. Yet no matter how much I try I can't seem to transform this longing into art! Unlike Borges, I chided myself, who, with the power of thought and imagination can conceive the constructs and constraints of a complete civilization instead of being enslaved by these erotic constructs and constraints!

I was under the weight that all my thoughts led to one thing, that is, a desire to produce pornography, that is, I was ensconced, more, prisoner, of images at whose mercy my mind trotted and art wasn't forthcoming to rescue them, no, Baudelaire, Dostoyesvsky, weren't rushing to the rescue, I was the prisoner of a mechanism which now made me nauseous, made me want to throw up, I was laughable, I don't even know why the stockings were black this time instead of white.

Buddhism teaches us all phenomena are mutually identified: one is equal to all and all is equal to one. The hidden and the manifest complement each other to make one entity. All phenomena are ceaselessly permeating and reflecting one another, like reflections in the jewels of Indra's net. This is a net said to hang on a wall in the palace of Indra. At each interstice of the net is a reflecting jewel which mirrors not only the neighboring jewels but the multiple images reflected in them. In this context, kissing stockings of beautiful women, more, kissing the soles of the women one loves, kissing your feet, my Imogen, is equal to all phenomena; one is equal to all, all is equal to one. The mystery of your stockings reflected in the dictator's eye in whose eyes are reflected the longings of the people; his longing for power is to raise the longing of the people from desire for stockings to desire for spilled guts and glory, statues with hands raised as though greeting the coming of the prophet. In other words, greeting a prophet with vague promises of an uncertain future, but pre-designed, instead of the certainty of the stockings salesman.

Yet could I be blamed by critics for repeating ad absurdum the ostinato notes of my delicious & delinquent desire?

As I said, I was meditating on the commingling of our ethereal bodies, diaphanous bodies, imponderable bodies, when the cream colored pool or paste on the wet gray ground on my stroll by the concrete steps I was passing like thick impasto, a word I learned from reading Van Gogh's letters, stood out in eye-catching expressionist abstraction relief across from the parking structure's waffley windows: it could be melted butter, or ice cream, I reasoned thoughtlessly, or merely the barf of a dog. It must have been my mood on such a moody day, to not accept it simply as an eye catching expressionist abstraction and admire the mystery of the shape and the deep impasto, the corrugated edge versus the flat of the concrete, the accident splurging aristocratically atop the contrivance, but to fall into the trap of interpretation by reason, that the most general eye falls into, you know what I'm talking about? when you're at the museum with Ma & Pa Kettle—this is very abstract already, I have no Ma & Pa Kettle kin, why would I oppress myself with thinking of them?—and they ask, no, not ask but, like the yokel before the Pollock, condemn, mock, sentence, with their: what is it? Well, I too had to ask, perhaps condemn, sentence: what is it? Well, a mystery, that's what it is, really, an unresolved mystery though I can't say I'm going to worry too much about it. But the impulse was there, for an instant, to rush tongue out and taste it. When I say I'm not going to worry too much about it, I'm being facetious. No, I'm being dishonest. Like I said, I will reveal myself to you completely. Tear out the brocaded redingote of fabricated facade, wrench away the houpelande of contrivance flung over the soul's meretricious assemblage, so you may see it—the soul—unadorned—the whole coterie of charlatan personages parading their colored cullotes in the couloirs of my chest; tear it out consistently, constantly, readily, so that it never grows back. I don't really mean that, I love this coterie of charlatan personages parading their colored cullotes in the couloirs of my chest; but I think for a moment I was pressured by the invisible coterie of personages bereft of personality cluttering the psychic passages of this protestant enclave. Yes, sweet Imogen, my Imogen sweet, it could have been ice cream. Though on the ground, perhaps dropped by a child, it would have still preserved, even mixed with the ground, a sweet pleasant taste. In that case, even bad ice cream would have tasted good. Bad ice cream, in comparison with good ice cream. I am philosophizing now. Because, even with bad ice cream, the kind whose taste you have no experience with before you take it home, you just decided you'd go for a new brand that evening, and, taking it home and expecting to be sent, the tongue flung out in welcoming embrace, but instead it shocks you with something disappointing, even with bad ice cream of the kind I just described, I can't give specific brand names for fear I would be sued, don't laugh, this could easily happen, even in private mail, that's the kind of world we're living in nowadays, and I'm in no position to pay a lawyer right now, even with bad ice cream, the surprise of the welcoming sweet to the tongue, sweet on the street, sweet on the sidewalk, that would have made it a good ice cream. The rains came last night, it is gloomy now but dry and it could be the rains washed well the ground where the ice cream lays, a creamy paste, cream colored, and what it is spotted with could be could be bits of chocolate or cookie crumbs, or crumbled little bits of pavement. On the other hand, if it is dog barf, the dog hurled one just before he crawled back into the house, or the forest, well, I never tasted that, dog barf, but a lot of the way we look at experience in general is contained in my hesitation. A lot of how we look at a situation when we're faced with embracing a new experience. Certainly before I jumped I would want you to appear from behind me, sneak up behind me and save me, grab me from the collar and opening your bra to me, your lace bra, you would have me suck that instead. (Note here that I began reading Freud's "Civilization and its Discontents" last night.)

I don't belong to society, but to passion.

Because there is this to consider, I am placing before you on a pedestal the philosophy to consider, it's important, it's important becasue, I don't know why I keep writing becasue instead of because and I have to stop myself and correct it all the time, but it's important because freedom is important. What I mean, impulse, because where does the impulse come from—I know dear dear Imogen, my Imogen, this is your slave writing to you—salve from your slave—and what is wrong with slavery, I ask you, leering philosophoes, mind excavadores—exposing all & mocking everything, leaving no stone unturned, picking up every stitch, I know that when I ask this question about impulse, a colloquium of tooth gnashing shrinks suddenly stop sucking on their pipes and prick up their ears, prick up their ears, or rears, and knowingly clear their throats, they know they've got their man—you would do well to mirror the faults of your own fashion rather than paint strangers with the bleary eyed hues of the perhapses that perplex your own lives—but is not their man, it is your man, my Imogen, it is me, your Julian, your man, your dear sweet man Julian, the man who loves you truly. They will leer and gnash, because what else can be expected of them to do with their lives except spend it in the function of their infernal profession as society's inquisitors, civilization's dandruff police, the mockers of the genuine, because how best to oppress and imprison if not by mocking, or by pinning a label on you, a label on which they painted their caricacature and gets the easy laugh from the nouveaux near literati, secret spokesmen for the common march, as well as from the leering muddy-mettled masses of ignorantis whose leering tongues are pre-fabricated adfixtures of the common march, but it don't scare me, I'm not the fool, not the masochist, not the fetishist, not the unrealist, not the idiot, not the general who betrays his army for you, who, against all advice, against all clues, against all reason, flings himself before you, places himself at your feet, do with him as you will, yes he is, he's placing all of himself before you, on the altar before you—can't they see I am simply a man who loves, yes a man who loves deeply, not as society dictates a man should love, not society's reduced man, civilization's quartered, but passion's man, not the reduced couvade of a passion engendered by TV ads but the true passion unleashed from the bone march of society's prison—the impulse I had to leap at the puddle of ice cream, the concoction I mean, whatever it was, on the ground of somber wet, where does this impulse come from if not from the stirrings of freedom at the root of my being, not the concept of freedom, but the true stirring of freedom, gnash on your pipes, you pricks, La Phantom du Liberte herself, always there, always goading me on to attempt new standards, leap at new experiences, etc, etc, the kinds of things that the stirring of Freedom herself goads one on to attempt, cut out etc, etc, the whole sum of which I can't think of this moment, but you know what I mean my Imogen. Yes, impulse to freedom, free unencumbered action calls, and you think what if it's dog barf. Why this desire to deny yourself by denigrating your aim? You're about to make a statement for freedom, against the straightjacket of society, against societal restraint, you're put in the position to break out of, with one single leap, the hopples of the common hora, and you think What if it's dog barf. And all the while teeter-tottering, balancing on the teeter-totter of making up your mind if you're trying to say dog barf or dog bark, I actually almost wrote down dog bark, and the closeness, the kinness, in sound, between the two is so uncanny at a moment of such moment as this, that it takes a long moment to decide which is which, which is it, dog bark, dog barf, dog bark, dog barf, dog bark, dog bark, is there even such a saying, a saw, as dog barf, or is it just like any other two words you'd normally couple in attempting to make yourself misunderstood. I meant understood. Take note, you barking shrinks, Fifi Freudian fanfaroons, Lacanian lap dogs, derisive Derridian Dalmatians. Yes, knowing there is meaning in both, with pen in hand, per- plexed because there is meaning in both, perplexed I stood on the teeter-totter, teetering to one side, dog bark, tottering to the other, dog barf, back and forth like that, perplexed on the teeter-totter, and all the while I was doing it for you, for you my baronessa, my Imogen, my queen, attempting to make it out, to distinguish it, out of the dark edge of my horizon, attempting to make a point for you, it was to you I was talking, there on a street in Amnesia, and perhaps, I had just vested myself for you, an instant before lounging at the liquid, the yuckster swill on the sidewalk, I had just vested myself in my slave's vestments, the doublet and hose, and here I was on the teeter-totter peering into the darkness, reaching fearfully into the centers of meaning in my brain, asking them to spit something out, to shine a light on the pickle of my dilemma, after bargaining for meaning for some time there at the border of all meanings, having finally severed the barbed wire of quartered meanings, finally the void barfed or barked out the correct meaning, as it always does, sooner or later, the void having chosen recently to be kind & generous to me: barf, dog barf. But the issue of freedom remains unsolved here, on the sidewalk, in my life: because this question presents itself: why make the assumption the barf before you, whether it's melted ice cream, or dog barf, or even child barf—a possibility I hadn't considered before—the child living in that house, or another house, walking by with mom, could have gorged, in spite of wiser advice, him/herself on French vanilla adorned with chips or crumbs and suddenly, whammo! booof!—why make the assumption

1. that it is dog barf

2. that it is, whatever it is, bad for you, and from a grander, more

    philosophical perspective that:

3. what's on the ground before you, because it appears to be the mere hurlings

    of an unknown another, that you should too ignore it, not study it, not

    research it, not even philosophize on pain of being monikered a saprophyte

    by fascistic Freudians, pipe-smoking Lacanians, derisive Derridians, and finally, perhaps most

    importantly:

4. excommunicate your impulse to the garbage bin of your unconscious, classify

    it as trash, as ridiculous detritus and not worthy of attempting, along with

    many other impulses which, were we to follow them, we would perhaps

    end up living a freer and more adventurous life. (see

Freud, prohibition against dirt, civilization and cleanliness).
It is true our life is made
   up of much to avoid, plenty detritus, but why avoid the
ground and not the
   television, for instance? (Here the prohibitive mother,
the interrogator of each and every impulse, is employed in
the service of the
   state). Can you convince me that the internetting
   of TV commercials in your brain is less damaging to your
system than dog
   barf? What if the dog had the ice cream? I think this last
is the most likely
   solution. A truly foolish dog.

I want you to know that I took longer than I thought I
would take with this above passage because the formatting
was difficult. However, after formatting it, I took a quick scan
and saw it necessary to make a few corrections and after
making some corrections on the corrections I got tired and
left the bits that got unformatted the way they ended up on
the page. Besides I saw a certain visual potential in it. (I am
transcribing my notes from the notebook where I wrote them
down in immediately upon experiencing this trauma.) Of
course, we must not neglect the thought which presently
disturbs us that there are those who will claim up and down,
(up and down?) that ice cream itself, whatever tributary
turns it might have took (I know I should have wrote taken,
but I just felt like writing took, 'cause it sounded better) after
forsaking its origins, dished out of the bins, spooned out
cartons, or splurting out of canines, is plain bad for you. But
there is no challenge there, no confronting a MOM prohibition, so to speak, in choosing to eat the ice cream, if you
choose to ignore the warnings of those prophets and
prophetesses of doom, who trumpet the sugar and the milk
composing the sweety frozen goo is poisonous and carcino-

genic, etc. After all, who'd want to fight with five thousand years of Chinese civilization? However, no regulation manuals exist to assist those spontaneously wishing to lick ice-cream barfed by dogs or others on the ground. Would it be any easier if I knew who the hurler was? In the background, at the piano, Mozart tinkles Andante Grazioso; you, on the brocaded couch amidst the pillows, where, from the bottom of your circassiene of sea green unbosom your ankles of white silk, while from the top, above the alabaster of shoulders, uncharacteristically, in sudden splendor, cascade, on the marble floor, the ice-cream not yet digested you ingested from the crystal bowl indifferent in your marvelous fingers, and the coterie, in couvadic stupefiando, burping with disdain; and I, whose love's imploring was disdained by you only moments before—admire me in the motion of my stirring prophile, the way I quickly cross the centuries for you, see the crimson heels of my pumps gracefully on the marble scuffling to the sofa; periwig patted I bow, and begging the bestowal of permission, I bend, unhesitatingly exposing burgundy breeches and buttocks to the rightfully awesomed assembly, & begin to lick your expulsion most delightfully. O Imogen, I adore you so! I keep on licking and licking and licking, on the floor and on the shoe and on the ankle and on the metatarsals showcasing through the silk above the toes, the metatarsals cleverly forced to showcase, to reveal, revealed by the clever designer of the shoe who deemed them to be revealed, who dreamed them to be revealed, showcasing through white of the silk of the stocking, jabot begrimed of your spew, the silk of my jabot feathering the silk of your begrimed ankle I now lick, and I lick and lick and lick long past the moment when all hurled cream is licked and long past the moment when all is clean, and it is not about cleaning here anymore, because I had already cleaned it all, it is not about doing the work of the servants, it was about surpassing the work of civilization, I had here surpassed, long surpassed what was proper, I had long surpassed making a point, I kept on licking and licking, it was not as though I wanted their world to be clean, because I had already cleaned, I had already licked clean your hurly, your cream hurly, your hurled cream, which was ice no longer, I just kept on licking long past proper, my jabot luxuriating in your hurled drool, the hurly burly of the assembly a distant rumory murmur, and only the precise curled angles of your ankles, delineated by the severity of the alabaster of your stockings, their insistence on assuming such surprising shadowy hues at the furrowy ripples of the metatarsals and the splashing of pleats circling the ankles, the rippling of metatarsal clarinets, yes, I minueted enslaved by the siren maidens hidden in the rippling valleys and hills there, but it was even beyond the implied eroticality of the moment even though I had removed your lovely shoe and had licked it, had licked its sole and hand licked its insides and had left that and placed it on the licked clean marble, and was now licking your silky soles, licking and licking and licking long past improper now, and you had understood, but it was even long past your understanding, even though you never stopped understanding and you let me go on licking and licking and licking your silky soles, in ostinato, cruising for a bastinado, you can see here that I was doing a thorough job of it; I must momentarily pause here to comment that you may feel as though, even I feel as though, I am wasting my time, that I already said what needed to be said. But how else, except through repetition, through incessant repetition, through mantric repetition, can I convey the intensity of what I am doing? It is the repetition repeated past what is tasteful, past what the assembly considers good taste, that the glue holding the assembly together can be made to come apart. Didn't the early Christians time after time walked to the lions? It is the repetition of their gesture which caused the Roman empire to fall, though it's a pity their philosophy wasn't a tad more imaginative, so that the Roman empire could not revive itself by incorporating it into its vampiric structure. In repeating my action, in doing my best to express it to you, I am also corroding the empire, lick by lick, transcending civilization and its discontents, lick by lick, long past improper and they could do nothing at that moment, that long extended moment, except to watch, and watch and watch, as I was licking and licking and licking, and could not even if they had wanted to, could not turn away, that was the moment of my inglorious glory, ingenious inglorious glory, as the sole licker of your soles before the assembly and its ilk, I licked the silk of your soles all the way to your soul, to their soul, I had your soul on the tip of my tongue, I had all souls on the tip of my tongue, I had transcended all of the western civilization with my licking, and eastern, I had licked it clean, with my tongue lashing, I was giving it a tongue lashing, I was giving its souls a tongue lashing, and you were a part of it, you and I together, we had transcended western & eastern civilizations, we had gone clean past it, licking with all my might way past improper under the stupefied stare of the assembly and its ilk, I had transcended the food, the consumption, the purpose of the consumption, and the intensity, the determined march of my action was such that no one could look away, my determination was a subterranean partisan forcing everyone to look, my determination was a guerilla force, my determination was Che Guevara, I was electrifying in my determination, my determination was de Sade, Danton, Artaud, Rimbaud, Lautreamont, Baudelaire, they were electrified by my licking action to such an extent that it electrocuted them, they were helpless hostages to the electrification which was engendered by my action of licking. Borges describes a scrupulous man scrutinizing the world for the engenderer of a gesture; a gesture of great nobility—soul's nobility—he observed in a scoundrel; a gesture he intuited was a copy; a copy of a copy perhaps, or of a copy of a copy of a copy; and he made it his life's work to scout out the originator, the engenderer of the original gesture, because he intuited there was such a person, and this person must possess the secret to the enlightened consciousness he was seeking. One late afternoon at the end of the world on the cracked pavement of a plaza in ruins a complete scoundrel of a pimp will be stealing a contemptuos lick of a dead whore's foot, one he just slashed, to amuse his companions; yet the scrupulous retina of a scrutinizing youthful seeker intent on piecing together a new world out of a vague notion, of something he only suspects will reflect a glimmer of my determinate action. Because I had transcended all prescribed and proscribed modes of social being, that is, I had transcended the straightjacketting of the being itself, thus I was deserving of a statue or statues to built to my acts whose repercussions and reverberations were to be many; there are the snorting gentlemen, like crows on a fence, and the ladies too all crowing and leaning to peruse through their lunettes, finding it progressively impossible to maintain the posture of insouciance in whose service the European Cultural Machine had invested its best teachers and teachings: the banishment of emotions in public! this banishment with its sister, shame, can only engender an inimical stance toward our own selves; the only conclusion we can draw is that we are no good and we must train ourselves against ourselves to feel good about ourselves; to feel good about ourselves being determined by how good a show we can put on in front of everybody else; this mode of behavior, this cultural construction, constriction, achieves its highest degree of baroque stylistics in macho, the Italian Mafia, the Mexican Mafia, Hip Hop, the black gangs, etc. They are forms most removed from the true ticking of human emotion, life itself. This leads to fascism: emotional displays such as group, or very large group singing and shouting at massive social events are enforced, shaped according to bizarre baroque stylistics of the lockstep mentality; but free displays of personal emotion is discouraged and punished. I don't mean by emotion the cinematic sentimentality true life is shunted into by films and TV, you idiots. As for me, in between licks, I am staring into your eyes, my Imogen, I am in the staring regard of your Imogen eyes, I float in the staring regard of your Imogen eyes, in between the licks, the passionate licks I commit upon your soles and even the marble floor, the smooth marble floors which I lick clean for you and for your sake so that you do not have to suffer the derision of the no longer insouciants, the humiliated insouciants, the insouciants whose insouciance I have destroyed through my public licking, through shifting a private act to the public domain, not simply gesticulating it but shifting it into the realm of a true act surging as it does from the life force itself, not mere commedia to be performed for public enjoyment and derision, but an expression of the life force of humankind itself, a new definition of the human being bursting free of social straitjacketing, stepping out of the common activity lockstep bone march leading to fascism and the corporatization of the being, using judaeo-christian entreaties to downtrod the inner being. Thus a statue must be built to me and you in which we will be represented in marble in our respective positions and we will be known throughout eternity for our transcendent act. And don't think this act is simply a personal transcendence only whose achievement is the achievement of others before me and no more. This is the original engendering itself, a wafting of the amber imponderable itself, not an act to be depicted on dowered porcelain china showcased in living room cabinets of formica, where the Watteau Directoire is depicted in alabaster and pink to titillate like silk undergarments underneath the industrial fist we're forced to raise to survive

A PHILOSOPHICAL INTERLUDE

(*Note to Imogen: This is going to be published in the next issue of the Corpse, in my weekly column "Skeuromorph Detective".* JS)

"With a disgust I have learned to ignore, I propel myself among these pre-staged personalities, among these unending dependabilities, male and female humans, dogs, schools, mountains, quotidian and faded terrors and thrills. For a few thousand years now you put forth this axiomatic humanoid of Oedipus, propagate it like an obscurantist epidemic, the castration complex man, the man of the natal trauma, upon which you prop up your amorous encounters, your occupations, your neckties and your purses, your progress, your arts, your churches. I detest this natural son of Oedipus, I disdain and abjure his pre-established biology. And, if this is so because man is born, then all that is left for me is to abjure birth, abjure any axiom even if it boasts of the appearance of a certitude. Upholding like a curse this quotidian psychology-consequence of birth, we will never unearth the potential of bursting into the world extrinsic of the natal trauma. The man of Oedipus deserves his destiny."

—Gherasim Luca, The Inventor of Love

i

Why would I want to go on living, why would I value my own life, if there is nothing "out there" which reinforces its essence? Why would I want to leave my couch? Even the erotic which, according to Freud/Marcuse, (*and you and I, my Imogen, we know this very well*), is at the core of my motivational strategy, is re-formed by advertising, in other words is given "form" by advertising men without any concern for what my own specific forms are. You've read Society of the Spectacle, you're a cultured audience. Thanatos vampirising Eros. What life do I have which is my own, what do I have which is not merely formed by demands of the shopping mall? Have I become no more than a mannequin to hang designer clothes on?

The shopping mall, the corporation now claims my body, that is, the exterior, and the interior is claimed by the medical profession: my networks of guts feed entire chains of state validated drug pushers in hospital green scrubs and all the associated penumbra of mercy whores in white polyester.

So if both your gestures and your intestines are plugged into the life support machine of others' purposes, others whose purposes you don't admire, others whose purposes are not your vocation, or call you from the abyss, the lovely abyss of a goddess who adores you and whispers you poems *(the goddess, my Imogen, the goddess you promised me you were)*: you would return to that abyss if your gestures were not trapped in flesh's birdlime, forced to perform according to straighjacketted gesticulations, in the service of the forces of manufacture, forces whose function you do not admire, whose function frightens us, whose function you loath; prodding you to march against your unique sense of yourself. And this is our present destiny, to place our restricted gestures in the service of manufacture; the manufacture of objects which are unnecessary, made from materials we could not love, foam which disgusts, in other words which our senses are revolted and dulled by; and our anxiety is caused by our recognition of the inferior purposes and materials which blend up to make up our mutual mundo; yes, our gestures, functions of our body, whose motions do not belong to us any longer, but to the corporation whose meaning is a stranger to the abyss that would love us. We have been cloned by the corporation into clowns hobbling in the service of purposes foreign to our purposes which originally gush out of the abyss, the lovely abyss of the goddess; we have become marionettes, robots, mannequins for the purposes of the corporation. Body = corpus = corpses = corporation.

ii

Still, one conjectures that inner life does exist but to what extent does one pay attention to the delicate eddies of feeling and thought unless ad men sell it to you as an emotional disorder to exhort you to buy the prescription drugs to fix it? Borges speaks of a threshold which lasted as long as a beggar visited it and faded from sight when he died; it is the same with our inner life. And those who are still poets, those who should point out to us those internal eddies and winds, who should be extolling them for us, edifying them, are primarily concerned with being published, making a splash at this reading or that, playing politics with possible publishers. And what good Dadaism any more, or Surrealism? Are they powerful enough now to restore our sense of inner identity? Do we still have enough faith in poetry now that the poets are all writing copy for advertising? Gherasim Luca leaps in the Seine at 80; his suicide note reads that there is no longer any room in the world for the poet. And the art institutions? If they don't nurture ad men, they train you to scratch filigree frills on stainless steel, emboss arabesques on styrofoam. (I just checked the spelling of "styrofoam" on my computer; spellchecker warned me I should spell it with capital S; but I refused, told the computer to "add".)

The same hippie poets who traveled Whitman's "long brown path" in the sixties are now selling us the clothes we should wear when we are to profess to ourselves that we're "born to be wild" while barreling down to the malls in SUVs. Can the Gap ever be bridged back again, Allen?

Speaking about the "long brown path" and about Borges, do you know the story "The Approach to Al-Mu'tasim"? In it Borges tells of a novel, or rather the second edition of a novel—the first edition of which, he hastens to add, he suspects to be superior—written by a Bombay lawyer about a Bombay law student, who "falls among people of the vilest class and adjusts himself to them, in a kind of contest of infamy." Amid the men and women of this vile crowd surrounding him, our protagonist detects—he is a seeker—a gesture that shocks and surprises him, "a tenderness, an exaltation, a silence in one of the abhorrent men". "It was as though a more complex interlocutor had spoken". Our seeker resolves to devote his life to seeking out this "more complex interlocutor". Along his journey towards Al-Mu'tasim, in his "insatiable search for a soul by means of the delicate glimmerings or reflections this soul has left in others", the student detects "at first, the faint trace of a smile or a word; toward the last, the varied and growing splendors of intelligence, imagination, and goodness." The novel of which Borges speaks about ends abruptly with the student drawing a curtain of beads leading to Al-Mu'tasim's quarters and, stepping forward.

I furtively wondered—feeling out of place, fearing perhaps it was inappropriate—after all it was Borges—what I am saying is I felt hesitant to rummage through Borges's purposes, as though stepping into a territory forbidden to me— why Borges did not paint a more specific picture of Al-Mu'tasim. Why we didn't meet Al-Mu'tasim. In other words, we are presented with, and our curiosity is piqued by a gallery of skeuomorphs—albeit an increasingly impressive one—but Borges, or Borges' writer Mir Bahadur Ali, holds back from us the original we crave. About to step forth into Al-Mu'tasim's abode, our seeker gazes at a glowing light, and is enjoined to enter by the "incredible" voice of Al-Mu'tasim. We don't know whether it is the light emanating from Al-Mu'tasim, or merely a lamp, or whether Al-Mu'tasim himself is light. (Or whether the student himself is Al-Mu'tasim.) We are never told. Al-Mu'tasim is presented to us, the readers, no further. Borges goes on with the story, concerning himself with matters other than those I wish to reflect on here.

Is it possible, I wondered, to portray enlightenment convincingly? In a story belonging to the realm of literature it is perhaps fruitless to attempt to render the glory of such a promising original, especially in light of the fact that the immediate predecessor to Al-Mu'tasim is a Persian bookseller "of great courtesy and felicity" and that the man preceding the bookseller is a saint.

For an instant, while reading the story, during that palpitating flash when we are told the student draws back the curtain of beads and steps in at the bidding of Al-Mu'tasim's incredible voice, a multiplicity of my own molecules filled with light. Perhaps that is enough. Perhaps to witness Al-Mu'tasim's light would be blinding. Yet I felt myself longing for a more lasting effect, for "intelligence, imagination, and goodness", and I kept asking myself, if I were to portray the original, how would I do it? How could I convincingly render the "tenderness, the exaltation, the silence? The varied and growing splendors of intelligence, imagination, and goodness?" Yes, I admit, I craved these virtues for myself.

Is it possible, I wondered, that a word or a series of words could have been rendered, mantra-like even, to explode me out of the realm of literature and into the transcendent realm? Perhaps this is not even the point of the story and as I said I don't wish to box with the purposes of someone like Borges. Still, I stunned myself with my own intransigent reaction, the intransigence of my craving to meet Al-Mu'tasim. How un-post-modern I am, I remarked, hypnotized like a simpleton by the mystery of the story and wishing for nothing but the apparent enlightenment the story promised at the outset? Did I hope perhaps, goddess forbid, that Al-Mu'tasim would burst into Whitmanesque verse, something like "Stop this day and night with me and you shall possess the origin of all poems", or "You shall not look through my eyes either, nor take things from me,/You shall listen to all things and filter them from yourself."?

I questioned myself as to the reason for my reaction. I thought of the novels of Hesse I read avidly when I was in college, and tried to recall the last person I had met who "emanated light". Borges is Argentinean, Hesse German; both have placed their seekers in India, because as we all know, that's the place where enlightenment was originally invented; the last time we westerners had seekers was in the fifties and sixties (when we effortlessly borrowed ideals from the east): the beatniks and their heirs the hippies, who were beatniks on LSD. (That was the last time I know of when you count on the kindness of strangers.) The beatniks were preceded by the hoboes, who in turn owe their obscure etiology to student travelers and troubadours of the Middle Ages. To be alone or with a lover at midnight in the open air where all free poems are conceived and all heroic deeds, as Whitman would have it.

iv

I don't think I know anyone in my immediate surroundings willing to undertake the arduous journey of the law student in Borges, to seek an original identity. Whitman's "call to arms", to take to the open road sounds inviting while I'm yawning with a nice glass of port, stretched out on the couch after a day at the office. But to take to "the long brown path before me leading me wherever I choose"? In case you didn't notice, the long brown path before me has morphed into a six-lane freeway, leading from one shopping mall to another. Free poems and heroic deeds in shopping malls indeed! And if there were an Al-Mu'tasim now, a being of tenderness, of exaltation, of silence? I am afraid that instead of the varied and growing splendors of intelligence, imagination, and goodness, you get the depleting and equalizing marching boot thunder of the followers of some death cult.

v

How can we even speak of a "long brown path taking me wherever I choose" now when our horizon has been flattened into a TV screen? When the "reality" of the entire world has transmuted into bombardment of electronic particles? How can we speak of the value of human action when, as Paul Virilio puts it, we have become inert in front of the voluntary prison of our TV screen's false horizons? What significance does the "real" horizon hold for us, the horizon which meant hope, imagination, seeking, adventure, our very future, the indefinite we so craved, when our life force is sucked into the malevolent electrons of the glass tube? Yes, we lug around with us our TV screens like an electronic malady, like a virtual transplant, a nightmarish growth we can't find the means to root out, screens where we mirror the network of our actions in the constricted gesticulations and monosyllabics, the insufficient mentality, of those we have relinquished our moral tonality to, those sterilized marionettes we have invested with the power of being our icons. We gesticulate, flail about in blinded constriction inside our breathing environment, while our internality is enslaved in debates with these electronic screen idols, attempting to negotiate with them for a semblance of unrestricted breathing space, a tiny plot of personal identity.

Where is the "long brown path leading me wherever I choose" now that the "the extreme reduction of distances that ensues out of the temporal compression of transport and transmissions"? Perhaps we can search for Al-Mu'tasim on the internet? Perhaps Al-Mu'tasim even has his own website.

vi

The deprivation and deprivatization of secrets on account of their free display on talk shows where one tells all for the prurient salivating scrutiny of others; thus inner life loses all meaning, is emptied of dignity when potentially treasured or painful personal events become the possession of all, while our true inner life, the places where we live, is exiled to the status of refuse.

Are there other horizons? "All parts for the progress of souls" says Whitman; what is the soul now, at the edge of human cloning? When philosophers themselves believe that technology is the continuation human evolution?

vii

The only real solution I can think of is simple and I am surprised no one thought of it before me. I would get rid of the body. If the body belongs to them, let them have it, like a lizard that sheds its tail. Adventure, surprise, the imponderable, are all impossible anymore in this body of physical flesh, a "resource to be mined like any other" in this world of "unending dependabilities".

What use is the body anyway except as erotic contour shaped by the imagination; otherwise it serves no purpose at all. Let them have the body, but let us reclaim what is ours. To engage the body in a world wide network of incessant production for the single purpose of feeding it, gaining it shelter and maintaining status for it? Absurd!

Yes, let us reclaim what is ours. There has got to be a way of freeing the body from the demands of the stomach, the need for shelter, from the demands of utility. The body as imagination only. The body as a field of intensities. Marcuse called for the reducing of production to a minimum so that human beings are free to follow their erotic destiny. But he lacks vision in his compromise with the body and its atavistic drills, thus he still, albeit willy-nilly, endorses the forces of production. But imagine if you will, a body made of imagination only, free to pursue its desires, unrestricted! Free to pursue and fulfill all erotic imagination! The body de-sausageified. A society, a world freed of the demands of the stomach! I could easily give up my status as a restaurateur for that! The flesh liberated of its coprophiliac predestination. Food? Who needs it when my body is made up of erotic intensities only? The tongue liberated to formulate words and give pleasure. The flesh made word.

And why maintain status when enslaving or being enslaved could be so much fun? Borges speaks in "The Babylon Lottery" of the delirious exhilaration of plumbing the vicissitudes of terror and hope, of a lucky drawing to drown you in the river of delights, or condemn you to the intimate custody of "the woman who began to disquiet him and whom he never expected to find again".

Yes, an immanent eroticism extending into all social affairs. A ceaseless erotic war between male and female, where prisoners are taken, because what is the family if not a restraining social contract? The human being loosened of the constriction of playing the male and female roles. The woman freed from the demands of motherhood and family, unrestrained in pursuit of her erotic fulfillment. Eroticism freed of the genital focus, infusing and pervading now the totality of the being. Incessant betrayal as erotic play. The body liberated of family restrictions, of social restrictions, of theological vows to unproven male superegos, colonels of mass blindings; I see military incursions, available to everyone, as erotic play; architecture and furniture incessantly constructed and deconstructed by imagination, a nomadic life freed of the search for state; tentative teamings in pursuit of erotic pillage; incessant switching of loyalties; betrayal as socially acceptable erotic behavior. (Acceptable or unacceptable, who stoops so low as to differentiate between them?) The body eternal, experiencing neither birth nor death, neither illness, nor old age. The body eternally youthful, more graceful and fluid than a ballet dancer's or a pantomime's. Eros sans Thanatos.

ix

Here I must detour to speak about sex liberated from its reproductive duties, ascending to its erotic mission. Or rather returning to eroticism. Borges says, quoting Bioy Casares, that "mirrors and copulation are abominable because they reproduce men." I could speak, certainly, of a new manner of reproducing ourselves, science has, as you well know, not been dilatory on this matter, a new manner which could resolve once and for all the time worn argument of copulation for procreation versus eroticism in the service of pleasure; perhaps it's here that the core of confusion lies, and it is here that the solution lies as well. And I am suspicious of eroticism for both procreation and pleasure. (Certainly I am aware there are those slavishly drooling middle way mediators who claim that it is to be used for both, but they are to be discounted from my book.) Let us look for a different manner of duplicating ourselves, if duplicating ourselves is what we need to do. I for one am not sure. Where we falter is to imagine that we need to reproduce at all, this worship of the man of mud demiurge who exhorted us to go and procreate. (The east on the other hand has held for ages that life is eternal, that there was never a time when we were born and never a time when we die, that a body does exist that lives forever.)

Yes, I opt for this eternal body, the body as an assemblage of intensive principles, the body destratified and destraight-jacketted of male superego significances and restrictive borders and boundaries, armadas of functionality, maternal imperatives, blinding logic of massmamalias and Descartes demarcations, freed of the subject/object separation ("here the profound lesson of reception".) The intensities that circulate through me, through space, without the separation between the two, no separation between desire and fulfillment of desire in its essential form; perhaps, if I grasp Spinoza, I'm not sure I do, a Spinozian infinite substance; I see you or you see me, I wish to possess you or to betray you, or to be possessed or betrayed by you. All is fulfillment, all is intrigue, all is idleness and endlessness.

> *Là, tout n'est qu'ordre et beauté,*
> *Luxe, calme et volupté.*

An eternal indolence. The endless play of a goddess. Our gestures, actions, formulations, all planes of intensity. Finally, a veritable global community.

X

How would you make a body like that? The ancients proclaimed our bodies are made of the four elements of earth, water, fire and air. Heraclitus countered by proclaiming we are made of fire only, which I like, fire and conflict, a fire that heats but won't incinerate, a fire flecked with algoric viridescence, a fire in its original, poetic state—here I must divagate to rage against Prometheus the Pyromaniac who in a feat of reverse alchemy reduced the essence of fire to mere arson and pyrotechnics. Borges too dreamed of a man of fire dreamed into the world. To the four elements the Buddhists added the void. The void, the abyss, is really a misnomer as it is not devoid of content, just as dreams, which are insubstantial, immaterial, are not devoid of content, are not devoid of experience. The void then is a virtual state where all the substances exist in their potentiality, their immaterialness, but they do exist, like a spring of incessant life. What we need to do is, by some new (or old) alchemy, return our material bodies to the eternal state of void.

How do we learn, or re-learn this alchemy to transmute us back to our original state? This state I might add that we crave, that we wish to return to.

But first let me divagate again, forgive me, but I feel compelled right now to itemize more of its benefits, yes, compelled, like a new lover returning the following day to reclaim last night's ecstasy, like a phantasy fabricant who stumbled on a brand new phantasy.

A divine Eros. No, not that. An erotic divine, rather. (Not that Eros was not originally divine, until they put him in the porno shop.) So the materials of the world I propose are materials infused with Eros, but Eros without Thanatos, an erotic abyss, an endless insubstantial substance which contains and engenders all substances, yes, the attributes of all substances immanent and inherent, a field of consistency, pleasure without discharge.

A general pervasive sense that we are ourselves but at the same time do not belong to ourselves, we relinquish all responsibility for ourselves into the gentle arms of the goddess, that each of our gestures are the fulfilling gestures of the goddess, that we are one with her purposes, that we are her purposes.

Each motion we commit ourselves to, each gesture we indulge in, is a slow deliberate abandonment, there is no purpose, no alarm clock, no one to save, no reason but the indulgence into the next moment of the abandonment itself.

Each particular gesture an invitation to levitation. All surfaces are erotic. The internal factory organs that we believe sustain the body are non-existent. No one wants anything, not because they've given up but because they have everything. Each action, unwilled, leads to fulfillment. Realize that my ideas are not so different than Spinoza's.

The prayer each of us would utter each day to the goddess: "I abandon myself to the sleepwalking abductions of your fingertips' purpose; I live each day as though ceaselessly capitulating to an abducting quicksand of silk and enigmas."

xi

We have two apparent choices here, to produce this body of Spinozian Infinite Substance:

1. To involve science to help us create another sort of a body. I am sure with the development of computer sciences, the internet and virtual reality someone must be already working on it. Bioy Casares expressed a similar sentiment in the "Island of Morel", though much less satisfying, in my opinion, as his envisioned life, though perpetual, is repetitive, and lacks the element of surprise, of abduction. Be that as it may, we must move forward and not be thwarted by old fashioned ideas of nature. Perhaps there is no such thing as nature; (what is nature anyway? a backlit landscape, with a clearing in the foreground, trees in the background, a shepherd, some sheep.) And perhaps evolution itself, Hegel's process, leads from "nature" to scientific manufacture, since the human is the teleology's end. And if we were created in the image of god, we can't help imitate the old man. The good book never tells us how he created the world, what exactly

sort of "science" he possessed; this is where the great lie lies, and the source of our confusion: this concept we have grafted to our core, gesticulating through life without questioning it: creation of something out of nothing: the belief that there is a force which has made us but who forbids us to find out how, not just forbids us to find out, but forbids us to ask the question how: and the literatures concerning themselves with this question supporting those beliefs by portraying tragic ends for those impertinent souls who make the attempt. And the corporation is nothing but an extension of that form of belief, drawing its power from our fear of questioning at the core of our perception of life, something concealed and occult we must avoid attempting to discern.

And we must certainly relinquish this self oppression that we subject ourselves to, not to question "His" purposes. (I only wrote his with a capital H to make a point, to make myself understood, not out of fearful respect, let that be understood.)

Still, since science is the tool of the corporation, I do not trust the sort of bodies it would make, the sort of purposes it purports to pursue, the sort of codifying these corporation created bodies would be branded with, infected as the present corporations are with His exhortations. Virilio: "And can we really contemplate in the near future the industrial breeding and all-out commercialization of human clones, destined like animals for a *living death* behind the barbed wire fences of some experimental farm in the depth of some prohibited area because there we wouldn't be able to see those fellows or hear their cries?"

2. Why, instead of spending all these years developing instruments of science, did we not work to develop our intuition? Instead of developing hearing aids, why did we not develop our hearing? Instead of creating jobs, whose day in and day out drills suction off our power of the senses, why

did we not make it our life's goal to develop our senses? To become pure sensing without the encumbering of their perception. Yes, to train ourselves so that we can psychically transmute our flesh into a substance which is less fleshy, less demanding of maintenance, "the incoherent and vertiginous matter" that dreams are made of; I am thinking here of Borges's dream man in The Circular Ruins, or his *hrönir*, from Tlön, Uqbar, Orbis Tertius; a flesh made not of gross meat—really a very bad idea from the start—here I have to blame once again the bad temper of the mean-spirited old man credited with creation for charging us with eating flesh, he makes clear his sympathies when he opts for Abel's burnt offerings (burnt flesh) but turns down Cain's (wheat, vegetables). And for centuries now everyone tightens a jaw and sneers at the sound of Cain's name.

xii

I am well aware that these ideas I propose do not stand me well in this myrmidon community contaminated with the tumor of the man of mud worship. Of he who told them to go and reproduce. To multiply. I also understand that the Hades family, yes, that's right, the Hades family, virulent front-runner of mass produced intimate attire in service of reproduction, finances—but in secret, a secret everyone knows—the Institution, the so called "art" Institution that finances the sustenance of my flesh. At times I indulge in solitary relish of this ironical stand-off. While I bear the aspect of one immersed in waywardness, of hobbling in contretemps, a stunning vendetta obsesses me incessantly.

The demiurge they worship in these parts, if you spelled his name backwards and read it out loud, you would get something close to "sausage". That figures, if you figure that dad is "dog". I hope you get my meaning. Next to the corner worship establishment where hymnals to their "sausage dog" blast out on Sundays—there is one on every corner—is a little cafe that boasts on a peeling wooden sign: "the best sausage dogs in the world". You'll understand if I can't commit myself to clarifying this matter any further. With glance askance I spy on the crowd at the meat counter of the local deli where I shop: more and more take on the aspect of stuffed sausages. Some are peppered with bits of humor and other similar spices so as to give you the illusion of intelligence, of courtesy, even of metaphysics, like a smile carved out on a dead turkey.

I stroll the empty streets at night and can only hope that the baroque turns of phrase I wield with my shadow tongue will make my thoughts incomprehensible to those who would pry into the penumbra of my personal events, those already wary of my intimate activities, activities I have camouflaged by having mastered the candid uttering of stirring language formulations birdlimed in a cloying doxology.

Until I have masterminded my alchemic abscondance, I need this source of fleshly sustenance. My contract with the Corpse brings me but little gain.

AMNESIA LOWER APPALACHIA,
APRIL 5, 1999

Dear Imogen:

The pre-Renaissance alchemists believed that, according to the principle *of ex ungue leonem*, in order to shift to an alternate world one has only to clearly and precisely imagine in their hearts a small detail of the world they wish to visit. What follows is perhaps, I don't wish to be too specific for fear of having my plans uncovered, what I mean is, I am creating a ramp, a bridge to this other world; but only by uniting our energies can we travel there. I wanted to start out by conferring the tableau to you, the architexture, the porticoes, the cupolas, sanctuaries incessantly unshielded to the night's faintest wisp of weather, the consistent triple music makers, duplicated irregularly and surging out of the ground's "carpet". But I don't want to give you more than a fragment; the reason being that I don't wish to circumscribe in print the limitless possibilities inherent in this world; I don't want to create literature but a ramp; and literature, no matter how surprise-filled it is, cannot replace the unrestricted life which is in store for us once we step over the edge to this alternate world and become Splendid Siegfried and Queen Imogen.

The text that follows resorts to this *ex ungue leonem* sort of details, to stir the imagination to portray intimate details, necessary for us to step over the edge; I suggest we do it while holding hands, having decided that the time is appropriate for us to do so.

You must understand what I'm attempting to achieve here. You must understand my purpose. Do you? Do I need to be more specific? Since you answer my letters so infrequently, I don't know where you stand regarding my attempts. Yes, it is true, you extol my word constructions, which you insinuate engender within you explosions of longing, you compare me with Artaud, but, nothing to suggest you grasp my true purpose.

If you do not wish to follow me (I'll be more perspicuous later) all is useless and all that's left me is to try my hand at literature. (Do you really presuppose my purpose is to simply glide along led by the geometry of lust, leaking at random across the page from my opulent lexical duffel bags? This is only a book, you denounce with veiled contempt, the substance of slavery to the yoke of pre-established concatenations of the afore mentioned lexical reservoirs according to pre-established syntax, with a nod to a few dead writers held dear in the writer's heart. Is that really what you think of me? No, you didn't say that, I did, I take pride in having said it, but, last night on the phone, do you think it was so hard for me to feel what you were thinking?) Then the comparison with Artaud is appropriate as a last resort consolation. But I have decided to leave literature behind, as I mentioned before, I decided to follow "ethics" and not "aesthetics", in Kierkegaard's parlance. What I mean is, this writing, I will say it again, is not literature—though my attachment to literature is as profound as a malady—but a bridge, a ramp. This is the later that I mentioned in parenthesis in the first line of this paragraph—I know you thought it might take a while for me to get there but I can't help myself, I have to tell you now. You know me, I have always been anxious, impatient. I have not changed. I will not change. You might have guessed what I have in mind already if you read a previous letter carefully, the Skeuromorph Detective episode; many thought it hilarious, what I proposed there, congratulated me on my humor; let them. It is best that they do not suspect how intransigent I am in my purpose, what a stunning wand my words are, though clues I have divined indicate that more than likely many of them may.

I realize as I write that, though indications abound, I have instructed you little into the world of the Splendid Count and Queen Vivian Imogen. What follows will serve as a sort of an "infomercial", (if I may be so crude as to use the language of those who destroyed our last resort, language itself), like an advertising for an exotic island, something to make you hunger for it. I am painting a picture so that you know exactly where we're going.

Perhaps a poem will help. I don't wish to paint a definitive picture, where all coordinates are set in stone, so to speak, especially as there is nothing there made of stone to speak of. (What materials is it made of?) I count on you to help me trace some of the details. You have always made me envious with your fine gift for the applied arts.

I copied this poem down while I was entranced in research, it's from one of the English poets, but I didn't write down his name at the time and I don't remember it anymore. Here it is. Maybe it's Milton, perhaps Marlowe.

> ... For spirits when they please
> Can either sex assume, or both; so soft
> And uncompounded is thir Essence pure,
> Nor ti'd or manacl'd with joynt or limb,
> Nor founded on the brittle strength of bones,
> Like cumbrous flesh; but in what shape they choose
> Dilated or condens't, bright and obscure,
> Can execute thir aerie purposes,
> And works of love or enmity fulfill.

Again at first I was disturbed at my lack of ability to sketch the architexture of the place. I don't know if it is inability or unwillingness. Because if I did trace in detail the:

... baseless fabric of this vision,
The cloud-capped towers, the gorgeuos palaces,
The solemn temples, the great globe itself...",

the whole "insubstantial pageant" of this place where "we are such stuff as dreams are made on", if I traced it in detail, then it would be painting, or filmmaking, it would be the job of the production designer, not the writer. And it is crucial that what I put down here is not subservient to the movies or any other art.

"...on a hill, an ant's perusal, through the grass, diffuse, as though through the fog, in the distance, impossible to discern how far, figures, as amidst fighting, as with rapiers, with curved scimitars, as though their movements purposefully slowed, as in dreams, a ballet of lovely violence.

A long pointed emerald hued slipper, of intarsia embroidered satin, the beribboned pantofle of an early Renaissance nobleman if you will—we are pandering to your dependence on rooting description, your contamination with cinematic phantasma, sucked into the phantasma of cinematic history, sucked into the plasmic haze of cinematic phantasma—alights leisurely into your principal perusal, perhaps even squashing the hypothetical ant whose initial perusal guided yours.

Here I have stop, my dear Imogen. I'll tell you why. Because squashed ants do not belong in this tale. And, what is now the ant's perspective was originally what the painters call a frog's perspective. But a squashed frog is even worse than a squashed ant, and far more disgusting—to refer here to our great master who taught us of 'the fortuitous encounter upon an operating table of a sewing machine and an umbrella'—though I'm sure the frog would have been able to leap away from the impending slipper sole and thus spare us the disgust.

And whether this is a tale or a poem it is of little significance. Neither does belong in it the grass's chlorophyll nor its potential for staining the alabaster hose of the beloved. Squashings and humid chlorophyll stainings do not belong in this tale. Poem. It's as though its substance, the substance of this tale, does not invite, no, it is revolted by squashings and stainings. Perhaps squashings and stainings signify for us the distressing climax of chronicles that quicksanded me to abandonment, vortexes like mothers in reverse. And then, an icy gust on a thigh, where abandonment to dizzy suck of clouds shifts transmutes to vitreous gravity.

That's the problem, I feel, I haven't studied architecture enough. Or art history, so that I cannot describe this environment convincingly. Do I need to? You know what I mean? I have to get back to what I'm writing.

White silky hose that gleams treacherously at the entrancing ankle's astrogolos; new seat of perusal, comfortably reclining in our tiny floating sedan we spy, yes, oh, the seams! cameoed sabery cruelleries, whips to lash at the core of a crave! The limbs are slender and long, calves well cambered as though intricately sculpted by endless austerities demanded by the mastery of a superb minuet; swirls of brocade of the slashed trunk hose, ballooning slightly to betray: the inciting spectacle, the curve of the…; and the same intarsia swirls on the emerald doublet.

Here's some more description of the thus far described:

1. His emerald locks cascade in curls and ringlets from under the beret with crimson ostrich tips, streaming the ruffled collar of alabaster.

2. He twirls his curls around an indolent finger, a lovely begloved silky finger, whose distended nail is rendered in

calculated viridian splendor, a violation calculated to enslave by its insouciant flirting with disobedience, with indolence, perhaps even, yes, impertinence.

3. Please do not trouble yourself, but more principally, us; and do not reveal yourself a linear simpleton befraught by dreaded logistical inquiries: we can discern the incipient squirming in your system of inquiries, already have we spotted you stepping on the soapbox to regurgitate constricting mental constructions, emetic constrictions whose tentacles you sport and spurt at us with the pomp of self-flattery, and, with salivating glee you shout to the marching myrmidons for the purpose of employing for yourself their own constricting straightjacketting, sans-remuneration, to goose-step in the service of your squirming enquiry system: how can you tell me, you shout, the distended fingernail is painted crimson when the hand is begloved? Yes, save yourself from our jeering, you twits, and the jeering of history to follow. Keep it zipped! We are returning to our tale from which your ignorance momentarily kept us. We'll take a short pause to disenclench ourselves from the smear of your salivating cogitation and return to the divine lexico-erotic acrobatics we crave.

Deep breath. Pause over.

He is the Ravishing One of Emerald and positions himself with the fingers of one hand delicately on the slender ballooning of the trunk hose while the other abandoning curls to support chin. This is the ill of describing: that it must be executed in sequence, chronologically, linearly; and we abhor it. No, we don't abhor it. We do it for a reason; and this reason is not literary. We're not going to reveal it yet. More, we are enmeshed in wishing to perform it upon you, upon ourselves, we crave it like agitated inamorato ephebes: the Ravishing One of Emerald—and please note it was the motion of the fingers abandoning curls to settle impudently in support of chin that led us to wish so desperately—rather his visage, his ephebus visage, is viridescent. A painted viridescence shadowed by a beckoning cheeky blush. Amber irises glowing under the obsidian of lashes and lids.

(When we say "desperately": desperation is an alchemical component of our precipitate to precipitate our abscondance.)

You can't help yourself: you too want to be his Amoroso! Let us then assume you are a spy, an Amorous Spy, an invisible caresser: o! to caress at will, unimpeded by the reproaches of the marchers in opinion imposing rallies! o! to kneel before the Beloved! Shameless retinas absconding to canopies of abandonment with miniscule creases at knees!

Here we will reveal exactly what we meant when we said that our purposes were not literary.

You crawl with languid sloth, the indolent glide of the marvelous fingers of the would be caresser, the wishful adorer you are, along the silk hose, mounting upwards to the curls; then carefully, almost as though you, the invisible caresser, in spying on dream lover, are fearful not to disturb him with breath and thus breach the borders of his countenance or even, horrors! give yourself away, you glide sideways to study his profile: the androgynous visage, powdered and rouged, eye-lashes cameoed with obscurity instead of contours, lips rouged to promiscuous prominence. Not that the promiscuous or the prominence weren't present before paint and powder; in truth, we know nothing of what existed before the powdering and rouge; but we wish to subjugate you by our skillful employment of description.

Oh my dear Imogen, will you still lash me that I am a literal minded painter, who doesn't see beyond the core need to represent? Will you despise me that the need is a crave which transmutes representation to fetish?

The irises, pools under the cameoed lashes, swirl with

private storms, reflected in, and reflecting, the action at the foot of the hill; you, the unseen spy, glide close, below the lashes you wish, of the one whose lashes you brave to imagine you might endure—you pause, peruse yourself, ponder into the echoing mirroring of meanings, and the tip of your tongue glides gently on and you wonder if you're indulging in too often and this forces you upwards to further glide unto the curlicue of curls and locks of the Beloved's peruke—and you stop to peruse peruke peruse peruke peruse peruke peruse peruke peruse, you amuse yourself by sing-song, by child-like divagation, indulging in language, then chide yourself for such simple-mindedness when the weight of chronicling awaits you—to peruse the spectacle the Ravishing One's vitreous humors reflect: again, as in dreamy motion purposefully slowed, you peruse now the action of the battle, as its focus becomes aggressively clearer, but as though glimpsed through burgundy and turbid water:

(Again you stop and ask: how can you avoid writing for the cinema?)

A battle of rapiers and scimitars frantically wielded by a maniple of agitated gallants contra a surge of heraldic demoiselles; the gallants are vested in a manner mimicking him in whose pools the action occurs; and they are succumbing one by one to the superior battle skills of the demoiselles; the demoiselles whose visages are erupting with flames of crimson, are one and each of a severe pulchritude equaling in exquisiteness that of the ephebes, and are vested in prolonged boots of vermilion, and lurid sleeveless doublets revealing shoulders and trimmed with burgundy brocade and fuchsia fur. Featured entrancingly above the top of the boot, as though the boot top were a socle or even a pedestal, is the piercingly alabaster filigree lace of the stocking top; we telescope, like a monocled sea captain peering through a golden lunette, to examine and investigate. (If the monocle were on the right eye, the lunette would be on the left.) We pause here to reconsider our perusal mode. Certainly in high cinematic fashion, a perusal of the gleaming boot surface from such proximity so as to elicit an imprecise self image; yes to mirror yourself in the act of your own worship, enraptured more by your own act of worship than by the worship proper, though no one in particular perusing through the golden lunette the could accuse you of improperly worshipping. There is no judgment passed here, we are ephectic in perusing, the worship of your own worship seems proper to us. But we are launching ourselves far too far into the future. Let us reconvene where we began. Or not. Not yet. We are suddenly forced to respond to academic pressure, certain circles of academic barracudas, Thanatos worshippers, to defend our indulgence in fetish. To defend the telescoping degree of our attachments.

In the final analysis, to defend the form of my love for you, my Imogen.

For instance, I hear that the demoiselles' boots being painted in such wide brush strokes, while Siegfried's attire is represented so thoroughly, that principally, in painting the boots in such wide strokes we are pandering to a pornographic mentality. A salivating erotomania stratified in the male psyche, and not the erotic transcendence we reach after, and which needs no defending. A salivating erotomania stratified in the male psyche and brought before the rostrum of recent critical studies; critical studies in the service of Thanatos; the stratified grin of salivating erotomania, plastered in flagrante delicto and brought before the rostrum of recent critical Thanatos studies. Yes, here I foresee rostrums of critical studies barracudas, worshippers of Thanatos, defenders of the man of mud worship, dashing themselves against my formulations, jostling me with jeers through streets and public halls; (and it is only my dire rapturous entrancement with you, my sweet sweet Imogen, rapturous entrancement providing me with such surges as to lift my lexical scimitar, against these barracudas who deplore my formulations to deplore theirs.)

Yes, but forced to paint the boots in coruscating detail, for instance in pliantly villous folds of vermilion; and for this I would once again be vilified for indulgence in fetish (as though fetish were a pejorative, as the painter said, as though fetish were something you can banish, as you laughed and defended me when from the poet's rostrum I called your toes arsonists.) I am floundering in an uncertain sea of flung pejoratives, dashed by barracudas, my Imogen, and it is now you need to rush to my defense…

I realize as well that I am floundering because I am incapable of writing all I imagine the dictators of the literary oblige me to write. Yes, meaning is "indeterminate, plural, diffuse, … every image woven out of every other image." It's like vivisection at the instant of the slash (my scimitar arm raised to vivisect): you spot the squirming events, still alive, and as you spot them they scurry off as they multiply in every which direction and you're at a loss which to follow because it's all of them you want to follow, all at once. Yes, my Imogen, I am floundering and I would sink if it weren't for the suck of your forgiving arms, my Vivian Imogen. The Ravishing One too could be Lancelot or even Merlin. I am sure somewhere in some library, though I can't be sure, a tome accounts for their accounts, listing them categorically according to time and place and symbology and I don't know what else, as you know my education is spotty, wayward, and my mantras squirm with indeterminate events that won't stay classified. Still, I can't be ignored, kept out of books, libraries, schools, the internet. "Consequently the imagery is fragmentary and obscure to the degree that it finds its resolution in other, absent and not always determined texts."

And is it enough to claim that our endeavors are literary? Have we conveyed then the quality of the architecture enough? Is it sufficient to simply say we are implying an Escherian Stimmung, or something sort of Varo (as in Remedios) to in fact enact the light of the Dämmerung? Are we here literary enough? Have we left no stone unturned, have we considered every facet, turned each synecdoche? And of our previous claim, that our purposes are not those of literature, what of that?

A quick dip out of the double pool, recall the double pool, to spy on the wanton lips of the Ravishing One: they curl heavenwards at the corners, as in a smile. Now the Adoring Spy, [you,] crawls up again, to plunge, again, in motion slowed, into the barbaric, conquering pools. O how the rapiers and the scimitars in the hands of the warlike demoiselles pierce and spear the doubletted trunks of the heroically overwhelmed gallants! How entrancingly their hose creases at the knee, these gallants, slumping into postures of magnificent supplication! Their irises too, pools to reflect cameo-like, the powdered & unforgiving visages, the striking arms of these invincible Madonnas of Conquering Madness! O, ode to defeat! O, at last, the longed for Languid Overwhelming!

The light of day fades leisurely orange upon this tragic scene of brutality... But the Enamored Spy does not keep us long in darkness. Long enough, the pause's length is nearly unbearable, long enough to make us reflect on our own longings, but tastefully so. No, hurray, hurray, the light of day has not forsaken us! The 'simulated' 'fade-out' was simply an effect engendered by the languid opperculation of the Ravishing One's lashes! Lids. We mean lids. We were momentarily deceived!

Yes, the Ravishing One's lashes, lids, are now closed as his slender and beringed fingers with painted nails fall like an autumn leaf in flight to settle upon the emerald of his short short trunk hose, where it curls under over the silk of the hose, to absentmindedly feather their brocaded velvet an inch above.... And then, suddenly, snap! The eyelashes of Siegfried, Count Siegfried, Splendid Siegfried, for that is our creature's name—the Amorous Spy, in fit of traitorous whimsy, impudent! lashes for him! has agreed to reveal this piece of information—yes, he knows more than we do—have popped open. Still, our Amorous Spy will detain us yet from enjoying the reason for Siegfried's disturbance; instead his glance swirls to show us the sprawling hill at the bottom of which the diminishing Emerald Gallants are doomed to the fury of the Crimson Demoiselles, one after the other pierced by their skillful rapiers and scimitars. And having wrenched himself from the grip of these booted demoiselles, a panting gallant mounts up the hill, flings himself supine on the ground before the Ravishing Count, and places his lips upon the pom-pom flurry of Splendid's slipper. And allows his lips to indulge, again and again. And again and again. Then his lips slide forward to graze the rosetta spokes of the milky metatarsals beyond the half moon of the emerald slipper's brocaded velvet.

He is befraught by an unending craving for the astrogolos, muses the Amorous Spy, amused at his sudden skill of lacing old Athenian into the Spartan tongue he is presently impelled to stutter.

"It's a massacre, my Lord. Save us. We are at the mercy of these Hades dwelling Dames. "

Yes, you, the Amorous Spy, present, presents us a Count Siegfried with eyelashes directed not at the Groveling Gallant but trained on his own slender and splendid fingers. His spellbinding stocking, disobedient! has evaded the grip of the bejeweled garter we assume—we assume—is concealed underneath the trunk hose—and with a shiver we assume it is bejeweled, the garter—and a strip of silky translucent alabaster glimmers above the disimprisoned stocking top. Yes, a strip of silky translucent alabaster above the filigree of the stocking top, as though the substance revealed by the accidental disimprisoning of the stocking top were insubstantial. This is no surprise to anyone inside this furious narrative but we are pausing to entertain yours, reader. How can we describe this insubstantial substance? Translucent, yes, perhaps watery, but not wet, we wish to assure you it is not wet, we could, should you wish us poke it with our finger to prove to you it is not wet, or even press our lips against it, but you must trust us. We feel compelled to continue with the course the narrative and do not discern it necessary to entertain your frivolous doubts; Yet, we are forced by an internal pressure we can't identify to be more specific in defining the apparently watery substance of the inner thigh observable above the filigree lace of Splendid's stocking top. Still, we are not going to. Yes, frivolous, the thought occurred to you, did it not, more than the thought, the urge occurred within you to place your lips upon ours to taste the wet, we congratulate you on your erotic temerity, and since you've gone this far—for which we congratulate you—we enjoin you to continue; but don't expect us to indulge you. Still, if you feel compelled to place your feverish lips upon that alabaster translucence, we'll not prevent you; we'll even encourage you: but don't surprised if you feel yourself sucked helplessly into a quicksand vortex of air, a sudden drown into a fiery volcano without reform.

And you, the other you, the Amorous Spy, are befrought in the grips of a tormenting predilection: is it the sight of the groveling gallant's lips lightly grazing the silky metatarsals of Count Siegfried it is proper to present us with? The crimson curve a flame kindling upon the metatarsals' snow! Or the disimprisoned stocking top now gripped by the slender fingers of the Splendid Count Siegfried? Or the Maddened Demoiselles having pierced every single one the Vanquished

Gallants and now mounting up the top of the hill to claim their long longed for prize, the Commanding Count, who for so long has led his maniples of powdered gallants to victory after victory against these flame headed Hades Madonnas in prolonged boots?

You—not you, the Amorous Spy, but you the reader—will perhaps note, if you're not too befrought in the grips of the narrative's tentacles, or if you haven't vanished yet as a result of your immodestly libidinous and heedless action—that this new information we are presented with in the second section of this last sentence, about Count Siegfried and his previously victorious maniples of ephebuous gallants against the Hades Madonnas, victories which have caused the Maddened Madonnas to aim for the Count's capture, more, for their Queen Vivian Imogen to demand and command the Splendid Count be captured alive and brought before her to the catacombs she inhabits, the weatherless catacombs of her Hades abode— fiestas should be held in catacombs, as the Great One taught us —is reportage which, in contrast to the immediate and presently observable reportage we have been presented with by the Amorous Spy, who is our witness, is general, not presently observable, historical. Why? And who is it that's presenting us with this new information? Oh, the issues of narration! they seem so labyrinthine, so billowy and undulant, so meandrous! It is entrancingly marvelous, we note, how incessant the echoing of commentaries, like the flutter of swift wings, like a flickering of nightingales! How they incessantly upon each other like serpents tails!

Oh, but to describe the disimprisoned stocking top! If only there were enough time! It's the disimprisoned stocking top he would opt for describing! If only the Amorous Spy knew that time is all he possessed! Then he would pay no heed to the Groveling Gallant peering upwards in supplication to the splendidly insouciant Count Splendid.

"Save us, save us as you always do!" beleaguers the Groveling Gallant positioned in kneeling magnificats.

"You couldn't fathom in fathoms," the Splendid Siegfried spills from his magnificent and becrimsoned lips, "the whirlpool of longing I am forced to endure when I fathom my nebulous stockings. My stockings are the imponderable clarinets of longing! My stockings are a weave of transcendent tarantulas, precipitate of feathery shiverings engendered by rumors of startling abductions! Here, lend me your fingers."

Yes, to abandon yourself utterly to the commands of description amidst the demanding rigors of the pandemonium! The Amorous Spy raises his imaginal lids and flutters his (also imaginal) lashes to the Imponderable, propitiating magnificats to engage the Imponderable's faculty of description in the weft of his own being. He recalls vaguely now, not his own memory, to be sure, how once a man before a firing squad was granted the writing of a complete tale. Certainly he would be granted a brief but somewhat detailed description of a single spellbinding stocking top! He turns to spy the Groveling Gallant offer his beglovéd digits to the Splendid Count. And shivers when Siegfried deftly leads them to fasten the silk stocking inside the trunk hose.

"But these booted Dames of Hades! They will pierce us in moments! We must save ourselves!"

The stocking, in mutinous uprising, refuses the attempt at fasting.

"Maybe they will pierce you. They will never pierce me! No, they will not pierce me. They will imprison me instead, and we must not be imprisoned with our stockings all askew, must we? Oh, my stockings! The translucent beckoning of azure, shook foil clouds transmuting to lower limb nebulae! Stratagems of limpid conflagrations!"

"But they will make us their slaves!"

"Bulwarks of secretive heron! My stockings are bulwarks of secretive heron!"

"Slaves! Next to piercing I fear it most!"

Siegfried snaps to attention then slaps the gallant across his powdered face.

"You are the captive of indistinct mental phormulations! Your philosophy has been served you on contemptible plates of Platonic platitudes. Yes! In slavery we would prove our true obedience to the whimsy of the Goddess we worship."

The Adoring Spy's thread of description is broken by the philosophy he hears. As in an involuntary mirroring of his own phormulations, the Groveler cries out:

"Oh, my lord, you have instructed me, time after time, in the highest teachings yet I do not learn! Yet, be not spare with your wisdom! I wish to become a follower!"

"Oh, for the sake of the Goddess, imprison this stocking inside the garter. I am afraid the Goddess will not have her worshippers in disrespectful stockings."

The disrespectful stocking, astir with the pandemonium of frantic fingers, glimmers treacherously and settles momentarily in mimick of obedience in the bondage of the assumed bejeweled garter.

The Adoring Spy notes not without a note of astonishment how Ravishing One places the silk gloved fingers of the Groveler Gallant inside his own trunk hose. Did you notice when we switched to the third person singular? We mean for the Adoring Spy. The astonishment you feel, not at the switch from first person singular to third person singular, leads you to take note of the visage of the Groveling Gallant. His visage, unlike yours, shows no surprise. Your astonishment leads you to look up at the wistful aspect of the Splendid Count: he flings his emerald curls backwards and gasps, as he intones in cant:

"Is this then a touch? quivering me to a new identity?
Flames and ether making a rush for my veins,
Treacherous tip of me reaching out and crowding to
                                                    help them!"

You quickly shift your sedanic position to ogle the bombastic trunk hose of the Ravishing One; to ogle it from very very close, as though reclined in the sedan gallery you shrink to fit the occasion and fly by surreptitious wit: the bombastic ballooning of the trunk hose swells and shrinks, amplifies and contracts, flares and withers, puffs and puckers, at an even and rhythmical pace. The quivering voice of the Silk-Gloved Groveling Gallant pierces like a fruitless prayer:

"But slaves? Is it not disrespectful to be a slave? Have
    you not taught us we must gain the day?"

"Yes, I have taught that it was good to gain the day

But I also say it is good to fall, battles are lost in the
    same spirit in which they are won

Vivas to those who have failed! And to all generals that
    lost engagements, and all overwhelmed heroes!

And to the numberless unknown heroes equal to the
    greatest heroes known."

The Ravishing One's tongue tip glimmers, slithering on
    a leisurely journey across the crimson cut of his
    upper lip.

"We are the slaves of the Goddess. Only the Goddess is
    worthy of respect."

"Then is slavery to the accursed dames the same as
    slavery to the Goddess?"

"These 'accursed dames' are made of the same matter as the Goddess. And we too are made of the same matter as the Goddess. Nothing that is is not the Goddess. My stockings too are of the Goddess! The bejeweled garter—"

—ah, our assumption proves to be correct! It is bejeweled! Magnificats to the Goddess! If now we could only glimpse it!

"—that serves these stockings and all those who shiver at their entrancing aspect, those who would shiver at their entrancing aspect, more, the shiver itself, all these are the substance of the Goddess."

Splendid Siegfried switches tone to intone:

"Oh, it is as though my stockings were fashioned of a rosy echo of dawn in a forest clearing! Praising them thus, I praise the Goddess."

The Amorous Spy, you, notes, note that for a shivery flash Siegfried's splendid stockings glow with a blush of rose, made suddenly flagrant by the vicinitous emerald... Perhaps the Goddess Herself has blushed at being so praised, he, you, the Spy, can't help but observe the curling like smoke of a poetic shiver within his, your, palpitating chest.

Splendid continues.

"Why is it when I awake from my trance my stockings are not the same stockings as those I adored ensconcing the contour of my limbs when my dreaming began? Why is it the pantofles I find besides my bed and which you slip over my toes are not the same pantofles I wore when my dreaming began, yet they are of a fit more perfect, as though the subtle substance of sleep itself had fashioned them? For sleep and dreams, are they not the Goddess? Today's stockings, as though sleep had competed with itself to fashion them of a wind, a mist more subtle than before, an alabaster more entrancing. Who conspires to dream them each time of a grip more indulging than before? Who conspires to so splendidly rehose my splendid limbs? Each day in every way I am made more entrancing, more intriguing, than the day before. Is this not, am I not, the loomwork of the Goddess?

"But how could it be so? I see it before me yet it baffles my understanding."

"The vestments ensconcing me are a mandorla."

"A mandorla?"

"An excretion and secretion of luminous desire."

(Note: the careful reader is hereby requested to picture the anabasis of the Flame Headed Demoiselles who are heading up the summit straight for the spot where this poeticophilosophical dialogue is occurring. These Vanquishing Madonnas of Doom are in fact very, very close, very close, to the position of the two gallants in the garter grip of their metaphysics. So close we might indeed fear for their safety. Will the Groveling Gallant be mercilessly pierced? Will Splendid Siegfried be imprisoned? Can we still fall to Slippered Ease and savor the delights of Poetry and Metaphysics when the Booted Dames—and do not forget their formidable piercing instruments—are a few short mini-fathoms away?

And again, please do not forget that the silk glove of the Groveling Gallant has remained at its post inside the Ravishing One's trunk hose. Recall that "its bombastic ballooning swells and shrinks, amplifies and contracts, flares and withers, puffs and puckers, at an even and rhythmical pace." Keep it in mind, this has not changed in the least while the two are in the grips of dialectical ejaculation. Could this be the 'metaphysics of ecstasy' the mystic speaks of?

Still, for those readers unaccustomed to the conceits of quantum time travel it might be difficult to conceive how it is possible that the viciously booted demoiselles are so vicinitous while the gallants have the leisure to resume their ecstatic metaphysics. Certainly, their seconds are numbered, the simple reader will philosophize. For in trenches we are all philosophers. For them, and them only, the author suggests a simple exercise. The Maddened Madonnas of Flaming Curls are to be pictured in slowed movement as it is used in the mass productions of motion pictures; that is, appropriately slowed to such leisurely pace as to allow the gallants to continue their metaphysical conceits. The author wishes to thank those readers for their patience and understanding and assure them that no contempt for their imprecise gift of grasping the Profounder Realities is implied.)

"Then, if nothing that is is not the Goddess, then why are we ceaselessly at odds with these damsels who are of the same matter as the Goddess, as, as you say, we are as well?"

"I explain yet you do not understand. It is clearly because the Goddess chooses to amuse herself through our constant skirmish."

But the Groveling Gallant is not to be persuaded. (Please note that from here onward, since we have plain run out of embellishments to describe the reactions of our interlocutors, we will simply condense their names before each of their allotted dialogue: The Splendid Siegfried is SS, while the Groveling Gallant is, yes, GG.

GG: "Let me then quote another, opposing source. Did not Zephyrus the Heresiarch (before he vanished along with his followers) teach us that we must submit, for fear of doom, to the demands of the demoiselles and their fury? Did he not presuppose in his prosody that we are inviting only disaster by resisting? Did he not profess that their Queen is the true aspect of the Goddess herself and by opposing her we will bring our own end? That by not immediately submitting to her in instant slavery we are courting the unleashing of her fury, a fury the likes of which we have not yet known?"

SS: "It is because Zephyrus is a Thinker and not a Believer that he is mistaken. He is not a practitioner of the Languid Overwhelming. Presently it is only through struggle that we worship her; that presently the power of the goddess is maintained through our disobedience; we must obey by disobeying her by defeating the demoiselles; if indeed doom is what awaits us, our reward will the punishment we'll presently receive through our disobedience at the hands of the demoiselles and the ecstatic transcendence engendered by it; but this, to grasp entire, requires a long and exquisite honing of our creed. We must fall on our knees and thank the good goddess and her whimsy each time we are punished, either intimately or as an agglomerate. The wisdom of the goddess is the whimsy of the goddess and the whimsy of the goddess is the wisdom of the goddess. The only practice of a Believer is to hone his belief in the Goddess by being ever alert to the whimsy of the Goddess which is the wisdom of the Goddess."

GG: "How does one hone one's belief in the whimsy of the Goddess?"

SS: "You are indeed hollow of understanding. Yet, in the Goddess there is hope and I humbly invoke her hallowed wisdom to penetrate your hollow grasp. Since the original nature of the Goddess is desire itself, to hone one's belief in the Goddess means to hone oneself to keen alertness to the slightest flurry of desire within; her most whimsical flurry is her dictate and as her followers we are to follow the slightest whims. The contest is who can discern her dictates in the utmost, who can distinguish the subtlest eddies of her dictates. Certainly one day her desire may be that her followers perish at the hands of an intimate enemy, the next that we imprison her."

GG: "But, since I am the Goddess, since my matter, what I am composed of, is the Goddess, then why do I not believe I am the Goddess? Does it not mean then that most of me is the Goddess, while a minute part of me, that part doubting I am the Goddess, is not the Goddess?"

SS: "Certainly the part which doubts is the Goddess as well. The disbelieving part is too the Goddess."

GG: "But then why does it disbelieve?"

SS: "The disbelieving part is simply the Goddess amusing herself. The general current belief is that one should not be afraid; but how could you have courage without fear? That which fears is the Goddess amusing herself too. Since you fear and disbelieve, it means that the Goddess has chosen you to amuse herself thus. You are that part of the Goddess that fears, thus the Goddess amuses herself through your actions inspired by your fears."

GG: "I understand. But if you speak of honing belief in

the Goddess, to where one is always awakened to the minutest detail of what the Goddess desires, then does it not mean that one is working against the Goddess by honing one's wakefulness?"

SS: "How can you work against the Goddess when you are the Goddess? Isn't every thought you have the thought of the Goddess? Isn't every word you utter the word of the Goddess? Since you are the Goddess can any awareness you have not be the awareness of the Goddess? Your disbelief is the joy of the Goddess."

GG: "But if I believe, will not then the disbelieving which pleases the Goddess be discounted?"

SS: "Belief, which is the honing of the awareness is not static, it is a constant honing of the pursuit of pleasure, which is the Goddess pursuing her own pleasure through you.

GG: "I am beginning to understand. You have removed the haze of my ignorance once again, the haze of my ignorance which I now see is also the Goddess. I see now that all that exists and doesn't exist is the Goddess."

SS: "Yes. What then is this summit?"

GG: "This summit?"

SS: Yes. This summit upon which you and I stand."

GG: "I am once more perplexed."

SS: This summit is my desire to view the battle from the appropriate height!"

Siegfried then intones operatically, (though you might ask yourselves, do they have operas?):

"To be enslaved by the woman I crave is enough

I go and put on my stockings and admire myself."

We have advised earlier regarding the envisioning of the slowed, leisurely pace of the motion of the Crimson Madonnas. They have now thoroughly surrounded our philosophical gallants and propped the points of their rapiers and halberds against their doublets. The rhythmical and bombastic ballooning of Splendid Siegfried's trunk hose, the previously witnessed—by you—flaring and withering, swelling and shrinking, puffing and puckering, comes to a sudden halt. The wistful aspect of the Splendid Count turns grave.

"How dare you pause amidst the fulfilling of a task?"

"I am fearful, my commander! Infinitely fearful!"

"That is as it should be. Courage is the contemptible vice of those who are fearful of their yearning for groveling. To be at the mercy of the Beloved, that is the true purpose. You will do exactly as you are told. Resume your task, I insist!"

"No! Let us alight from this cursed summit with the swiftest of mobility!"

"I order you! Resume! This is my command! Obey!"

"But look, the Maddened Dames have placed their piercing points plunk against the brocaded velvet of our doublets. They will pierce me! Oh the horror, the horror!"

Siegfried snickers, riveted to perusing the splendid swirl of his fingers.

"Oh, tis but a sleep!"

"Yes, but in that sleep, what dreams may come... "

The Ravishing One forces the Groveler's fingers to resume their rhythmical motion inside the trunk hose. The Groveling Gallant shivers in the sheathing a fruitless protest.

Splendid Siegfried raises his voice and chants in panting cant:

"On all sides prurient provokers stiffening my limbs,
Behaving licentious toward me, taking no denial,
Deluding my confusion with the ecstatic of capitulations.
No consideration, no regard for my draining strength
    or my anger,
They all uniting to stand on a headland to witness and
    assist against me."

The Groveling Gallant steps forward in a brusque motion

and addresses the Flame Headed Madonnas of Defeat:

"Confine then to the ecstasy of capitulations, this wicked commander you wish"

Splendid, the Ravishing One, continues undaunted in his panegyrics to the ecstatic:

The sentries desert every part of me,
They have left me helpless to a crimson marauder
(Oh, dainty dolce affetuoso I!)
They all come to the headland to witness and assist
    against me.
I am given up by traitors,
I talk wildly, I have lost my wits, I and nobody else am
    the greatest traitor, I went myself first to the head
    land, my own hands carried me there."

"No", replies the Groveling Gallant, insidiously shifting his traitorous retinas "it is my hand that carried you there." and jerks Splendid forth by the prize he has trapped inside Splendid's trunk hose to present Splendid as prize to the piercing Crimson Madonnas of Doom. The Splendid Count, Ravishing! now ravished, shivers while his curls fling backwards and his lips curl to the Imponderable. Please, patient reader, picture simultaneously the multifarious components of the picture presented forth for you; you, yourself do so, as the Enamored Spy, suddenly snapped off duty by his entrancement stares in ecstatic despair at the meticulously miniscule curls the hose of Splendid forms behind his splendid knees; do not count on his further reporting of this event. He too would fling his curls backwards and arch his supine spine, in imitation of his Beloved would be Ravisher; he would be Splendid, Ravished & Groveling Ravisher, and if truth be spoken, if this brief candle allows a flash of confession, not a few of the rapiered Dooming Madonnas to boot, in the waning of the Crimson Dämmerung.

"You villain touch!" shouts the Splendid Ravishing Count.

"What are you doing? my breath is tight in its throat,
Unclench your floodgates, you are too much for me!"

Recall now, prisoner that you are in the unclenched floodgates of this narrative, try to disenclench to recall the picture presented before you:

1. Spellbinding Splendid with spine curled backwards, curled hose behind splendid knees.

2. Groveler with spine curled backwards, fingers fidgeting on Spellbinding Splendid's prize, presenting him as a prize. His hose too spellbinds by miniscule curls behind knees, though slightly less, as expected, meticulous.

3. Bespelled Amorous Spy with spine curled backwards in perfect alignment with the above two.

4. The backdrop, the surrounding Demoiselles, the pointed rapiers, the crimson Dämmerung.

5. The backdrop of fiery crimson smoke

The simultaneous sequence of events we are forced to describe in sequence by the circumscribing nature of narration.

a. "You villain touch!"
shouts the Splendid Ravishing
"What are you doing? my breath is tight in its throat,
Unclench your floodgates, you are too much for me!"

b. An beryl hued smoke suddenly surges like a multi-toned Vesuvial fume from inside Splendid's trunk hose, quickly engrossing the surroundings. To obtain full impact of events reported in previous sentence, the reader is encouraged a second reading of it.

c. Splendid's fingers suddenly gripping a surprising and treacherous Stiletto. They, the fingers, thrust the Stiletto in the side of the previously Groveling and presently Treacherous Gallant. A thin stream of multi-hued crimson smoke issues. The traitor shouts, then wobbles, then fumbles, then falls.

d. The traitor's purple lips intoning through the thick smoke: "the horror, the horror..."

e. Fulgurations of cerulean and beryl branch across the horizon with booming reverberations. The beryl smoke surging from Splendid's trunk hose envelops the scene so that we presently see nothing but beryl smoke, multi-tones, with a slight wisp of crimson smoke tingeing it—recall, this is the crimson smoke emitting form the Traitorous Gallant's side pierced as it was by Splendid's Stiletto—contraposing the edges of the scene where the crimson of the Dämmerung can still be slightly glimpsed. The entrancement we feel at the pure beauty of the abstract blending of colors is.... is... we're awfully sorry that we cannot engage the superior descriptive powers of the Enamored Spy. As we lack his ability of description, we are challenged to mostly list with just a mere dash of lace filigree of our own to spice the mix.

f. Splendidly Rapier-fitted Gallants in Emerald phorm themselves from the beryl smoke issuing like a Vesuvius from the prized prize. An ejaculating surge of Splendidly Rapier-fitted Gallants in Emerald. They come to life and quickly overwhelm by piercing the Crimson Demure Demoiselles. A detailed account of the brief battle is unnecessary, we feel, in the absence of the superior reporting faculties of the Amorous Spy. However a quick note is needful if we are going to be unconditional adorers of truth; in the quickly victorious battle, one Emerald Gallant was pierced. He was pierced, arched his spine, and tumbled. As he was in truth Splendid's ejaculation, Splendid too arched his spine as though pierced; but while the gallant only arched his spine once, then tumbled, Splendid, though he didn't tumble, arched his spine twice, as though he was not pleased with the first arching; he was not pleased with the second one either; from the folds of his sleeves out comes a looking glass; for the looking glass Splendid repeats the arching of his spine ten, twenty times, until he is satisfied with the effect. And the battle ends, with all the Crimson Demure Demoiselles pierced.

g. Splendid intones:

"From the smoke-strewed threshold I follow their
  movements,
The lithe sheer of their waists plays emerald billows
  with their fluent sleeves,
Overhand the scimitars swirl, overhand so slow, over
  hand so sure,
They do not hasten, each pierces his target,
Leaving a mist of lily.

What follows:

a. Splendid peering into the small looking glass rouges his Ravishing lips.

b. The Amorous Spy, on his knees admonishes self in derogatory manner for having once again abandoned reporting duties, and solemnly promises He-Who-Employed-Him-To-Spy that, should he be allowed yet one more chance, he would not phail so miserably.

c. The lashes of the pierced and fallen traitorous Gallant suddenly flutter and the lids fan out. Yes, the lids are fans that flourish and thrive and flutter in the entrancing fingers of the woman we adore, the man we adore, or like a glimmer of a splendid stocking."

AMNESIA, LOWER APPALACHIA,
APRIL 16, 1999

My Imogen,

You may be wondering what happens next: the Groveling Gallant awakens; and so do the rest of the pierced gallants; the hole in their doublets (did I mention blood?) produced by the rapiers and the scimitars mend themselves, as though the fabric from which they were fashioned were a live substance, no different in its essence than the fabric of which the gallants are composed of; no different in essence but perhaps serving a slightly different function, though the 'surfacing' of substances is to be noted here: people made of a cloudlike substance, yet maintaining erotic contour; but more of this later.

Another version of the story goes like this: There is sudden thunder and lighting and Queen Imogen Vivian's grave aspect surges out of the fulguration. It is a solemn moment and the Gallants and the Demoiselles all fling themselves anxiously to the ground before her path. She floats to face Splendid who is silent and stupefied. I'm thinking here of the Heavenly Messenger in Inferno's Canto IX, looking neither to the right nor to the left, undaunted in purpose.

Vivian Imogen waves her arm and Splendid lifts, floats and settles a foot above her head, facing the same direction as she is. She floats off with Siegfried in tow.

(Which reminds me, I forgot. There is yet another version of their meeting. If you'll look again at the "novel" fragment above, the Splendid Count, in the grip of the gloved hand of the Crimson Demoiselle, unclenches his flood gates while a "beryl hued smoke suddenly surges like a multi-toned Vesuvial fume from inside Splendid's trunk hose, quickly engrossing the surroundings", and "Splendidly Rapier-fitted Gallants in Emerald phorm themselves from the beryl smoke issuing like a Vesuvius from the prized prize. An ejaculating surge of Splendidly Rapier-fitted Gallants in Emerald. They come to life to quickly overwhelm by piercing the Crimson Demure Demoiselles."

In the new version, Queen Vivian Imogen materializes just when Splendid Siegfried is about to shout:

"You villain touch!"
What are you doing? my breath is tight in its throat,
Unclench your floodgates, you are too much for me!"

Vivian Imogen herself grasps his prize in her alabaster fingers, while Splendid intones:

"Here, take this gift,
I was reserving it for some hero, speaker, or general,
One who should serve the good old cause, the great
      idea,
the progress and freedom of the race,
Some brave confronter of despots, some daring rebel;
But I see that what I was reserving belongs to you just
      as much as to any.")

I don't wish to retell their encounter in unnecessary details. The general overview of the significant event is enough for now. I merely wanted you to meditate upon, be enthralled by the image of Queen Imogen solemnly floating with the presently imprisoned by her splendid magic Siegfried the Splendid above her; I find this image entrancing, though you know me well enough to know that I despise mere description, general overviews. I don't know why I indulge in it now. I am not even sure I want them to meet then, though once I clearly witnessed their meeting in the circumstances I described above. But this line came to me, this exchange of lines between them, where he asks her: "Are you the Empress of these catacombs?" and she replies: "I am the Queen of Murmurs and Concealing."

It is not even important that his name is Siegfried, it might as well be Merlin, or Tanhauser or Tristan, I don't wish to indulge into the unnecessary details, she could be Morgana, or Isolde, Venus, even Morticia, etc, etc, I'm sure somewhere in some library, though I can't be sure, a book accounts for their accounts, listing them categorically according to time, place, symbology, etc, but my brain squirms incessantly with indeterminate events that can't be forced obediently into folders. To return, perhaps the general overview of the significant events is enough for now, though you know me well enough to know I despise general overviews of events, I said that, being in particular partial to the minutiae of the coruscating detail, one that has the force to transcend beyond the controlling vice of mere overview. Because, should I merely recount the general overview, as I said, I would be blamed for recounting only for the purpose of enthralling, for merely sketching the outlines of a phantasy meant to induce no more than erotic arousal, mine first, then I don't know whose, and I don't know that writing should be about that unless I wrote a pornographic account meant clearly for erotic arousal and nothing else, with no pretense to attain to the palatial enigma of art, no attempt made at the minuet of metonymy, say, or poesy. An event I stage is circumscribed by its edges, that's the nature of the stage itself, it circumscribes, I stare at it and it strains me that it is finite and confined; it is confined within its definitional frame, a frame formed by its purpose; I am afraid its purpose which I share with you that it is my purpose, I am squirming inside the definition of my purpose; I am unable to shift to a perspective where my squirming transmutes to, say, gliding or glissade; the perspective that I am merely sketching for the purpose of arousing. It is a plane of immanence I'm seeking, really, I am not a pornographer, it is the imagination of the goddess erupting in incessant transcendence, to avoid the tar of dominant opinions; because if a definitional system achieves status, becomes state, the trick is to shift velocity, to torment with sudden tornado boudoirs, assign it to tasks of detailing delusions...)

As I wrote, I don't wish to be assigned to the task of detailing, not detailing, but chronicling events, details actually, that can be construed to be so merely for the purpose of arousal. As there is no history in this world I detailed for us, as I initially called for an abandonment of history, thus a surrender to Eros that incapacitates any proclivity for aspiration to heroism or the performance of noble acts, the drama in which history is made, the drama where aspiring heroes strive for heroic acts, is meaningless; only the erotic Now has meaning.

Here I wish to state clearly my tastes, splay my derision at those who merely inflame by marching their premeditated boudoirs before the palatial enigma of my architexture.

You'll say Siegfried is a reductive human being, from whom the feathers of tears, laughter, etc, have been removed. I say no. Because there people are a field of intensity, and the degree, though consistently intense, changes quality, quality of intense feeling changes, incessantly shifting. The consistency of the person, which is an intensity conductor, pipeline, is there simply to admit the passage of intensity.

Plunged into an infinite mud, quicksand, which, in seizing you, even against your will, belongs to you, like an abductor who becomes yours just as much as you are his/hers. In other words there is no loss here, there is no vampirism in the abduction, as you are replenished through the abduction.

"I feel myself looked at by the things, …, which is the second and more profound aspect of the narcissism [removing the constraining carapace of guilt from narcissism, seeing its positive aspect]: not to see in the outside, as others see it, the contour of the body one inhabits, but especially to be seen by the outside, to exist within it, to emigrate into it, to be seduced, captivated [captured, abducted] alienated by the phantom, so that the seer and the visible reciprocate one another and we no longer know which sees and which is seen." Merleau-Ponty.

Smash the state: in executing this gesture with utmost presence, in absolutely indulging in this moment's motion.

We have spent time ad nauseam speaking of, say, the entrancing popliteal crease at the knee, shifting our plane of reference to this minute detail. We have so far enjoyed many planes of reference all at once. Are we tired? And again, we can come back to ask the ultimate question: the question that obsesses us: are we horny? Is this text an excuse to document, to detail and outline events for the purposes of infantile prurient inflammation? (It has been whispered that I am merely gorging on the disorder of infantile sexuality. But infantile sexuality has not been sung enough; it's only societal straightjacketing—that's where the disorder lies— that condemns it, as though you could fashion it like plaster to fit their attachment to christian chokeholds.) Yes, certainly, I feel distraught at the lack of the elements the art prescribers have prescribed for us: form, content, sacrifice, altruism, revelation of an inherent humanistic nature which can overcome all ills, tragic flaws which in turn cause tragic events, oedipal complexes, encouragement for the needy, engaging plots to keep the masses captivated, noble gestures, courageous deeds, I think at the moment we've run out of categories. But look: once again I forgot Myself, and I wonder why I consistently disappoint by constantly forgetting Myself: once again I strayed as a child longing for a spanking;

once again I need to be reminded that we are not here to make art, to create aesthetics to please the aestheticians, like flies are apt to please the fly catching glue; this is not the new novel. I am here, this text is here for no other purpose than to build a bridge, a ramp if you will, but a bridge is better since bridges stand for symbols, as for instance getting to "the other shore" in Buddhism, though I think in Buddhism they swim, I am not aware, searching my memory, of there being a bridge. This is, I repeat, not a work of art, this is merely a letter, why this agonizing obsession with aesthetic principles and purposes?

Yes, the purposes I plunge into are profound, I strive for pelagic immersion, its distinguishing indwelling dharmas have been enumerated by the messenger from Montevideo and that is perhaps enough. And humor? I had once even conceived of the disobedient garter disimprisoning his stocking when the Queen appears, and she comments ironically on it, and even wrote it in before I deleted it, struck by horror at the humor, not appropriate for this moment of mystical moment. On the other hand, it would be delightful to indulge in Siegfried's horror at being discovered by her with a disimprisoned stocking. Still, again, should I merely sketch an outline for the reason of recounting, for the purpose of inflaming a phantasy, (which could be construed by some critics to be mine as opposed to yours, though what critics, this is only a letter to you, this is the *ex ungue leonem*, the oneger-like detail to catapult us to the alternate worlds, why am I so obsessed with the literary criticism section of the bookstore?) I would be diminishing what I wish to accomplish here to suddenly delve into the pornographic, an event placed on the page's pillow and presented before your eyes to merely inflame prurient interests, I would be admonished for proposing a salivating erotomania common to the stratified male, not the erotic shifting of levels. (I concentrated on the minuscule details of the erotic phantasy, the phetishism. The elements of eternity we'd rather avoid. Still, I am aware of my limitations as an artist; the fact that I question my own work in my own work, makes my work, in my eyes, post-modern. Perhaps to turn the spy glass upon ourselves, upon what compulses us to extract enjoyment out of certain events. But here, for a moment, our pen dries up. Here, during this present moment, we are speechless. We revolt at the compulsion to indict ourselves for our compulsions. We sneer and snort at the compulsion to view ourselves under the oedipal spy glass.) You see, they will not grasp my purpose, will take my word construction "significant events" which I used above and use it to default me, as though I only intended to paint a significant event in regards to a picture to be used to inflame. This is merely a love story, the love story whose significant events throb in catacombs as yet unobserved by the clusters of conglomerates that sheen the patina of pre-ordained coagulations of events in service of their global circumscription systemata. If their systems of duplication were to detail our love, it would only be to detail the curious detail, to indulge in salivating entrancement & mocking of my curious erotic perdilections. Perdilections is on purpose. Not even psychiatry would put me under the belljar of perusal. At best the academia would list me as a minor disciple of de Sade, or Sacher-Masoch. No revolution would have the foresight to claim me, in spite of my thorough philosophical calculations, as my vision, they would claim in blindsight, lacks force, is bereft of blood and spilling.

To return to the erotic question, only those events are included which cause joy. Why should I castigate myself as an atheist for creating pornography? For creating a masturbation machine for myself alone out of images I stole from my psychic events. Why should I apply societal/religious categories to my actions? I am what I am...

(I had this note to myself: Describe the boots of the

Madonnas of Madness as they mount up in anabasis. We would paint the boots in wide brush strokes, without the entrancement of the minuscule detail, the seduction of the synecdoche, without the glimmer of the Dämerung in their reflective shine. And when I say reflective, you could see yourself in it—like my dominatrix friend Layson would say—and comb your hair and brush your teeth and shave in them too, *une invitation à toilette*, but here I am beginning to describe a dominatrix boot, again the brush strokes are too general, I'm painting a dominatrix simply to get the inflaming erotic thrill from the audience, you simply have to write dominatrix boot, to get the desired response, from the readers I mean, and I would hate myself for that because if it doesn't somersault into metalanguage, if it's not exquisitely synechdochetic, or metonymic, it's anemic, it's just another event in linear time. In describing the demoiselles, as writers we are compelled by voices emerging scoldingly from silvery amphoras, from amphoras tipped over by present literary disgusts,

> amphoras filled with sleepwalking cascades,
> spider web glaciers contaminated by mutinous genu-
>   flections
> perused in the limpid lakes of unsuspected erotic
>   curlicues
> compelled, as mentioned above, to indulge into genu-
>   flections,
> mutinous genuflections to the lustrous leather of
>   synecdoche

Is there a sun? Is there weather? I don't know. "I have lucubrated by luciferease to squeeze an answer." "I have loathed the noon and midnight of this planet, I have ached for world without weather, without hours and the horror that bloats them, I have loathed the moans of mortals under the burden of the ages." (My translation of Cioran, because I find

Richard Howard's lacking.) Perhaps this takes place in the sun. I mean inside the sun. I have never given in to the scientific claim that the sun is a mass of gaseous substance, claim meant to cause us to abhor its physicality! I believe this claim is in itself detritus transmitted to us no doubt to doubt our true identity, which is that our "life on earth", our perception of it, is merely the reflection of the sun's life, where we truly live, our veritable domicile. We've become so accustomed to the burden of flesh, we must now shift awareness to our solar identity, our solar mass. Because mass in earthly terms means weight, gravity, the grave. But sun is light. I have craved to tell you this face to face, eye to eye, lips to lips. That you and I are one creature only made two in this grave nightmare. But in the sun we're one.

You will worry, I am sure, about the flagrant homosexuality on display, splayed exuberantly across the page from my promiscuous lexical duffel bags. Not true. (And, no, I have not turned "gay"!) Here are some details. The anus, both "male" and "female" is a bona-fide vagina. No memory of it as excremental organ. Never an excremental elimination organ, that is a pure perversion invented by the forces of lack, Ananke, when they also trapped people into needing to eat, turned them into molar beings. (That was the myth that coagulated us into mere physicality, the creation of food as sustenance for the bodies. The idea that food is necessary for the sustenance of bodies is the primary problem of humanity; and the idea of reproduction through the o(ri)ffice of the woman. If there is to be such a thing as reproduction, it is preferred that they should grow on trees. The fruit falls to the ground where a kind of dehiscence takes place, the loculus of the rusty fruit cracks open dehiscently and out pops the fully phormed young one, ready to be enjoyed, and eventually to form where it could enjoy. Much superior is the Buddhist concept that we have always been, the entity is never born nor destroyed. We have always been; and mothers, so proud of their off-spring! All fodder for the meat factory! All marching into the grinder to come out a sausage on the other end! Sure, they have hired a few sausage sculptors, to whittle out a few different shapes, big deal! To infuse with slightly different admixtures of spices; some are infused with a little more humor, but where is that humor coming from? It's from an admixture of humor which is already pre-established, all pre-fabricated humor with no connection to the whimsy of the amber imponderable!) Still, my critics reading this would impute upon me that I write out of a veiled homosexuality; like psychiatrists of the predominant system, they are blind to the original ur-state of androgyny at the core of the universe. What I had envisioned, what was envisioned for me, to be exact, though to be exact is by no means my purpose, was that the orifices of the anuses were shaped like lubricated vaginas, replete with clitoris, the anus itself is celebratorily fitted with a clitoris and meant only to give pleasure. Yet, the psychiatrists of the predominant system would impute I bear the banner of opposition to the "continuing the chain of reproduction". Psychoanalysis proposes—presupposes a liberation so that a continuity might emerge. This liberation presupposes to engender a freer shifting through the world, obtaining more pleasure from the process of living, unencumbered by the delusory magnetism of the past. But in society, liberating that original freedom which is in truth the freedom of the pleasure principle and using it to shift through a performance principle society, where does it lead to? Can one have regard for a performance principle society after liberation? Society does not prize you for the creation of any liberation devices, it prizes you for slight and essentially useless improvements to the performance principle. Something to engender more sales, not to improve life itself. The psychiatrist is like defender of the faith, the priest: no matter how nice you try to be, no matter how soulfully adept you become at listening to one's sorrows, no matter how you might relieve him of momentary pain by skilful listening, you're ultimately doomed to working for a god who's an insidious and contemptuos absolute: can it be that when you return to heaven you're tip-toeing on egg-shells because the old man is a moody malcontent? Certainly, and going to heaven is irreversible; once there, there is not even a round trip to hell and back to gloat on the sorrows of some ex-co-workers. The priest works for this inherently consumptive construction; he has to defend it: the priest cannot be your friend because ultimately he works for Him; even if the priest sympathizes with you and your doubts, there is nothing he can do to give you courage: he doesn't work for you; he works for Him. He has to go against himself and re-convert you to Him. It doesn't matter the priest has read a few 'new age' books which claim that man is not originally sinful and whose content he uses to spice up his sermons; how can he believe that after St. Augustine, who stated that little children were Satan's issue before baptism; and how can we fail then to put St. Augustine on the same rung as Hitler?

A certain sort of mystical moisture occurs, a lubricant for the silky motion to occur; yet to describe it as moisture destroys the effect I'm after, as its essential nature is one of smoke, of whirlwind and silk. The creation of a new being, a new world thus, not homosexuality, but using the being to its utmost, not even, which I do, to express rebellion against the subjugation of sexuality under the order of procreation, and against the institutions which sustain and promote this order; what with this new craze in re-design, the moral aspect gets squared away and we finally admit that desire is supreme, I think this new phorm of being will prove to be much more conducive to happiness.

(I had mentioned to a former lover how it would be both provocative and productive if my fingers, if anyone's fingers were created to exact pleasure from touch; if we followed our impulse then to feel pleasure and exact pleasure from each other by finger touching, which would have the power of pleasure that the localized sex of the Approved Orgasm had, under the Order of Procreation. If men and women, men and men, women and women, met on the boulevard and inter-laced fingertips, just to experience pleasure; I mean the fin-gertips, of both men and women, outfitted with alternating tiny penises and vaginas to interpenetrate; but minus the anxiety of pregnancy; I mentioned this to her in the huff of passion; my former lover expressed disgust and rushed off in a huff, though it was midnight, under pretense she had to attend to a dying dog, a dog that had been dying for years; but I still maintain it would be beneficial because it would bring people together; but I don't disagree with her that it is in reality disgusting; it would feel disgusting to me to feel pleasure from so many people I despise.)

    Inside the vagina, a mixture of fog
    and silk
    and whirlwind
    and fountains
    anus: velvet, volcanoes and leeches
    velvet volcanoes and ocean depth
    the creation of substances
    poetic substances
    materials created from poetic images
    which are words
    in certain admixtures
    since all is sensation
    the world of poetic image
    sensation
    which created by the poet
    in opposition to the fixed world
    of the materialist
    the producer of materials
    of petroleum, of plastics

yes the creation of new substances
from poetic images

The vagina, like the mouth, like the ear, secrets this precipitate of ocean, silk and whirlwind, ocean, silk and
volcano, which does not need to be captured so as to be precipitated by the production engines. It produces itself, it is
the work of the Goddess.

A bit of necessary history for you, I have mysteriously
waited until now to introduce: the women live in catacombs,
a well ordered world, with a queen, Queen Imogen, of
course, and a High Priestess, whom I will call Alcina, who
insures the inhabitants are reminded to live according to the
dictates of the Goddess. How do I know this? This history,
which never ends, is incessant, with the complex internetting
of events incessantly occurring, was passed to me conspira-
tionally in vessels containing ecstatic liquids, amphoras from
which I imbibed daily, inkwells of ecstasy in which I dipped
the pen that pens these lines for you, only for you, my sweet
sweet Imogen; are they only for you? I don't know if they are
only for you but I do know you'll understand; I have always
haunted the threshold for these liquid events to be handed to
me, or perhaps I was haunted by the threshold, life itself, its
events sculpted in the concrete of the quotidian has been of
secondary importance to me, life in the concrete quotidian
interests me, certainly, but only vaguely, like reruns from a
miscast mini-series vaguely perused on an airport's television
set. I used to think myself a man enslaved by his maniacal
erotic imagination, his priapic scepter a lever to conduct his
non-apparent self through the maze of phantasms, a pipe to
channel the cosmic phantasmic, both sender and receiver.
Erotic imagination nothing but a conduit into a world they're
trying to keep you away from by designing inferior models
they can sell you, by those who are multi-duplicated as
twirlers of the caduceus of values, you're made to chew on a

popsicle of ethical standards forged in another's heaven, you're made to view your own model as sub-standard, by calling your attachment to your model monikers which would cause it to glare unimpressively in your own eyes, they would never call it, for instance, a palatial substance of enigma, which is what it is. With St. Augustine and the rest of the neo-freudians arming them up with words to defeat you of your own intimate imagination, your own palatial substance of enigma, your own conduit to a mystery you long for, the one that has not been designed for you by others, true freedom. (Perhaps here the fear of turning Siegfried into a holographic signifier, because it would not be an infinite world, but a circumscribed one to a merely one hundred thousand reticulations.)

So the Queen and the High Priestess, who is the servant of the Goddess, are intimate, these are events that were handed me as I mentioned, I am not altering one bit, they are exactly as I received them, they are lounging with each other, the Queen, vested as Siegfried, is reclining on the recamier; she is being implored by the High Priestess: the High Priestess explains to her that the men's world does not exist in fact but was dreamed up by her, the Queen, in expectation of it; she reminds the Queen of the past Era of Inner Unrest, when, in order to quell the ennui that had gripped the demoiselles, and in order to infuse fresh significance into their catacombic mundo, the High Priestess had prayed to the Goddess for a solution; the Goddess came to her in a vision and told her to transmute mishap to peripety, to prevaricate, to invent a false world, a world which does not exist, of the missing half, she described the men, the ephebes, to her in their coruscating detail, and the demoiselles must form an army which will conquer and subjugate the ephebes so as to reunite with the missing half and thus to use them simply at their pleasure; the demoiselles, whose essential culture is the cult of the Goddess, were given to activities, such as wrestling contests, constant and incessant competition sports as erotics, would find it easy to overcome and subjugate the men, who were essentially fleeting, more fugitive than events and easily dismayed, given to philosophy and to poetry, to religious sophistry, feeding on the substance of clouds; thus the demoiselles formed an armada to march on the ephebes; "Let us deplume them of their fripperies" was their battle cry, "Let us adorn our own selves". There is a substance, they were told, which the men possess but must be dematriculated of, and which ingested, it would cause them, the demoiselles, to obtain soaring and wafting, travel by flight. So the demoiselles formed the armada, which after traveling for the duration of, but to speak of time is immaterial, because to be here is the same as to be there, to be there is to be here, and yet the demoiselles understood travel, comprehended intuitively a form of meditational peripatetic purpose; so they mysteriously manifested themselves inside the palatial substance of enigma which was at first apparent as the carpet from which musicians emerged and played the entrancing droneful incessant tunes which maintains their world.

Here, dear Imogen, I feel compelled to paint a picture for you. The grass, the so-called grass upon which the battle scene I spoke of in a previous letter is occurring is actually carpet. Out of the carpet grow musicians who play upon flutes and sing a soothing drone which is in fact the frequency which is the cause of the events shuffling themselves into the order of the words upon the page. The music keeps the world in its place. It's an idea I partially stole from a painting by Remedios Varo as explained by Janet Kaplan in her book. But maybe instead of flutes the musicians issuing from the carpet plink upon strings that surge from the sun and are fastened on the other end to the carpet, another Varo concept. Perhaps we can't even discern whether they are sun rays or carpet strands. (But I am fearful this could be made into an animated movie and I wanted so to write the reflection itself, so that it cannot be sold as another media. I cajole myself with the thought that no one would want to transplant this into a movie.) Here, by the way, are some notes I made that I just found in a folder I forgot about: "I have thought of adding this element to this world, that of musicians, for instance, which, just like in Varo, emerge out of the carpet, a carpet which covers everything, an incessant carpet; and it is music which keeps the world together, a quiet and distant flutelike drone, which if ever it should pause—in the same way that if the sun were to stop illuminating in what we consider to be our world—their world comes to an end. (That perhaps their world is infused with incessant anxiety on account of this fear the music might stop.) That it is the music itself which engenders the world, that the world is the music which expresses itself through the musicians (and the flutes) which materialize, so to speak, from the carpet. (This line came to me and I will include it here for you, and though I didn't originally imagine Siegfried singing, now I say why not, as Siegfried would: "I could not resist the beckoning of an allusion which once escaping the sheathing grip of my well-trained lips invaded the sequence of myrmidons like an alluvial fan": 'The Adored One intones to replenish his fulminating colonies.') The carpet itself becomes them, is them, they are the weave. And when I say carpet, I don't want you to think of the sort of carpet that you're used to in apartment complexes, the prickly off-white or cream pile, the weary weft depleted of splendor, that you've got to dust or vacuum and that if for any reason you're obliged to think of in your secondary, non-utilitarian thinking and you stopped and cognized how you really feel about it, you would shrink from in disgust at its un-erotically conducive, rough surface and its dust and its imprint of disgusting lower limbs and your own lack of taste for accepting such inferior sort of a material in your own life; and I'm not even thinking of the overpriced rugs shrewd Middle Eastern salesmen would try to sell you at the bazaar. I feel as though I am forced to give you a sense of what this material feels like, like for instance, it is loomed with ceaseless fulgurations, because I am sensing you're getting bored and you need something to hold you glued to the story, something to inflame you, at least partially.

What the demoiselles didn't expect was the counter attack from Siegfried, who, upon defeating the demoiselles by unexpected skill of guile earns his moniker of Splendid.

In the skirmish the demoiselles manage to capture a few of the ephebes. (A few of them are captured as well.) These captured ephebes are placed in display cages for all to peruse and wonder. Many forays follow into the world of the ephebes and multiplies the number of the captured; but no final victory, not the dreamed of subjugation, the demoiselles always return defeated by the superb military skills deployed by Splendid.

What happens in the world of the ephebes? Secretly, like a malady that contaminates them, they begin to dream of being abducted by the demoiselles. In their erotic encounters, though I shouldn't call their encounters erotic as opposed to non-erotic, it is what they do, their daily social life—though they have no days and I despise myself for attempting to describe to you their life from the point of view of the coagulated quotidian rather than the other way around, (Octavio Paz, in speaking about Cernuda says: "if desire is real, reality is unreal") but I console myself that this is only a provisional praxis which certainly will not continue once we have achieved our threshold crossing), some begin to take on the apparel and even aspect of warring demoiselles and indulge in abduction. This becomes a matter of public concern and these behaviors are outlawed by their High Priests. But more about this later.

The captured ephebes introduce poetry and flight to the world of the demoiselles; for instance, here's an event I witnessed: one of the ephebes is brought before the Queen; he is commanded to produce a line of poetry. The poetry is never written, only recited, always spontaneous, never remembered. (Though for me to say "never written, only recited", I am merely circumscribing myself to finite data, this is a strategy I wish to avoid. I have always sneezed even at axiom, even if it's mounted high up on a socle, and gesticulating backbone, bragged of brotherhood to apparent certitude.) The poetry's value is measured by the intensity of the subsequent flight it engenders. The ephebe flings himself on the ground before the Queen, a gesture he had mastered with ease: "I long for you, oh Queen of coming to be never there and ever vanishing." The Queen produces a translucent soft and bubbly substance between her fingers, places it around the ephebe's prized prize and causes him to ejaculate a cloudy yellow fume while he sighs with pleasure, moans with dolor; the bubbly substance fills up like a gigantic soap bubble and she soars away holding unto it. As she wafts into pure air travel, (though can we speak of air there as we speak of air here?) there are many others wafting through the space of the tall hallways of the catacombs, which abound with display cages filled with captured ephebes. Though many of the demoiselles may suddenly plunge to the ground on account of impotent poetry.

The multiplying forays into the territory of the ephebes does not fill the increasing demand for them. Air wafting becomes an emblem of superior social status; tumbling leads to social disrepute and ridicule. Great poets are in the highest of demands.

Two classes of captured ephebes emerge: the great poets, whose skills are to be used for travel by air only; mediocre poets, merely for penetration. The great poets may crave penetration, but this is not allowed them. As there is no currency of exchange, the ephebes cannot be bought or sold; however they can be stolen, captured, concealed. This creates social unrest in an society that had experienced only internal peace until then.

The only solution is to entirely subjugate the ephebes. (Colonialism seems to always be the solution to internal unrest.) And the only way to subjugate the ephebes is to abduct the legendary Splendid Count, the Adored One, Siegfried himself.

The Queen finds herself ensnared in the dreaded Quicksand of Yearning; yearning for Siegfried.

She interrogates all the demoiselles who caught sight of him.

She interrogates the captured ephebes.

She wears the same vestments as Siegfried in her private chambers, though it has been decreed against the law for the demoiselles to sport the vestments of the ephebes.

Here I must pause and explain. When I say "wears the same vestments" I don't mean that, for instance, she despoiled one of the gallants of his doublet and hose. The costumes these people wear are a "mandorla": an aura, like the numinous luminous, an emanation of the psychic body. But even I say "the costumes these people wear" I realize that I am in error. There is no separation between the wearer and what she wears. They are one and the same. We do not go somewhere to pick up clothes that someone else, or an inter-textual context of someone elses has created, vestments to cover our nakedness; there are no materials whose exploita-tion, whose transmutation led to the formation of these vest-ments. The people are the clothes, but in saying that I am not passing judgment, I am not implying that the people become inferior by being likened to clothes; all I am saying is that there is no separation between the "mask" and the person, you are not parading your lower limbs veiled in frantic nebulae of silk, your lower limbs are the frantic nebulae of silk, you do not, as it is your custom, "strip proper decorum down to the steel skeleton", you are the proper decorum.

Kant separates the work of bees from the work of artists. The work of bees (their regularly constructed cells) he says is the work of nature, you can't declare that bees are artists, you only compare their work with the work of artists because you already have artists to compare them with; while the work of the artists is "artificial", the free work of "reason", making rather than being. Bees can be squeezed when caught and the substance of bees is a disgusting moisture when squeezed, like squashed frogs, while the substance of reason is a circumscribing terror at the threshold of the abducting imponderable, (I don't call it "free" as Kant does, it is not free, here is where he and I differ, he thinks of reason as a means to get free from the tortuous quicksands of imagination), leading to the contempt for the "work of the bees", the puny attempt to circumscribe subject to a few pre-established parameters, imprisoning parameters. I for one don't bear the strain of subject well, but today's not a good day, I'm in no mood to delve into and expound upon the reticulating networks of my entanglement with the intrigue of intercontextuality.

I don't separate the two because there is no such thing as nature as opposed to artificiality, between river or frog and entrancing weave or boudoir, there is only Imagination which is always creating, weaving, but they are not two, Weaving and Imagination, there is no separation between Imagination as desiring to weave, and the already coagulated weave of the pre-established principle where it is a transgression in reverse to introduce the Imagination's fresh weave, especially as it is implied in the coagulated quotidian, that Imagination is a frustrated weave, desiring for a weave that will never be weaved, because desiring and weaving are one and the same, the tension between the two has been transcended, or rather, it has always been one in this world into which we will be catapulted by the oneger of our mutual desires once we cross the transgressive threshold, and it is only in the coagulated quotidian where you are matriculated into compulsory mode, which is to perceive it as two separate events forever forbidden from uniting.

Imagination being simply another name for the Goddess and her manifestations. And I repeat, when I say I don't separate the two, I mean they have never been separated except in the mind of coagulated physicality, its constricted motion too impeded by ballast to ascend to the light of magnetic surge.

Yes, what we're speaking of here is Imagination. But when I say Imagination you will question these people that I speak of and their reality, ah, you will say, they only exist in your imagination, nowhere else. But you are wrong, not that I blame you completely, but you've been made to believe that the Imagination is secondary, unnecessary, while the stratified being of flesh is the essence, where "real life" takes place. But you've got to understand that's the illusion, that it is the Imagination which is supreme. That our being of flesh is nothing but coagulated Imagination.

In imagining Siegfried, Imogen simply transmutes into his attire. Effortlessly. As light here has no source, but is secreted from within, neither do the clothes, they too are secreted from within, anything can be imagined, or rather secreted, Imagination and secretion are one, as a spider secrets its web. (What are shopping malls but the shouts of concentration camp victims? We must discover for ourselves by listening to the murmur of our intimate weave, what really brings pleasure and benefit, what costume is best for us to consume.) This the bliss body, freedom of Imagination, imaginal body, freed through indulgence in fetish. (Though when I say fetish I am using a language that does not belong in that world. The pedestrian world is, as I think I mentioned, the coagulated imaginal; and the forces of coagulation constrain magnetic surge by obnubilation of fetish through definition, fetish being a trapdoor to expand into surge. Solidity being only a conspiracy. Religion then is using the mystery of existence to subdue by fear: by inducing fear of the mystery, the corporation's use of religion is to subjugate. Sausegization equals amnesia. Yes,

no love is more powerful than governmental control
in the tentacles of corporate control
not even the love of mother for her child.

The High Priestess Alcina, who is now losing power, abrogates the Queen to stop adorning herself as Siegfried, she insists it's blasphemy; she insists it's blasphemy to insist that the ephebes exist. The penis itself she insists is engendered by the longing to fill a vacancy; it does not exist in and of itself. The ephebes too, she reminds her, do not exist, they were simply a vision which the Goddess had infused her with to circumvent the ennui which had infused the demoiselles. That the ephebes and their world were found is only to attest to her, Alcina's power, by infusing the demoiselles with vision which came true. But it was only a vision, which now has gone too far, we are in danger, Alcina announces, of angering the Goddess, who would forever destroy this weave we are presently part of. You must allow me to institute abstention. I will institute abstention in order to decontaminate them of the ephebes. The Goddess has spoken again, yes, and she advised me to abandon all the ephebes and imprison any demoiselle who sports or conceals one. Now that we have abdicated boredom, we shall abdicate boredom anew by ascending to abstention, and by a forced return to engendering ecstasy from one another. Yes, if we stop lusting after the joys of the ephebes, non-existent to begin with, we will return to the state of serenity and happiness that was always ours. She begs the Queen to allow her to satisfy her like in the past. The Queen allows her but is not satisfied.

The queen retorts, to Alcina's horror, that she has plans to stage a full campaign to capture Siegfried and subjugate the land of the ephebes; she longs for poetry, for culture, for the "The cloud-capped towers, the gorgeuos palaces,/The solemn temples…"

Alcina threatens the Queen with the fury of the Goddess. The Queen replies that it is the Goddess herself who desires this, it is the transmutation of the desire of the Goddess. That the Goddess, in giving her the vision of the world of the ephebes, withheld the full truth from her on purpose. She imprisons Alcina, in spite of her imploring, in a barred cell with ten ephebes who are mediocre poets simply to teach her a lesson, to prove to her that the ephebes do exist. She, who, next the Queen, yielded the highest power in the Queendom, becomes a mere slave to the imprisoned ephebes.

(This will also reverse the pre-dominant Biblical value: in this narrative ephebes emerge out of the phantasmic of the demoiselles; Yes, a reverse of the Adamic man and the myth of man engendering woman. All I'm really suggesting is the elimination of the judeo-christian idea of original sin.)

As you can see, I have not been slothful on research. Here are some samples from my copious notes; they are notes only, I have not sifted through them carefully, some are, as I mentioned above fragments from unfinished letters I didn't send you, so forgive their repetitious nature, you will be trumping through the text in elliptical boots.

You will suggest, you the reader, that I should commit some of my time to investigating kinds of architecture (the cloud capped palaces, etc); or, architexture; thank you for your suggestion; my reply to you is, do your own investigating; I'm not even getting paid for this; though I've got to say, don't think I haven't thought about it, I mean the architexture. Still, to proffer lists, one executes oneself of one's duty: huge rich billows of fabric, in the style of the great Venetian artists, or canvass awash with Venetian colors; as though plunging into incessant languishment. (We're languishing in language.) Though we are not attempting a definite landscape as necessary for the movies—what we're attempting is a *langue*scape—we have not hired a production designer, nor will we. But something suffused with the uncertain, with tentative tentacles, suffused with evanescent architexture. I have dreamed about investigating the "cloud capped towers, the gorgeous palaces, the solemn temples, the great globe itself, all the stuff as dreams are made on." Yes, I was once of the opinion that I should have production values in this book, that I should indulge in well described production values. And I have spent many a sleepless night gleaning information from the pages of: Visual Arts, a History, by Hugh Honour and John Flemming. But perhaps because of my lack of erudition in this area, I couldn't settle on one specific style, and though I have thought of fusing styles and even engaging the help of an architect friend of mine, I finally gave up on the idea; (or perhaps because there isn't one specific style I wish to circumscribe my world to, I didn't wish to imprison it in the derogatory demands of one particular style.) I considered using the work of M.C. Escher as my guide, as I do see my characters inhabiting those constructions, M. C. Escher's constructions were always imbued for me with an erotic mystery of death I wished to explore. But I gave up, just as I gave up on Remedios Varo, she comes the closest to the colors I might have envisioned, or might have agreed with—note here I say 'might have' rather than directly 'envision', or 'agree with'. The reason being, as I mentioned, I don't want to fixate on any specifics. I could say look up Escher, look up Varo, look up the magical world in Varo's work. But that's not the point. First, as I mentioned before, this is not a blue print for a movie or a painting. (You have clearly seen my demonstrations of my descriptive powers, that's not the point, if I wished to describe, well, see one of the previous chapters where I speak about this more elegantly, stylishly.) And more than anything I hate indicating, this is not a reference manual. And even more, this work is a work in itself, not referable to something outside it. So, these words that I am presently formulating, they are not an expression of frustration with description, if you think they are, you are wrong, it is you who lacks imagination, this is not a colorless text I am presenting simply to fill the page's empty space and add more volume to the book I'm writing. I mean I could say emerald, burgundy, alabaster, obsidian, would you feel more satisfied then, would you feel more imagination is infusing the text now? And once again I am forgetting who I am writing this letter to, you my sweet sweet Imogen, or you the reader, someone I don't know but whom I hope to entrance and enlighten with my tale; and more, I keep forgetting this is actually a ramp to take you somewhere else, to a world you crave, and I feel I am getting more and ensconced in a text I don't adore. And the weight is upon me, the same question weighs constantly upon me now, how can you insure they don't say "he's just inscribing his phantasies", they won't even say phantasies, they'll say fantasies, they won't even say erotic, they'll say sexual, which you hate, how can you insure they'll know you're making a political state-ment? Because the reader will surely wish to venture into gloating over the idea that these represent in some manner the author's own fetishes. The critics will take on the duty of judges and lambaste or castigate the author for his indul-gences, more, for his conscious luxuriation in fetish. (I could of course forced by the dictates of others occupy myself with more "valuable" enterprises: I could get a job for the habitat for humanity, I could serve soup to the homeless, I could work for racial equality, I could start a revolution. Yet as a matter of conscious choice I choose to unravel this tale which is at the core of my existence; I know in confessing this I will be judged by many as superficial, I run the risk of being judged after death as having squandered my greater gifts in favor of personal attachment to fetish. But in my vision I surprised them straining themselves in the mirror of self disgust, their precepts crumpled snow in the drawer.)

The air, I said, is a fetish none of us could do without; or at least that's what science reveals.

My other fear is they will find my manuscripts and use them to create cinema. I am locating a method to transcend cinema. A text they categorically cannot use to create cinema. To say no one would pay you any money to make this sort of a movie is not enough because the movie then exists in a potential state and it is conceivable that in an alternate world, or even a future world someone could make a movie of this story. I am against the making of a movie; I must make sure I create a record of events that could not be filmed, that acquire their energy only when read on the page, and not as description. Certainly, you must interact with it, certainly I want you to become enfolded in its compulsions, impulses, convolutions, implications, sucked, no, abducted into its catacombs. You must feel as though you are abducted into its costumes and customs, that their gestures are your gestures, that you are glued to it irretrievably, stripped against your will of your "ideas and utility, your accustomed routine, your knowledge, your prayers". Things must be done to you against your will, it's only then that my art will be valid. We must ensconce the petty philistine in the doublet of speculative cobwebs, steep them in the hose of ecstatic transcendence.

(The doublet I wear is not the straightjacket of delusionary formulations. My stockings do not ensconce me in sources of prevailing understanding, dominating opinions. They are the sources of elucidating understanding, pythons of discernment.)

Yes, a film no, but you will ask what if they want to turn it into a video game! Not a video game but interactive software! The most sophisticated game of holographic virtual reality you ever could imagine. I am generally not a fan of Borges's poetry, though you know well how much I adore his prose, but these lines from him captured me a moment ago while I thoughtlessly leafed through "A Personal Anthology":

An enormous diamond in which a man
May lose himself most fortunately
Through ambits of indolent music
Behind the scope of his flesh and name.

Yes, to free the erotic, but only part time, into this holographic virtual reality, while for the rest of the time to remain tethered to the tentacles of the performance principle, sort of like a post-modern re-interpretation of the Hashishins, who, coaxed by the promissory pact of temporary hashish and young maidens lure, would murder at the beck and call of Hassan ben Sabbah. That is not at all what I had imagined! In other words, while I have sought to permanently eradicate the performance principle, they would seek to maintain it by endearing it, to package it by seasoning it with artificial flavor of prefabricated erotica, a technologically spiced erotica to splash an elastic sheen on the procrustean bed of societal constraints. To turn Siegfried into a holographic signifier! You step into him vicariously, not vicariously but cybernetically, the dreamscape of my phantasies turned into the cyberspace of a mass consumption game, oh Imogen, it's sickening, everything I believe in obliterated! An infinite world suddenly circumscribed to some smelly scientist's imaginal limitations! Don't even think about it. And this could occur, my Imogen, all they'd have to do is suck up the contents of my hard drive. Technology as a continuation of nature. No, let's not even think about it.

Movies on the other hand, yes, there are certain considerations, certain options I mean, certain stipulations, contingencies, which, if made operative, if I were, for instance to be promised these stipulations were to be made operative, I would consider a mass market movie of the adventures of Siegfried (though now I think more and more of calling him

Astolpho, but maybe not) and Queen Imogen, of the Groveling Gallant and Adoring Spy: as their erotics, a world of lovely erotics, engendered of itself, pose a threat to the enforced sexuality of the dominant system, the mass market presentation of their erotics might have the effect of a veritable revolution. At least, I would plant in the mass market audience the seeds of incipience, the ur-crave for this alternate world, for origins, really; but presently, their bodies and minds made as they are into instruments of alienated labor; their enslavement of the erotic, of the playful; alienated from their own selves, and their desires, it's now impossible for their sausage bodies to perform successfully in the phantasy world I created. To suspend disbelief requires a heavy dose of drugs which, used repeatedly, constantly, would lead to a slow but sure erosion of the ability to dream effectively and to perform effectively; and then society blames those who cannot function according to its dictates, calls them losers; they cannot function as the priests of the sausage machine god; the sausage machine god, the god of the jews and the christians. But perhaps trained by the erotic drills of my movies they may be gradually freed of their sausage mentality. I might even be convinced to leave aside my obsession with style for the sake of this revolution.

Yes, at first I was disgusted by the idea that this would become a movie, you know how much I hate the cinema, the tool of domination of the forces of the performance principle. Because while the word is infinite, the visual circumscribes; you force a single Siegfried on everyone. Especially someone who disgusts. Paul Virilio: "'The cinema involves putting the eye into uniform', claimed Kafka. What are we to say, then, of this *dictatorship* exerted for more than a half a century by optical hardware which has become omniscient and omnipresent and which, like any totalitarian regime, encourages us to forget we are individual human beings?"

But then I thought, what a great way to introduce this

idea, this concept to the public, like a contaminating virus; because, this is the only way it will catch: like a virus, like a contamination, because that's the idea behind a contamination, it is irreversible; Ghandi spoke of the world being contaminated by his ideas, by the movement. I dreamed at first, of course, of literary glory because the words I penned are so entrancing, I dreamed, no, I creamed over the words of a creamy critic creaming over my alphabet gumbo; but soon I realized I'm not literary glory seeking here but revolution, a total complete revolution of the world, and I am mobilizing all my forces to incite it.

But I would have to, first and foremost, have complete control over the screenplay, direction, editing. (And this may mean armed revolution.) Not only that, direct control over distribution; and, direct control over the presentation. What I mean: each member of the audience, before the film starts, is tethered to his or her seat; more, each member of the audience has to hold hands, interlace fingers that is, with his or her neighbor. But if a couple comes to see the movie, it is separated at the entrance, so everyone must sit next to someone else he or she doesn't know. And their hands are also secured together with binds, so that they may not, for the duration of the performance, disentangle their interlacing fingers; and their feet as well are secured with some form of velcro binds, I have seen those in certain catalogues. In this position they are now forced to view their repressed sexuality on screen, as the lives of Count Siegfried and Queen Imogen, and The Groveling Gallant and The Adoring Spy, and the rest of the cast of characters. A man, who for sintance, I mean instance, has cultivated the malady of machismo as his permanent allure, armored himself in the predominant culture's atavistic breastplate, must view the supine Groveling Gallant placing his eager lips upon Siegfried's slipper; he must be forced to view this shameless unrestricted worship, without being allowed to turn away, in order to prevent him from his customary refusal and conscript him to give free reign to his alternate erotic identities. He must be shocked into entrancement with unsuspected erotics. Because just like in dreams, in whose events, while they are occurring, we are participants with an even higher sort of involvement than the so called "real life", movies elicit in us such an intense sort of inner life that we are willing to abandon everything else to imagine ourselves participants in it. (That is why the predominant system uses the film industry to choose for us the vehicles for our journey: people whom the present system deems worthy of transporting us across this pre-designed landscape.) Because you have the internal world and the only one to have meaning at all, the only one where you do not shun or shunt your true desires, where no one watches you and you can allow yourself to feel its true desires and where you are absolutely free, and you since you have to have a body whose functionings depend on its interdependence to the rest of society, where you have to masquerade by pretending that these desires you have do not exist or if they do you're willing to declare up and down— this up & down disturbs me, what does it mean? that you have to walk up & down your block and make these declarations to everyone in your neighborhood?—they are evil and they belong to the devil and they are nothing but temptations and it's better you not have these desires so you can belong to god and go to heaven where for the rest of eternity you'll not have these desires. And that this life of the body is temporal but your soul is not which means that your soul which must be what you feel, etc, etc); as I said the audience would be secured to the chairs and to each other. By the way, that, I feel, would make for a powerful communal experience; this is an idea that should seriously be considered for a method of true bonding of a community; certainly, many would protest: they are the ones with the most hang-ups who would profit the most from this process! I think that experiencing something so pleasant together, but forced to experience it in such a compromising manner would cause the community to, force them to bond because they would not be able to evade or avoid how they actually felt, they would not be allowed to retreat into their own heads and discount the experience. They would experience their shame together, that's the meaning of true bonding. It would be preposterous for anyone to protest while being tied up to everyone else and experiencing this.

Siegfried struts in. There is no governmental edict, no cloistered pretext in his gait. If I were to trace on paper the motion in time and space of the billowing sleeve of the doublet I envision adorning my arm, an arm which only exists as a doublet sleeve whose liquid interiority billows uncloistered, (you must not fabricate in your imaginal factories an image of silk, an image of velvet which is engendered artificially through the office of exploited workers, Marx, commodities, are inappropriate here and I would slap you if you brought them up—though to say natural, to say artificial, to separate these two, as I said, it is a grave error), but a doublet of pure sensation, a visible doublet sleeve, and as sensation, pure sensation, as though my arm has mastered the art of eternity, i.e., the art of each motion, on account of its existing as fullness in the moment, on account that nothing else is necessary for that moment except that motion – and by the way, this is really how you smash the state, by hungering for the present, not by placing bombs, which the state actually wants – and though you are reading this in time, as I am writing this in time, these words placed significantly one after the other on paper...

The Amorous Spy is compelled to leave aside style and simply enumerate; because how to describe every slipper he would like to kiss, every entrancing stocking? How to describe shiver at the sight of the fold of trunk hose above the upper echelons of the thigh.

"I can't help perusing his stockings which now are perhaps of another hue which I can't fathom with the force of my description; but the clinging glimmer of the stockings, the clinging glimmer of the stockings is soft and warm and unsettling, like a womb perhaps, or like an egg. There is a surrounding sea of stockings whose warm clinging glimmers are a womb—a womb I'm in—just as entrancing as Siegfried's stockings."

What are these people made of, you might have wondered, I'm sure. "If I were the Groveling Gallant I would fling myself on my knees at Siegfried's feet." But I'm inside this body whose pre-designed system of posturing cannot deviate even a millimeter from the circumscription of the Common Activity Drills. It's always easier to let others perform these feats of desire with the kind of indifference we execute our daily actions. The Immutability of the Void! I, under the sign of the Mutable! Let us gaze with contempt at others perform what we should perform ourselves! What are these people made of? These people populating this story. These fashionable creatures in stockings and doublets, thousands of them perhaps, having paused to greet the vanquishing emerald of Count Siegfried. As an aside, 'people populating' has an entrancing sound, especially since 'people' and 'populating' are probably rooted in a similar etymology. They, these people, are made of a poetic substance; the original, poetic ur-substance; they have broken free of the body which imprisons us and which we inhabit as though it were an obligation, imposed upon us, to maintain;

> the desire to sustain the self,
> the desire to sustain the self of flesh,
> is an obsession born
> out of a consciousness of values
> entertained by the hysterical

cloning binge out to perpetuate a need,
an echolike cloning of catacombs
of mysteries, this fanfare
auxiliary to the sausage man
at all turns
determines
conducts
the cadence of his uncertain
and awkward
fandango

an obligation to who? The füehrers of signification, which is sausegification, that's who; those who have an interest in us maintaining the circumscription, the straightjacketting, of this concept of body which we now drag around like a grave. This body and its networks of circumscription. This body belonging to insurance companies, advertising companies, drug companies, credit companies, this body whose system of motion and gesturing cannot deviate an inch from the circumscription of the Common Activity Drills; this body whose desires are designed by the füehrers of the marketplace which will promise fulfillment at a price the price of which is enslavement to the market; so this body whose natural desires are re-designed, standardized, packaged, and re-sold back to it; this body whose natural desires and longings need to be pre-approved by the networking pretexts—cathexis to reticulation of imaginary and actual systems of punishments—in which it is circumscribed; ("Thus:", says Cioran, "to abandon everything, without knowing what this everything represents; to isolate yourself from your milieu; to reject—by a metaphysical divorce—that substance which has molded you, which surrounds you, an which carries you./ Who, and by what form of defiance, can challenge existence without fear of punishment? ... the will to undermine the foundation of all that exists…"), this body forced into a reticulation of marches specifically pre-designed to tend to its maintenance; towards a system of maintenance which will not maintain it because it is only concerned with maintaining itself and in order to maintain itself it uses only a miniscule, partial function of the body's infinite potential; this body finally a slave to the ravages of time; this body which is then buried and forgotten. Etc, etc.

So then, my Imogen, Imagine, before you discount what I am suggesting, Imagine what it would be like to have eliminated birth, old age, sickness, and death. Imagine being a body suited only for pleasure; no other consideration exists, except pleasure. This new body is immortal; it is never aging; it never has to worry about being born or dying; never has to worry about earning a living—that's part of what is defined as illness; (ask about born or dying - if we always exist, then why not just do that) it never has to worry or complain about ailments, (here goes my nosology) indispositions, disorders, afflictions, infirmities, disabilities, defects, handicaps, deformities, blights, hopeless conditions, brain death, ill-health, sickliness, feebleness, debilities, decrepitude, invalidity, infections, contagions, contamination, epidemics, plagues, pestilences, pandemics, scourges, tuberculosis, seizures, attacks, accesses, abscesses, blockages, stoppages, thrombosis, strokes, ictuses, apoplexies, spasms, throes, fits, paroxysms, convulsions, epilepsy, lockjaw, trismus, tetanus, laryngospasms, laryngismus, vaginismus, cramps, fever, feverishness, hyperthemia, neurasthenia, circulatory collapse, anemia, ankylosis, asphyxiation, anoxia, ataxia, bleeding, hemorrhage, colic, chills, hot flashes, dropsy, hydrops, edema, morning sickness, fatigue, constipation, diarrhea, flux, dysentery, indigestion, upset stomach, dyspepsia, inflammation, necrosis, insomnia, itching, pruritus, jaundice, icterus, backache, lumbago, vomiting, nausea, paralysis, skin eruptions, rashes, sores, hypertension, high blood pressure, hypotension, low blood pressure, tumors, fibrillation, tachycardia, apnea, dyspnea, asthma, blennorhea, nasal discharge, rheum, coughing, sneezing, cachexia, cachexy, tabes, marasmus, emaciation, atrophy, sclerosis, myopathy, collagen disease, connective tissue disease, deficiency, nutritional diseases, vitamin deficiency diseases, genetic diseases, gene diseases, gene-transmitted diseases, hereditary diseases, congenital diseases, infectious diseases, eye diseases, ophtalmic diseases, cataracts, conjunctivitis, pink eye, glaucoma, sty, ear diseases, otic disorders, otic diseases, deafness, earache, otalgia, tympanitis, otosclerosis, vertigo, Ménière's syndrome, apoplectical deafness, respiratory disease, upper respiratory disease, lung disease, white plague, phthisis, consumption, venereal disease, VD, sexually-transmitted disease, social disease, Cupid's itch, Venus's curse, dose, chancre, chancroid, gonorrhea, the clap, syphilis, pox, cardiovascular disease, heart disease, heart condition, vascular disease, angina, angina pectoris, cardial infarction, myocardial infarction, cardiac arrest, congenital heart disease, congestive heart failure, coronary, ischemic heart disease, coronary thrombosis, heart attacks, coronary, heart failure, tachycardia, blood disease, hemic disease, hematic disease, endocrine disease, glandular disease, endocrinism, diabetes, goiter, hyperglycemia, hyperthyroidism, metabolic disease, acidosis, alkalosis, ketosis, gout, podagra, galactosemia, lactose intolerance, fructose intolerance, phenylketonuria, maple syrup urine disease, congenital hypophosphatasia, liver disease, hepatic disease, gallbladder disease, kidney disease, renal disease, nephritis, neural disease, nerve disease, neuropathy, brain disease, amytrophic lateral sclerosis, Lou Gehrig disease, palsy, cerebral palsy, Bell's palsy, chorea, St. Vitus's dance, the jerks, Huntington's chorea, headache, migraine, multiple sclerosis, Parkinson's disease, sciatica, sciatic neuritis, shingles, herpes zoster, spina fibida, paralysis, impairment of motor functions, stroke, apoplexy, paresis, motor paralysis, sensory paralysis, hemiplegia, paraplegia, diplegia, quadriplegia, cataplexy, catalepsy, infantile paralysis, poliomyelitis, heatstroke, heat prostration, heat exhaustion, coup de soleil, siriasis, insolation, calenture, thermic fever, gastrointestinal disease, disease of the digestive tract, stomach condition, colic, colitis, constipation, irregularity, diarrhea, dysentery, looseness of the bowels, flux, the trots, gastritis, indigestion, ulcer, peptic ulcer, nausea, nauseation, queasiness, seasickness, mal de mer, poisoning, intoxication, venenation, septic poisoning, blood poisoning, sepsis, septicimia, toxemia, pyemia, septicopyemia, autointoxication, food poisoning, ptomaine poisoning, milk sickness, ergotism, St. Anthony's fire, allergy, allergic disorder, allergic, rhinitus, hay fever, rose cold, pollinosis, asthma, bronchial asthma, hives, urticaria, eczema, conjunctivitis, St. Vitus's dance, cold sore, allergic gastritis, cosmetic dermatitis, Chinese restaurant syndrome, Kwok's disease, allergen, skin diseases, acne, sebaceous gland disorder, dermatitis, itch, psoriasis, skin eruption, eruption, rash, efflorescence, breaking out, diaper rash, drug rash, vaccine rash, prickly heat, heat rash, nettle rash, papular rash, rupia, sore, lesion, pustule, papule, papula, fester, pimple, hickey, zit, pock, ulcer, ulceration, bedsore, tubercle, blister, bleb, bulla, blain, whelk, wheal, welt, wale, boil, furuncle, furunculus, carbuncle, canker, canker sore, cold sore, fever blister, sty, abscess, gathering, aposteme, gumboil, parulis, whitlow, felon, paronychia, bubo, chancre, soft chancre, chanchroid, hemorrhoids, piles, bunion, chilblain, kibe, polyp, stigma, petechia, scab, eschar, fistula, suppuration, festering, swelling, rising, wound, injury, hurt, cut, incision, scratch, gash, flesh wound, stab wound, laceration, mutilation, abrasion, scuff, scrape, chafe, gall, frazzle, fray, run, rip, rent, slash, tear, burn, scald, scorch, first degree-burn, second degree-burn, third degree-burn, flash burn, break, fracture, bone-fracture, comminuted fracture, compound or open fracture, greenstick fracture, spiral fracture, torsion fracture, rupture, crack, chip, craze, check, crackle, wrench, whiplash, concussion, bruise, contusion, ecchymosis, black and blue mark, black eye, shiner, battering, battered child syndrome, growth, neoplasm, tumor, intumescence, benign tumor, nonmalignant tumor, innocent tumor, malignant tumor, malignant growth, metastatic tumor, cancer, sarcoma, carcinoma, morbid growth, excrescence, outgrowth, proud flesh, exostosis, cyst, wen, fungus, fungosity, callus, callosity, corn, clavus, wart, veruca, mole, nevus, gangrene, motification, necrosis, sphacelus, sphacelation, noma, moist gangrene, dry gangrene, gas gangrene, hospital gangrene, caries, cariosity, tooth decay, slough, necrotic tissue; imagine no more concerns about germs, pathogens, contagium, bugs, disease causing agents, disease producing micro-organisms, microbes, viruses, filterable viruses, non-filterable viruses, adenoviruses, echoviruses, reoviruses, rhinoviruses, enteroviruses, picornviruses, retroviruses, bacterium, bacteria, coccus, streptococcus, staphylococcus, bacillus, spirillum, vibrio, spirochete, gram-positive bacteria, gram-negative bacteria, aerobe, aerobic bacteria, anaerobe, anaerobic bacteria, protozoon, amoeba, trypanosome, fungus, mold, spore, carcinogens, cancer causing agents; no more sick persons, ill persons, sufferers, victims, valetudinarians, invalids, shut-ins, incurables, terminal cases, patients, cases, inpatients, outpatients, apoplectics, consumptives, dyspeptics, epilectics, rheumatics, arthritics, spastics, infirms, the sick, no more carriers, vectors, mechanical vectors, Typhoid Marys, cripples, defectives, handicapped persons, incapables, amputees, the halts, the lames, the blinds, no more anemics, chlorotics, scrofulars, epileptics, diabetics, variolars, malarials, lepers, encephalitics, consumptives, rheumatics, no more acute conditions, allergies, atrophies, autoimmune diseases, bacterial diseases, blood diseases, bone diseases, cardiovascular diseases, childhood diseases (no more childhoods), pediatric diseases, chronic conditions, chronic fatigue syndromes, circulatory diseases, collagen diseases, congenital diseases, connective tissue diseases, contagious diseases, infectious diseases, deficiency diseases, degenerative diseases, digestive diseases, endemic diseases, endochrine diseases, endochrine gland diseases, epidemic diseases, functional diseases, fungal diseases, gastric diseases, stomach diseases, gastrointestinal diseases, deficiency diseases, no ariboflavinosis, no more genetic diseases, geriatric diseases, glandular diseases, hepatic diseases, liver diseases, hereditary diseases, hypertrophy, iatrogenic diseases, intestinal diseases, joint diseases, malignant diseases, muscular diseases, neurological diseases, nutritional diseases, occupational diseases, ophtalmic diseases, organic diseases, pandemic diseases, parasitic diseases, protozoan diseases, psychogenic diseases, psychosomatic diseases, pulmonary diseases, radiation diseases, renal diseases, kidney diseases, respiratory diseases, skin diseases, urinogenital diseases, venereal diseases, viral diseases, wasting diseases, worm diseases, deficiency diseases and disorders, anemia, beriberi, cachexia, legionnaire's disease, famine fever, anyway you get the basic idea, no more environmental and occupational diseases, no anoxemia, anoxia, anoxic anoxia, anthrax, woolsorter's disease, cadmium poisoning, frostbite, lead poisoning, mercury poisoning, radiation sickness, no more bombs, atomic or hydrogen or any kind, no more science, no more sunstroke, no more traffic, no more smog, no more medicine, no more insurance.

Yes, the only solution for mankind: to become Immaterial, or rather of a different Material, of eternal youth, of infinite means of the imagination which constantly multiplies itself into the forms which this Material will take. No more birth, old age, sickness, and death, what the Buddhists classified as the bane of human existence. No, the idea of flesh is not a good one. Perhaps that's what the saints meant when they said flesh is evil; while on the surface condemning flesh, they had entered their world of the Imagination; (not bereft of all) what possibly could they have meant when they spoke of union with god? God is Imagination! (I am not speaking here of saints like augustine, augustine presents us with an interesting problem: how to cure us all of our humanity. A non-existent god as a new form of imploratory erotics. An ownership of a nothingness. In this way he prophesized the future: he knows very well that his pathways to god are empty of words, there is nothing but empty praise; his life of sin is well more beckoning. He's actually prevaricating, mystifying god like he does, with his insistence on praising that borders on sick languishing over a non-existent god—god, that consoling blank!— compare here Julian's languishing over the minute details of his erotic phantasies, Buber who said that god can be found in perfecting, or working at perfecting something, what about perfecting one's phantastic inner life? is there something to be said about perfecting something of no apparent value? "...phantasy... remains free from the control of the reality principle—at the price of becoming powerless, inconsequential, unrealistic." Is it of no apparent value because the valuer does not value but perceives his erotic phantasms as a negative? From whose point of view? Neo-Freudians wanted to cure him of them; but what about actually validating them, enjoying them without the stigma? Man has the right to be happy. Man is not a curse.) They spoke of a union with Imagination; but if they called on the world to join them on their Imaginal journey, what would have happened to the world? Certainly they had to leave behind writings, and if you read these writings carefully, you will see what I mean.

And shame on those who speak of the erotic standing in for the sacred. The erotic is sacred! The only issue here is the flesh, and the maintenance of the factories which maintain the flesh; the meaning of revolution is simply that you dismantle these factories; that's it. Why maintain them? What are you trying to stay faithful to? To the factories of concentration camps this world has become, maybe has always been?

So, what are these people made of? They are people of the fire I spoke of earlier. These people belong to a civilization which has always existed. A people living a life whose impulses we have constantly felt but relegated, circumscribed as we are, to the abnormal; yet it is we who are abnormal, we who are the scum and the dross.

We have chosen to opt for the flesh, for carnality, for the immutability of the carnality, and naturally, for the corporation, in the original sense of this word, this word being rooted in the Latin 'corpus', i.e., body, for the design of the body the corporation has come up with for us, the design they have come up with for our body. We have decided that the only way to live is to commit mass suicide by allowing the corporation to pre-design our lives for us.

But this is something you already know and it is not the corporation I want to speak about. It is about the people in the story I wish to speak about. To speak about the life I love; the only unrestrained and uncircumscribed life there is, life in its original state.

To be more specific, these people are made of light; they are not lit by a light source; each and everyone is a light source. Their existence has been recorded in the esoteric literature of the past. Corbin speaks of "mundus imaginalis". In other words, a world made completely of imagination; imagination as a kind of "matter"; a more essential matter; but when I say 'imagination', you'll instantly think of a world of prohibition, a world which is not to be taken seriously, perhaps a world relegated to the insane asylum by the füehrers of the flesh; that is why the corporation does not condone the personal imagination, though it makes allowances for a severely circumscribed form of imagination which serves its purposes and is in fact the secret religion of our time and is force-fed to the populace through television and the media, with its pre-designed heroes and heroines, pre-designed issues, pre-designed sexuality, etc. That is why what I am writing you about is dangerous information.

I'm pointing to, again, Corbin here, "a world to which the ancient sages alluded when they affirmed that beyond the sensory world there exists another universe with a contour and dimensions and extensions in a space, although these are not comparable with the shape and spatiality as we perceive them in the world of physical bodies". "...the mystical Earth of Hurqalya with emerald cities; it is situated on the summit of the cosmic mountain...". "...the visionary geography of the ancient legends which tell us of a race ... ignorant of the earthly Adam, a race similar to the angels, androgynous perhaps, since without sexual differentiation (...), and hence untroubled even by desire for posterity (...) they have no need of outer light, whether from the sun or the moon, the stars or the physical Heavens.". "... a world", he continues, "made wholly of a subtle "matter" of light, intermediate between the world of Cherubimic pure Lights and the world of physis...". Elsewhere he mentions these people exude an unearthly beauty.

(I want to clarify the declaration that these people are "perhaps" androgynous. While it is true that they are neither imbricated in masculine scales, nor forged in the frantic sub-missiveness of femininity, they exhibit separate male and female organs; Corbin's conviction they are "untroubled ... by desire for posterity" is true but in another sense: they are eternal. They don't need to be troubled by desire for posteri-ty, they are unplagued by time. They are eternal and maintain the contour and nature they have always possessed; they were never born, nor will they ever die.)

It is possible that in the fluctuations of the eternal now, which on account of the constraining frame of our ability to grasp timelessness I can't present in any other way but within a "time frame", there was a period in which these beings made of this cloudlike poetic substance were androgynous, in other words the "males" and the "females", the "andros" and the "gynos" contained each other; they were given to the "contemplation of the essences', a fine manner of whiling eternity away. In the process of contemplation, which is essentially self-contemplation, and since "androgynous" means the 'one' that contains the 'two', "androus" and "gynous", the contemplators arrived at the discovery of their dual nature. Being of a substance which manifests far less "density" or "aggregation" than our substance, i.e., the substance we have made ourselves of, really, the signified sausage substance we have opted for to obtain our uneasy passage through this particular mundo we now inhabit and which I spoke of above,—as an aside, I want you try to perceive "our" world from the point of view of "theirs" and not the other way around—the androgynous beings divided simply on account of the mere contemplation of their differing natures. Should I say the two natures, becoming, on account of the contemplation itself, separate: I can't pretend to know, so I can only conjecture this, but their increasing awareness of the separateness of the "androus" and "gynous" parts, caused the whole to separate: thus, the "males/andros" and the "females/gynos".

You may ask how it is possible to cause a separation simply by contemplation. Think then how something comes into being when you pay attention to it. Try sometimes to listen attentively to someone: you'll have a friend for life. The same with a child: if you listen to its being, that being will begin to take its own shape. Contemplating is equivalent with watering, nurturing. I mentioned Borges before. In "Tlön, Uqbar, Tertius Orbius"—and by the way, notice the echo-like sonar mirroring of Uqbar with Hurqalya—Borges speaks of a planet and a people which are "congenitally idealist". Psychology then as the basis of all sciences, but a psychology where value is placed upon, attention is paid to, what the ideas are actually doing of their own want. Thus even lost objects can reappear as near look-alike clones, and some objects are brought into being simply by hope. Objects on Tlön even "tend to lose detail when people forget them." The classic example is that of a "stone threshold which lasted as long as it was visited by a beggar, and which faded from sight on his death. Occasionally, a few birds, a horse perhaps, have saved the ruins of an amphitheater."

(Again, here I don't want you to conjure up, when confronting the word "ideas", simply some passing ideas that appear and disappear at will and are devalued by our system of values simply because they bring no monetary return, no one else pays attention to them, in other words they are no armament to use to build a statue for yourself, a grave that is, in the amphitheatre of forced common activity. "Psychology then as the basis of all sciences", but a psychology where value is placed upon, attention is paid to, what the ideas are actually doing of their own want. Unrestrained ideas, following their own paths.)

Certainly it is difficult, engorged as we are in the tentacles of our conception of the flesh, to imagine how a single being of flesh could divide upon contemplation of itself; like I said earlier, these beings' original nature is not the signified sausage; the sausage is the result of the "concentration" of the self contemplation: a sort of clotting aggregate compression. The clotting, followed by clogging, of contemplation matter, the sclerosis, is so extreme that it cannot but contemplate itself in ways other than, or out of, its coagulated state. But at the level of the matter, the light matter—light in both of the senses of the word—that "timelessness" is made of, division by contemplation is easily achieved.

The idea of this separation is not new. Plato, in The Symposium, presents us with a somewhat similar vision. Though a convert to grave matters, this Plato, his vision of the separation will come out of the mouth of someone with light words. Aristophanes, that is, his nemesis. And Plato would like us to take those words lightly. In other words, to discount them as a light entertainment, a non-truth. Yes, Plato would like us to be grave. We have been grave ever since. (Though Nietzsche tells us that just pre-grave, Plato kept Aristophanes, not Socrates, under his pillow.) To be fair, our gravity has even graver roots than Plato.

I happen to see a little more into the speech of Aristophanes than Plato himself does. I am inclined to believe that Aristophanes was inspired, touched by the Goddess when he spoke, though maybe he himself didn't believe it, as his purpose at this party was to primarily entertain that gay drunken crew. Essentially Aristophanes holds that the split occurred not on account of self-contemplation but it was caused by an outside agent: the ever interfering, ever intervening male Zeus who, for some personal motive I don't right now recall, was jealous of the androgynes and cut them in two. Still, the allusion to the their original integral nature and their being split is what I wanted to get to.

Why are they warring then? Why are the andros and the gynos at odds with each other? The answer is simple: the separation could not have taken place without incident, as any awareness of difference would create; on the other hand, as mentioned above in the example from the Symposium, the two parts were originally one integral whole: they cannot help but long for each other.

Though a contemporary psychiatrist would define this split as schizophrenic, the original split arrived at in the self contemplation of the androgynous being, I view this in another way. The psychiatrist as a tool of the signified sausegification, in other words as tool of the maintenance of societal strait-jacketing, societal control through creation of false definitions, false definitions meant to bind, and to obstruct the clairvoyance of wholistic grasp, the psychiatrist needs to live up to the definition of his role and thus infuse into the sausage the "spice" of ignorance. He needs to continually work at stoking the virulence of the spice by obstructing any process of clairvoyance. Thus the sausage maintains itself as sausage, without aspiration to the essence. But perhaps, and this is how I view it, he too is a function of the Goddess: because, as Siegfried has stated, everything is the will of the Goddess, because everything is the Goddess. So the psychiatrist represents ignorance. But from the viewpoint of the Goddess, the split is a unity in intent, in other words, the Goddess's intent to amuse herself. So, ignorance is a necessary factor in maintaining the split; in order to amuse and continue to amuse the Goddess, the split needs to incessantly continue to cause itself to splinter; and each splinter continues this never ending process of self-splintering. The sausegification is actually a splintering to the nth degree. In other words, we are so far gone that it is impossible for most people, steeped as they are in such a heavy syrup of sausegification, to even conceive what their ur-nature really is. For what better way to (unreadable, from my pocket note-book) than to incarcerate the very being into a view of itself which is heavy with dense matter? To rack and pinnion the being into a sausage identity? To pillory, to guillotine, to sentence to the Iron Maiden all those who point the way out of this "concentration" camp?

As a matter of fact, here in Amnesia, should you publicly declare, even in jest, some of the thoughts I mentioned above, is considered just cause for incarceration.

So, what is my function? Why was I chosen? Because things have gone too far. The splintering has got out of hand. And Amnesia is the center of sausegification, the hub of it all, the home of the Hades. The splintering gone so far that fixed roles are rigidly allotted to the "androus" and the "gynous".

The Goddess has compassion for her children, the splinters. A clairvoyant must appear at particular points in time to re-balance things, to tip the scales back to the origin. As an aside, I find it amusing that "origin" is starts with an "o". The ur-O, the seminal vagina, the original engendering mystery, the catacomb, the grotto, the grave. The dungeon even.

What happened to the contemplator?

Though the males possess male organs and the females female organs, these are not for reproduction; and neither are the males or the females circumscribed by a pre-designed male or female behavior. Thus the male attire is endowed with the 'femininity' of the Renaissance attire worn by the males which is intrinsically "feminine"; and their movements are not restrained by the limited gesticulation imposed upon the contemporary males. The female attire, also rooted in the male attire of the European Renaissance, is less "feminine" and more spiced with andricity, viragous, and their gestures as well, if I can allow myself that indefinite manner of speaking; but in private and in public they each feel free to exhibit an even flimsier attire, expressing their spontaneous eroticism. Their entire lives are dedicated to unrestrained eroticism.

As I had mentioned in the previous lines, you must not think of the erotic manner in which the males act with one another as a form of homosexuality as defined by our present mentality. Remove the stigma absolutely. (I want to place their way of living entirely outside of contemporary judgment, whose stigmatizing mentality is incapable of grasping the underpinnings of this world.) The anus, as well as the penis, is adorned with a surface which enhances pleasure, ecstasy. It is the same with the females: both their vagina and their anus are pleasure centers.

Though the original ur-state is that of the Goddess, she contemplated herself "against" herself; i.e., created the male God of the Bible; the male god of the Bible with his obvious insistence on damaging the woman's reputation, clearly he had his own agenda; the bible's tree of life, which he wished to keep for himself, was in fact the Goddess, with her emphasis on the pleasurable and ludic aspects of life; this "God" with his back turned to the world, attempting to enjoy his captured trophy, the Goddess, like someone watching TV all by himself in the corner (see Nietzsche, the malevolent god in the corner).

As to the matter of the 'shape dictated by desire': the ugly mass of meat which is our internal entrails, it is explained about it that in order for itself to reproduce it had to cover itself in an attractive shape, thus, our human shape, thus the clothes, cosmetic industry, deodorant industry, everything that is prosthetic to the human shape and mode of locomotion; my opinion is different: the meat stole the image which was already there. Beauty was already there and some meats stole it better than others. Maybe it wasn't theft, maybe it was commerce; the character Skull in The Palm Wine Drinkard rents an irresistible aspect, all its separate parts; my personal view on this is that Beauty, or rather Entrancement, the true name of the original shape was forced by circumstance to lend itself to the insidious purposes of the flesh; for the flesh could not entrance itself to continue, it could not find a good reason to continue without the entrancement of beauty; without entrancement, period; when the god in the bible chooses the flesh gobbling Abel versus the granola chewing Cain, he betrays whose side he is on. The mythologizing necessary for the cover-up betrays itself in this detail. Though to uncover the original cover-up, I don't know if I am capable of it, but I will try, I will try...

This is not a pursuit of spirituality mantled in the veil of eroticism. This is eroticism, pure and simple, shameless, if you will, at the center of all action; this world—freed from birth, old age, sickness and death—does not need to validate eroticism with a veil of spirituality; this world accepts its nature; I say shameless and pucker up my jaws and cradle my tongue while the left corner of my upper lip curls upwards to lick the beckoning of the Imponderable's whirlwind; the Imponderable, like a fragrant leech, never fails to lick back: siphon off the clouds, chameleon clarinet! it whispers. Someone observing me and forced to report on my actions would write on his meager square leaf that a smile appeared on my aspect, and its nature is an ironic one.

So, viewing eroticism as the central vortex, I see the Splendid Siegfried as being deeply religious. The act of lifting the stocking, for instance, which is postulated here as pleasurable to him as it is the appositioned parallel the act of perceiving the elliptical curves of the cambered calves. Each act is dedicated to the reception and the giving of pleasure.

He is perceptive of his pleasurable sensations and inwardly pauses to thank the goddess. The Groveling Gallant at his feet reminds him of the pleasure of danger; to be captured by the Maddened Demoiselles, there is nothing more pleasurable to him, and he envisions it with relish; as the commander of the army of gallants, it is supremely pleasurable to dream of defeat, to be wrenched from his high position and be made a slave to those whom he has defeated in the past; it is as pleasurable as victory and as enslaving those whom he has defeated. And the thrill engendered by danger, deepens his sensations of pleasure, and he further thanks the Goddess.

Siegfried's name, when he is not executing the gesticulations of a military commander, is Astolpho. He is in fact Astolpho at all times but simply by poising himself in the position of commander he is Siegfried. But now that he has returned once again from battle he is once again Astolpho. He reclines on the recamier of indulgence and languishing, which is his customary posture, in his brocaded booth at the opera. And when I say he luxuriates, he reclines, indulges and languishes, you will, I am certain you will, wonder, inappropriately so, how can he be a military commander if he doesn't work out. If he doesn't exercise. But he doesn't need to exercise, either his body or his mind, his imagination, there is no impe(n)ding flesh to thwart any of his gesticulations, he is not separated from his desires by the gravity of flesh, desire and action are one. He doesn't need to lug around a "body". The continuity of desire and the world it engenders. More, Astolpho defies the king and the High Priests and advisors who surround him by adopting the dress of the demoiselles in public. He defies them in plain sight because he knows his power at the court, there is no one else capable of subduing the attacks of the demoiselles. Still, he is being accused by the High Priests of complicity with the demoiselles; why is it, they ask, that in recent skirmishes, it takes him longer and longer to subdue the invasionary excursions of the demoiselles; it as though the Splendid Count, in counting on a last minute solution to exact victory, is inviting defeat. And moreover he refuses the lead the ephebes in an incursion into the catacombic mundo of the demoiselles to subdue them once and for all, as the High Priests have demanded. He laughs inwardly at the High Priests because while they are attempting a political solution to the issue of the attacks of the demoiselles, he simply practices the art of honing his fusion with the Goddess by following his desires; he is fearless and needs no social construct, no collectivity to protect him; the issues of the High Priests are of no concern to him, he refuses to allow his intimate paths become tangled into the pretext of "social" issues. He is indifferent to apparent victory or defeat. Either is pleasurable to him. He reminds the Priests that he is the "artist" who crafted the first victory against the demoiselles, when everyone else cowered and was willing to be subdued; their present arrogance could not exist without his exacting the first victory. He has no regard for his own safety and when they chide him for allowing the last battle to come so close within defeat's reach, he perplexes them with statements such as: "I do not attempt to win, I simply worship the

Goddess." And in truth, as Astolpho, he revels in being the leader of the transgressive movement of the ephebes who dream of being abducted by the demoiselles. Now he reclines in his recamier at the opera where his worshipful follower ephebes have staged an avantgarde melodrama for his luxuriating pleasure while from vicinitous booths the invidious king and the High Priests glare at him.

The melodrama, or the fanfaronade: consists of an ephebe and a demoiselle entranced in each other's erotic gifts and gesticulations. This is high political drama of the subversive sort in the present situation of war. Astolpho enrages his enemies by ordering the Groveling Gallant to masturbate him as he watches. The melodrama ends with the demoiselle imprisoning the ephebe behind bars. Siegfried's followers cheer while the High Priests are outraged and term the melodrama illegal. Siegfried shouts before the assembly that the High Priests are "fanfaroons of philosophical fatuity", as they are also ambulated by the staged fanfaronade into the realm of the amorous; the High Priests demand those responsible for this outrage, along with erectile Astolpho, whom they suspect of connections to the fanfaronade's artists, be imprisoned. Suddenly a maniple of demoiselles invades the opera house. The terrorized ephebes fling themselves in submission before the demoiselles, (You have never seen so much panic, the ephebes making no attempt to summon up courage, but giving in to their fright with exquisite abandon, as though their ability to indulge in fear was a great inner treasure which was now fully revealed to them by the offices of the invasion like an enlightenment they now they have the opportunity to embrace with absolute relish) while the High Priests, trembling with horror and on their knees, implore Astolpho to save them. But is too late, the demoiselles invade the booths and capture the High Priests, the king and Astolpho himself, who calmly suggests that the best course of action is submission to the demoiselles. The demoiselles bring the king, the High Priests and Astolpho on stage before the frightened ephebes. Queen Imogen materializes too before the assembly and informs that the state of the ephebes now belongs to the demoiselles and the ephebes too belong to the demoiselles, that they are nothing but war booty and outlines a plan for their delivery as slaves. At this point Astolpho's arm reaches laterally in the indicative mode: his fingers draw entrancing circles in the air and the demoiselles reveal themselves to be nothing but ephebes in disguise; this was Siegfried's plan from the start, part of the fanfaronade he conceived to avenge himself of the ungrateful king and High Priests. In the confusion that ensues, Astolpho disappears. If this were on opera, and don't think I didn't think of turning this into an opera, I have not frequented the opera as often as I should in my life, but I plan to now, so if this were an opera, Siegfried/Astolpho would sing an aria detailing his desire to leave the land of the ephebes and trek to the catacombs of the demoiselles in search of Queen Imogen. His aria would be a long musing on his pelegrinage past the transgressive thresh-old into the indefinite catacombs which border the cata-combs which the legendary demoiselles are presumed to inhabit. He sings of his identity as traitor (see Cioran on his definition of betrayal); he betrays a pretext for of a higher order: he needs no pretexts, he creates his own values; he only wishes to follow the dictates of the Goddess, moment by moment.

He embraces his betrayal like a new and entrancing lover; he closes his eyes and allows the radiance of betrayal to engulf him, to caress him, to frighten him; yet he betrays without fear of punishment, and he immerses himself in the imagination of possible punishments; and he knows that the ephebes without him are at the mercy of the demoiselles, and this too entrances him. Yet without the Queen, he sings, he would be nothing; because in the past he has been the general and without her attacking he would be without the status he has; he gloats on his present nothingness; and now because he loves and because he is giving everything up for the Queen, he would be again nothing without her. Maybe she will love him, maybe she will make him her slave, or both; he is ready. Because what he is now as he strolls through the reticulation of catacombs is determined by the next step his foot abandoned to its silk leeches and undisclo-sure, purdahs of pre-suspected intrigues and the allure of imminent abductions, captivity.

"If I am another when I arrive than the one I am now, riveted as I am to my stunning aspect, who will it be who is riveted to stunning aspect when I arrive? More, as I spotted the undulating I before arrive, as the I before arrive twisted to call attention, who will I be when I arrive, who is the I that arrives? I must simply be the hope of the Queen as it arrives at the desired destination to fulfill the mandate, no, the desire of the Goddess.

Perhaps it is not only a shift from road to vowel; a vowel may attract our attention, may suck us in like the fragrance of leeches and quicksand, but it's surrounded, like knife wounds simply to astonish us. Suddenly vowels are leeches, echo-like abductions, and the meaning of placing the vowels and consonants in consonance with one another entrances him; to become absconded by the echo of new meanings.

From the forced match of the common activity into the unexpected vowel:

"Are you the Empress of these Catacombs?" he asks

"I am the Empress of Murmurs and Concealing", she answers.

"And, if this is so because man is born, then all that is left for me is to abjure birth, abjure any axiom even if it boasts of the appearance of a certitude." Gherasim Luca

"What is now proved was once only imagin'd." William Blake

Amnesia, Lower Appalachia,
April 28, 1999

My Imogen,

In order to eliminate the Performance Principle you need to eliminate any sort of production. I spoke at length about the clothes they wear. How did these particular sorts of clothes occur to me? I spoke to you when we first met about the particular predilection I have for Renaissance clothes as my erotic wear. What I perceived for years to be a fetish, an embarrassing desire I couldn't speak of as an erotic need to a potential lover for fear I would be thought of as a pervert and abandoned and later spoken of with disdain and ridicule to people who possibly knew me or people who knew people who knew me, I now realize it was the work of the Goddess, has always been the work of the Goddess. The Goddess making a reappearance and having chosen me to do her work. Like I said, I've always held my actions suspect in the eyes of their God always feeling as though I were an arcane adherent to the cult of Kali. Freud mentioned how the gods at the Dämmerung of one period are relegated to the status of demons in the next. Imagine them being relegated to demonship. Yes it was the work of the Goddess entrusting me with a mission. Mankind is at a crossroads. This man I contrived in the previous letter, Count Siegfried, the Splendid, is the man of the future.

For I do not think, I do not see this man, this being, this consciousness, as a contrivance, though I, the Manipulator, the Imaginer of the Imagined, I the Contriver, the Manipulator, yes, though I was the Contriver I was not really the Contriver, the Manipulator, but rather the Rememberer. That's it for the qualifying capitalizing. The rememberer, yes, yes, the rememberer but the memory too. Don't ask me to explain. I was a memory, that's what I was in my non-contrived mode, uncontrived self. I was a memory, a memory, yes, a memory of this being, albeit an Active Memory, sorry, an active rememberer, the rememberer as well as the memory, a memory remembering itself and longing for its actions in the future, yes a future memory. A memory like a star, so clear, a center of energy, that had existed, had existed somewhere, maybe in its essential ur-state, we're splashing in the puddle of metaphysics here, had existed because otherwise how could I have remembered it? Invented it? No, one could only discover it like an archeologist. But a psychic archeologist. Something that has existed in the mind, in the memory, but the dictates of the present system of formulations imposed upon us by the tar of Hades FreightWerks prevented this memory from being recalled, brought to the fore. And yet, a memory of something that had not yet existed. A memory yet to exist. Was I, was the meaning of my life, was *that* the meaning of my life, the deliverer of this memory? Was I to be that? A messenger? A being, this memory, I craved to be, a being to be wrenched from this memory and yet to be projected into the future. A being I was contriving, conceiving, no, discovering, revealing, as in a memory, to be projected into an uncertain future. A memory for whom I alone was the ferry, a being in memory in my fare, welfare, only in *my* care—in my care alone—with the express charge to discharge it into the uncertainty of the future, sowing the seeds perhaps of a new cultural assemblage, I flatter myself, a future civilization. Maybe you'll think I am flattering myself here, giving myself prophetic airs. Yet, this being, this being and this, his, world, because as a being to be the being he was he had to be in a world from which he could not be wrenched, extricated as a segment, could not be separated, he was, is, an organic, wholistic, part of, because you could say, if you were to become philosophical, I guess, and to be philosophical I wished to be so as to give this being a validity, so as not to disvalidate him, and his world, so that no one tries to disvalidate him and place him in the realm of fiction, erotic fiction, erotic science fiction, realm of affliction, which could easily then be discounted and disvalidated and placed on the shelf of the ridiculous,—o how the soul of its own want wills to twill my hiddens and thus enthrills me—so as not to expel him to the realm of ridiculous phantasy, ridiculous erotic phantasy which belongs in the pornographic shop, which is cackled at, ridiculed, treated with contempt and exiled into the realms of the subconscious which is exiled from the subconscious itself by the professors, which is as annoying as a swarm of mosquitoes, which must be exiled so that we could built the monument which is the pretend life we have agreed on calling our modern world, which must be exiled at all cost, expelled at all cost, so we can go on pretending, so that the court of appointed and unappointed, self appointed and disappointed men and women whose business is to be discounters, in whose court the discounting of this world takes place, in whose court the discounting of this man, this being and his world that I'm speaking of takes place, and whose power is to appoint their dispatchers to dispatch their exiling and expelling, with weapons and batons if need be, to discount and dispatch and expel and exile with extreme prejudice, to excommunicate, the dispatchers and discounters and expellers and exilers and excommunicators of this sorry planet, I could argue in their court, if their court had any interest for me at all, if I didn't myself discount this court of discounters, if I were to get on the stand of this discounting court, to stand before the discounters themselves, I would take the discounters to task, philosophically I would discount their view, their filthy unhealthy unnatural view, I would do that, it's my purpose to do that. What I meant to say here, the philosophical point I was going to make, is that you cannot wrench this person from his world, that he and his world are one and the same; perhaps he is not just himself but also all the characters of this world of his. But what is even more revealing, what is even more stunning to find, is that this world could not exist without you, my Imogen, as though this world was phormed in its Diaphanous Material state—the Immaterial Materiality of this world I spoke of earlier—by the union of you and I, as though as this world grows out of my heart, it grows out of the spiritual union of you and I. When I say spiritual, I mean nothing of the religious sort of spirituality; I mean nothing about spirituals praising their lord jesus, or the chants of the gregorian brothers of labrador, or some such merdure the corporation is trying to sell us to circumvent partially the angst of living with one another in the metropolis. I am talking about this material of immateriality which so clearly exists because I am creating with it, or rather it is creating itself through me, or no, through our union. Except that I am the one who's pregnant here. A poet I know once wrote a poem in which he considered, ironically, as though tossing a drink at a party, but bitterly too, that the gender of the poet, the male poet, is female, as he hopes to get pregnant with inspiration from his relationship with a woman. I found his idea no more than amusing; and almost insultingly so; it's clear from his ironical tone that he himself finds the idea of the poetic cum drag amusing, but no more than that; that he himself does not even take his poetic inspiration seriously, he sees it not as being of moment, not a moment beyond the words spoken in jest and passing, hoping to get a chuckle at a cafe gathering of drunken poets. Me, on the other hand, I speak of a discovery more momentous than, say, the discovery of penicillin, the birth control pill; more momentous than, say, the ancient Greeks finding that it is the sexual union, not the wind, that leads women to get pregnant, though we're still not too sure of that. The discovery that the future of the new world perhaps lies in our union and that our union made me pregnant with it, our union which still continues in spite of physical distance, has engendered, in me, the seeds of a new world, with you as the father, me as the mother. (But let us not restrain ourselves to such commonplace notions, such restricted binarity of definitions of all that we are.)

This world which I engendered with your and my essence, this world which will be nothing but a still born baby without you... Think, I am now at large in Amnesia, large with our baby!)

These are, I feel, serious issues. You may wonder why I spend such inordinate amount of time in attempting to decipher the baroque turns of a phantasy. No, that's not phair. Do you like this spelling of the word? I love you and I trust you and I feel safe in your arms, I picture myself in your arms as I unravel these journeys to you. My heart glows like an orange sun. I was going to say a Van Gogh sun but the implication of agony wasn't there in my meaning. Only ecstasy. But there are others. Should these letters be found and read— think about it—I could easily be put away. My sanity would be instantly questioned; yes, it's the first thing they'll do. We're like bugs here, under scrutiny, could be squelched at any moment they see fit. And if they wished to get rid of me, these letters to you, my Imogen, would be my very end. The fact that I thoughtlessly place myself in your hands, like a penitent places his life in his god's hands, is a matter of conscious choice. All is so tenuous, you see. It wouldn't matter I protested for instance these letters are a novel I am working on; artistic immunity is not granted anymore; they wouldn't even ask me to prove it, that these are the notes to a novel. The feeble protests from a few artist friends would be useless; and these few artist friends would never fight all the way for me; they would be happy I was put away, it would only confirm the events imagined in their own paranoia and it'd give them the best excuse to exercise it. They would have something to beat their clumsy chests about. No, artistic immunity would certainly not be granted; look, would they want someone with these thoughts in his head roaming at large and free amidst the general population? Should he choose to repress himself in most instances, would he not still exude these ideas, would he not ooze them at all times, in all places, in one form or another? He would certainly infect, more, contaminate, those about him, I mean after all, is he not in contact with young people? All is so tenuous, you see, all depends on such a delicate interweaving of events, on the orchestration of this tenuous armada of events in constant march to, to where?

Take these thoughts deeply to heart.

Eagerly awaiting your reply,

J

My Imogen,

I was told there is an item about me in yesterday's Amnesia. Though he who told me couldn't remember the nature of the information it contained. This item I assumed being a unit of information amputated from my life's infinite continuum. An explosive unit of information, I assumed, charming enough for the diversified metropolis but deadly in the tar of Hades-owned Amnesia, Lower Appalachia, for otherwise why would Amnesia bother with it. Amnesia Spectator, that is. And shaking him up as I did, I rattled him really good to get him to recall, his eyeballs bulged in afflictions of graves as I slapped him manneristically numerous times and he crumpled in the corner, whether it was a panegyric, or an attack, a spoof, an honorable, or merely a passing mention, the listing of my name in relationship to something I was observed performing that he or she digested according to particular purposes into a unit of information, explosive unit of information, that is, that someone connected to the paper, or someone else connected to someone connected to the paper and who observed me, thought merited attention and thus mention. I left him in a green pile on the floor and nearly urinated on him; though neatly urinated on him could work as well. Or, the urgency of the craving to obtain the paper prevented me from spurting out my right shoe, an Italian gray suede loafer, much admired, and when I say much admired it's as though I am permeated by an emerald glow, more precise, as though I nurse on purpose an emerald glow in my heart, my gondolas as I sometimes whisper to myself, my frogs, into a seminal area of his somatic formulation, so to speak, this sort of magna cum laude treason is not tolerable to the assemblage of my symptoms, I mean you know me well I think, and headed for the little concrete island at the corner of Amnesia and Brood to track the young shaman damsel who sells Amnesia there. Brood Creek Road, that is. But everyone here, I find it, just calls it Brood. Its meaning like the creek's itself beaten unconsciously into concrete. Once, before it became a thoroughfare, before they forced it into the demands of the Utilitarian Orders, abandoned lovers reflected themselves in the creek and watched their visage shapeshifting in azure by the mini-ripples of intoning spring peepers. I won't tell you how I found this out and though Hades Concrete (it is not only Hades Hose—the sort that those afflicted with the masculine disorder prefer—they own everything in this damn town) conceals it now they couldn't prevent the entrancement which still wafts to the surface and permeates and the sudden hazy driver fractures a telephone pole. At night bright orange men with the chalky neon Amnesia Bell logo on the back spill out of vans and replace the pole and no one speaks about it any longer. It's quiet in Amnesia. Agglomerations of obese people gorging on the just-in Doberman at the sleepless counter of the all-you-can-eat Roadkill Cantina, spitting out pieces of still blinking amber glass from the freeway yellow stray caught in the headlights. Sailors with a mild blend of vertigo at most, but not a one to train you into the flames reclaiming mystery. Don't think I didn't think of assuming a vocal stand. But each time I promise myself to do it, because someone has to assume a vocal stand, because you shapeshift into constricted urethra otherwise, I forget the next moment and don't think about it till one morning I pick up some Amnesia from somebody's front lawn on my walk to Amnesia Park and there they are again, the orange men in black and white. And I promise myself again, and again, I forget.

The young shaman damsel selling Amnesia broke her congress with the sun while her neck swiveled as though on rusty hinges when my Maxima screeched to a stop. The rusty hinge and the screech made me think of thick orange impasto beneath a splatter in yellow and for something no longer than a tiny significant instant I envisaged the veritable mystery of abstraction, and the enigma of synesthesia unfurled before me like a kiss. This time she clashed her combat boots with black fishnets, with seams! as though to turn, I mused, the battlefield into a boudoir; the ballerina chisel of her well cambered haunches strutted the concrete like an arresting officer's; and I was curiously stabbed by the likeness of those haunches to haunches I was bewitched by in another recently. Yes, I had spied them a few days before adorning Candora, the modern dance student for whom I stealthfuly wrote a paper on Hamlet for Eric Rudner's "Will's Androgynous Violin" class in General Studies, in actuality he wanted to call it "Shakespeare and Bi-sexuality", blah!, I convinced him to replace it with "Will's Androgynous Violin", suddenly he's flooded by music and drama students, dance students, because who doesn't secretly dream of being a gypsy violin?

They were the exact identical haunches! You want to know what I wrote? You'll love it. I had her falling for Hamlet! I was messing with Eric here, "Someone should coin a word for it", 'she' said, "this entrancing state of indecision that Hamlet flounders in; if no one named it before, I would name it Hamletism. I know there are those wrist-shaking closet cross-dressers, who, with feigned fury, called Hamlet to the floor to chide him for his prolonged dance with ambivalence; I do not join their frantic chorus; I find the shaking of the counterfeit lace on their colonial wrists a turn-off. It is nothing but an ass-shaking couvade; as for me, I too call Hamlet's ass to the floor: we would make a lovely couple, waltzing to the hesitation blues, doing the shilly-shally hully-gully, leaping a faltering pas de deux as I would slap him and he would whisper the sweet 'coinages of his brain' in my ear. Yes, Hamlet, why don't you step up to me with your "doublet all unbraced, and your "ungartered stockings down gyved to your ankle"—oh how this bent disposition of his entrances me!—yes Hamlet, I'll ungarter your stockings if you'll ungarter mine—yes, take me by the wrist and hold me hard, and "do fall to such perusal of my face", you'll see then your tristful visage turn to cheerful and infinite jest, you'd know then how this too too solid flesh could melt, thaw, and resolve itself into a dew, and the uses of this world would perhaps not seem so weary, stale, flat and unprofitable.

Oh, hush, hush, sweet Hamlet. Let the very coinage of thy feverish brain wax desperate with thoughts of me. It's a fair thought to lie between maids' legs, I'm no ditz-head Ophelia withholding her feminalia. Come to me, my Hamlet, my lexical prince, come, come to me. Yes, it's a fair thought to lie between maids' legs. This maid. Come to mama."

Then I quoted Cioran, seamlessly braided Cioran and Shakespeare into the text, confident that Eric, the cross-dressing was a personal attack, I knew something about him and he didn't know I knew, wouldn't spot the ruse:

"Once a man loses his faculty for ambivalence, for Hamletism if you will, he becomes a potential murderer. Scaffolds, dungeons, jails, bombs flourish only in the shadow of action. No wavering mind, contaminated with Hamletism, was ever pernicious; the principle of evil lies only in the incapacity for indecision. More matter with less art? When Hamlet, forced by circumstance, finally decides, everyone dies. The history of mankind abounds in certitudes: suppress them, suppress their consequences, and you recover paradise; murder is the result of having forsaken doubt and sloth, vices nobler than all virtues."

Next day. Just had my yogurt.

And then, two days ago, I'm supposed to meet her to hand her the paper and she doesn't show up. I'm sort of freaking because what if she told the Vice-Canceller in Charge of Student Affairs I'm writing a paper for her, what if she suspects I spied her cambering calves, more, what if she went to the founding Vice-Director of Rational Behavior and drew a sketch of me as one who incessantly delights in craving them in the solitude of his symptoms, they force you then to strip on a stage of ridicule, they can bust you for bare-ly a creeping inconsistency shifting within, once they publish your name, or worse, what if she spit it out in spite to June, the whole campus suddenly oglehaunts you the instant that, under her crocodile eyelids, June in Student Under-Affairs secures a rumor in her incisors. They'd paint me in the unprincipled hues of a velvet pre-nuptial ejaculator before of an assembly of alabaster ballerinas! And now combat boot intruded upon the emerald abductional haze emanating from the fishnets. Yes, the only way I saw out was to begin a con-versation in the epistemological mode and so inquired whether the clash of shank versus foot wear was a conscious choice, that is, was she making an ironic statement, clashing combat with boudoir; yet one combat boot closer, fishnetted shank gliding leisurely in tandem with its elongated shadow against dawn's radiance, and I clearly grasped the extent of my miscalculation and upbraided my self icon for not instantly appraising the penury of her training in irony. And then, are you with me on this?, it took me no longer than an explosive instant to flash on it. It was the instant previous to the one her grim visage infringed through the window and I shouted from terror. She was identical to Thea! Her sympto-matic splendor had been amputated but the outlines pre-served as though through a contouring system of mesh wires camouflaged in chalcedony tinged plaster and further veneered to a semblance of rouged porcelain and mascara eyeliner!

Maniacal mannequin whose present wireless beam was the outcropping of a Frankenstein's fingers twisting a rheostat in the kryptic catacombs of Amnesia!

Perhaps I didn't mention Thea yet, in fact I will admit it right now, because I have no other wish right now than to expose myself to you. I am on bended knees before you imploring forgiveness. I was hesitant to speak to you about her because she's been my lover these last few months. Please try to understand, it means everything to me to share this with you, please don't stop reading. I thought of you constantly, I fought it, but

she instantly abducted me

in her solar catacombs

and I am nothing

if not a corporal of amber

abandoned to drown,

if you'll refer to the essay I sent you, "In Praise of Absence", which by the way, was published in "Syllogism" and I forgot to send you a copy, she is the willing lover I prophetically surmised was arriving from Europe in section x. Actually I didn't forget, and I want to admit this to you now because I never ever want to lie to you about anything ever again and if you wanted me right now you could have me, I mean Imogen, my Imaginatrix, you could if you wanted to take me away from any woman including Thea any time you wish no matter how enraptured I was, you could step right in and demand me as yours and I would give in. I didn't actually forget, I just didn't want you to see it because I didn't use your translation of "Ode to Joy". Instead I used my own. And applauded myself for my resourceful fabrication. Remember how emphatic I was at first to involve you in the translation? You were cloudy at the time, you were turbulent, you presented an aura of quicksand, and I was still scintillating with the sort of beryl haze hue you had trapped me in.

The translation you finally delivered was thwarted with

the chemistry of pre-established clouds; but I adore you madly like in the book by Breton and didn't want to send you off into the well-beaten quicksand; and it haunted me that I did it and couldn't send you the magazine because I think you would have loved it. It's some of my best work. Actually I did send it to you, didn't I, what am I saying, I just remembered, why did I think I didn't send it to you?, oh no, it's the essay I sent you not the magazine. Remember?

This is what I wrote: "I don't buy that sort of Oedipal acrobatics. For me the breasts are orchards", I wrote, "and a willing lover is arriving form Europe." That was Thea.

Only I don't know how willing she is! Oh Imogen, she breaks our dates, she mocks me. I fell on my knees before her and kissed her feet and asked her to marry me! Of course I wanted to lick her feet, they are to die for, but I abstained. And she just giggled. And then I told her I wanted to be her slave and she emitted with gleeful glow and said, you are my slave! And repeated it. You are my slave. And her glow permeated me and I begged her to say it again. And she said: you are my slave. You must do whatever I tell you. And I agreed. Then she pushes me on the couch, she straddles me and promises we'll make love the next time she comes over. Two months now of these games! Then she calls to say she's not coming over because she has to practice, she plays the viola de gamba for the Amnesia Symphony, a graduate student here at the school, yes, she is from Germany, but East, she's from Dresden, we share the communist past, except that she's now NATO and I'm not. Then why the hell did she promise she'd be over, didn't she know beforehand she had to practice? This unbearable arrogance of the NATO nations! The next night she calls, Are you still mad of me? she asks. Can I come over? You noticed I wrote "mad of me", not "mad at me". It is how she speaks, her English suffers. Though "mad of me" is correct, because I am 'mad of her'. Then she's one hour late, If you're going to be late why don't you just not come at all, I'm too old for that shit, and then the doorbell, and I'm on my knees again! This time she pushes me on the bed, unfurls her blouse, we're agitated, she fidgets out of her skin tight jeans, she outmaneuvers me with black lace like an exquisite Don Juan, then she hops on the bed, she straddles me, she doesn't demure a murmur when I unfurl her brassiere and she is flaunting grace's echoing indulgencies! And then she rises and her panties dissolve. Dematerialize. Dissolve into "thin air". Though I dread the use of the "thin air" cliché, imagine yourself being forced to face and muse upon this miracle. But I was snatched from musing. Imogen, as I live and breathe, and you know how much I hate this particular figure of speech, how I loathe to be suddenly pitted against myself as a speaker of tropes, there was a little penis hanging between her legs! A miniature one, but it's a real penis, and suddenly, impudent! rises like a tiny tower!

Dear Imogen, my Imaginatrix, I stabbed myself at times in a hideous face—a proletarian suddenly ambushes you from behind the countenance a dreamy madonna, which amuses on a casual acquaintance—the sudden jag on a lover I had just moments before been plunged into. It was daunting, I admit, and I had to resort to the unforeseen factories of the Imaginal. But this, how can I place it before you without deflating my eidolon, I had almost expected it, I admit I had even once phantasized it, and perhaps it was not phantasy but prophecy and when she said turn around I obeyed automatically, because I craved to abandon myself in surrender to her and I knew then what Raimbaut the Jongleur Poet of the Provençal Troubadours may have felt, not my Arthur this one, who has no 'a' after the 'R' and no 't' at the end but a 'd', when he spied on his yearned for amorette abandoning her Beatrice vestments, flinging a sword into the air, then deftly apprehending it, and wielding the skillful Excalibur right and left and causing him to swoon and declare himself as her forever slave. Which she accepted because he wrote her the following poem:

Well, I can't find the book with the poem in it, so I'll go on.

No, not the twilight mist-embracing hermaphrodite of Lautreamont, her, as she inserted herself with her tiny audacious tool! Oh, it was a little excruciating at first though I said she was tiny, no more then a suppository, I had to stop suddenly just now to answer the phone, I'm back, when I hung up I was captured by the aspect of the telephone's antenna, fourth of an inch thin, two inches long and while plunged into the current of words weaving themselves for you I caught myself placing its surface to my two lips, thinner than a suppository perhaps, it was a purgatory of catacombs she had ambushed me in as I undulated like a submissive duelist. And what a pleasant cool rush like a stream in the shade on a late summer afternoon when she gushed. A little too soon I might add. And I don't want to, what I mean is I want to dissolve from your perception the coordinates you might have formed of an antenna, of utilitarian plastic material, no matter how expressly smooth to the lambency of lips its surface, no matter how insinuating its deliberate shaping, yes, utilitarian industry has its own artists, artists engaged to march to the trumpet of its mandates, engaged by it expressly to mold the dilemma of Eros into deliberate cushions. Perhaps in presenting the sudden quicksand the antenna held me in I was in a rush to list an obsession with size, (the remains of the masculine disorder still grip me), and thus prematurely dissolved the silky countenance of murmur and vertigo this exquisite miniature might have engendered for you, though I fear that to venture to portray emphatically might once again deflate my eidolon.

Oh but to be thus vanquished by her, what, am I complaining? And I was suddenly scented with the swift impudence of iguanas, and swiftly switched. Yes, how long had I contrived to attain this sort of indolent impudence! Oh yes, to attain impudent indolence like an enlightenment, who can brag of that nowadays? We who rose our choruses to those altars! We who abandoned faith! And if we should encounter someone who has attained it, who impudently sports it, that languorously indolent arm that leans and loafs at its ease, who could ever say no?, the steep amber drown of vitreous humors, don't we secretly crave to worship at her or his court, don't we fashion them into the statues of our secret mahatmas?

Next day

Her father is the mayor of Dresden! A conservative ticket I don't endorse and which I choose to ignore in her, along with her fervent Catholicism! Or maybe not, as they are permeated with the plasma of the phantasmic, they are woven into the wedding of Ares and Eros, if you get my disturbing meaning. But while I rub a little Ares on my Eros to season it, they season, no, marinate their Ares with Eros. Thus the empire. Her tiny tool like a soft soldier now in the somnolent arms of indolence, the citadel door inviting invader and I thought about the time she told me how as a child at Christmas she would walk to mass through marxist Dresden, her childhood's heels tracking a blanket of fresh snow, and they were singing Mozart's Requiem, her tiny tool secret as a faith. And I was on top now, and told her you're my slave, you must do everything I tell you and she said yes my king, I am your slave and will do anything you tell me, I mean she was still on top, but I was saying all this to her. But I didn't mean it, it was just that I was in the momentary grasp of the masculine disorder, a disorder I don't endorse, what I wished to say was a poem I wrote her then:

I am a butterfly in your misty
Semiramis gardens
                              drowning

in the reverse gravity
of
 steep amber perfumes
and

penumbra

And then she shuddered, she keeled over me, soft, and said you killed me, I am dead now. And then again, I am dead now. O but I forget myself, I'm back to this other, fabricated Thea I'm facing now, my Thea's limbs are delicate, supple, entrancing in their lace-like delicacy but non-muscular, strong, from tightening about the viola de gamba, but not muscular, certainly her calves are not ballerina calves. I even once absentmindedly wished for the two to be spliced together, Thea's wistful eyes, that was before the incident I just mentioned, and Candora's haunches. When I say absent-mindedly I realize I am condemning myself. Who am I kidding? Absent-mindedly, in a misty haze, with a crimson-sky-at-twilight background, while "mermaids laugh and fishermen hold flowers"! Hah! The amusing phantasy of a Frankenstein! Murderer! And now I hadn't heard from her since Tuesday. Same I hadn't heard from Candora. I had assumed it was another one of her moods, these moods she tortures me with. And then with an explosion I realize it was I who had wished her limbs were more like Candora-like! My notorious obsession with form, with enticing contour! I should stab myself! Had I caused this? This transmutation? Could they now read my mind and thus spliced together this amorous monstrosity out of the two of them for my sake, in order to unhinge me? My left hand was suddenly inside hers, how did it get there? when did this occur? The interior of my mouth had desiccated like in a movie I once saw with John Wayne and Sophia Loren when they were crossing the dressing, the desert I mean, and I wondered what the hell she ever saw in him. I could have revved up through the red light as she shanked up to the window. I question here the nature of my forbearance, of forbearance in general: why did I not rev up and hazard across the random traffic on Brood and risk the drab yellow stab of the Texxon marquee and leave this demon babe behind. She made me forget all about the listing of my name in Amnesia, but she reminded me too: "Looking for yesterday's paper, California?" It was a double stab: she knew what I was looking for and she knew I had come from California. Or maybe she spotted the license plate, but I didn't think so. She wasn't the reading type. Her forefinger's sinister fingernail was sketching incessantly delicate circleloids on my palm. Yes, she had been spliced for my purpose; Thea and Candora, amber pupils and cambered shanks, inductors so propitious to my entrancement! And the religious terminology was not lost on me either: Thea, from Theodora, meaning love of God, and Candora, love of Truth. I needed to pause and recapitulate. Why was I here? Back to the listing in the Amnesia as I mentioned in relationship to something I was observed executing that someone connected to the paper, or someone connected to someone connected to the paper and who observed me, thought merited mention. Like I said, the someone connected to the someone at the paper must also be connected on the other end to someone or to an institution, more than likely an institution, whose purpose is connected in some sense to what I was observed doing; looking back now, it is to my credit that instead of running I opted for forbearance and didn't give them a chance to think I beat a hasty retreat. And besides it would have been foolish of me not to assume they were watching me, and to beat a hasty retreat meant to stage myself as dismayed, more, incurious, an inclement sketch of me they could post at random, though I, as I mentioned previously, I do not make it a custom to fetishize myself as an armored exemplar on posts, have no truck with the masculine disorder.

I quickly shuffled through my repertoire of spellbinding intonations while attempting at the same time to powder up a smile and rouge irony into the left upper lip which I forced in the direction of the clouds to mimick the indifferent wire of a paper clip excused of utility and condemned to the fate of doodles, while ordering into enticement the verbal construct 'You got yesterday's Amnesia?' She leaned an elbow on the window and peered in while I dissolved the smile hoping that only irony remained; however irony without the smile was like nothingness without being; I rushed to rouge the smile back on but she spotted me doing it and snatched it away from me before I could get to it. I had no idea she could sing: Who needs yesterday's papers—she crooned surprisingly Jagger-like. Her lips were, I suddenly noticed, of a full Jagger-like cut, perfect like a skilled plastic surgeon's slash into raw meat, her teeth splendidly burnished and even, and her amber pupils, for one quick moment, almost made me think of the purple yours. Almost. No other pupils can. Like I said she was Thea but she was doctored and the chisel of the lips was Jagger's. The only alternative left me was to screech off to the right on Brood, illegally on red, 0 to 60 in 5, and be done with this sorceress before she scooped me up in her fishnets or massacred me in her Amnesia bedroom battlefield; I couldn't be sure just how much damage had already been done to my psyche, as it was clear this was a psychic attack and that she had be en my god Imogen, this 'en' wasn't there an instant ago when I stood up to go to the bathroom! And the fact that 'en' means absolutely nothing, there is no referent, my whirling formulations are at a loss for something firm to grip on, that is what makes it even more frightening, to be plunged into the agitated mouths of the serpent of obscurity! But I can't stop now, here's the last sentence again, I couldn't be sure just how much damage had already been done to my psyche, as it was clear this was a psychic attack and that she had been set upon me by others; and it wasn't farfetched to assume she had been doctored up for my sake, that she had been spliced that way. The ballet shanks were a ruse whose magnetic force upon me could not be denied; somewhere in the krypts of Amnesia a doctor Frankenstein matched a ballet student and an unfortunate match girl, (that's not what I want to say if I am to stick close to the truth, but the match girl bit wafted in from my grim childhood) for a purpose whose ramifications included excluding me and whose roots I needed to extirpate to prevent the conclusion of my exclusion. It was then that she took my hand in hers, her left thumb and forefinger, an exquisite set of translucent crabclaws, picked my left forefinger from my hand dangling negligently at the end of my left arm I left carelessly perched on the car window, all the while her quicksand corneas sucking up my vitreous humors across the expanse of the fifteen centimeters separating our faces. Her fingers were exquisitely sculpted! They were just like Loony Linda's! I don't think I ever told you, did I tell you about Loony Linda? the lude freak, Loony Linda, this is part of the poem I wrote about her years later, I am opening up the file with it, here it goes, and by the way I didn't include it in my book Transgender Organ Grinder, and once at a party she was so fucking stoned I had to drag her away but she was intransigent and tried to exit through the refrigerator door, the guests, all New Yorkers in exile to L.A., all contemptuous to and of the locals, all looked away and snorted, and Linda noticed, Linda was a local, Linda had been a groupie and once fucked Mick Jagger, maybe all the Stones, for sure all the Monkeys, L.A. woman "do" style down to stilettos, the New York film crowd in exile to L.A. was scum to her, she once sucked Frankenheimer, so she outstretched like jesus her fingerless black satin gloves enshrouding arm to armpit and crowed like a fanatical rooster just to unhinge them, because she could, see, they were contemptuos of jesus as well but at the core they were all frightened, I'm just like jesus, see, she didn't believe in jesus either in case you're wondering about that, but she'd crow, see, I'm just like jesus just to unhinge them. Or maybe it wasn't to unhinge them but she was incrementally awakening to an indigo twilight resonance she had always sought and which presently promised to erupt, unexpectedly as these resonances naturally do, when they finally season to a level of maturity. Linda was over six feet tall and Jagger's a little dude and her arms stretched out into infinity, the edges nearly wounded you, the fingers were long, the most exquisitely sculpted fingers you have ever seen, skin like velvet, fingers so long and so chiseled you wanted to pray to them, those fingers, which once when I got fired from a film placed a lude between my lips and pushed it in, fingers with silver rings and long black fingernails, fingers that brushed my hair as she held me and hummed a Tom Waits tune, fingers that touched Mick Jagger. And fishnet's fingers were chiseled just like Linda's, replete with black fingernail polish, as she fished my forefinger between her thumb and forefinger and imprisoned my palm in hers, it was warm and soothing in spite of my boiling with silent protests whose bubbles were fluttering about my lips like butterflies as she placed my hand under her black leather mini and into her crotch and like a sudden soldier tightened her grip! The fishnets were barbed wires to my skin and while I still had time to ponder I pondered on how such entrancers, such promoters of the path to the boudoir could be so jagged; and the connection between Jagger and jagged didn't escape me either, perhaps she had been spliced for my benefit, grafted like that, do not mean benefit but undoing, those nutcracker gams to tight me in their grapnel grip and crack me, but her crotch itself was surprisingly unprotected, there was no jagged barbed wire fence around it, it was removed post factory from the Hades fishnet thighs; and the pudenda, ascondida beyond the protection of undisciplined bush wires was soft and moist and warm; palm imprisoned in the barbed wire of the fishnets while fingers dissolving to freedom and ecstatic convergence! I meditated on the metaphor the dichotomy of the placement of my hand presented as she tightened her thighs' grip: had the light turned green now and I stepped on the accelerator I would remain while the car would shoot forward without me and its burgundy crash into the poles holding up the drab yellow stab of the Texxon marquee; the Texxon marquee above which I had just spotted the brand new billboard, whose content I forced myself to ignore; yes, there I sat and forced myself to ignore though chided myself too because there was no way you could say to yourself this doesn't appear before you, sat there in that particular space which was not any other space, this time which was not any other time, I was a prisoner of space and time, but yes forced myself to ignore it, time after time, in full concrete knowledge I would not succeed; yes, I would be wrenched out through the open window, my fingers dissolving in the warmth of her ecstatic fluids while my palms hacked and sundered by the barbed wire strands of the stockings! Seams like sabers! I wished to shout. I would be found wrenching in bloody dolor on the concrete island on the corner of Amnesia and Brood. And all this because of a mention I was told about in the Amnesia Spectator; and because he who told me couldn't recall whether it was a panegyric, or an attack, a spoof, an honorable, or merely a passing mention, the listing of my name in relationship to something I was observed doing that someone connected to the paper, or someone connected to someone connected to the paper and who observed me, thought merited mention. Certainly, the someone connected to the someone at the paper must also be connected on the other end to someone or to an institution, more than likely an institution, whose purpose is connected in some sense to what I was observed performing. A breath of soft wind caressed my burning cheeks. I had left my passenger window open, it had been open all night long while night embossed Amnesia with its chalcedony balm; and what if now Linda, in her fishnets, yes, Linda was fond of fishnets too, she sometimes forced me to try on her fishnets on pain of no satisfaction, and she had some enrapturing gifts such as a penetrating tongue, she could for instance penetrate the core of your heart with it and dissolve any maternal childhood trauma, the oedipal was nothing to her but conceptual constraints and she could take you past civilization's discontents and into divine acceptance if you abandoned ypourself to her needs, shit, I can't even fucking type, it's yourself, and now she had suddenly manifested on the passenger side and grasped my other hand! Linda too sported ballerina calves, Linda too once inserted my fingers with her fingers into the silky and wiry concatenation above the kid leather edge, and it was as though now past and present were braided to each other as one, my left arm was in the grips of the present while my right in the graft of the past and the future I had hoped for in the light that might turn green, the tights I mean lights in Amnesia are very long and waywardly irregular, I don't know if I ever mentioned this before, they seem to be controlled by brooding rather than the reoccurring intervals we've adopted in what you've come to define as the civilized world, so the light turning green was hope I had suddenly become desolate of. My only future was here, a jesus in the grips of the present and the past, this would never have happened had I not left my right window open, I'm just like jesus see, I'm just like jesus! With superhuman effort I wrenched myself from the tenterhooks of an emerging temptation to regard myself as a religious dilemma. Already the gelatinous substance which felt so lovely to my fingers was inoculating them with absorptive fluids. Could they have already sucked the contents of my hard-drive? And then, for what reason go so far as to post them on the Hades billboard I was facing? "No longer fascinated by the performances of souls delusional of the undermotion of phenomena, she steps to a music she alone can hear." These lines purloined directly from my computer's hard drive! And then, Thea, yes, Thea, how would they find out about Thea? She only came at night driving her '76 Impala through the core of the ghetto I'd told her to avoid, Thea, arms raised to the light source, visage same, this is a tights ad, an ad for Hades Hose, in the foreground, twirling so as to hoist up her skirt against gravity by the centrifugal force of an à la Monroe twirl and present us with the lovely coruscation of gams, Candora's, the light reflexive of the hose glimmers reflected on her visage in coruscating splendor, while the disgruntled male's unshaven visage unglows in the shadows. He is perusing himself in the mirror, neck downcast as though in shame; next to him, shimmering under the sienna fawn of candelabras, the unmade bed, on which, if you inspect carefully, you'll see a black cat; his presence conveys, I am never mistaken in this medium of the message: what have I done to be thus left behind? And he wears stockings, garter belts and stockings! Though his face is in the shadows, it's clear that face is my face. How could they have found out? Unless they were spying on me. Thea had disappeared two days earlier. This is what happened, I might as well tell you. I don't know what you'll think of me now but I have to tell you. Thea and I spat a little ire at each other, so to speak. She hates my cat! She gave me an ultimatum, either you get rid of the cat or I leave. There I was, firmly secured to the bed posts, she had shown up earlier and cooked dinner, she was wearing the black silk stockings I had bought her, I mean she showed up ready to cook dinner and dressed like that, these stockings under the long black skirt she wielded with such force, she made me feel the garter belts by taking my hand and placing my fingers against it when I kissed her when she first came in, and me intoxicated with rapturous gliding across fields of anticipation of contact with nebulously mantled lower limbs, she was smoldering in her melanoid oblivion stance, into which I was plunging, oh, your stockings of blended snakes! I plunged the "binarity of my knees" before her and gazed up in adoration of her tyrannical allure. She motivated her long wrap to collapse like an army. "O my Queen of Diaphany! Your tyrannical lower limb nebulae are the metric which can be applied directly to happiness!", I hissed in adoration, anyway I won't bore you with everything that occurred between us, it would be impossible anyway, solely a gathering of fragments, a suctioning of sections, I sport doubts in my skills of hand to hand description, Rimbaud would have forbidden it anyway, but she was the Queen-Bewitcher bedighted in tyrannical allure and vestments he speaks of, being of legendary elegance, she who may consent to whisper what she knows and what we'll never find out, she was suddenly as though born of Rimbaud, no, she was a transfigured Rimbaud for me alone to worship, Rimbaud whom I've always craved to worship, and I could only aspire to a destiny of being her lifetime slave, suddenly I was secured to the bedposts, and just before that she breathed a haze of black silk stockings on my legs, oh I can't deny it, I watched her do it, it was divine, "my stockings are getaways from abduction by chronological forge", I murmured, "undulations into an aurora where you might throttle me", I was plunging into the destinal foreboding of garter belts and she was a Gaudi goddess sprinkling me with lovely rivulets regarding the allure of my lamellated contours against the gloaming, and then my black cat Sabrina hops on the bed and nuzzles herself against my stockings and starts purring. "Until the sabrinas at the barriers of enigma surprise you without your stockings." This line of lovely verse came to me for no apparent reason I could discern and I smiled till it thunderbolted on me I was too bound to write it down. And I demanded she untie me so I could write it down. This erupts her ire, and she demands that I kill the cat. She will untie me if I kill the cat as a sacrifice to her. I am aghast on account of her demand, as she had in the past demonstrated an erotic affection for the cat. But now she re-demands I kill the cat as a sacrifice to her, she would love the fur for a collar, she purrs, because don't I call her my goddess? And I refuse categorically, and here I must give myself credit for refusing categorically while entirely at her mercy, a prisoner of this plunge into the rigors of the ecstatic, and still, I refused, while drowning cavalierly in the ecstatic storm of her displeasure, I refused, (not the tedious te deums of the propitiatory for me! I wished to shout but didn't on account of her challenge with the high-wire of my lexicon), and I demanded in the name of the muse of poetry that she untie me so that I could write down this line and she wants to know what the line is, such an entrancing line making itself apparent to me more than likely because I refused propitiation, the poet as you know is the antagonist of the propitiator, I will not reveal the line! I shout. She says if I killed the cat (and how well you know that at my core beats a cat!) she would marry me, which she made me beg her for the day before and then she said maybe. Ok, so I bend a little and opt for giving the cat away to a sympathetic friend, I told you about Renata in Rapturous Oneirics en quotes, for sure she would take pity on it and adopt it and I could visit her there, Renata only lives a few blocks away, but she insists I kill Sabrina. If you really love me, you'll kill the cat. Sacrifice her for me. I refuse, we hiss, and though the means by which the actual sacrifice is to be carried out are never discussed, she suggests we do it while we're cross-dressed, and then suddenly she storms out, and there I am firmly secured to the bed posts and wearing stockings.

For a while I find this enrapturing, I've been hopelessly plunged into the river of delight, but for sure she will return, the cat was a total ruse to enrapture me, she only wishes to enrapture me even more by this thunderous storming out and abandoning me secured to the bed posts like that, the stockings felt as though I was abducted by the transgressive mystery of obsidian ballerinas, I didn't even attempt to squirm out of the binds for fear she would return to find me free (free!!!) and thus disrupting her aims; and what would those be? A few nights earlier she was sleeping, I was twisting and turning in bed because I couldn't sleep because I was so angry with her and was meditating on leaving her because she had flirted with a young boy at the party she had at her house for the Bartholdy String Quartet after their show, a young boy I might ass, I mean add I mean, the "s" is right next to the "d" and I wasn't looking at the keyboard, a young ballet dancer I thought for an instant it might be nice for us to share, only for an instant and didn't think about it again, only because I imagined she would have liked it, and the moon was full and its light cast itself pale on her face, I can't figure how I could discern her face so clearly solely by the light of the moon, it was a face I had never seen before, she was the androgynous Indra, well, I am not sure it was Indra, but a figure from an Indian landscape of mythology that you've spotted in reproductions and though I wished to leave her, something I was seriously meditating on, something I had actually made up my mind on, she seemed like Indra, who is androgynous, didn't it ever occur to you how androgynous these Indian figures look even when the title says these deities are male, that's how she looked backlit by the moonlight, and it occurred to me that if I left her I would be leaving a god, or a goddess, whom I am supposed to serve and worship and by leaving I would only be bringing a curse on myself like a backslider in faith, an infidel, that so what if she flirted with the young boy, it was my own constriction I got jealous, after all it is me she slept with afterwards even though I had to go home and wait for her to call me when she finally got him to leave, it was me not him she was sleeping with, and I looked at her, she was Indra, an Indian deity sitting on a cloud surrounded by servants and lovers and worshippers and perhaps there was no separation between them, perhaps I had entered a course in obedience, supplicancy, veritable service, because what good is service as commodity, nothing but the fulfilling of an obligation, transgression outfitted with a chastity belt, not the ecstatic trance of supplication before the goddess you worship; that perhaps the tricky issue was the fact of your outmoded democracy (which is no more than demographics, the approximation of the human being), "The more readily he recognizes his own needs in the images of need proposed by the dominant system, the less he understands his own existence and his own desires", where is the freedom to obey the lover you worship, the ecstatic commitment of supplication which you despise in principle, but in fact it is only so because you are committed to the desiccated balletics of restriction, permanent position in diorama, frozen pose in the plaza, tenure in the temple of self-disgust, and suddenly here I was, she was goddess Indra teaching me the meaning of forgotten arts, such as irrational obedience, ecstatic suplicance, diaphanous idolatry, magic, these very elements of hyper-Fragonard erotica, erotica that transcends the concrete the quotidian is composed of, I was being trained to, I had been chosen to be trained for a higher calling, no longer the pedestrian pedagogue merely straining for the alabaster entrancement of sudden abandon to the beckoning burst of the vajra violin, I was being tested for a master in the sudden abandon of the beckoning burst of the vajra violin, Leila Ferraz's perpetual encounters and ancient recognitions and Evening Gypsy legs were erupting at my core as a beam of light poised from her forehead like a viper's tongue glimmered like a mandorla: "Magic is the cultivator of the very desire that makes it 'beyond good and evil' in a sphere belonging to enchantment and violation—the feeling (or rather *sensation*) of power that transforms *what I have* into *what I am*, hurling me against everything that seems to obstruct my self-movement", and still, here I was, could I forgive myself, giving in to my reluctance, withdrawing into my sorry state of concretized dignification, me abandoning her? No I was giving her reasons to abandon me by my disobedience to the task itself, yes I realized now I had judged her according to the restricted motions of the quotidian, that I had been chosen to transcend its limitations and here I was retreating! And I realized that I had judged her yet again, told myself she couldn't possibly be Indra, that it was only some poetic illusion, (only some poetic delusion! I could stab myself for that!) I had given in, without even realizing it, to the standards of the quotidian masquerade, to the rule of the utilitarian order simply because she was such a premature ejaculator! One touch Imogen, one touch to the underside of her tiny penis and she would squirt! She commands me to run the tip of my tongue on its underside and splash, a faceful of come. A faceful, I'm exaggerating here, it was merely a tiny squirt and she'd shriek like a rhesus. I know, I know what you're thinking, that she's abusing me and it's undignified, that I am the fool of a con, but you can't deny the desperate pleasure I feel; I mean certainly I wouldn't go to the office and brag, I couldn't 'hang out with the guys' and brag, I couldn't express this in conversation with my boss Das Goot (I don't recall if I ever mentioned him to you, but I will if I didn't), so what posture could I take, what societally approved value could I adopt to paint my eidolon in? (As I mentioned, the masculine disorder is not entrancing to me.) Except, of course, fulfillment. Yes, fulfillment. My whole being vibrated and I can't say it was merely 'pleasure' the way pleasure is undignified through democratized pornography, why is 'pleasure' wrong? Yes, my entire being vibrated with fulfillment as though all aspects of the universe were contributing instruments to a symphony of joy and abandon being played inside me. "I am not merely one who approximates pungencies!", I wanted to shout in submission in order to be forgiven. "Not even yet a murderer of syndromes! I will be the myrmidon in your conquests", I muttered with glottis in flames. "Yellow smoke swelled out of my vampirically costumed melodramas, in intonation of gazals to her majestic turbulence".

But now the hours were passing, perhaps, I reasoned, it is her season to make me panic by exaggerating this ruse, how could I ascertain whether she imperiously intended this comedy to be horror, to linger for the duration of mere moments or to persist for interminable months, she alone held the key to this convulsive melodrama, who was she? a sinister soul pirate, plundering demon, appropriating me in her stockings, abducting me in her stockings, encapsulating me in her stockings, sequestering, sequestrating and confiscating me in her stockings, abandoning me in her stockings, these stockings, which, though initially palatial substance of enigma, were now beginning to itch, what if they caused me a rash, and suddenly I am assaulted by a drill of lines I couldn't make any sense of but which coerced me to write them down, lines such as:

"Reality being too much like sausages inspired with pre-established humors, too much for my network of internal inventions, my frightwork of catacombs, I crept nightly to my queen in the guise of a cinderblue aviatrix."

Or:

"Siphon off the clouds, chameleon clarinet!"

Or:

"Strive for the unclaimed unredeemable"

Or:

"A few stragglers coagulated into a no more than an April idea of pavements."

Or, and this one I liked a lot:

"Nocturnal midgets dust off the chimerical tattoo and mold his chambers by recitation of new solar entreaties."

I am repeating each line over and over again so as not to lose it to amnesia, as I am no position to write them down, and I recall, apropos the line stolen from my computer I was facing now on the billboard: it was also very possible that Thea had inoculated my left buttock with a very tiny object because earlier while she was twirling her right finger inside my anus I felt a minuscule metal prick on my left buttock and it could easily have been her left fingers inoculating a foreign substance in there, though I can't figure what the purpose of this could have been, if they can make a tiny cell phone that can track you wherever you are, they can certainly insert in your plasma a minuscule gadget to discern even your thoughts, and, could she be working for them too? I could only assume it was a microphone, everything is so tiny now, so undetectable, it may be more than a microphone, I am not familiar with the latest developments of science, I have ignored my studies in science, especially those concerning espionological forays, it was a computer chip perhaps, connected to who knows what sort of Hades retrieval system, yes she could be working for them too, I am very behind in these studies, I confess my ignorance here, of which I am not proud, knowing how technology has developed the last few years only, and everyone but me is an adept at technology, and it makes me feel they learned to tolerate me, and accept me and remunerate me simply as a "creative type", there must be something they are trying to extract from me, there must be something, what she inserted in my red buttock, I mean my left buttock, while I was squirming as she twirled her finger in my anus. My right leg was curled inwards at first, foot against my left thigh, but my left thigh then elevated in a dancer's graceful arch lifting to the sky, something I had actually observed Candora execute on stage before she and I met and her grace had entranced me and I was left unwittingly wishing to perform it myself with the same grace, and because she had performed it before me on stage that grace invaded me and persisted as an enriching element part of my assemblage, though I never imagined the opportunity would emerge for me to express it by performing it myself. I assume that is what happens with the arts, they inoculate you and become part of your daily routine without you even realizing it. Something occurs to me here, in discussing the arts and their meaning, that it was the sole reaching for the sky, the sole, what sort of meaning could this comprise, sole to the sky rather than hands, the bottom up, as though I were wishing to stand on the sun perhaps, I recall Heraclitus and his "the sun is as big as a foot", I thought of 'sol' as in sun versus sole, 'sol' as in terra too, but this held no meaning for me momentarily, so I won't explore it, but I did feel it was appropriate for me to perform this particular gesture, my sole to the sol, and though I couldn't see Thea behind me I sensed her and gave in to the mastery she commanded, I solely wished to be her Juliette, I abandoned myself to being her Juliette. And this would be another statue I would put up in this town. But more about that later, something to do with statues I've been pondering about. I feel that the graceful arch of the leg curling upwards would make the statue bewitching in bronze or maybe black marble. And I recalled the painting by Max Ernst, "Virgin Mary Spanking Baby Jesus", and how could I forget this, oh Imogen, this is frighteningly close, Virgin Mary in this painting resembles Thea very closely, Thea, though she is teutonic, she looks exotically Asiatic, perhaps she is endowed by an atavistic return, perhaps Egyptian, perhaps Hindu (and as you know Ernst is teutonic too) and she had her hand raised and about to bring it down towards baby Jesus' butt as he lays on her lap, his legs arching upwards just like mine were, toes curled in obvious delight, just as her right foot is drawn back, it is an intimate moment shared between mother and son, and it's the only time in my life I wanted to be Jesus, more, I craved to be Jesus. But more later, like I said. Still, I can't help but wishing to pause so as to cause my words to render the painting itself, not merely describe it, but I am impelled by the imperative that drives this narrative I am imparting to you to return to the plight in whose grips I was presently trapped, so you must run to the library or the bookstore and get the book of Ernst's paintings yourself, as I said, in the past I would have rendered the painting with my words, not merely describe, but now my words must cause you to rush to the bookstore or to the library, or perhaps if you possess an Ernst, you must go to your shelf for it, so that perhaps, I use perhaps a lot, because I don't know the source of, what drives, the imperative that propels to push forth with this narrative, or its purpose, the presently privative that impels me to push forth, the demigorgon in whose grips I might be, is it a source whose purpose is to force me to extract an event, to return to an event, an impending increment to reveal to me what I was looking for at the incipience of this narrative, who knows, perhaps to abstract a concept to illuminate my plight in whose trap I was presently squirming, here and now, hic et nunc, as I now could not wrench myself from this memory quicksand machine they spliced and concocted in the form of a frightening fishnet Madonna, as my memory strands were melting, this detail they quartered from my life's continuum, which they placed amidst the rest of the quartered details, concealed inside the rest of the tortured and quartered details imprisoned inside the Amnesia

Spectator, this fragment of my life floundering as it was now in the fishnet of their manipulated interpretation, like a contortion detailed and glimpsed in the twist of a distorting mirror and which acquires its significance simply because it is sectioned off through its distortion, suctioned off too, and there is an instant of glimmering recognition in the distortion which you would never spot in the morning's toilet mirror or even in the common activity utilitarian mirror of say the airport's bathroom, or any other public place where quartering and restraining our mirrored image is part and parcel of our taking our assigned place in the forced common activity utilitarian march, this detail, yes, which now they could mirror and entrap me in for their unscrupulous purpose. But why, I did consider this, why should their purpose be unscrupulous? Because, if they wrote something about me, their purpose was to define me. Let's go back for an instant here to the Socratic "know thyself", not that I am fan of Socrates, but the sentiment itself is one I admire, no, I despise Socrates for how he is always "right", how he always wins arguments by trapping you in the quagmire of his restrictive "reason", and to think that for millennia we've allowed him to oppress us inside the avuncular cavities of his superego mentality, but still, know thyself is good, I too have since very young desired to know myself, but perhaps out of a character flaw or lack of concentration I have been unable to do so. To this day I still don't know myself; perhaps the trap is to believe you can; as for me there have been a few character attributes, flaws really, I have spotted in passing, some of which depressed me or infused me with low self esteem; but essentially I didn't believe them, because I thought that at the core I am a much finer character, and what I was experiencing were only tests I hadn't yet passed because my time hadn't yet come. And if a newspaper places an article about you in its entrails, for the public to observe, it must mean that, since newspapers are written for the people and by the people and for the purpose of educating the people, that what they wrote about me is the truth, there must no insinuation even, no feathery insinuation that intrigue is at work here, intrigue which grows verdigris on the truth, because how could you impute upon a publication which claims to tell the truth for the people that it tells untruths about the citizens of its own community. And thus if the newspaper presented a fragment of truth about me, I should then be grateful to them for it for it was helping me to find myself, to know myself, in other words. Because I didn't want to take on the view that this is a rat race, the cynical view that everything is corrupt and that everyone has an agenda they want to fulfill and that in order to fulfill it they would resort to any means necessary, that they would manipulate the public opinion through the newspaper, for instance. They would make me an object of ridicule, for instance, by placing in the newspaper this event segmented from my life, a diorama on view for the education of the public (and my own), a view into the depth of the human soul, with the long-range purpose of improving the state of humanity through self-knowledge, no? But was their intent really to reveal my inner self, exploding as it does out of the abyss, the mysterious, the miraculous, the true, to create a mirror for everyone else to look into to delight in their own inner selves? Something to make them reflect upon the marvelous? Create an event in diorama, which, upon perusing, they would exclaim: How whimsically marvelous life can be! Or to create a mirror which to shame me and shame others' desire to perform along the same lines as me? A segment representing an area whose borders must never be crossed for fear of being placed on public display as object of ridicule. Because if you recall, I remind you, we're talking about the listing of my name in unequivocal cathection to this detail, an incriminating increment, sectioned off, something I was observed executing that someone connected to the paper, or someone connected to someone connected to the paper and who observed me, thought merited mention and certainly, the someone connected to the someone at the paper must also be connected on the other end to someone or an institution, more than likely an institution, the institutionalization of a purpose cathected in some sense to what I was observed doing; what I mean, the purpose which they institutionalized was supported by what I was observed doing; by what this someone, or this someone else connected to someone, both of whom indoctrinated in the interpretational mode whose survival depended upon extracting a meaning inimical to it from the detail wrenched from my continuum

and here I must pause to mirror my plight in the eyes of those whose purposes mirror mine, such as Paul Klee: "To define the present in isolation is to kill it",

an extraction through a refracted
interpretation of an incriminating increment, this act that I was observed committing. Thus I reasoned then, and perhaps not wrongly so, when I knew a little less than what I know now, simply through deduction due to the chain of the above mentioned events; that is, something I was observed doing appeared to the observer at the moment that he or she observed me doing it to serve the purpose of his or her purpose, in the sense he or she perceived it to be the same as the purpose of his or her superior in the hierarchy of the institution he or she belonged to and thus of the institution herself, and hoped to advance towards leadership in, the hierarchy of the institution, this institutionalization of a purpose I could not clearly at the moment discern, (fishnetted as I momentarily was, with the fishnetted spliced one melting my fingers on my left and Loony Linda, fishnet shanked Loony Linda melting my right), but a purpose which, as I noted above, the increment they extracted as a

refraction of my life's continuum was inimical to and thus necessary for its survival; the institution he or she (the observer) belonged to and whose ladder he or she hoped to climb, all at the root a detail wrenched from my life's continuum by this someone's interpretational mechanism, detail which, for me, were I to be able to track it, would mirror for me the original event which they quartered through manipulation to obtain it, I realize right now just how far they have gone in wrapping my vital wiring in the cotton of amnesia, no, it is not yet time to consider this, yes, no it is not, why should it be so difficult to, no I must, and I was resolved to get there before I met with incarceration or internment in the asylum they had just finished building and now Amnesia was notorious for; or even death by dissolution, as it awaited me now before the red light in the fishnet grips of my captors; the obvious thing to do next was to find once again the person who had originally spilled the news to me, the person who originally announced to me my debut as a 'public figure' in Amnesia, and shake him and rattle him some more. Or why not, and this idea came to possess me, to rely on my own command of alchemical implosion because for an instant I ecstatically inferred that perhaps the centripetal force of my thought spinning would suddenly spill out for me, the quickening speed of the spinning would spill out the event I was in search of, unable as I was at present of availing myself to any means of ambulation. Fishnets had wrapped her Jagger lips around my tongue while her tongue was a spigot suctioning my memories! She was a construct! A spigot for suctioning memories, memories which, once spigotted into her hard drive they could access and make use of any way they saw fit! A hard drive disguised as a demon spliced in the guise of a Jagger lipped ballerina shanked and fishenetted nimphette-fatale; they had been watching me, they had discerned my fatalities; And Linda, Loony Linda, long exquisite tongue now shooting right into my right ear lobe, how did they reconstruct her? Only from my poem, which they had found in my hard drive? There was nothing I could do as I was being plunged into the quicksand they had prepared for me; I thought of counter-acting with Rilke, and how "every angel is terrifying": but is that the sort angels he envisioned? "that even one of them should embrace me and take me close to her heart, suddenly I would dissolve before her greater being." Instead of angels, the divine, the greater being being an institution in whose devious purposes I was floundering. My flesh would be found a few days later quartered in plastic in a trash can in a parking lot in Amnesia while my suctioned and digitized memories stored in a warehouse below Amnesia belonging to the Hades. Or perhaps, more likely, being put to use for purposes I couldn't discern and for certain wouldn't endorse, like my puppet's sudden appearance endorsing the purposes of someone whose purposes I despised, more, who were inimical to the singular weft of my formulations and symptoms. This incriminating increment, solidifying duration to be presented on a stage of ridicule. As Bergson would have it: "And while we can no doubt, by an effort of the imagination, solidify duration each time it has elapsed", i.e. place it in parenthesis, on stage, diorama, between quotes, frame it as a picture or a news item, "divide it into juxtaposed portions each time it has elapsed, and count all these portions, yet this operation is accomplished on the frozen memory of duration, on the stationary trace which the mobility of duration leaves behind it, and not on the duration itself." And have you ever attempted to fix the frozen memory of duration? The invading neighbors, a haze of militant psychic substrata, the reticulation of an advancing and retreating armada of psychic events which battle you if you try to speak of them, and who knows what happens if you try to speak to them. But I digress.

These different concepts then were only so many intersecting standpoints, the circumnavigation coordinates from which we could consider the event extracted in order to frame me. The error they commit in simplyf(l)ying (I couldn't resist the lapping of the 'l' in parenthesis, it purled like a pelagic vagina) the perceived by dividing it into inner and outer is infuriating, their affable inability to realize, and to continue their research along these simplification lines! That inner and outer, I wanted to shout, are only ways of simplifying and simply to say that "it's an admixture of the two in different degrees" is, which is "true", is an over simplification because you start from the viewpoint that inner and outer are actual (opposing) coordinates, when in fact they are merely simplifications, reductions really, and this is what raises my ire, reductions of a conceptual kind, reductions which serve only the masters of utility in their protestant attempt to produce. (I'm looking here for the source of their ignorance, I muttered, the better to spew my contempt at them, these children of fat luther, ingestors of grease at the counter of the all-night-all-you can-eat Roadkill Cantina.) Because the metaphysics they have created is meant to exist as a structure, which is stricture, which exists outside the human being, to daunt it and thwart it, so much did they mistrust the spontaneous exploration of the human being, to present the construction, and not only present it but impose it, through their schools, their churches, their cathedrals, their chairs, their cars, their architecture, their structures, to inoculate into the human that what the human being feels, senses, dreams, desires, is not reliable as a system in place and must be replaced, reduced into a formula and preserved, and why? Our behavior is, like I said, infinite, yet out of this infinity he or she could have snipped (or snapped) (or sniped) a so-called event; the event he or she would have snipped would be, like a fish out of water, fried and placed on a plate with lemon on the side, not the true event anymore in an infinity of events which should not be separated in events but seen as a harmonious continuum. The fried fish on the plate serves a valuable function, (and I have no clue if I'm speaking of the jesus fish they paste on their bumper stickers) and by the way the fish image is by no means arbitrary, once again Bergson: "It starts from the immobile, and only conceives and expresses movement as a function of immobility. It takes up its position in ready-made concepts, and, endeavors to catch in them, *as in a net*, something of the reality which passes." Yes, let's call it a flounder because of the entrancing name, which suggests a graceful billowing in the deeps of the ocean among the waltzing seaweeds and the vanishing octopi, I do not deny that, I am not the one to deny, at this late stage, the value of our civilization, the value of eating itself, which is primary component of our civilization—since the air is still free, not good, but free—like fried fish on a plate, which is not free, I am merely making a case for an alternate one, an alternate civilization, and it should not be assumed out of hand that just because I am making a case for an alternate civilization, the seeds of which I have described in previous letters to you, I am calling for the destruction of the present one, if I haven't yet I will soon, the one which you are now inhaling, inhabiting, I am only calling for abandonment, not even en masse, ok, en masse if you will, certainly en masse, and it is for these ideas which I have not widely propagated, not yet, not propagated en masse, but still, at a party, or with my students during class, in the hallway with a younger and more impressionable instructor— these, to take time for an aside here, are more than likely the readers of the Amnesia Spectator for whom they (my opposers) wished to discredit me, while working with a student alone, at a moment when I happened to be most convincing, the ambiguous feather of my fingers on her or his wrist, when the force of my ideas suddenly penetrated her or his internal landscape, you, my Queen, have just curled your toes at feather, I know, absentmindedly crossed your feet, rubbed the toes of one silky foot against another, your lovely white feet I still wish to kiss, when the feather of entrancement had the best of me, when I was in my most enticing mode, I dropped a hint, a mere clue, the shading of a trait which glowed for an instant like the gliding of the stocking of the one longed for observed in passing through the crack of the bedroom door, dressing for the artifice of the opera perhaps, perhaps merely the perfume she wore then but you scented unexpectedly on a fleeting someone else entrée-acts and accompanied by the pang of the (assumed) long vanished longing, as though trying to hold onto a live flounder or imprison a perfume into wall of reinforced concrete, out of a continuum of events to choose one is to imprison it for naming it, it is to scoop it out and place it in the past's plate for those whose job is serve interpretations at a price, paid by those willing to pay for interpretations, which are nothing but an amputation of the infinite, powdering the imponderable, so necessary for the latest wave of imprisonings, for those who cleave clever cracks into the continuum of meanings, yes, those who quarter the infinite, powder the imponderable, to let all this loose on an impressionable someone of the sort I described above, is to corrugate from within their faith in the present civilization, is to detach them from the tentacles of the fish fry civilization, the molar civilization, and allow them access to the world I suspect and of which I will speak about, a world I have yet to reveal, a world of a material more critical than the material of this world of which they think you and I are a part of, what its maladied priests call the 'real world', I am not talking about, when I say priests, about men of the cloth, yes that's one material too, so in a sense they are men of the cloth, mere cloth, men of the trade, men of the industry, men of the earth, all these men in the food chain, all the big fish consuming the lesser fish ad infinitum, ad absurdum, ad nauseaum, men of your consumption, men of your production, all of you, and your poets, the poets of your world, marshalling

their ideas neatly into the rank and file march of commonality, yes, advertising men, you will all go to hell, along with
the men of cloth who inform you that your counting god,
accounting god, discounting god, incremental god, god of
incremental mercy, vengeful god willed it, this god, meat eating god, I am detaching the world from you as though
pulling off the bloody bandage, your coagulated blood world,
my world is of much more critical cloth, an imponderable
cloth, neither born nor ever dying, a cloth I constantly secret
and which your industry may crave but never attain to, my
body not in need of your agriculture to sustain its form, its
cloth, to support the balletics of its motion, to engender the
poetry of its gestures, no, "I breathe the air of pure poetry,
and it is sating", not in need of you, not in need of your man-
ufactured, yes, even air, and your incriminating increment
you extracted by quartering a piece of the material of the
continuum cloth of my behavior, a piece engendered by the
throttled breath of your perception, your amputated eye
wired up to your arrested cardiac quarter, your amputated
cornea camera, amputated by your quartered understanding,
you realize my Imogen, my sweet Imogen, that when I say
you, I don't mean you, I am by no means speaking of you, but
them, it is them which I am calling you, but do not mean
you, but them, I am, was for moment addressing them.
Whose world is a spell I refuse.

Let me recapitulate. On my left Fishnets was extracting
my memories through my now melting left fingers. Or no, I
retract, fishnets had wrapped her Jagger lips around my
tongue while her tongue was a spigot suctioning my memories. So much had she flexed forth that the straight line
formed by my left arm, which was the dispatch for my fingers
that earlier had served as the siphoning pipe, was now forming a right angle. And on my right Linda, Loony Linda, long
exquisite tongue now shooting right into my right ear lobe,
so that my right arm, again, straight earlier, had now also

become a right angle; before me, the billboard with the picture I described above, with the purpose to brand and discredit me, and with the line, my own line, purloined from my own computer: "No longer fascinated by the performances of souls delusional of the undermotion of phenomena, she steps to a music she alone can hear." And below: "Read all about it in the Metro section of Amnesia Spectator". The light not about to turn green. And the indignity that they contrived to taunt me with, which afflicted me more than the purloined line, the suggestion that it was me who was the "soul delusional of the undermotion of phenomena", when it was them I had written the line about. Turning it against me, as though I were that soul, delusional of the undermotion of phenomena, as though I were that soul! because how could a passing peruser of this billboard discern the line was my original brew? My alchemical concoction I directed at them! I would have shouted if I could that I was being dispossessed of my own words, had I not been aware that they weighted lexical aurora by the pound, that it was not a luminous factor on the scales of their dun-dawned estimation. The whole sad weight of Amnesia was suddenly intrusive like a hard breathing convict pressing a crowbar across the constricted throbbing of my cardiac muscle. At least if my arms were still extended, I mused, perhaps ironically, for which I instantly upbraided myself, as this was no time for irony, (the ironic era had already passed, as I was fond of shouting at parties, I was too aware of that), I could have reverted to viewing myself as a religious dilemma. Or at least I could view my condition as a "work of art", as the shamans of corporate spirituality are calling for. Thus I would strike back because subversive symbolism could have charged my plight: a statue, I would strike back by becoming a statue of subversive symbolism: their beloved jesus (and here I must confess that I spent the last half an hour on this particular word, performing innumerable keyboards commands as the computer would not accept the j word except with a majuscule. No computer, I hear, can be sold in Amnesia unless the software program is outfitted thus, but is anyone assuming a vocal stance? So I figured a jesus in silk stockings might prove anti-emblematic enough to them to lead to internal upheaval. Unhinging. Fortunately, though progressively desiccated of memories, I was still keen enough to write down what follows before performing the innumerable keyboard commands, so the word construction parading before you is a paste.) Yes, here I was a potential jesus in silk stockings being manipulated by two, one on each arm, fishnetted madonnas, my long locks too would contribute to the jesus mystique, but my widespread arms had been collapsed to right angles. And I was disturbed by the symbolism of the car; or lack of it, rather; do you know Kienholz's sculptures? Had we not once perused them together at MOCA in LA? I thought of Kienholz sculptures, I thought a life-size Kienholz sculpture would be appropriate to give meaning to my condition. Were the Maxima and us to retain our position as statuary, there would still be enough room to veer around it, especially if they cut partially into the empty lot on the right, where the abandoned hands of Gentlemen's Paradise still molest. Except of course that since my jesus condition had been collapsed, no contriver of meanings might reenact this situation as biblical without proper elucidation. I was looking for context here, as I sensed that as it was, my condition had no context I could discern, social or historical or otherwise, not even the solitary pathos of the transgressive in the downtown hotel of a major metropolis that Kienholz had promoted. I was afraid that my pose was purely pornographic, sans even the pathos, though pathos is clearly not my path, I opt Bretonianly for the chorus of corybantic coruscation, and I reproved myself for this momentarily longing for this stance. I craved the vertiginous plunge into vision, into the redolence of disobedient emerald clarinets, eruptions of vatic balm, and instead was presented on a stage of pornography! And my vehicle too, what meaning can be extracted from a burgundy 1994 Japanese car? What context? Across the junkyard of a mythologically parvenu universe whose showrooms boasted the James Dean Porsche. In a haze of desiccated butterflies, I leafed in despair through Kienholz's fanfare of vehicles, mostly American, like the Americana of his foreshortened Dodge '38, belonging to his father, which he used on his first date, (see, you have some history here, but me, it was another dun place to be a meaningless stranger from, I have no such architextural memorabilia to root me to locus), the one, do you recall, with the coital couple in the back seat, already, so suddenly, ambered in the mausoleum of myth, the strewn beer bottles on the ground, the forensic peep show; but my Maxima, abstracted from any history, as was I, in Amnesia, so inappropriate was I in the sepulchral burgundy of my Maxima. At least if it had been a crimson '57 convertible Cadillac. And why was I embracing Kienholz? Why prop myself up with his pathos? Yes, the tenuous jesus mystique was all I could come up with, and now with the jesus pose collapsed, that was gone too, (not that I opted for symbolism either) who would ever grasp it or try to, now with my arms no longer spread wide but bent at right angles; all I had left going for me was the obvious irony, the juvenile juxtaposition, I upbraided myself—though on the other hand I could, couldn't I? somewhat justify it by calling it dadaist, something in the vein of Man Ray's flatiron with nails sticking out of the flat surface, and thus invalidating its obvious utilitarian purpose—the juvenile juxtaposition of the jesus in stockings and the two madonnas in fishnets. This as statuary before the Hades Hose billboard above the yellow stab of the Texxon marquee serving in tandem as propaganda for the Amnesia Spectator. If I could only widespread my arms again. That and the fact we were in the middle of the intersection in Amnesia's ghetto and soon enough the locals would gather and begin to peer in, I had forgotten to mention this, and me affronted by the cruel taunt of the purloined line pasted across the intersection with the implied taunt of Thea's allure to invalidate me, I would have to fling back retorts at their rude jeers directed at my amorous array. Which I doubt I could have under this condition I was in, what with the forays conducted against my psyche and the belligerent blasting of the hip-hop, boiling disgust pounding like lava underneath the chokehold of christian conditioning. Yes, at least with the jesus mystique going for me I would have served some local purpose, much like Man Ray's flatiron with the nails sticking out and invalidating its utilitarian purpose, a jesus outfitted and made up like a whore, because suddenly I recalled, and confirmed it by quickly glimpsing my face in the rear view mirror, Thea had outfitted me with rouge and eyeliner and mascara, and most of it had not yet rubbed off, (I must admit here that though my age was partially apparent, I found myself entrancing), yes, what with the locals such fanatic worshippers of their utilitarian jesus programs my appearance would have certainly caused their belief system to implode. Perhaps, I mused, to attach a computer screen to the car with this letter to you and a mouse to facilitate scrolling might have solved the problem partially, the way a title completes the picture, it would have informed regarding my previous jesus position, now collapsed, and that may have been fraught with meaning as well, the collapse itself from a previous state of grace, but who reads nowadays? Who has the inclination? Who the lexical leaning? They would more than likely steal the screen, on assumption it was a TV, because who would hire an off-duty cop, in this land where jesse helms, to protect art, especially art unendorsed by the program of their utilitarian orders jesus supporters; more than likely the off-duty cop too one tarred by the benighted cognition of their utilitarian jesus orders and finding himself face to face with the commingled enigma of the unendorsed art. And here we are, incapacitated sans the legal apparatus to the rescue on account of colloquial benighted cognition; they have their statues downtown, to honor the posturing of veteran fascistics, those they understand and endorse, their postures in the service of their restricted utilitarian orders. Rousseau who called for statues of men who defended their country or those greater still, who enriched it by their genius. (Though I doubt they would see my dada statement as genius.) Yes, perhaps I needed to presently simply opt for a dada statement, and abandon any obsession with a pelagic understanding of my position I might crave as well as a need to extract a meaning which might have done more than enrage the locals with impudent performances against their modes of restricting belief. I don't know if I should continue speaking to you regarding my ideas concerning what I felt should formally be done with this statue; but on the main, at risk of being ambiguous I chose to remain conceptual. I would stay close to the simplicity of the wax figure, or the mannequin, which would lend it the macabre aspect so common to the B-movie I feel it should preserve, along with the persistence of a near life-like quality. My arms outstretched, perhaps Fishnets and Linda piercing my palms with their penetrating tongues. I would replace the burgundy Maxima with a crimson '57 convertible Cadillac, convertible because I should stand, because perhaps jesus would be pointless when crucified sitting, it would deplete the drama, the spectacle; and with me standing they would see a jesus in stockings, it would cause them to become inflamed in spite of themselves. And as for me, transmuting personal fetish to mission and into the ontology of culture! After that, would I still be sketched by critics as one rehearsing ad nauseam absurdum the ostinato notes of his delicious & delinquent desire? After that, was it still the rigor to delve into a visual history of the arts to fish out a deliberated model for my position to emulate? Tradition be damned! To shuffle through its entire repertoire for a mere posting in Amnesia was beyond the call of present duty. Still, tradition, though somnolent, made a weak attempt at visitation; yes, though I had studied art history in college, its only appearance was in the form of Albrecht Durer's self-portrait, facing the viewer full on, an honor reserved only for jesus. I didn't recall any other pertinent jesuses, though I vaguely flashed through many. Certainly no cross dressing jesuses. There was Bunuel's Duc de Blangis jesus in L'Age D'or as a sex murderer, but he wore the conventional plain robe. There was another Bunuel Jesus, this one as a hippie. There was Serrano's Piss Christ, a crucifix jesus dipped in bubbling piss. And then, a couple of weeks before, the imaginal Condom Christ, which I phashioned from the creases of plastic wrapping painted on a poorly painted table whose brown intended to render the wood hue but made me recoil as from an unexpected encounter with human excrement on the dining table—the table cloth made of plastic was inadvertenly painted so that I it made me think of a creased and abandoned condom to drop christ in—when I junketed through a spurting of galleries and took refuge in the single one that invited the peruser with cheap vino and pink cookies, and the oversized wooden crosses the artists bore around their necks of implied penitence, the cheap vino and pink cookies, I surmised, being christian charity to make up for the poor art, still, I confess, I can't say I didn't partially enjoy the cookies and the vino, we hadn't had dinner, and if it hadn't been for Serrano's Piss Christ I might have congratulated myself as a veritable original thinker. Still, the fact that I dropped Christ inside a condom—I will not pause here to comment on the symbolic bubbles of this image that sizzles out of the words I splattered across the page—which occurred to me while viewing ineptly rendered creases of plastic cloth should be enough for me to merit permanent statuary on the Dadaist Hall of Fame. And so far, I was the first cross-dressing dada christ, the first to meld jesus and eroticism in the bible belt. Serrano had merely dipped him in piss, but I got him to swing, I eroticized him. People of the future will grace me with gratitude me for this act of liberation. Still, though I had craved for profound significances, I was starting to settle, and gloat, for seminal dada shock.

Meanwhile I became aware that I had progressively become immobilized, that though I was alert to the agitated motion of my cogitation, I was unable to gesture though the imperative to do battle against the enrapturing plunge that was operating at maximum, when suddenly the Maxima, along with the pavement where Fishnets and Linda respectively stood on my left and right, had lifted off the street level, with loud cracking noises, and we were suddenly hoisted up possibly 12 feet in the middle of the intersection, a statue, I mused, exposed to the perusal of the two way traffic and the flurry of oblivious pedestrians. The right hand side mirror having been partially inverted to face downwards on account of Loony Linda's maneuvering to insinuate her spittling into my ear and the cause of the upheaval became instantly and to my horror clear. I have spoken to you at times of my entrancement with spiders, I recall how it fascinated you at the time, when you still were entranced with my gesticulations, that I had lived with one for a time, she watched me (or didn't, perhaps it was incurious in this matter) taking a bath each dawn for two years, and even warned my cleaning lady to not disturb its network of silk on pain of becoming paralyzed by her nocturnal ambush habits. I had even composed a poem about it, though I don't remember it now, a juvenilia partial to symbolism where I blasted the utilitarian order; that though the spider had been placed by the utilitarian order under the rubric of the vampirical, in that it sucked its victims dry, in that it survived not by its industry like the myrmidonic pismire it fed on but by stealth, it was the utilitarian order that was the veritable meriter of the moniker vampirical. I had written that had the spider secreted strands of sturdier silk it would end up stunted in the restricting drills of the cultivation camps; and in the poem the spider herself, to avoid this tragic destiny, though it was certainly capable of producing the sturdier strand, necessary for the weave of the entrancing stocking, essential factor in the order of human reproduction, had opted for secreting only the precarious strand that we are familiar with and which utility was forced to despise and refuse, and that, more than anything, was the reason for the spider's vampirical moniker. And the poet was likened to the spider in that her coruscating secretions were also despised by the vampirical order of utility. The ancient Chinese were aware of this and the appearance of a spider was thought to herald good fortune. And certainly, do not think me ungrateful, I have not forgotten Breton: "The fabric of adorable improbabilities must be made a trifle more subtle the older we grow, and we are still at the stage of waiting for this kind of spider".

So why was I horrified? The torn patch of concrete I spoke of on top of which my Maxima now rested precariously was supported by the carapace of a giant amber violin spider which the right hand side mirror had made all too apparent! The sight of all its eight eyes made a straight line to the surface of the obliquely pointed right hand side mirror and ricocheted right into my own two eyes! Her Malpighian tubules began to intone in the manner customary of violin spiders, her pedipalps were not frantic as the Hades had warned, but fibrillated with a soothing hum that caressed and entranced us with her intricate pulse and led us into a frequency of trance we secretly crave but consistently forget, a state of unattained imagination and unrestraint and reticulating inner exultation, and though I can't repeat exactly the exact words she intoned, this is the gist of it: she is the Spider at the center of Amnesia, the one who sucks up memories. The true strands of her silk are made of oblivion, out of suctioned memories, though no one is known to have worn a pair stockings made of this strand, but the one who does will become the true poet. Hades Hose puts up tent here in hope of harnessing the spider, vain attempt to match the unmatchable spider, but the spider is wise and ferocious and avoids capture. Hades' cotton fibers, historic result of local slavery, and petroleum product fibers, result of international slavery, are merely an imitation that will never match the original, a cause of never-ending frustration to the ruling Hades clan. She told me she respects me and my attire and in her mirrors I was her champion and that my spider poem and my friendship with the she-spider in my bath are known among the company of spiders, who communicate by fibrillary auscultation throughout the universe. "You are the spider's stratagem", she intoned as she handed me back my memories, "and you will make yourself the worshipper of my purposes. Here are your memories back, made savvy by my hatching. And here's a pair of silk stockings, imponderable obsidian clarinets, for you and for Thea, and a poem, for which she will always adore you: do not give her the stockings without the poem, do not give her the poem without the stockings. The stockings are neither hers nor yours but that which will always keep you together. You must do so on a moonless night while you enthrall her with your discipleship to me and to midnight. Then you will be forever young, so will she, and she will never forsake you." I perused the stockings. A creeping transparency barely more dense than nothingness. Liminal lower limb lamellation. Consistency slightly more constant than absolute inconsistency. Mandorla of solar and selenic clarinets. "The simultaneously luminous and embracing mandorla is a mysterious image of concentration upon the light that shines from within."

I thought of Thea and how she left me and I wished to protest that Thea had already left me, that she despised me, not only me but my cat, but the Queen-Spider began intoning the poem she spoke of, so I rushed to carve it in my reconditioned memory:

Your stockings are a moonless chalcedony sky
ambrosial mist of terrified disciples,
and I fear I will swoon
before I gain the river of night.

Suddenly the Maxima precipitated to the ground and the desiccated Fishnets and Linda collapsed by the sides into colloquial dust. The light had transmuted to an emerald glow and I was about to step on it when Thea and Candora manifested by the sides where Fishnets and Linda used to be, penetrated beyond the doors, and we were off with Thea at the wheel. She looped about, reversed charge across the intersection barely avoiding collision with oncoming traffic even as I glimpsed the rear-view mirror to peruse the Hades marquee so inimical to my eidolon transmute into the glorious piece of dadaist propaganda I conjured, with me as the jesus paraded atop the crimson '57 convertible Cadillac in my delicious valkyrie attire and Thea and Candora as the crucifying Madonnas. This presentation as an ad for Hades Hose, a blow to business and about to evince a new bible garter belt rage. "You fucking nutcase", I shouted to upbraid her for having absconded with our erotic ludism to such unforeseen levels of belligerence, I had actually conceived an arcane reprisal for her, replete with years of subjugation in possible commonplace matrimony but with a finger to my lips she stilled me: "If you never love in life", she sermonized, "you'll never take the memory of it into death—which is a prolonged phantasy (as life is)—till you're born again." She was about to return upon the hour, she then explained, only meant to entrance by fright as I had suspected. It turns out her viola de gamba guru, the gangling Gunther Marmosette, founding member of the noted Bartholdy Trio, in residence at the school, had broken his thumb attempting spectacular new head stand asana in order to combat an attack of the jaundiced eye of begrudging (which, as is well known, along with his closeted heterosexuality, he had made it his life's work to eradicate), and had called her in to replace him in the trio for pre-sold-out New York performance. She was rushed to the airport in a limousine without a cell phone to arrive just in time for coruscating performance, with the audience forcing seven encores and another show where her viola de gamba auspiciously intruded itself as a sonar salamander salivating for passengers, and thus transmuting her into the star I knew she already was. In a moment of jealous frenzy her guru, still in the grips of the begrudging attack, had chopped off his thumb to spite them and she was instantly appointed in his place. It turns out they never had a taste for his sacerdotal teutonics in the first place. She rushed back from the airport to give me the good news but finding me gone, her divining clairvoyant sensors, enhanced as they were by the eruption of her instant glory nodes, had told her where I was and that she was to save me. No, she had never opted for sedition as I had paranoically suspected. I wanted to fall on my knees before her and call her my goddess but my position forced me to abandon this plan; instead I recalled the indignity Candora had subjected me to and I shouted: "You bitch, it took me four fucking hours to write your ignorant paper!" "Yes", she yelled, "It must be tasty, can I have it? You were supposed to meet me today behind the Vice-Cancellery to hand it to me. Where were you? It's due later today. I waited for four hours, then in despair I rushed to your house where I ran into Thea whom I had long aspired to from afar. Thank goddess we found you!"

They drove me home. There was much to do over my new stockings, especially by Candora. Thea was more austere in her rhetorical displays and I am sure her caution was no more than pure entrancement transmuted to a momentary bow to envy: "I have stockings you couldn't endure", her lashes glamoured, "someday I'll wear them for you." Following the spider's admonition I vowed silence in this regard until the auspicious moment arrived to present her with the *cadeau* cum poem. Who was I? Now that I had transmuted my masculine disorder entirely. Was I fated to be a mere hierodule to these Corybantic Cybelles?, I wondered and yawned. I should be a recipient to the ordination of the highest degree of ambiguity, I laughed. Candora marveled at Thea's tiny penis and took it between her lips, but languor had already overcome me. I called in sick and then I slept.

AMNESIA, LOWER APPALACHIA,

Dear Mother,

I debated for a bit whether to start out this letter to you by saying dear Gisele or Dear Mother. I opted for dear mother because it is to you as my mother that I am writing this letter; Gisele is your name but if you were simply just Gisele and not my mother it wouldn't mean that much, there wouldn't be such an emotional charge as I assume there is in my heart regarding you as my mother. I hesitated for many years to write this letter to you as I didn't feel I could reach deep enough and "plumb the depths" of the emotions and the, I assume, "emotional baggage" that exists in my heart regarding you. Last night Diane, who teaches modern dance here at the school, suggested, after an intimate conversation she and I had, that I should write you this letter; she was so sincere in her intent, I was impressed by the sincere and intent manner in which she stared into my eyes, and I knew I should follow her advice. Also, Sheila suggested I should be speaking to you, I spoke to her on the phone about two weeks ago or so and told her of the heaviness I still carry in my heart in regards to you and she suggested that I should talk to you; I tried to talk to you while in unconstrained congress with the imponderable, I can communicate with the entire universe when I am in congress with imponderable, but nothing much happened at first; then the other day the poison exploded and I didn't feel it was appropriate to spew such poison at you while in congress with the imponderable and I tried my best, in spite of the heaviness gripping my heart, to tell myself that there is something I have done in a past life that merited my having you for a mother; the line from a poem by my friend Will Alexander occurs to me now, the sun cut off in my heart, that's how I mostly feel and I feel that it has something to do with my relationship with you. As I am here alone with my computer keyboard and the screen and I will write whatever comes to me in regards to you and the many things I wish to tell you. What I hope for is that I have a catharsis of sorts and that I feel there is a final understanding between us, whether we're going to see each other again or not. Speaking of seeing each other again, and relating this to what I said a little bit earlier, about past lives, once, many years ago, it must be about twenty years ago, while in congress with the imponderable, I had a vision of myself as an ocean brigand. As a sea brigand I practiced the paramita of white slave trading; the time, I assume, was about 1300 or 1400; I was wearing a breast plate, it was a dark and cloudy night, I recall the thickness of the clouds and the indigo sky and the molten sea; and I drowned in the sea a young woman, a blonde who had been my lover; someone perhaps whom I had kidnapped; she was crying and imploring but I had no regard for her fear and didn't listen to her imploring; I enjoyed the power of cruelty; or the cruelty of my power; even now to think of it I feel a kind of an erotic excitation, just like I felt another time when I saw myself in ancient India, my body trembles now to as I write this down, a subtle silk-like shiver, walking through the bazaar, a large dark man, living only by my senses, a ravisher, content with myself, rubbing my belly with satisfaction as I traipse down the paths between the booths at the bazaar; and I suspect that these are some of the acts I committed in the past to get the karmic retribution of having a mother like you who persecuted me and who was not a real mother to me, whom I don't see right now as having been a real mother to me; though it is difficult to accept these acts as the cause of my effects, I still wish to blame you for the sort of mother you have been. I know that while you were alive, if I told you about reincarnation and past lives you might not have believed me, or you would have been hesitant to accept these ideas; but now you probably have had a chance to see for yourself, and if you're not yet on your way to being reborn and you're still in state of insubstantiality and you're listening to me and paying attention to what I'm writing, you will understand, you do understand; and I want to get this out of the way. I wanted to write to you in Romanian but since I have a better grasp of the English language and since you understand English well I will write to you in English, and perhaps sometimes revert to Romanian if the case calls for it; because since Romanian is my "mother tongue", meaning that you as my mother first spoke to me in Romanian and Romanian is the first tongue I heard, from your mouth, I assume the core of my emotions are in Romanian, are associated to the Romanian language and so perhaps writing in English is not such a great idea; but the words are coming out in English right now and I feel a degree emotional intensity as I write them so I will continue to write in my English.

Perhaps on account of what I might have done to you in past lives you tried to subjugate me and dominate me. Not long before you went to the hospital for the last time, I think it was mid-July, when you went to the hospital, that is, I just went to look it up, it was in the first half of July, but I wanted to check because July 16 is Thea's birthday, but more about her later, we had gone on a drive together, it was one of the few times I took you for a drive and I was angry with you and frustrated because I couldn't tell you anything, our commu-nication was always thwarted, you were as always stubborn and unwilling to conciliate, and I brought up the fact that once when I was maybe 5 or 6, I couldn't be sure right now how old I was then, I had done something which in your eyes was the wrong thing to do, I didn't behave according to standards, I did something for which I needed, according to you, to be punished and you requested that I get down on my knees and beg you forgiveness and kiss your feet. You said, what imagination you got, you wouldn't admit to it, though I remembered it clearly, certainly I can't be too sure right now because I mentioned it to you so it's only the memory of my telling you this and not the true memory, because each time we remember something it is already a copy of the original event so the next time we remember it we remember the remembering and not the original event, we remember the remembering and we remember to remember how it felt so along with the memory we remember the attached feelings, it's a whole package deal that we recall. And then at times we recall something and share it with a friend and the interpretation gets attached to it then because of the interpretation of the friend or acquaintance; the friend or acquaintance is someone who means something to us and their interpretation becomes part of our interpretation; this is a letter I am writing to you so I feel obliged, I feel pressure not to get involved into a philosophical interpretation of my memories; but on the other hand it is me writing this and I can't tell for sure what it is that you want to hear and I will write what I feel I want to write and that's that. Why do I want to remember all this? It's not just writing the letter to you, I am using this letter to remember something that perhaps lies at the core of my being which prevents me from developing further, some form of amnesia at my core which prevents me, prevents my psychic emotional life from opening up, something perhaps I don't want to see, look at, experience, feel. This word amnesia and the word mother seem intertwined at my core and my present work, which I am writing right now, A Spy in Amnesia, may be suffering right now because I am not yet able to plunge, to dive freely, into my amnesia; so far I have explored only my erotic phantasies, which certainly I would never have been able to share with you. My erotic phantasies started when I was a very young, though again I don't recall when they began, the exact age, that's not important except to psychologists and social scientists who follow demographics. But they began perhaps, more then likely, when I saw a comic book style history of Magellan and his travels, I think I only recall a mysterious shiver before then, a new guilt to disorder me; there was a some sort of mutiny on board of the ship and one man was putting another under arrest. Both men wore Renaissance dress, long vermillion stockings, they all had thin and well shaped long legs, it's clear now the artist had an interest in sketching such entrancing legs, it doesn't matter whether they belong to men or women, the entrancement cannot be denied by any societal entreaties, and the arresting officer had put his foot, ensconced in a dainty shoe sporting a silky tassel, on top of the to be arrested man's foot, also tassel shod, as a sign of dominance; and this picture remained with me till now and became the material source of all phantasies produced by my erotic factory. My desire to wear Renaissance clothes and stockings is still as strong an obsession now as it was then when my erotic phantasies began to take root. I was cata-pulted into ecstatic transcendence by the influence these images exerted on me and my internal phantasmic factories went to work to produce elaborate dramas into which I immersed myself each night, both as participant—I played all the characters—and as observer. The switch that turned on the lights on this drama was within easy reach inside my pajama pants. At the time you told me that masturbation is bad for you, both you and David told me that, though I can't recall exactly what it is that specifically you told me about masturbation; I can't even recall the Romanian word for it, though in street parlance a masturbator was called a "labag-iu", a pejorative, someone who worked it with his paw, "laba", the Romanian for paw, in order to downgrade you to the status of an animal. Still, as soon as I discovered mastur-bation which was the switch to my new found phantasy fac-tory, the two of them would not have worked without one another, I began to masturbate every single night; though now to think of it, according to the world I masturbated while according to me I engaged my life into, my life was abducted by entrancing and bewitching events; at the time, in the beginning, there was no sperm that spurted out of me, but a dry orgasm which was more pleasurable than anything I had experienced till then and the only source of true pleasure and fulfillment that I can recall at this moment that I experienced at that time. Everything else seems obscure, all the events of that time which are significant to my life, which were significant to my life then; I will perhaps return to the phantasies, which, after all these years, still make me uncomfortable to speak of, and which I am still looking to fulfill. And I am wondering what you're thinking as I tell them to you as I am wondering if you know what I mean, as I am wondering if you knew then what the content of my imagination was; I can't picture you accepting this content of my imagination then, I assume you would have taken me to the doctor, you would have worried I was insane, you would have gotten council on my aberration from my doctor aunt Mina or someone else, I don't know if the political situation at the time, circumscribed as it was by the chokehold of local Marxism would have allowed for such imaginal content; (and the thought occurs to me, what if, say, you and I had a relationship at that time where I could have told you about my erotic factory, I didn't know at the time they were "erotic", what did I know at the time?, and you said what an incredible imagination you have, please continue to enjoy yourself, you'll get many years of pleasure from these phantasies, they will be unimaginable wealth of delight for you, your whole life will explode out of those marvelous phantasies! Or perhaps, you are a great artist, you should attempt to eliberate yourself of masturbation, you should use these imagination to create great art!) but not only was I not prized by you and David for what I was, you expected me to be someone else and never really bothered to investigate or be concerned about who I was, what I was about, what my life needed at the time, at this moment I too wonder what my life needed at the time, my destiny seems to have been that there was no mentor at the time to guide me, to help me esteem my life for what it was, was my life only composed of this over-whelming erotic imagination, nothing else? Because other-wise, what was I? What value had I? I had no social value because I was not prized as a soccer player, I was cursed on account of being a murderer of their christ, I recall wishing to not be a christ murderer, one who on top of it all mastur-bated, I recall being with non-christ murdering friends in the neighborhood, I can't really define them as friends, more like other kids I hung out with, I recall being with them and thinking it would be good if they thought I wasn't a christ murderer and just then someone says he's a christ murderer, I remember being perhaps with Florin and this thought occurs to me out of nowhere that christ murderers are bed-bugs, I don't know why bedbugs except they are intransigent and of a disturbing yellowish color and you get rid of them and Florin says, for no reason at all, out of the blue, christ murderers are like bedbugs, I don't know what caused that comparison either in my mind or in his mind, something to do with the lack and debility of the masturbating christ mur-derer, in my mind I associated the christ murderer with lack and debility and with masturbation,—the thought occurs to me that this system of beliefs, about masturbation and debil-ity and christ murderers existed in the culture itself, Andrei told me once that the order of St. Michael, a fascist right wing organization, claimed as its eternal foes all homosexuals, masturbators and christ murderers—each time I masturbat-ed in those early days, right after the climactic moment of ecstatic transcendence, I inspected my mental state to see if I was still sane by asking myself my name and the name and number of the street where I lived and there was something else I inspected for, because I remember that David said I would go crazy if I masturbated, he pointed to me the crazy guy down the street and said he was like that because he was a labagiu and I don't remember right now what you said, I think you said that I would lose my memory if I masturbated and then I checked to see if I still remember where I lived and what my name was. But maybe there was something else you said and I inspected the condition of my memory in order to check up on my sanity. I don't know why it is you never understood what I was, not even a bit, you only understood it in terms of accusations and comparisons, you're like your uncle Hirsch, you said, you have a persecution complex, and uncle Hirsch was also, in my opinion, inept, unsure, spineless. And all my soccer playing friends called me a sissy and even when I was born, I recall you told me this, my grand-uncle Doctor Wolff, who brought me into this world, sprinkled me with dogbane and wolf-hound blood, so I don't end up being a sissy.

Anyway, you're at a point right now when it won't help you to say that these things I speak of are gross, that you don't want to listen to them.

There is a line by Bob Dylan in one of his songs, Ballad of a Thin Man: There ought to be a law against you coming around. I feel as though there were a law against me coming around, but "we'll make an exceptions for you, but don't you forget it." I think this is at the core of my life, I feel as though they want to chase me away, hunt me for sport, everywhere I go, and I am always afraid for my life. Is this how you felt? Is this what you gave me? What happened to you during the second world war? Did you get raped by he Germans? The local fascists? What is it that frightened you? Why were you always so frightened? I don't know you and now you're so far away and the past is so far away; I don't remember anything, the memories are so vague, what exactly did you do that made me hate you like that? Was there one event or a series of events that cemented this hatred I have of you? I hope that by dissolving the cement I will recall the event and will let you go and I can be free.

You know, once while I was in LA the first time, in 1968, I was hanging around with some friends and I said my mother didn't give me birth, my mother aborted me; I said that about you, I was complaining a lot about you at that time; I was switching back and forth between hating you and hating David. I don't know now why I hate both of you so much. Recently though, after the flu and the winter which was so difficult on account of my relationship with Thea which, if you've been watching me, you probably know all about it, still I will tell you about it, while in congress with the imponderable I spoke to you and promised you that if I get Thea to marry me we will have children and you will get to be our daughter; afterwards I had doubts, I don't know if I can take another lifetime with you, not so soon anyway, but I wanted to tell you that in case you didn't hear it then.

But did you feel that same way, that there was a law against you coming around? In that we are sisters. (I say sisters because you used to say that you should have had a daughter, whenever you were displeased with my behavior—I must explore at some point this concept of 'behavior'), I want to tell you about one of the erotic practices between me and Thea: I wore stockings and garter belts, the same stockings and garter belts that I bought for Thea and she put her finger in my anus to try to fuck me there, though her finger didn't go all the way in. My anus was tight. She tried and I squirmed, I sighed like a woman and asked Thea to tell me I am her woman and her whore. I am getting turned on just to remember it now; is it upsetting you? I don't think it is because I hope in your passing you transcended the chokehold of civilization's discontents. I suppose that now you have no more inhibitions. You were always so inhibited. I was always curious what your personal erotic phantasies were, you never shared any of that with me, you never spoke about this, not to me, I doubt you spoke to anyone about it, though I feel towards the end, your end, last couple of years, you were confusing me with David and you had a sort of erotic fixation on me, there are two times when you were "way out there", when you entered a sort of a Nervalian (as in Gerard de) dreamscape, when you had mostly abandoned any reason to grip onto the constriction of reality, I mean the time when you showed me your naked body in the hospital, you dropped your gown right in front of me and said to the nurse I was your husband, and this was shocking to me, but the surprise was that for a 92 year old woman your tits still stood up pretty good, I wonder why or how they could have done that, preserved themselves so well at that age, but still I found it disgusting, I found your wrinkled old skin disgusting, I found you as a threat to my erotic life, but you were always a threat to my erotic life, I recall once when I was maybe seven or eight and I got into a fight on the street, somewhere on Negru Voda and it was a fight that kids usually have (actually a fight that occurred with an intransigent loather of christ murderers) and you came in and tried to separate us and I remembered you started to wail, whimper and snivel, you stupid woman, I wanted to say and slap you, you stupid stupid woman; and I recall once, maybe about the same time, that I said to you sometimes you make me want to slap you and you became livid and wouldn't speak to me for a long time, a few days, which was a long time when you're a child, you wouldn't forgive me even though I asked you to forgive me, because I needed your love not because at heart I believed I did something wrong, I asked you to forgive me, that was real big with you, this begging for forgiveness, you were such a self righteous bitch, that's why I hated you, you were such a believer in the institution of 'mother' that you forgot to be a mother, more recently while in LA a few years ago you told me how a cat that you tried to befriend scratched you and you did something, what did you do, something where you showed your stubborn self-righteousness to the cat, you got your revenge on the cat, you were so proud of your stubborn self-righteousness, and how I despised you for it, anyway what surprised me since the flu is that I missed you, I missed you before, I would suddenly miss you like a part of me that was suddenly missing, not that I missed you with longing but I missed you, and during the flu when I felt such loneliness I realized that I couldn't talk to you anymore, that I couldn't tell you anything anymore, that there were things I wanted to tell you though it was vague what it was I wanted to tell you, I wanted perhaps to share my life with you and also I was thinking of the time when a close friend told me who the hell are you writing for if not your mother, and you were gone, you weren't there and I felt as though my life was meaningless because I couldn't tell you all these things and there was absolutely no one else to tell these things to, I couldn't tell them to Thea because at that time she wasn't listening to me, we weren't as close and loving then as we are now, not much later

What is it that you wanted from me? especially in those last two years, especially towards the end, is that what you were feeling, this loneliness, this despair that I felt too these last two weeks? This feeling of meaninglessness, lack of life force? What did you do to merit this destiny? To end your life this way? Was it my fault, did I fail the test that I couldn't give you any affection? That I couldn't soothe you? I felt so disgusted by you, by your constant demanding, complaining, lack of gratitude, stubbornness, you had no graciousness at all and I hated you for growing so old without acquiring any wisdom, without any ability to speak to me about anything, you didn't take the time to speak about anything that was going on in your mind; I understand your complaint that no one calls you, you complained that no one calls you; I understand because no one calls me either; yesterday the only person who called me outside of a wrong number was Thea from San Francisco, which I was so happy about; and there was a phone call from Renata who left a message from Pennsylvania. That's all; my loneliness is unbearable too, and I felt my life force waning during the flu, during the whole winter with the relationship with Thea, going so rough; even now as I write, my heart is a tight ball, and I feel depressed, I only feel happy when Thea calls me, or when I get a vibration from Thea. I don't know why I feel so depressed, I wanted a mother to take care of me when I was depressed but you were never a mother to me, whenever I was in trouble you only scolded me, you never took my side when I was growing up, you were never on my side. I could always count on being scolded by you, yes I got in trouble a lot but you never thought about how I felt, you were a mother, you were supposed to think about these things, but you were only an authoritarian bitch, a cold hearted bitch is what you were, so few were the times I could count on you to soothe me emotionally. Your whole life was symbolized by that story you told me that you were so proud of, when you were a little girl and you brought that glass of water to the friend of the family who asked you for a glass of water, the gentleman, as you called him, I don't know why I pictured him in a gray redingote and top hat and cane, and he slapped you for bringing him the glass holding it by the rim instead of the correct way, which is on a plate, and you were so proud for him doing that and you related the story to me so proudly, so as to reach me, as though that punishment you received is such great thing to treasure, you never gave me any self esteem, maybe you yourself never had any self esteem, why do I forget so much from those days back in Romania? It's there, at the edge of my heart, perhaps that's why my heart hurts, but for the times that my heart hurt over the years I never told you about it except once, and then I regretted it but I won't bring it up now, it was perhaps my pride not to tell you as I wanted you to think me a man, an independent being, someone who could take care of himself, someone independent of you, so much in my heart, so much turmoil in my heart, so much pain, sure you have pain too but as my mother shouldn't you have tried to have a conversation with me about my pain, shouldn't you ever tried to advice me concerning what my concerns were, were your concerns so far removed in time from mine that you didn't understand it, why was there such a gap between us?

I hated you for always putting me down, how you always demeaned me, how you never had any faith in life. How when I told you about a great possibility for a new job, you instantly leaped to advising me that it was a bad idea to take a new job, that I should keep the old one, instead of congratulating me on the fact I was offered a new job. Your advice always made me ill. Whoever gave you the right to give advise? How when I told about my new teaching position here, you began gesticulating histrionically like a mad woman about to have a heart attack, with back of palm to brow, only worrying about what would happen to you. Yes, I know, there were the eighties when I had such a hard time and I was so unhappy and I couldn't get work at all, and it is true that that you gave me money, you secretly smuggled me money that David didn't know anything about, it is true, but you did everything with such constricted dolor in your heart, you never once gave me encouragement that things will change; all you did was complain about my unrestricted contraband with the imponderable, my incessant congress with the imponderable, which you resented so that it eventually sucked your life force. You tried to make me sick with your sickness, everything you did made me sick; you were so restricted in everything, and you tried to bring me down to your restricted level, you would have been really happy if I hadn't succeeded in life because you would not have lost control; everything was for you, not a thing was for me; that

I have such a tough time now with my self esteem is because you never paid attention to me and to who I was; I feel helpless now to rescue myself, I will go on with my life yes, but I don't feel there is any use to it, I need to rescue myself from this low self esteem that you contaminated me with. And I hate to continue this letter with negatives only, but right now I feel sick to my heart and I need a drink or to smoke dope to get high but I don't drink anymore, I am feeling so restricted, I am feeling my restriction because you never valued me, except as a toy, I was never a human being with my own feelings and my own ideas and thoughts, and then the defeats I had in the eighties, you held those against me, you held unto those because it was the only way you could feel victorious, perhaps your incessant inner dialogue had to do with the fact that it was just another way you were betrayed by life, that now that I am successful, that I am making a living doing what I want to do, I disrespect you, I pay no more attention to you. You tried to steal, suck out whatever life I had created for myself, the life that I got back by plunging into the imponderable, you tried to take that away from me too; I am so sorry that I am pointing these things out to you but in the last years there was absolutely nothing that I liked about you, nothing, nothing where you gave something, where you showed a little bit of gratitude, where you tried to give something without destroying; even when I tried to tell how proud I was that I drove directly from Louisiana to here without a stop for fifteen hours, you said don't do that anymore; how I hated you for that too, that you took away everything from me, I suppose that it meant something to me that to get your approval, to get some praise from you, I guess it does, perhaps I am weak in that I want that, and now realizing that you died and you never had a real conversation, we never had a vindication, I feel so meaningless, I feel like what's the use, I feel like nothing, I feel like I need to be validated; you were a dog always biting at me, biting at my heart, my feelings, my life, you hated me for being successful no thanks to you, you hated me because I didn't give you credit for raising me, but my whole childhood you never praised me, you praised cousin this and cousin that, but you never praised me. And at the end you were so needy and I hated you because you constantly crowded me, you wanted to take my life from me as you did when I was growing up, you always wanted to deprive me of my life, you needed and needed and needed from me but you never gave, sure I recall that when I had a bad hangover when I was a teenager you spent some time with me and soothed me and once when David was working nights we watched a Laurel & Hardy show, the one where they end up all distorted at the end, while in the same bed and we loved each other, it felt pleasant to be together, yes it was pleasant I recall, it was a moment of love between us, it was almost like being in love; and then, you're the one who remembered this, you said don't you remember when we watched Laurel and Hardy once, when I brought charges against you that one time on that ride not long before you died, that you made me kiss your feet when I was a child in order for you to forgive me, which you wouldn't admit, which you denied, though its meaning you understood because you told me how you pro- tected me against Bella's abuse when she picked at my penis, she grabbed my penis supposedly, which I don't recall, but no matter, you countered with how much we loved each other when I was a kid, how we would butt our heads together and stare closely into each others' eyes till all looked distorted and say eyeneye, let's play eyeneye, you remembered that, I am sorry perhaps to take away from you that illusion that you may have been a good mother, so late in life, must have destroyed you, I understand how one feels if life has lost its meaning completely, believe me I really do, I experienced it lately, it was horrible, I understood what you meant when you said you wanted to die, why can't I die, I wanted to die too and I accused myself for not being more compassionate to you these last few months, that I couldn't put away the disgust you caused in me, the suffering you caused in me; still, I look now at the ugly shape of life at the time, how you climbed lower and lower on the scale of life status, it broke my heart to see it, I couldn't do anything about it and cursed my fate that I was left alone with you, that I was the only one to witness this tragedy, no one to share this with, worried about being destinally punished for abandoning you, for perpetually losing my temper at you; and I must say I was impressed that you did change, that when you reached just about the lowest point, when you were at the rehabilitation center, you showed some gratitude, I recall especially the intense feeling of gratitude you showed, how your face lit up when you heard my voice when I returned from Switzerland, perhaps I hoped then you reached some sort of peace with yourself, you lost need to be looked after, except in the most basic physical manner, you had perhaps had some sort of an internal change because what is a human being once he or she gets to that point when there is nothing to do, nothing to create meaning with, when there is nothing left in life except the present moment and the present moment offers no distraction, no creativity, no fulfillment, no friends, no love, a son yes, one who comes to visit every few days or weeks, but what else is there, to die among strangers, among people who have a different religion, a different manner of being, different values and when just being nice has no more meaning, where you have no understanding, where there is no peace, just the incessant inner regurgitation of life's unsolved situations and issues, the incessant rehashing in the mind of the past, of the could have beens and who done me wrongs, etc etc etc. I know that sort of hell you must have gone through, I know, I know lack of love, I know being abandoned by the women I loved most, I know the fear of abandonment, I know how fragile love can be; at least you had a life long companion, you had this companion for 57 years, he gave your life meaning though I am not sure I know what really went on between you two because I was kept out of your lives almost completely, I was a stranger, I can't feel myself, looking back, being a participant in your lives, your lives were completely separate from mine, you never invited me to be part of your lives except as a kind of a guest, we never shared, I was an uninvited guest, that's all, certainly certain things were shared but over all we weren't a family, I am writing and writing and I don't know if I am writing to you, whether you're hearing me, and I don't want to cause you pain, which is bread in French, and I don't know the state you're in, I don't know the sort of understanding you have in the state you're in, I hope you are at a higher state then the one you were possessed of in your embodied state, with that disgusting old body of yours which you finally shed, but I hope that asking the imponderable to come to your aid helped, I hope that you are not in pain anymore, I hope you have realized some wisdom, though to say I hope you have realized some wisdom makes me feel arrogant, but I do hope that you realized some happiness, some sort of ful-fillment, that you are fulfilled as a human being presently, that you will be reborn in good circumstances, hell, I don't even mind right now having you for my child if it means to have this child with Thea, this Thea whom I love so much, I love her more than my life, I say that and maybe I even mean that, but I do love her so much, she gives me so much meaning, and maybe I want you to rejoyce in my love for her and maybe I ask you to help me in any way you can so that this woman marries me and that we have a happy and long life together. I hope to have a happy and long life with Thea.

Thea is now in San Francisco; she had an audition for the San Francisco conservatory of Music; she plays the viola; do you want to know more about her? I feel I can tell you now because you can't criticize me anymore and you can't put a hex on our relationship; because one reason I didn't tell you things is because I felt you that simply telling you would put a hex on it; I assume that where you are you can understand what I mean when I say hex, though I don't know if you knew enough English while embodied, to know what a hex was. The funny thing about it is that you're the one who taught me this superstition, that I shouldn't tell anyone anything that I have presently brewing, especially an opportunity I hope to succeed with until it happens. You're the one who taught me about hexes, and whether it is a superstition or not I don't know to this day but on occasion I told and I won anyway. I met Thea (again) seven days after you passed away, and I think this is perhaps significant because seven was your favorite number. Thea is German, which might give you reason to be upset, and she is twenty-seven years old. I don't know how you feel about that, her being German and her being twenty-seven. You might be upset by the fact that she is German on account of what you had to suffer from the Germans during the second world war. I don't know what happened to you then, I don't know what sort of humiliations you were subjected to, I don't know what sort fears you went through; I understand it must have been awful and that on account of my limited experience with, in other words because I never had to endure that sort of trial and tribulation, I can't imagine what it must have done to you; I know persecution of christ murderers to some extent, but still, it was contained, it was mostly covert though sometimes bubbling over into the overt. While I was at school comments were addressed to me a few times; always feeling that I didn't belong, as I said earlier, I felt there was a law against me coming around, that I was un uninvited guest; I never felt this place is mine, this world is mine, these people are my people, I always felt their customs were not my customs; not that I felt that your customs were my customs either, I didn't feel that the table manners you taught me, though to tell you the truth I don't remember too many table manners you taught me, except perhaps to cut the meat with the knife then switch hands and put the fork in the right hand so I could lift the morsel of meat to my mouth, which was cumbersome to me, I never understood why you just couldn't lift the meat to your mouth with your fingers and just bite and to this day I still am not sure whether this custom of not putting your elbows on the table is still observed. (But that Thea now drills me daily in these table manners...) And as far as my introduction to society, which was supposed to be that you taught me how to dance, yes, you spent an evening or two teaching me the waltz, the tango, and the foxtrot, perhaps David participated in this too, I have a vague memory of it in the living room which was also then your and my bedroom, or perhaps by then I had my own room, I don't remember, I just recall a vague living room and I don't recall at all the dance, or perhaps there is a dance and I didn't know how to keep the rhythm or the step, the trend at the time was parties, you were trendy if you were invited to parties, I don't even remember how to say parties in Romanian, what was the Romanian word for parties, I was never invited to parties, I was always chased out of the world's community, if not chased at least not invited, or if invited, only very rarely, and if invited I didn't know how to talk to the world, had no idea what to talk about with the girls, didn't know how to kiss, I didn't know anything because you didn't teach me anything, maybe it's always like that, maybe it's like that everywhere, that parents don't teach their children the most important things, so I didn't know nothing, I was an idiot, I always felt I was an idiot, I saw no value in me, even if they had invited me, I have no idea why they would have invited me, there wasn't even anything that interested me, not politics, not reading, sure I read a little Jules Verne, but who didn't, a few mysteries, a little from Tom Sawyer, a little from Huckleberry Finn, why didn't you guide me even a little back then? You admitted, after David died, that both of you never communicated with me, never tried, you admitted that was your mistake, but after that you never continued with your self-reflection, you never attempted to right any of your wrongs, in terms of the higher teachings what you have is a constricted life state where you cannot see beyond your own self, beyond your own needs, which in your office as mother is a very bad qualification to have, you do not qualify for office as mother with qualifications like that, still, perhaps I do not recognize or remember the good things you did for me, perhaps I only remember the bad because perhaps it is not a matter of remembering the good and the bad things, perhaps this is only putting things on the scale, counting, accounting, and you know how I despise accounting, counting, measuring, the thought occurs to me that David was an accountant, but that's too facile a connection to make, what we're speaking of is a condition of life at the core of the person, an ability to be open to life itself, as a mother you need to be open to the life of the child, but you were constrained by your social program, the social program you were raised on along with your own constrainment, along with your own addiction to the self-punishing rules you were made to swallow and learn to like, along with your own distorted manner of feeling and thinking, but the teachings I believe in say I must take complete responsibility for being born in this circumstance, here I am, a Whitman being constrained by being born to a constricted mother like you. Perhaps it is the reason I was born with you, to enlighten you through my own example, o it was so painful to be with you all my life and especially the last two years you were here. Because you were my mother, and you tried to bring me down to your level, you were my mother, which no matter how you look at it, it causes a man an incision right into the heart, I had to live, I was forced to live without a heart, you tried to destroy me, though I don't know whether you knew it, but maybe that's all you knew, maybe it is at the heart of being a christ murderer to destroy the young, to squelch the life from the children, all that remains is a mind that may contribute in some degree to society, but nothing else left, without life force, without vigor, without personality, nothing left inside them, left to be encouraged, goaded on only by women they don't truly love, to be encouraged only by drinking and smoking marijuana. You were one of life's curses. It is why I carry so much pain now, so much discouragement, I have no love for you right now, I look inside and I feel your rankling, you only knew how to rankle my heart, rankle and rankle, like the barking of a rabid dog. Because the mother is so connected to the sun (son), it's a live connection as though there is an umbilical chord attached to the heart strings and you know how to pull at it constantly; beleaguer, harass, irritate, rankle, pester, plague. Rankle especially, I seem to recall thinking rankle, you know how to rankle, I spoke to myself as I walked up the long hallway to your little apartment at the retirement home. I had the inkling to look up rankle in the dictionary: from Middle English, *ranklen*, to fester, via Middle French, *rancler*, via Old French, raoncle, festering sore, via Medieval Latin, dracunculus, diminutive of draco, serpent: to cause anger, irritation, or deep bitterness. You are a vengeful bitch, calculating, you believed in an eye for an eye a tooth for a tooth, it's hard to believe you were so ugly inside, so small-minded, yet so timid, so repressed, so reserved, so well trained in the arts of social charm and gossip. The way you smiled with strangers and recited from your repertoire of charm, you even surprised me. Like when you first met Sanda, no one would ever guess that small minded self of yours from the way you comported yourself when she came over and you met her for the first time... Were you vengeful and calculating because you were masticating on the wrong deeds done to you by David's mother? I know perhaps I am doing myself harm by concentrating on your small mindedness, by blaming you like this, by not accepting the fact that that's how you were, that I shouldn't expect more than that from you and I should just simply aspire for your happiness and thus change whatever is inside me that caused me to be born in this circumstance; but it is a shock right now even to me to discover this disease which I see is still now in my life; because I want to open up my life, I want to open up my heart and be generous, I want life to circulate through me freely, I want poetry and art, and I feel your energy is dragging me down; I just recalled right now what a friend told me, that they can try to drown you, they'll get their arms around your neck, they will try but they will never succeed.

I lost the train of thought because even though I had planned to write this morning I didn't. Thea came over and she stayed the night and we woke up very late. She was very nice to me last night, and I gave her a back rub with the body, mind & spirit relaxing oil. We made love for a long time afterwards, and in the morning we held each other for a long time and it was comfortable to hold each other for so long and then sleep like that. It was so nice that I wondered how could it be so good, especially considering the fact that the whole of the winter it was so horrible, she treated me horribly, I can't think at this moment everything that she did but I will, in the writing of this letter some of the ways she behaved with me. I suffered horribly yet I continued believing I would turn it around. I feel that I should tell you these things which make me less of a hero in your eyes because I wanted to be a hero in your eyes, I wanted you to see me as a man and there is a network of actions which supposedly make one a man, an accepted member of one's imagined society, one that is considered to be a top member of one's society, a strict code of behavior, the living up to a strict code of rules, keeping face I guess, so that one does not become someone who is laughed at by others, though the standards of others could be despised by one, one still tries to live up to these standards, like being known as a great lover, being seen with lots of women, being thought of as the boss with the women; you must not be seen as feminine if you're a man, you must not be seen as someone who is pushed around by women, someone who sticks around with a woman if she treats him in a demeaning manner, like Thea treated me; I guess I could easily tell you all these things now because I am confident I will not hear the dreaded advice that you always gave me, the advice from hell, because I don't believe you're there now, an advice which paid no attention to who I was, advice which demeaned me, advice which took no consideration of my circumstance, of my feelings, of the content of my heart, advice meant to do nothing but rankle the heart. Where exactly did that advice come from? What part of you did it come from? How could you give advice when nothing worked in your life? Your life which you used to distress others with. I must have done something really awful in past lives to get you as a mother. Perhaps you were raped by a German officer and I was that German officer and was reborn as your son. Still in thinking this way I feel no relief; and my purpose is to get rid of you, to get rid of the poisonous influence you have on my life, like a rabid dog's bite on my heart which won't go away, whose mark remains, whose pain remains, whose consciousness-reducing influence still remains. In discerning this, as I discerned it yesterday and the day before yesterday, I saw what a sick person you were, how low the status of your life was, what an animal you were, and was hoping that by understanding it I would be able to overcome the effect of this bite which just doesn't seem to go away. It feels as though this bite is a scar tissue, has hardened to the extent that it's not allowing the flow of life to circulate freely. It is made of judgments and of frozen voices, it is made of your incessant barking, it is made of your evil need to hurt and destroy, it is made of your lack of empathy, your lack of vision, your lack of trying to raise yourself to higher level of being and to a being like me who is made of air, who is made of poetry, who is made of vision, this sort of being that you're made of can only be poison; I need people around me who are also desirous of transcendence, of light and air and who are not made of the cruelty which is the fabric of your being. As I write this do not think that I do not think that someday this will become a novel. It hurts me to say these things directly to you, and I don't know anymore if I am being truthful right now or whether I am attempting to be a Thomas Bernhardt. I don't know how you feel hearing these things about yourself, I am sure they hurt you a lot, though being where you are perhaps you have achieved a great serenity, where you are you're not affected by these things anymore and you look upon my plight with great compassion and empathy; perhaps it is due to your help that Thea is so nice to me now and she loves me so much. Perhaps on account of your encounter with great king Yama of hell but having been able to escape that hell very quickly on account of my intervening with the imponderable for you, you have been able to achieve great peace and you are smiling upon the sausage world; perhaps this lightheaded bubbles I feel upon my head right now are the beneficent vibration you have set in motion with the power of the insubstantial imponderable where you live now. Perhaps you are laughing at my accusations, they are nothing but the purling of a brook in a shady spring forest on sunny day. Who knows; I just can't imagine that you are facing my avalanche of accusations and shuddering in torment and fright at their violence, realizing now, in front of king Yama's mirror, their frightening truth, truth which you did everything you could to avoid looking at while you were embodied; perhaps I make a mistake to think of you as the shriveled old woman I knew you as in the last couple of years of your life, this image of you that I can't shake, that sticks to me like gum to shoes; perhaps on account of my intervening with the imponderable for your sake you were able to shed that countenance and you are now a purling brook, you are mountain air, you are sea, though I can't see you as sea, you are wind, which is a great improvement for you, for I couldn't see you as wind, it's a great imaginative leap for you to be wind, perhaps yours, perhaps you have become the laughing waters of a small river that winds through a forest where you can rest in the shadow, for I can't picture you as a large river, as the Mississippi for instance, a public river, you were always a private person and on that you have not changed, though you may have allowed yourself to become wind, you certainly have not become a public thoroughfare, albeit a watery one, and to think of you as the great Mississippi is something I wouldn't impose you, no, because it's a filthy and polluted river and no matter what you did, I wouldn't wish that on you, for no matter what you did, you are my mother and I love you. I didn't want to write I love you but it came out, "it wrote itself", before I could stop it, I could have perhaps stopped it, but didn't, either because something within me meant it or because I felt guilty. Maybe you have completely changed and it's all because of me, maybe it's all because of my intervening with the imponderable. Still right now I am not sure, with this bite in my heart though I can tell you that in the last few minutes it certainly lighted up, it certainly became light, much lighter anyway, and I am grateful for that. I don't know if we'll ever meet again, I certainly asked that we never meet again when you were alive, I said it to my friends, that if I never see this woman again I will not miss her; I was certain of it then, I was certainly very certain of it then but I am not certain of it now, I felt it in my heart that there was so much that was unsaid, and with you gone, I felt there was no reason for me to say anything anymore because it was you I wanted to say it to, perhaps it was you I wanted to write A Spy in Amnesia to, in spite of the fact that it was mostly about my erotic phantasies, which I would never have told you about when you were in life, I almost said that I would never have dared to tell you but when I thought to write dare I felt ashamed because certainly, I tell myself, I would have dared, what am I afraid of, a wrinkled helpless old woman? Perhaps if I had told you my erotic phantasies it would have offended you, or you would have been very upset, it might have made you dizzy or very sick, very ill, there is the inner life and I doubt you paid much attention to yours, or what I'm trying to say, there is the approved inner life which you are taught it's acceptable to have going on inside of you, and the disapproved inner life which you are told it's not acceptable to have going on inside of you, like erotic phantasies for instance, or "immoral" thoughts, the desire to kill, or maim someone, or hurt them, you see I'm shedding a lot to share this with you, especially now that you can't reply, or maybe you can but you can't criticize what I say, you can't judge me, you can't worry that I'll turn bad for society, that I will embarrass you with you my behavior and thoughts, I will turn out to be a nuisance and that part of you which is me will cause you pain and embarrassment and suffering. It will embarrass you in society, people will speak ill of you because of my behavior, as though you were the mother of someone who turned out to be homosexual for instance, what if I did turn out to be homosexual? Thea has put her finger in my anus and twirled and tried to get it all the way in but didn't succeed because I guess my anus is really tight; but we'll try again; and she put stockings on me and garter belts and it felt absolutely supremely divine to feel their light softness against the skin of my legs; and when she tried to insert her finger in my anus she did it as though she was fucking me in the anus, as though she had a penis, she really intuited I wanted that, that I had an erotic need for that, and I felt somewhat like I was at her mercy which felt like such a relief, release, I wanted the pain and to be totally hers and I said I want to be your woman, I said that to her and she said you are my whore, you are my whore and I said I want to be your whore and I was trembling with pleasure, I said teach me how to be a woman. I can say this to you now that you're not incarnate and I hope you're beyond any sort of judgment and see beyond civilization's discontents; I mean I know when you grew up societal strictures were far more prone to be enforced, not necessarily by the authorities as by the people themselves; you for instance were ready and willing to march for these strictures, you had adopted them from whoever taught them to you. Was it your father? Mother? Girlfriends? Did you ever think to fight against them? Did you ever think to protest? Or did you just take up the flag of restriction? What was it that coaxed you into restriction, into denying your imagination and opting for the plaster of societal behavior? Why were you so willing to give up your life itself? Because if your erotic imagination is not your life itself, what is it? What is life? Sacrifice? Heroic deeds, to save the life of the people who restrict their lives? To save the life of a society that kills life? Since I know nothing about those days of your life, since you told me nothing except the few trifles, that's what I think them, a few trivial non-details about how much fun you had, how you spent your time with your friends skating and walking up and down the boulevard in Braila when you were young and the young men admired you, I saw some of your photographs from that period, all of them so casual, you were sitting at restaurant tables and laughing, that was your life and you said about it it was a good life, but what did you really do then, it was all trifles, you squandered it all in trivial games. Then the war came, and you suffered, and I have no idea what you did then, I have such few details, why did you choose to tell me so little, why did you choose not to share that time of your life with me, why wasn't I part of the family? Who did you recognize in me? It feels as though you didn't believe that I would turn out to be something worthwhile, that you didn't want me to become someone out of the ordinary. As though there were no stars to announce my birth, no great omens. Was there no one around to believe in me, someone to intervene on my behalf? Why did you decide so early I had no talents, what did you see in me that caused you not to try any further? I fought with Sybil, I got into some fights, I don't recall all I did, was I real stupid? Was I all that average? Why so much pressure on my getting good grades? Will he be a good student? Was it perhaps because your own self esteem was so low, your expectations of yourselves were so low? I know that David had singer aspirations, you told me once that he had writer aspirations, we had talented people in the family, my two uncles for instance, published writers. Certainly, they were in prison during the first years of my life and that I suspect must have upset things quite a lot; what did you all feel then? You spoke to me so little about those days. You were, in the last years, more concerned about how David's mother treated you, how badly she behaved towards you, how she slandered you. I need to figure these things out. I need to understand, to get a sense what happened then. How your life functioned, what was going on in there, in that head and heart of yours. Can you speak to me? Perhaps in a dream?

I had no dreams last night, I don't know why I'm telling you this, but since you're my mother I should be able to talk to you about anything, no? Perhaps I am disappointed I had no dreams, perhaps I should blame you for not giving me any dreams but on the other hand I was up late and only slept three and a half hours and so how could you have dreams when you sleep so little? I am going to turn some music on before I come back to write so that between the last word of this sentence and the word starting the next sentence there will be a short pause, though they will be in the next paragraph. It is Stravinsky, Symphony of Psalms, conducted by

Stravinsky himself. I don't feel like writing anything to you right now, I don't feel like dealing with this, maybe because I slept so little last night, who knows but I just don't feel like writing you right now. Thea is late, we are going to Charleston today and were going to leave at 8 am but she woke up late and I was going to pick her up at nine and then she called me again and she said she is making the sandwiches and she will not be ready at nine. Nine thirty I said? Yes. That's fine I said, I'll pick you up at nine thirty. I love Thea so much, I can't tell you how much I love her and I am so happy to be with her. We never resolved last time the German thing, Thea being German and how you feel about it, it's not a question whether you agree or not because whether you had agreed or not that she is the woman for me wouldn't have mattered but to say, for you to say you have my blessing is not bad, though on the other hand I feel resentful that I would want to hear that from you, because I don't need your approval for anything because I am not a mama's boy, never have been. I don't know how you feel about that, but that was an issue with me and I am not feeling too enthusiastic confessing that to you right now. How are you right now? Are you enlightened? Do you understand the nature of the universe? Are you staying in the state of non-substantiality for a while to watch over me and be a protecting angel to me? If you are enlightened maybe you see that, from the enlightened standpoint, you and Thea are related to each other. As I am writing this letter to you, where the primary interest is to share information particular to you and I only, information which only you and I should be interested in for the purpose of sharing information, for the purpose of gossiping perhaps, for the purpose of getting to know each other better, I can't shake the feeling that I am superficial, that I should be writing something a lot more, I mean a lot deeper, because what I have in my heart right now is that I really want to write literature, I am expecting this to be a part of A

Spy in Amnesia more than a letter to you, I feel that this break from A Spy in Amnesia is necessary to be able to write A Spy in Amnesia better, to open up emotionally more, to allow the circulation of ideas and emotions through this opening up to you, allowing the flow and circulation to travel through me, as Diane said on Saturday, you don't mind that Saturday is not spelled with a capital s but what do you know, I wasn't looking and the computer changed it to capital s, anyway, what I was saying is that what Diane said is that I won't be able to go on until I take care of this matter to write this letter to you, so I am writing and writing though I don't feel this is accomplishing any purpose, I am perhaps just wasting time before my trip to Charleston but I rely on your indulgence—perhaps 'dulce' which is 'sweet' is in indulgence, it's also close to 'emulgence' which is milk, since you are my mother after all, since you are in the universe and perhaps right now know more than me because by now clearly on account of my congress with the imponderable, for you are enlightened or somewhere close to that, perhaps you and David are together right now, which reminds me, I gotta stop this and put some rubbers in my bag in for Thea's and my lovemaking tonight, just in case you're planning to make an unexpected appearance before your time, be right back, I am back, indulgence yes, because indulgence has milk in it, like emulgence, lapte, the l is what does it though the g is sort of a rough spot like a scratch in the throat, I don't think there should be any gs in milk though if I say gggggggggggg holding it between the tongue and the lower palate it is a nice vibration that travels throughout the body and refreshes one, it's actually the upper palate, I don't know why I thought the lower palate, actually originally I wrote the upper palate but thought I was wrong. I am doubting that I am really addressing this to you, I don't know I feel the pressure of pressing events, as though there is something very serious that I must tell, I must fess up, as though I ma, see I wrote I ma instead of I am, anyway I don't know, maybe you just want to be entertained right now, maybe you are the womanhood of the universe, I just thought of Lucille Ramieu and I will have to write about her later because it is time to go right now but Luv=cille is a French woman I still phantasize about.

A couple of days have passed since I wrote last; I lost the thread of thought I began and will just begin again, dear Mom. I wrote something down in my notebook, on Thursday morning while driving with Thea towards Charleston, I wrote that "you should be happy, freed as you are of any duties, where your only concern is play and display, freed for instance of motherly duties, you should not be presented with any reason for suffering, you're freed from your own time and so consequently you are free of any sort of judgment as well, so you should easily understand what I am after in A Spy in Amnesia, no?"

Last night while Thea and I were watching TV and planning an erotic encounter later in bed, you came to me and disturbed me. The vision of you laying on the hospital bed after your operation, when I came in to visit you the day before I went to Los Angeles last summer, and you whispered to me, kiss me, and it was only later I realized there was an erotic element in the way you said it, in your intent; and I also remembered last night, the vision of you came to me as a libidinous ghost, a disgusting libidinous ghost, you were imposing yourself on my sexuality, I recalled the time that you were in the hospital about maybe two years ago and I walked in and you dropped whatever it was you were wearing and revealed you naked body to me, I think just before then you told the nurse I was your husband, though I don't know that you really thought I was David though somewhere in your subconscious you confused me with him, you corrected yourself and said he is my son, but still the embarrassment remained because I was left with the sense the nurses thought that I was really your husband and laughed behind my back because they thought me some sort of a strange weird person for marrying a woman as a old as you. That's yet one more thing I resented you for, you could always be counted on to embarrass me, like for instance when I brought Nancy to take you shopping, I did it for you to do you a favor, and I told you she taught Italian at the school and you told her that we lived in Italy when we first left Romania and how I went out on my own and that the girls who lived at Signora Ballestra's told her I should be careful because there were so many homosexuals in Rome and how you were worried about me.

I had to interrupt this letter to you because I didn't feel like writing anymore yesterday afternoon. I felt a lack of desire to continue, though I overall I feel as though I should continue this letter to you, which I am continually questioning, whose purpose I am continually questioning. I am questioning it because I don't know who I am writing this to anymore, do you still exist, are you still concerned with this part of the living? Rilke, the poet, see, I feel compelled for instance to explain, I can't just write Rilke, I have to qualify it by saying the poet because I don't know whether at this point in your development you know who Rilke is, whether after you died you suddenly gained a wealth of knowledge you didn't have before, or whether you are just like you were, this person for whom I had to repeat everything two or three times and then still didn't understand what I meant, so at some point I just had to give up the desire to communicate at all. You never tried to listen so each time I even began a sentence you said huh? before I even had a chance to finish what I had to say, which was ceaselessly unnerving. But perhaps now the veil of ignorance has fallen and you can hear, though it shouldn't matter to me right now, I only wish to communicate out of my heart, and if you don't wish to listen or hear what I have to say, well at least I'm saying it; though I really shouldn't take such a negative view or assume that the communication will be so impossible once again. So anyway, on the way back from Charleston on Friday afternoon I read to Thea from Rilke in Imogen's translation and I wish to share this Rilke with you: he says:

> Of course, it is strange not to inhabit this earth any
> longer,
> to no longer put to use a few freshly learned customs

here of course the customs you could no longer put to use were customs you repeated over and over again over a whole lifetime. I feel hesitant to speak to you about your customs, about the nature of your existence, I sense a horror in it, in your existence, some deeply unresolved conflicts about your sexuality, about the nature of your sexuality coming in conflict with the social stratification at the time, you were obsessed with certain themes perhaps but repressed them because you were so needful of appreciation, so needful of approval, so needful to be part of the group, so little you were your own person, I need to understand what was at your core, what exactly moved you as a person? Rilke says later:

> In the end, they don't need us any longer, the early
> dead:
> one gently grows out of all earthly things, much like a
> child
> is weaned from the softness of his mother's breasts

And you, do you need me still? Was there something you still need from me? Is there something deeply unresolved in you which you still need me to help you with? Do you need to help me resolve something? You see, I am not so horrible after all, because I do believe in your soul's progress. Have you and I terminated all business or is there any business left? Though I hate to say 'business', I wish to remove the concept of trade from all this. Yes, all parts for the progress of souls, as Whitman says. The belief that there is such a thing as a soul, if not a soul then something that wishes, something whose need and desire is to perhaps become more human, more wise, more compassionate, more understanding, more fulfilled, something more than us perhaps but which contains us, which we perhaps are part of, because I am hesitant to say we contain it as perhaps it is uncontainable. (I have to admit that I am feeling bad right now, I'll tell you why: because I have this agenda that this letter will turn into a novel and that it is now becoming a little too "new agey" and unlike Rilke who is profound and profoundly moving, I feel my writing to be trite; but I have got to recall that I am simply writing a letter to you, that I believe Diane when she said that I have to do this first before I can do anything else; it is now almost as a superstition; well not a superstition, because I may have mentioned to you earlier that I wanted to communicate to you, so I shouldn't resent having to write this letter even though it might not turn out to be a novel, and shouldn't resent having to waste my time writing it though it impinges on my writing time for A Spy in Amnesia. Still earlier, working on a A Spy in Amnesia, I felt that I couldn't write anymore, I felt as though I had lost the gumption to write, because it was you I wanted to write for and since now you're gone, there is no one to write to anymore or at least that's how I felt until Diane made me see things in a another way, close to what Sheila had said a couple of weeks earlier, to speak to you.

But us the living ones make the error of drawing too
many distinctions

The eternal stream tears through the boundaries of all
ages and absorbs them with overwhelming sound

So it could very well be you're moving in a reality that's not too distant from mine and it could be the joy and the lightness I feel right now is actually you. I feel a happiness I didn't feel when I woke up this morning when I actually felt sad, I felt despair; perhaps the painful joint between us has changed and I don't need to write you anymore; on the other hand I am feeling so joyful and light because I am writing you, and it is possible that I felt as I did because I didn't write you. Maybe you're looking down at me for writing such tortuous sentences, that my thoughts are frought by such tortuous, meandering paths. But maybe not; since I am your son, you perhaps admire what I write; but on the other hand are you still my mother? If you have given up customs you learned, if you are free from your name, from any duties, from your wrinkled form, are still my mother? I am made uncomfortable by your masquerade as mother, I am made uncomfortable to think of the time in the hospital when you dropped your dress and presented your wrinkled old body to me; now you are not that person anymore, you don't have identification with that body anymore, you are not that body anymore; in writing all this I don't know whether I am writing to you, whether I am communicating anything to you or whether I am simply rehearsing ad absurdum my personal obsessions, my own horrors; it must be, now that I think of it, thinking how seeing your wrinkled ancient body makes me feel, that I am protecting myself against the idea of dying, of my own dying, my own extinction, when I feel disgust thinking of your wrinkled old body which now gone, which is not your body anymore, yet it exists as memory, as dream in my interior landscape, but you perhaps now are free of all this, of your crone body, of the ravages of time, you may be living where there is no time, what was the purpose of your presenting me with all these images I hated? What was the purpose of your presenting me with images that tortured my formulations? Were, do you think, my formulations so limited that they needed to be challenged? Again, I don't know if I want to go this route, travel this mental path; but right after I began the last train of thought I wondered if I am only following my own mental formulations or whether I am really addressing you, and then Thea showed up with the apple cake that she made and as I sat with her in the kitchen I wondered again the same thing, because I had thought I saw from the corner of my eye something shifting by the window and I don't know whether it was my own thoughts or my own mind shifting or whether something was really moving, and I wondered just how healthy it is to be only following the train of your own obsessive thoughts rather than being free to observe reality, to observe what goes on in front of you, but how can you really observe if there is so much to observe, that it is so infinite, besides as Emerson says, not for nothing does a certain ray of light make itself apparent to you alone and not another. Still, that is what I wonder, how healthy it is for one's mental, or really, soul's progress, to be so immersed only in following the path of your own obsessive thought patterns, I think this may be what is called hermeneutics rather than phenomenology, see, there's even a philosophical movement named after my thought patterns. Because following your own thoughts' path, does it lead you to more awareness, eventually, does it open the way to more awareness? Because at some point if you continue to follow this obsessive train of thought, does it not lead to nothingness, or suicide? Anyway, who are you now, where are you? I am curious about you. I don't even know whether I should follow up on your past trying to decipher it, you are finally engaging now, since you are dead, since you are in a state of insubstantiality, since, we hope, you are not needy anymore, since you are, this is what I caught myself reasoning, in debt to me for how you behaved towards me during my life with you, that, if it is true you are now in possession of some truths I need to know, some poems I should be writing and taking the credit for (oh I shouldn't be so harsh with myself, so self critical) you may be able to provide me with this knowledge, this information, no? I feel now you are only imagination, or rather, imagination only, though I question myself on this, what is my imagination, are you my imagination only or are you a being beyond my imagination, is my hermeneutics simply a manner of revealing my questions to myself, are you a transubstantiated substance which I have felt today as I felt a few days before, touching me? And what am I at the core, that, now looking back, I wasn't able to help you, comfort you, partially because you were such a wrinkled old body whose presence eliminated my sexuality, a wrinkled old body I felt demanded my sexuality to perform for you; and how could you? Though I suppose you were at a point in your life where you didn't care, where propriety meant absolutely nothing, as a friend said, or if it did it was only a means for you to manipulate according to any concept of propriety that occurred to you at the time, that you could use to your advantage, your only means was to manipulate by guilt because you had nothing else and you didn't know anything else, this manipulation, such as it is possible, how is it possible to behave in this manner, how can a son behave like that with his mother? So at the same time I could ask you, when your eroticism demanded satisfaction of me, is this the way a mother behaves towards a son, but all this was immaterial because you took no propriety as your mode of behavior, you were beyond any consideration of your own propriety; your life could cause only suffering to others, me, that is, but you were only concerned for yourself; as I write this I have no great gumption to continue writing about this, primarily I think because right now this subject doesn't concern me very much, because I am tired, or rather, since I went to bed real late last night after having drunk more than the regulated amount—I went to the academy award party at Lucky 32 and was planning to only have one glass of wine rather than the three or four that I had—and then woke up early, after going to bed at 1 am because Thea and I made love for a long time, so I am partially without energy and unless I come up with a subject that whets my interest, I don't want to go over material that I have gone over before, and perhaps I am feeling guilty about accusing you after having accused you so many times in this letter, I am feeling slightly guilty but I am even feeling too lazy to feel too guilty right now but anyway I will try to start with something new, such as the note I asked Thea to write down for me last night when we were driving to Lucky 32, and the note was: the essence of an event versus event as gossip. I was thinking of something I wrote earlier yesterday in trying to define what your life was about; and was thinking that I am writing down mostly theories about your life without giving specific examples, examples which I don't know because you told me so little about the specific events of your life and I am not feeling at this moment imaginative enough to come up with examples of my own but only with theoretical abstractions, for which, as a poet I am blaming myself, but last night while driving I redeemed myself in my own eyes because what are specific events but gossip and what is gossip for but something to whet the sick curiosity of the society of the spectacle, the members of "what happened then" crowd who need this information to gossip with their companions, who need to be perplexed and thrilled by these events, fuel for their bad-mouthing cravings. So now by devaluing events thus I am excusing myself from having to come up with the actual events, because if I come up with these events I am only creating fuel for these bad mouthers; but on the other hand what if these specific events are truly necessary for me to unearth in order to solve the problems I posed for myself at the outset of this undertaking and by saying that events are gossip I just make excuses for my inability to imagine, for the lack of imagination I am seemingly presently befraught with and on account of which I greatly despair and demean myself for; and the only reason I am writing all this in such great detail and with such great painstaking care is because I am hoping that by doing so I will elicit the imagination to emerge, I will seduce her to come out and inspire me to write something that inspires me. But I don't know just how interested you are in this, if this amuses you, or if it has the power to accomplish what I set out to do at the outset of this undertaking, namely to plunge into amnesia and unearth past events whose influence still holds me in their thrall and thus hinder my soul's progress. And I am feeling myself to be nowhere near such events, I feel myself to be nowhere near intuition, I feel myself to be trapped into the mundane, quotidian, a mundane and quotidian consciousness, a slothful consciousness and I despair that I will ever emerge out of it, I despair that the walls or the veils that conceal imagination, poetic imagination, from me will never consent to shift position and reveal to me magnificence; and I am bitter that all that is easily available to me is my erotic imagination to which I have access right now and so since it is the only event oriented consciousness available to me I will relate to you the phantasy I had this morning while attempting congress with the imponderable. This is a variation of a phantasy I have had for many years. In this kingdom whose primary function is erotic and whose primary erotic display is the Renaissance dress that men wear and the lingerie that women wear, the long stockings being the essential mode that I crave, it is the custom that the sons and daughters of nobility, once they reach adolescence, are taken below to the Land of the Whores to apprentice with the whores; there is a trap door and a stairs leading to this place; and the Grand Whore runs the show from below, because the king is erotically enslaved to her; and at this point the king brings his son to the Grand Whore to be apprenticed, really the son becomes a sort of a Lad in Waiting to the whore and must do whatever is demanded of him according to the demands of this world below which is dedicated only to eroticism, and where all the noblemen and noblewomen descend to satisfy their eroticism and where they allow themselves to be at the mercy of these prostitutes, while the sons and the daughters of the nobility have to as well act as prostitutes to male or female nobles and have to obey the demands of the Grand Whore who selects the right partner for the right customer; and I was the king's son, wearing my long white silk stockings and doublet and another one of the sons of the nobleman came in to my chamber or perhaps it was the chamber of one of the whores to whom I was given to apprentice, he was incredibly beautiful, a little older and taller and stronger, and he walked up to me and ran his long fingers on my thighs, over my white silk stockings and then cupped his hand over my penis, and kissed me and it turned me on, he did so and suddenly I was face down on the bed and he was over me with his penis in my anus. And then I wondered if I was homosexual, if I wanted to perform this in 'real life', which I really don't, the phantasy is much more entrancing and I need to validate the phantasy and the joy this phantasy gives me, which I might even share with Thea and she could perhaps walk in on us and save me, chase the young man away and do with me what she will. Or even imagine Thea as him. What I wanted to tell you is that when I first began to phantasize erotically, I don't recall how old I was, I was overwhelmed by the word overwhelmed, which I saw in the comic book about Magellan, Magellan's sailors were being chased away by the natives, men in stockings being, as the text told it, overwhelmed by the natives, some already lying dead face down with native lances on their backs, others running for their lives towards the ships, some just about to have a lance thrust in their back by some close following native, and this excited me to the point of being overwhelmed by this excitement and phantasized about it every night till I came (though at the time there was no cream spurting out, just a dry orgasm) and phantasized about being chased by a native, and I would fall on the ground and the native would play with me; and finally I changed this phantasy at some point after hearing someone, it could have been you, it was you, speaking against homosexuality, so I changed the native men to women, whom I dressed in all sorts of variations of male Renaissance dress, never were they without stockings, and there didn't seem to be such a difficult transition from the male to the female, (I enjoyed the female much more I feel, something far more infinite, while the male is finite, the female containing the ocean), being overwhelmed in all sorts of wars where the females were dominant and overwhelmed the males who became their servants and slaves. And this phantasy world was at the core of all my childhood, my one place of relief, my only single joy, my obsession, the extent of my world, the only world invested with any sort of energy, the only world that had any meaning; the rest was just 'chaff', a world in which I had to make do to live according to the demands of others, to live according to the expectations of others, please him, please her. There was nothing to live for, nothing to conquer, no other reason to live or make a name for myself, not that I thought I could make a name for myself, I didn't have that much self-confidence, I had no idea of what I could do, was supposed to do, nothing coagulated for me, no one praised me, no one validated me, I was nothing but someone who was easy to blame, easy to criticize, a nothing to wipe your ass with, a nothing to kick, to make fun of, to ignore, an absolute nothing, immaterial, your world had no use for me except if it needed someone to blame or ignore or laugh at or make fun of or beat up, I had no value for your world except the value you wished for me but which I couldn't deliver, you had no vision to infuse me with, no preparation prepared for me, you gave me no arms to fight with the world, you didn't believe in me except in the way in which I didn't fit in your schemata and so it frustrated you. Perhaps because of the lack of sleep, perhaps because I have exhausted the blame I have been daubing you with, perhaps because we have made our peace in the previous pages, I am investing no great energy in this blame now, though on the other hand I am feeling my life now to be nothing, (I don't want it to be nothing, I want it to be something meaningful), to be all the nothing things I mentioned above, I am seeing no value in my life, no great fountain of wisdom or joy or imagination spurting out except for this phantasy world which I am presently, I mean at this moment, not too enthralled about entering either, as I find it limiting, though to tell you about the 'novel' I have been writing, A Spy in Amnesia, it is this life which I have delved into and hoped to raise to the level of art, no, more than that, because the world means nothing me, I don't know if that's true or not, I love Thea, I would do anything for her, she means the world to me as I told her, but to escape the world by leaving the body behind, transmuting the physical body and being only the erotic self which feeds on what?

Pheeds on phantasy, that's what. This is the theory I will advance to you: I know that while you were alive you would not have understood this theory, or if you had you would not have taken it seriously but now, being in the position that you are, which really I don't know what it is, but I am assuming that you are in a position to understand, your consciousness is at a higher place than mine, you can certainly see more, you more than likely already faced the mirror of king Yama, and you would understand my point about eliminating the physical body and maintaining only an erotic shape. Imagine the freedom one would experience. Anyway, I don't know if still I feel like talking to you for a while. I don't know who you are anymore, whether I have released you or what, or whether that's necessary or not; I don't know whether there is something in our past which I need to uncover and release, the main thing I am feeling right now is a restlessness and a desire to get back to A Spy in Amnesia. Bye for a while.

AMNESIA, LOWER APPALACHIA, 4/28/2001

Imogen,

I wish I could say Queen Imogen right now, (certainly to say my Imogen would be a lie, not that I am one committed too rigidly to an absurdly austere version of the "truth", I have no commitment to that truth any more than I am committed to anyone's "untruth", that is not what causes my imaginal glands to unfurl in an agitated manner, no I am not one to adhere to a protestant abstinence from, say, the severest form of flattery and shameless flaunting displays), but it's just that I can't because I don't phantasize about you any more. Sometimes I want to, for the sake of this piece I'm trying to create. But I stopped phantasizing about you when I met Thea. Thea whom you gave me the blessing to sleep with. To share Rilke with.

Because how can I solidify my desire for you? How can you solidify duration? It irks me that I can't, this is disconcerting because I was counting on my continued ability to phrantically phantasize about you in order to bring this piece that I am writing to conclusion. But the images I have phabricated of you stir me erotically no longer. These images made of concepts, made of mental phormulations, which form the attraction core I have for you, had, the corybantic cybelle, it passes, it doesn't last, it has duration, but can two years, almost three years, away from one another be called duration? It was during the time that I conceived this as a "novel", though I don't wish to confine myself to calling it a novel, because I don't want to be confined to a phorm I have to follow, I don't wish to be forced to pay respect to a phorm I don't respect and which would constrain me or confine me, it was during this time I felt within my formulations an excitation, an impulse to write, I agreed with all the ideas that occurred to me, was enthousiastic, that's it, enthousiastic! Notice too how I spell enthousiastic. But events interfered and I was forced at times to put the work aside only to constantly and consistently think about it, pray about it, yes pray. I admit. And now coming back to it, I feel no enthousiasm at all. When I look back, it all started only because I felt I should start a diary detailing our "affair".

In any case, how can I continue to observe the moment by moment life of Siegfried? What I mean is, Siegfried is my invention, one that was engendered by my phantasies of you, he was our child, with me being the mother. But what if for instance I get tired of talking about him, or the Amorous Spy changes his purpose? What I mean is, this actually happened. Because, as I said, I stopped phantasizing about you. And while you had the chance, you didn't help me "stoke the furnace".

In presenting you with a window into that world, I planned to elicit in you a desire for it; and I have been successful in eliciting the desire within you. I know you smiled and sighed because you know, you know this world so well, but you didn't bother to consider the fons and origen that certainty comes from—that it was possible to climb over the window I opened and gain complete access to that world. That was your fatality, maybe mine too, to be so circumscribed by gravity. Walking down the street, has it ever occurred to you that if you mustered one more ounce of faith, you could actually lift off and float? Because the desire to float is legitimate, it is a desire like any other, why should you not be able to fulfill it? It's not a sin to betray gravity just because everyone else is ensconced in it. Now we will grow old, our flesh will decay. We will be "friends". Perhaps it my fault I have not been successful in seducing you, contaminating you, in taking you to a point of no return. That was my primary purpose. You were amused by the shamelessness of the eroticism, its absolute freedom, unrestraint, permeating all endeavors and actions. You were amused but you didn't stop to consider this world as veritable possibility, as a place you can actually exist, free of the fetters of the dying flesh.

And what if in fact everything has been said, exhausted, about Siegfried and Imogen, I mean everything has not been said, their lives continue to be weaved and implicated, but do I wish to follow? Do I wish to cater to the needs of those salivating fools whose only intention is to be captured in the pliers jaw of dramatic development? Yes, to crawl at night unseen, invisible, over unknown terrain to catch another glimpse of the glimmering seam of Siegfried's stocking, tortuous journey he must undertake to find the Queen, Queen Imogen; and should the journey be tortuous, torturous? And why at night, not at night but at late and crimsony Dämmerung? Because 'late' and 'crimson' occurs to me right now and has occurred to me before, when I thought of it, say, yesterday. Still, I feel that I owe some explanations, but to try to continue to reveal this world I began, no! Because I had planned to detail this blow by blow chronicle of Siegfried and Imogen; (and don't imagine that Imogen is you while Siegfried is me!) But now I am bored, besides I only write for my own phulphillment; and it doesn't phulphill me to keep on.

No, I don't feel like going on with this; Thea, who has just moved in with me, (Thea is not her real name, nor does she sport a tiny penis) has called me to help me move a shelf, and I love her madly so I'll do it with pleasure just as I'll do anything else she asks me, like arranging my books according to categories, like making sandwiches and bringing them to her when she works at the library; I even wash the dishes everyday now. She calls me on my cell phone and says, Julian, I am hungry, can you bring me a sandwich? And I say yes and I am happy to do so, I really am, and she says can you go to the Fresh Market and get some butter, but not just butter, butter mixed with yogurt, I want that on my sandwich, and I say yes. And I make the sandwich and take it to the library where she works. And then when she comes home from the library after 11 PM she notices the $5.59 price tag and she scolds me for spending $5.59 for the yogurt/butter admixture, anyway I'm tired of this book, it's been going on for close to three years, I think I'm done with it now.

But, in ending the book like this, leaving you with the image of Thea calling me to help her move the bookshelf and me gladly leaping to it, I leave you with the belief that the narrator has changed for the better, that is, progressed from a life of 'phantasy' to one of 'reality'. Then the book will be viewed as a redemption story, the story of a man who "improved", and this was the furthest thing from my mind. There are those who feel that art has no value outside the social function, that art is "for the people", to help them improve, just like a doctor or a lawyer or a handyman. That art has a moral value and by moral value they understand the disguised procrustean societal entrapment in service of utility; these people who always busy themselves serving you their euphemistic hors d'oeuvres on insipid plates of platitudes. I spit on the manner in which they clap you on the back when they feel you shed your wind assassin mantle to weigh as one of their ranks. Their purposes are not and will never be my purposes. I refuse to improve because there is no one and nothing to improve for; improvement is a fatality I don't condone.

I keep coming back to wondering what this book might have been had I not stopped phantasizing about you, had I still believed this book was a bridge; had I not been hesitant

to cross over the threshold; did I destroy it by my lack of resolution to cross over forever? What if I hadn't met Thea? I
have no more interest in Siegfried and his world now. I have
no desire to step into his world, or perhaps his world has no
more desire for me. Perhaps a couple of chapters out of me is
all it needed. Maybe someone else will take it up from here,
like a relay race. The wall I could step through at will has
turned now to cement; and this insouciance, or perhaps it is
fatigue, somnolence, like a dream you won't bother to write
down. If I continued right now, I would be fabricating, as
though out of a clay that's close to drying, a repetition of a
repetition; did I squander Siegfried for purely personal
entrancement? And have I become 'normal'? Am I reduced to
marshalling my visions neatly now into the rank and file
march of commonality? To simply cook or wash dishes with
Thea is a great joy, and I worry. Siegfried and his events were
my life, my body, infused with a joy that was transcendent,
infinite, multi-layered, a life I channeled, a mysterious and
endless life essence that chose me as its as playground. But
now, this world I could enter at will, this world I thought
would always be alive to my observing and perhaps participating in was only an elusive moment whose facets I only
captured incompletely and whose access is now denied me,
have I betrayed it? Am I now inside the wall, am I "cabined,
cribbed, confined" back inside a tomb of oblivion, until I
have served a sentence and Siegfried and the Queen allow me
back? Or am I awaiting for the doorway to another citadel of
words to suddenly fling open, for the quicksand of another
enigma that needs me?

I am worried, I am worried. Because while I (so proud to
have done so) had transcended the Oedipal to prove that
Siegfried existed not as a reactionary malady but as an eternal transcendent being, a will of the Ultimate Goddess, while
I had believed that I was chosen, that this life is merely a
coagulation, a temporary illusory density, have I now proven

I am merely Oedipal and that Siegfried is merely an illusion? His psychic entity, so potent, so electric, the way it would unexpectedly gush out me like an inner surge, a clear spring, when I was on walk, or driving, and I would pause to write it down, or just be forced to pull over, it was so real! And now this inner enthousiasm is dead! This spontaneity of images that sustained me! And now it seems as though apathy to Siegfried has taken hold of me. These images, whose legitimacy was authenticated by the spontaneity of the surge, a fulgurating vitality, utterly unpremeditated, have I really squandered Siegfried for motives of personal entrancement? Is it a kind of punishment? Will I be able to expiate my transgression against the spirit of Siegfried by re-immersing myself into the text in the hope that through the repetition of the contact my inner life of Siegfried will re-emerge in full bloom, and I'll be off again, ready to step over the threshold into that infinite world? And yet, Thea's love for me, it infuses me with such pleromatic redolence. We're saving money by cooking together! We go shopping together, we eat vegetarian. Yesterday she added, unbeknownst to me, three chocolates to my sandwich lunch bag! I do not suffer at my loss of Siegfried, but is this something to worry about? Or if I have indeed betrayed this world I was given to write about, will I be forgiven and thus be given another chance by another in need of its chronicler? And if I have failed but will still be given another chance, will it be a chance with a minor, insignificant circumstance to be chronicled? Or are the two chapters I snatched from the citadel of Siegfried enough of a witness to have exhausted the purposes of That whose call to words I obeyed, was so proud to obey? Enough so that the next chance will be a more privileged significance in the eyes of That that will choose me again? Or, to have Thea in my award, have I been awarded to a yet greater realm? A realm I had not even suspected? Or will I be simply left in the award of Thea? Will my fingers anew be the smuggling wires for words I hadn't yet expected? Concatenations of words I hadn't even dreamed existed? And once the smuggling has been accomplished, will That whose purpose has been accomplished in the smuggling abandon me again? And if they go will Thea stay? Will it be enough? Will it? Will it?

Bye for now.

Appendix

IN PRAISE OF ABSENCE

Doodles chiseled on the imaginary margins of a hypothetical urn

"And yet this creature of absence lives; and his life is a sketch of mysteries."
—Edmond Jabès

i

There are two orchard-like rows of trees separating Europe: Europe before the first world war, Europe after the first world war and before the second world war, and Europe after the second world war.

There is also an erstwhile wall separating Eastern Europe from its Western counterpart. It wasn't part of the plan to start speaking about this wall, but something made me. I think perhaps it wanted to speak of itself. An erstwhile lover from Western Germany absconded with a purloined fragment of it. It whizzed past my ear once, and nearly severed it, before she was erstwhile, and after it, the wall, was erstwhile; now both lover and wall are erstwhile; if you look up "purloined" in the Roget Thesaurus, you'll find that one of its numerous synonyms is "abstracted". She abstracted the fragment from the erstwhile wall, but it was concrete while it whizzed past my ear. This writing is not about erstwhile walls and their present fragments. However it is in the nature of doodles to meander at will, theirs; but you must give me credit that I am doing my best to return to my trees; there is no indication in the writing itself that I am, but I am; trust me; on the other hand, I am bound by no duty to do so; besides I warned you from the start I would be freely doodling. If I didn't, I'm doing it now. My memory's not very good.

I don't know what sort of trees the orchards separating Europe are made of.

The separation does not take place on the map of Europe you are familiar with; if it did, you would be inclined to place the Europe before the first world war in the west, with perhaps the first row of trees separating, say, Spain from France. It is not like that at all. The spatial map of Europe, the one you have spied in passing (and now remember only vaguely) in the offices of posturers who sport an extravagant globe on their somber mahogany desk, or a framed-in-matching-mahogany map of the world on the wall is no match for my map in time; the map in time occupies no space, but it does: a space inside my head; and my mind & its spaces are more worthwhile to me than any map of Europe; I don't give a damn about your pre-established map of Europe, I don't care who drew it, in space or in time. If my mind chooses to form this map of European history, I won't start a war with it; and I won't attempt to exile it either, to a Siberia of absurdities; its truth, I, will not deny; you're struggling with my words right now, I know, you would rather that this map of Europe's history is the map you know; you may choose to hang on to the map of Europe's history found in the common issue history books. But I will do my best to remedy that. Still, since beginning these doodles, I did question my trees and their nature; and please understand, it is you alone and nobody else I am sharing my doodles with; perhaps you will have dinner with me afterwards, a glass of Cabernet perhaps. Should I explain this to those for whom the imagination is a quicksand they don't endorse, except when it is slapped with the stamp of pre-approval, they would, I assume, classify me as wayward, erratic, delirious. They might rush in and attempt straightjacket me inside the restraint of their pre-established definitional systems; they have plenty of these systems which they keep at the ready for just such occasions; and wouldn't hesitate to use them on me, they never do, they would place me behind the bars of the definitives they worship, like a childhood's pillow. Let them; I am not responsible for the imaginally constricted. The prison bars of their pre-established definitives is enough of a punishment for them.

I have at times been informed by others the orchard's rows are made of olive trees; I am not convinced; their biblical symbology is lost on me; and neither are they the biblical apple trees, in case the thought occurred to you, though I confess that once when my confidence was shaken, I did try to replace my generic trees, furtively, with olive or maybe apple ones; though I found the task, which I should never have undertaken, too troublesome. My generic trees would not budge. They categorically, intransigently, refused. More than that, I could not remember what olive trees looked like. Perhaps, some would advice, I should not have set about the task without first researching olive trees; that indeed it was a foolish thing to do, to attempt to recreate the historical map of twentieth century Europe without having first armed myself scientifically with the proper tools of research. One thing that occurred, which again, I repeat, I am sharing with you and only you, because I trust you, partially, is that the trees whispered to me they are not generic trees, and I realized that indeed they weren't; it's just that I didn't know their names; their chiaroscuro whispering was faint and vague, with dissonant acciaccatura accenting in the background, and only among themselves, as though I were being purposefully absented; absented from my own imaginings! Imagine! It occurred to me that perhaps it was not me who imagined them, but they who imagined me, and, like God himself, weren't too certain of what they wrought; it left me feeling like an outsider, like I needed to propitiate them to be included into the realm of their mysteries, or like courting a lover you've decided, mistakenly perhaps, that you don't deserve; I don't know, but I suspect these trees will always refuse definitions. I suspect they take pride in assuming the shapes of vagueness. Perhaps, too, I was wrong to use the lover metaphor. But perhaps not. These are my doodles and I can do anything I want to. On the other hand, one morning upon awakening, the trees themselves surprised me and confessed to me that just as the substance of lovers is made of forgetfulness, they too are the trees of forgetfulness, or maybe I only imagined they did, confess that is, these trees, incessantly fabricating subterfuge out of the quicksand mirror of our being.

ii

Edgar Allen Poe, in his Eureka, his lesser-known-to-most-but-seminal-to-me metaphysical treatise, which he calls a prose poem, proposes the following recipe which you must follow precisely if you want to get at *the* truth: you climb atop the Mount Aetna, and while there, you whirl on heel so as to "comprehend the panorama in the sublimity of its *oneness*". The effect of this whirling, according to Edgar Allen, is that the surroundings will become, instead of bits of unrelated and diverse pieces of perceived events, a bowl-like twirling wall, which, on account of your spinning, will reveal a mystery you didn't expect and not inherent in leisurely & slothful perusal your stationary posture would engender. I became intrigued by the idea of a bowl which is engendered by your spin alone and has no existence otherwise, and thought of attempting this exercise myself; and since presently unable to travel to Mount Aetna, and since to spin on Aetna you run into the distinct hazard of tumbling into the crater and leaving behind you only a pair of wounded sandals, I decided that spinning in my own home is a good start. I knew I had antecedents: the whirling dervishes, for instance, or the spinning nahuatls my friend the poet Will Alexander speaks about; there must be then, I reasoned, numerous others like me: twirling necromancers, circumambulating thaumaturgists, wambling obeahs, swiveling erzulies, roiling moyles, swirling weird sisters, and, who knows, maybe even, pirouetting enchantresses, though Poe spoke only about heel and excluded, purposefully I suppose, though I could be wrong, toe rotation; still, I personally couldn't see why a pirouetting enchantress could not be included and obtain just as much benefit from participating by spinning on her toes.

iii

All scientific knowledge is contained within the two juxtaposing concepts of time and absorption. How clearly they juxtapose I am not certain I can disclose. However, as the Romanian philosopher E. M. Cioran clearly stated: "Nothing desiccates a mind so much as its repugnance to conceive obscure ideas." Let it be known I'm not one to look away when an obscure idea glitters on some tree. Certainly space too is necessary—and I have heard a scientist speak of the time-space continuum—as the scientist must, say, sit down in a chair for a spell for the purpose of study, or stand up in the lab besides the trough on top of which they keep their test tubes, waterclocks and clepsydras. Absorption, though, is another thing altogether and far more difficult to come by. This, however, is when eroticism and science, two rubrics never compounded in the same test-tube, find themselves the tenuous soul mates.

If I take my place in space, i.e., sit in a chair and study, or stand in front of test tubes, and while attempting to solve a problem of science with waterclock ticking and while being overtaken by scenarios with an imaginary or erstwhile lover, and the scenarios with the imaginary or erstwhile lover conquer any desire to continue with any gesticulating commanded to me by the rigors of the scientific study or experiment, I might conclude then, since eroticism has such instant claim on my attention, that eroticism is more important than science. Recall here what I mentioned above: how much I value the fabrications of my own brain, how much I prize them above all else, above all the pretexts of your world. I would then built a statue and place it in the town square to celebrate the scientist who leaves his books and his test tubes behind and gives in to eroticism. This is how I see this statue: first, I would somehow hoist it up high in the air, perhaps on a peduncle of crystal, shooting out and twisting like the curves of an enrapturing dancer, to serve as a wayward altar, so as to force the casually quotidian peruser to view the statue from below, as though in a kind of aspiration to an unpremeditated worship. Its size, the statue's, would be enormous, three or four times the size we have come to commonly agree matches the conventions of our world; I would have the scientist turned away from his table with the test tubes—the table swept away and at an oblique, athwart angle, as though it is half way to crashing to the ground as a result of the scientist's sudden turn—and leaning forward to touch... a pirouetting enchantress just slightly out of his reach. It would be the crowning monument in the center of town, placed there for the daily perusal of the incessant two way traffic and the flurry of agitated pedestrians.

iv

You will raise your hand to argue with me that science is from God and eroticism from the devil; I say, let it be then: the devil is so insistent, and I never had the heart to refuse anyone who insisted. You might insist then that it is natural that eroticism is easier, since it comes from the devil; science is harder since it comes from God. But your argument ruptures like the roots of rotten old trees in an insubstantial hurricane: and the system of beliefs that your world is founded on ruptures just as easily. Listen to me. The word "science" is rooted in the Latin "scire", to know. And if we go by the words of your Bible, whose words are the roots your quicksand-like concepts of God & the Devil spring from, the roots of your belief systems, man (and woman) originally were living in heaven, i.e., in a state of unrestricted eroticism. The Bible says "they were naked and were not ashamed." What exactly were they doing all day?

Contrary to what you believe, "original sin" has nothing to do with eroticism, but with knowledge. Had Adam & Eve opted for their God-given eroticism, we would have no 'science' today. Their downfall came when they gave in to the temptation to "know", i.e., take a bite of the apple fallen from the Tree of Knowledge; it was the snake—the devil—who convinced them it was a good thing to "know", i.e., to have "science"; trust me, I know: the symbol for medicine, is two intertwined snakes, and the most intriguing computer of our time, the Apple, sports as its emblem a near circleloid in the shape of an apple with a curved portion missing from it, suggesting, I assume, the Bite that spit us into Time, and Knowledge. Or the other way around. These things are hard to figure out.

Still, I am beginning to have doubts about my statue; it is humorous, I agree, but something is missing; perhaps I am disturbed by how easily he, the scientist, abandons his experiment to reach for his pirouetting enchantress; perhaps the overturning table should be catching on his foot and tripping him, as though it's the tripping itself that propels him forward toward the pirouetting enchantress; he himself maybe should show some regret for the experiment he leaves behind, yes, his head should be twisted towards the over-turning table; and perhaps we need to pay more attention to details in the kinds of things we place on the table: a book with an indicative title perhaps, perhaps a globe, now about to crash and shatter on the ground. And let's not forget the shattering waterclock and clepsydra. I feel compelled to search for my book of symbols but it is very late at night and books are piled up everywhere. It is night in the realm of ideas too and my doodles are flailing arms grasping for per-hapses.

v

Thus, he who created us, unhappy with the issue of his test tube experiment and in an abrupt moment of poetic fury, cursed us with existence in time; thus we assume the work of purposeful science is an attempt to reverse this original curse, to re-transmute us to our original substance of eter-nally erotic unrestraint, unending ecstasy. What other purpose would science possess if not to return us to the incipient condition of pure pleasure,—after all why would we long to return to it if Heaven were nothing but an anti-septic region of moral restraints—to improve what we agree to be the bane of our existence, i.e., to take away the dolor-ous, and replace it with the pleasurable. We then have come to agree that pleasure was once our natural, original state, because otherwise how could we foresee, if not by remem-bering, that pleasure will wait for us once we remove the obstacle to getting to it? Plato warned us that all knowledge is remembering. It is an erstwhile state of original pleasure persisting in our psychic formulations that we constantly crave. We are intransigent in our refusal to unlearn ecstasy.

In my doodles it was whispered that scientists have been spotted whose purposes were those of pure contemplation; I concede you may be right; but pure contemplation is reserved only for the poet; for the mystic too, but the mystic is under the umbrella of a dictator: he takes himself and his eternity far too seriously and puts bars around its unrestraint; he is nothing like the poet who is grateful for his "eternities of the moment", come what may, whenever or wherever he or she can get them.

Which reminds me: what about that other tree? Do you know the one I mean? In Bible lore it has gotten the lesser press; yes, conspicuously absent is any discussion of that other tree; that other tree whose fruit God did not want us to take a bite from: the Tree of Life; panicked that we would become just like him, and live forever, God placed a Cherubim with a flaming sword "turning every way", spinning that is, to prevent access to the Tree of Life.

It occurs to me that the Tree of Life is our access to art. It makes very good sense. God sends Adam & Eve into the world to till the soil and to multiply; to till the soil and to multiply, these are the usual excuses why people won't pursue the arts; parents tell their children to find a career first, or to get married and have children. The Bible abounds with lovers, adulterers, rapists, sodomites, sodomite rapists, onanists, but, where are the artists? Yet, God didn't say you can't have the fruit of the Tree of Life: it's true, panicked, he put a Cherubim with a spinning sword in front of it, to prevent anyone from obtaining the fruit; (and by the way, as an aside, we don't know if the Cherubim himself is spinning or not, but it's conceivable that he is.) All that it means is that the mastery of an art is difficult to achieve, not that you can't achieve it. Freedom from prohibition is necessary; I mean the inner prohibition, the sort of prohibition you've placed on your imagination. "If you can't get in through the front door, use the back; if the gate is locked, jump the fence, or break in."

vii

Recently I witnessed an enforcer of prohibitions speak about the penalty one might incur by using falsified identification papers, particularly for the purposes of purchasing those liquids whose consumption leads one to achieve an inebriated state. It occurred to me to ask him what the penalty might be if you just thought you were somebody else. It occurred to me to ask him, but I didn't. Still, I thought about it, and he continued riding his train of thought—while I whistled—inwardly—about the multiplication of penalties to be imputed upon adults who purchased inebriating liquids for those who are prohibited from partaking on account of their tender years; it occurred to me as I whistled to ask him—and again I didn't but thought about it—what the penalty might be if my poetry were more intoxicating than alcohol. Would my mind be classified a concealed weapon? Would I have to register it with the Department of Tobacco, Firearms and Alcohol? With the Federal Drug Administration? With the Ministry of Culture? Could a poet ever invent a more self-flattering thought?

My doodles got away from me again. I'm back now, though. Is it not then immortality the artist craves? Is that not the reason God panicked? "...lest he put forth his hand, and take also of the tree of life, and eat, and live forever?"

What sort of drunkenness would eating from the tree of life bring? And is it inebriation I'm after or the mastery of an art? I don't wish to seem as though I am prescribing a course in intoxication, but the king of poets, Baudelaire, hands down a ready made and useful recipe:

"And if sometimes you should happen to be awake, on

the stairs of a palace, on the green grass of a ditch, in the dreary solitude of your own room, and find that your drunkenness is ebbing or has vanished, ask the wind, ask the wave, the star, bird, or clock, ask everything that flies, everything that moans, everything that flows, everything that sings, everything that speaks, ask them the time; and the wind, the wave, the star, the bird and the clock will all reply: 'It is Time to get drunk! If you are not to be the martyred slaves of time, be perpetually drunk! With wine, with poetry, or with virtue, as you please.'"

Rimbaud the vagabond and god of poets who imparted to us that "'I' is another", and without whom none of us would exist, is even more precise in his recipe, in which he commands us to become 'seers', to *make* ourselves into seers.

"The poet makes himself a seer by a long, prodigious and rational disordering of *all* the senses. Every form of love, of suffering, of madness; he searches himself, he consumes all the poisons in him, and keeps only their quintessence. This is an unspeakable torture, during which he needs all his superhuman strength, an during which he becomes the great patient, the great criminal, the great accursed—and the great learned one—among men. For he arrives at the *unknown*.. [...] other horrible workers will come; they will begin from the horizons where he has succumbed!"

I leave it up to you to decide, is it inebriation, or the mastery of an art? Are these poets tracing a route of drunkenness for us? Or are they telling us that there are ways to squeeze past the Cherubim's flaming sword?

viii

I am spinning faster and faster and losing track of the details I originally began to trace for you. The great 12th century cabalist Giambattista Almodoverroes, who foresaw the

Renaissance and whose apocryphal writings were seminal for Giordanno Bruno, told one of the disciples, his best: a bowl spun quickly turns into an urn. The velocity of the spin accelerating, the bowl will certainly turn into the urn. It's not difficult to discern what he meant: the centripetal force of the spin forces the squatty shape of the bowl into the fusiform of the urn; what it doesn't explain is how the clay of the bowl transmutes into the urn's pewter. Or silver! Or gold! Yes, I would like my urn to be at the very least made of gold! Encrusted with jewels, of amber and emerald and sapphire! Imponderable emerald, imponderable amber! Imponderable sapphire! I'm getting so dizzy from spinning I don't know what I'm writing anymore. It is not me, anymore, pushing the power book's keys. I is another. There is a pirouetting enchantress pushing the keys for me, causing the letters to form one next to the next one; to pause for insignificant instances to form words, which group to coagulate momentarily into meanings which you're dying to grasp, in the vague manner that we remember maps, like falling in love, helplessly, but not forever, with an entrancing vampire.

ix

"Professional women singers are said to enjoy the adoration of all men, but they are inconstant and distressing wives or lovers. Their real lovers are their spiritual guardians, and in many cases they have sacrificed their ability to have children in exchange for beauty, voice, and songs. They can cause men to love them above all women, but they are fickle and prefer to go from one man to another. They are proud and show humility to no one. In this they do not behave like the ideal Gola woman should, but their powers protect them, and their abilities bring such enjoyment that they are allowed to be as they are."

Have I doodled for so long along the lines of the plight of pursuing the arts, that I disclosed not a thing about the rewards to be reaped? Well, here they are. In the course of copying down the above quote, certainly about my pirouetting enchantresses, I fell in love, helplessly, at least once or twice. My poor, poor scientist from the statue,

"Bold lover, never, never, canst thou kiss,"

to quote from the other writer of urns at the turn of the century two centuries back,

"Though winning near the goal—yet, do not
                                              grieve;
She cannot fade, though thou has not thy bliss,
Forever wilt though love, and she be fair".

"There are some older women who are professional singers," continues the writer of the quote previous to the one by the other writer of urns, "but it is an arduous and dangerous life. Most professional women singers give up the work when their beauty fades. Some become despondent and die; others marry and bring prestige to the households of wealthy families."

"When I'm dead", I loosely quote from he who lost an ear by own cooked hand, "and they look at my paintings, I want them to say: 'This man felt deeply.'"

An ear lost to one's own blade or severed by a sharded abstraction hurled by an erstwhile lover from Western Germany, and my thoughts are unfurling like an enormous bandage that never ends.

X

In an overly casual conversation, away from the incisors of logic's mongrels, I might acknowledge the revelation that strayed in echo-like from the catacombs while taking a siesta from my doodles: he who pondered weak and weary over his curious volumes of forgotten lore while seeking surcease of sorrow from the absence of his lost Lenore, is a distant echoing of my absent-minded scientist. Yet Poe in the poem is nothing like the Poe who brags about the precise science of his well-wrought verse, like an acanthus cut in stone: "It is my design to render it manifest that no one point in its composition is referable either to accident or intuition—that the work proceeded, step by step, to its completion with the precision and rigid consequence of a mathematical problem." The somnambulistic doodling of Poe's thoughts, intransigent like a dungeon prepared specifically for you, or wayward and irregular like his life, doesn't resonate with his recipe. Besides, drunks will never tell you the truth.

Thank god that Poe had made that other suggestion, the one about spinning. I took that on as my working praxis. The faster I spin the more my doodles splatter at random; am I then the sorcerer's apprentice on the sorcerer's day off? Unskilled in any art, wayward, and absent from your world, I spin and doodle, splattering rainbows at random, dreaming the effect will be bewitching, while fidgeting I might be making myself a subject of ridicule with my rubber band rhapsody.

Yes no art except the spinning; don't even try to spot figures in my doodles; though I'm sure a psychoanalyst would. He'd slap the stamp of truth on them. The orchards are breasts, he'd shamelessly declaim, and Europe the warlike mother that gave you birth. I don't buy that sort of Oedipal acrobatics. For me the breasts are orchards and a willing lover is arriving from Europe.

You noticed I started the paragraph before the previous one with "thank god". It's only a figure of speech, and god knows how I would hate to be caught doodling one on my twirling urn of words. Besides, which god was I speaking of? There are at least two that I know of, that are proper to speak of in doodling on urns: Plato's and the Flood Plotter.

> "Plato thought nature but a spume that plays
> Upon a ghostly paradigm of things",

wrote a poet I don't admire. Plato, king of philosophers and ur-scientist, phantasized an original urn, the urn in its original state, an ur-urn if you will; his urn was made by god; we would never get to drink from it, or posture it on our mantelpiece, but god might; we must be satisfied with the imitation, which, will never match the original; we're always stuck with hierarchies. Plato is responsible for that too. As for me, I don't want my urn to match the original; my urn is an original; I am reading to you from my urn; I want these doodles to be an infinite urn of words, like in a story by Borges.

My knowledge of history is wayward too and I can't be trusted with it; which God came first? Plato's, or the Flood Plotter? Suddenly, for no reason, I told you I was wayward, I'm thinking of my scientist on his downtown peduncle: yes, to stand before test tubes and to dream of sex; no closer to knowledge than to pleasure: what a predicament for humanity at the turn of the millennium! Good neither at the science we hoped would resolve the anguish brought about by the memory of our original eroticism, nor at the eroticism we hoped the development of our science would bring us! How could it be otherwise? We inherited the hatred of our flesh from Plato's god, and of knowledge from the Flood Plotter. It's the Flood Plotter who spit us into time and cursed us with making imitation urns because we wanted to know, which is what Plato said he wanted as well, while his god cursed us because we didn't want to know and opted for eroticism instead. Imagine picking up a fortune cookie that says: "There is a rumbling thunder of fire and brimstone that will unendingly beleaguer you."

According to Plato's god, evil comes from the flesh and its urges. And from the poet, because the poet stirs up the flesh's urges. The poet is quartered away from his fascist city state; a poet better use a fake I.D., if he or she wanted to get in. But there are penalties for that. Better to pretend you're somebody else.

Perhaps the solution lies in the Flood Plotter flooding Plato's urn? We don't know how big god's urn is, so perhaps a flood might fit in it. Plato's god's urn might be fit to fit in the Flood Plotter's flood. Try to say that real fast.

But I wanted to speak of god and history! My spinning is mixing everything up! I'm lucky if I get hold of one fragment as I rotate! One just whizzed past my ear! Imagine the head-lines: God Floods in Plato's Urns.

When the Flood Plotter spit us into time, part of the spit ended up in Plato's urn.

If Plato's god and the Flood Plotter both created the world from nothing, one must wonder exactly who must be responsible for evil; it is not they, they claim; somebody must take the blame however; we must search everywhere to find him (or her) because, after all, somebody needs to be pun-ished; I suspect that is the reason for the invention of the black sheep, sacrificial rams, scapegoats. How the devil changed shapes from a snake to a goat I don't know. Certainly one could trace the origin of it, and maybe there is a place for that on my urn. But I am taking my urn back from the pool of urns engendered by the ur-urn of Plato's god. My urn is made neither of clay nor of pewter but of spinning and words; if you find the performance of my reasoning ridiculous, it is you whose imagination is quartered by a manner of reasoning infused into you by Plato and his allies.

xi

Perhaps there are no gods at all but simply a reflection of our self hatred; our flesh? A sausage painted azure, or in turbulent melodramas, invested with corporation issue identity. The poet then is a criminal, a contrabandist who smuggles the void into the coagulating quotidian of the corporation; and hurricanes the only criminals you can't imprison.

The corporations, that is, organizations of flesh, are organized much like Plato's overly regulated city states; but instead of excluding the poet, they gave him a job writing copy for advertising; hatred of the flesh can be profitable: my shoes are Air Thunders, my Laundry detergent Tide, my dish detergent Dawn. Our gods and goddesses show up on billboards selling underwear, and gentlemen prefer Hades. Dante went there too and that's where he found his favorite poets.

On the other hand, my shorts are NWO, or New World Order. I bought them at Wal-Mart. It is only fitting this spinning episode would wind up the same way it started: with the new world order and a wall, which is now a market. I wouldn't be surprised to see Wal-Mart sell pieces from that erstwhile wall, which held the old world order in place, and whose memory is now for sale.

I said this spinning episode would wind up, but I also said my doodles are out of control. They'll wind up when they want to, if they want to.

xii

What were we hoping for when we stood upon that erstwhile wall and sang the words of Frederick Schiller to

Beethoven's ninth? It was a shard of concrete that whizzed past my ear, a shard abstracted from a concrete abstraction; we stood upon it while it still stood, at the point of its dissolve into abstraction, while the two abstractions it separated alloyed into a newer, perhaps even more deadly abstraction; and yet, in that one moment we stood upon the concrete about to dissolve to abstraction, singing, to the music of Beethoven's Ninth, Friedrick Schiller's words:

Joy, delightful inspiration,
Daughter of Elysium,
Drunk with ardor we're advancing
Oh, empyrean asylum.

That was our moment in the sun, at the start of this decade; we sang for ourselves and we sang for our camera-does who stood and sang the same at Tien An Men square only months before, facing the bullets of a concrete abstraction and then didn't stand any more. We sang for our confr-eres in Paris in 1968, who, with Rimbaud, declared that 'I is another'.

Yes, we abstracted our moment in the sun: maybe that's all we get, perhaps we should be grateful for that much.

Well, it's been a sad century, and an even sadder decade, and someone is needed to sing our sad dirge. I for one am tired and want to go to sleep; I worked too hard on my spinning word urn; I wanted to say an urn is a hora celebrating the downfall of a dictator, or perhaps an erstwhile lover, or a prohibition whose contoured edges are a canvas for us to scribble our furtive graffiti of defiance or insurgence. After that I would go to sleep, but my urn is spinning even faster; I don't know what it will turn to next but don't try to stop it to look; I would sing as I spin but even Beethoven's Ninth has turned to fanfare music, and I'm bored and I hate marching band music. Whatever you choose to march in favor of, leave

me out, unless it were absentmindedness, or flesh waywardly abstracting to phantasy's catacombs. Your worship of
marching to an armada of ideals is a necrophilia I don't
endorse, an azure betrayed by the stain of a coagulating
morality. No, I am not enraptured of your drills to a
necrophilia of ideals the engineer of your strings entitles you
to.

Perhaps it is time to get drunk. Still, I spin. Accelerando,
on my heel, or on my toes, on Mount Aetna, or in my room;
I will spin to resonate with my hypothetical urn; I would go
to sleep, but instead I'll spin; I will spin so fast no corporation could claim or duplicate my urn; don't try to stop me, or
my urn. Don't try to earn on account of my urn, neither. Yes,
if my urn spins any faster, I don't know what it'll turn to. If
you want to know what's on it, you spin as well; spin twice
as fast, or even sing as you spin. Maybe you'll spy something
I haven't seen yet. If you spin with me, I will spin with you.
Or maybe I won't, I was going to write. But I didn't.

JULIAN SEMILIAN is a poet, translator, novelist and film-maker. He was born in Romania and presently teaches film editing at the North Carolina School of the Arts, School of Filmmaking, after a twenty-four year career as a film editor in Hollywood where he has worked on more than 50 movies and TV shows. Among the films he edited are: Death Wish 2, Scanner Cop, The Landlady, Daddy's Girl, The Secretary, Distant Cousins, Captured, etc.

In the fall semester of 2000 Semilian taught a film editing class at Duke University. And in 2002 he taught at Columbia University.

As a translator he has published the work of Romanian poets, concentrating chiefly on the Romanian avant-garde. Among the published poets translated by Semilian are: Paul Celan, Gellu Naum, Tristan Tzara, Benjamin Fondane, Stefan Augustin Doinas, Tudor Arghezi, Urmuz, Gherasim Luca, Ilarie Voronca, Mircea Cartarescu. In such magazines as: Exquisite Corpse, Suitcase, Arshile, World Letter, Mr. Knife & Miss Fork, Ribot, Transcendental Friend, Syllogism, Callaloo, Sun & Moon, Kenning, Urvox, Trepan, LACMA and MOMA catalogues containing writings by the Romanian avant-garde.

Andrei Codrescu has this to say about Semilian's translations of Celan:

"Paul Celan, the Jewish, Romanian, German, French poet, has become the raw material of so much critical processing, it has become difficult to read him without hearing the voices of commentators. The continual buzzing of the interpretive chorus around Celan's poetry has nearly added another layer of pain to work that is already written at the synapses of raw nerves. I say "nearly," because happily there is Julian Semilian who translates the poetry as if there are only two entities in the room: Psyche and Echo. Celan would have been proud to be thus refreshed."

S P U Y T E N   D U Y V I L

The Farce   Carmen Firan
ISBN 1-881471-96-9 $10.00

The unique hybrid creatures that have emerged from the cracks between millennia have been captured here in all their eerieness. Andrei Codrescu

Spiritland   Nava Renek
ISBN 1-881471-57-8 $13.00

Her exquisite descent into hell is recorded with such a poetic realism it reads as if Dante himself had updated *Let's Go Thailand 2002*. Arthur Nersesian

Acts of Levitation   Laynie Browne
ISBN 1-881471-94-2 $14.00

An ultra femme, absolutely exquisite writing/vision. Acts is extraordinarily imaginative and remains with me as a luminous benchmark. Lissa Wolsak

ARC: Cleavage of Ghosts   Noam Mor
ISBN 1-881471-79-9 $14.95

Possibly the most phallocentric protaganist since Philip Roth's Portnoy... Rain Taxi

6/2/95   Donald Breckenridge
ISBN 1-881471-77-2 $14.00

Fifteen characters travel through New York City on a single day in 1995. Their paths intersect in a finely choreographed Altmanesque dance. The New Yorker

The Fairy Flag & Other Stories   Jim Savio
ISBN 1-881471-83-7 $14.00

These stories will be appreciated by a wide audience, as they evoke wide ranges of emotion, from the violent to the poetic. Foreword

Don't Kill Anyone, I Love You   Gojmir Polajnar
translated from the Slovene by Aaron Gillies
ISBN 1-881471-80-2 $12.00

Polajnar may become something of a Balkan Irvine Welsh... Library Journal

Ted's Favorite Skirt   Lewis Warsh
ISBN 1-881471-78-0 $14.00

The heroine is a hoops-shooting, Madame Bovary reading American kid trying to figure it all out.

Black Lace   Barbara Henning
ISBN 1-881471-62-4 $12.00

Detroit circa 1970. Eileen skips out, forsaking any desire she might once have had for a regular family life. Village Voice

Little Tales of Family & War   Martha King
ISBN 1-881471-47-0 $12.00

King is a minimalist with a difference. Where much minimalist prose is dry and detached, King's is richly detailed. American Book Review

Warp Spasm   Basil King
ISBN 1-881471-54-3 $14.95

... I must refer to Warp Spasm to help me put a few words to my perceptions, or better still, to help me watch the images change in my mind's eye. Now that is a joy. Hubert Selby, Jr.

The Desire Notebooks   John High
ISBN 1-881471-33-0 $14.95

...accurately conveyed desire to make a novel tell the story of love and death, always and everywhere. Publishers Weekly

Day Book of a Virtual Poet   Robert Creeley
Track   Norman Finkelstein
Columns   Norman Finkelstein
A Flicker at the Edge of Things   Leonard Schwartz
The Long & Short of It   Stephen Ellis
Stubborn Grew   Henry Gould
Identity   Basil King
The Poet   Basil King
The Runaway Woods   Stephen Sartarelli
The Open Vault   Stephen Sartarelli
Cunning   Laura Moriarty
Mouth of Shadows: Two Plays   Charles Borkhuis
The Corybantes   Tod Thilleman
Detective Sentences   Barbara Henning
Are Not Our Lowing Heifers Sleeker Than Night-Swollen Mushrooms?   Nada Gordon
Gentlemen in Turbans, Ladies in Cauls   John Gallaher
Spin Cycle   Chris Stroffolino
Watchfulness   Peter O'Leary
The Jazzer & The Loitering Lady   Gordon Osing

Spuyten Duyvil Books are distributed to the trade by
Biblio Distribution
a division of NBN
1-800-462-6420
www.bibliodistribution.com